**Dante smiled, b
edged with imp
danger that even Willow could
recognise was sexual.**

'That depends on you and what you want.'

'What *I* want?' she said faintly.

'Forgive me if I'm mistaken, but I thought
that you were as frustrated by your sister's
interruption as I was. I was under the distinct
impression that our fake relationship was
about to get real, and in a very satisfying
way. It would certainly be more convincing
if we were properly intimate instead of just
pretending to be. So, are we going to play
games with each other? Or are we going to
give in to what we both clearly want?'

The Billionaire's Legacy

A search for truth and the promise of passion!

For nearly sixty years
Italian billionaire Giovanni Di Sione has kept
a shocking secret. Now, nearing the end of his days,
he wants his grandchildren to know their true heritage.

He sends them each on a journey to find his
'Lost Mistresses'—a collection of love tokens
and the only remaining evidence of his lost identity,
his lost history…his lost love.

With each item collected the Di Sione siblings take one
step closer to the truth…and embark on a passionate
journey that none could have expected!

Find out what happens in

The Billionaire's Legacy

Di Sione's Innocent Conquest by Carol Marinelli

The Di Sione Secret Baby by Maya Blake

To Blackmail a Di Sione by Rachael Thomas

The Return of the Di Sione Wife by Caitlin Crews

Di Sione's Virgin Mistress by Sharon Kendrick

A Di Sione for the Greek's Pleasure by Kate Hewitt

A Deal for the Di Sione Ring by Jennifer Hayward

The Last Di Sione Claims His Prize by Maisey Yates

Collect all 8 volumes!

DI SIONE'S
VIRGIN MISTRESS

BY
SHARON KENDRICK

MILLS
BOON

First Published in Great Britain 2016
By Mills & Boon, an imprint of HarperCollins*Publishers*
1 London Bridge Street, London, SE1 9GF

© 2016 Harlequin Books S.A.

Special thanks and acknowledgment are given to Sharon Kendrick
for her contribution to The Billionaire's Legacy series.

ISBN: 978-0-263-92135-9

Printed and bound in Spain
by CPI, Barcelona

Sharon Kendrick once won a national writing competition by describing her ideal date: being flown to an exotic island by a gorgeous and powerful man. Little did she realise that she'd just wandered into her dream job! Today she writes for Mills & Boon, featuring often stubborn but always *to die for* heroes and the women who bring them to their knees. She believes that the best books are those you never want to end. Just like life…

Books by Sharon Kendrick

Mills & Boon Modern Romance

The Ruthless Greek's Return
Christmas in Da Conti's Bed
The Greek's Marriage Bargain
A Scandal, a Secret, a Baby
The Sheikh's Undoing
Monarch of the Sands
Too Proud to be Bought

The Bond of Billionaires

Claimed for Makarov's Baby
The Sheikh's Christmas Conquest

One Night With Consequences

Crowned for the Prince's Heir
Carrying the Greek's Heir

At His Service

The Housekeeper's Awakening

Desert Men of Qurhah

Defiant in the Desert
Shamed in the Sands
Seduced by the Sultan

Wedlocked!

The Billionaire's Defiant Acquisition

Visit the Author Profile page
at millsandboon.co.uk for more titles.

For Sarah-Jane Volkers, who will know exactly why this book is dedicated to her when she reads it!

And to the brilliant Rafael Vinoly, whose words painted such a perfect vignette of Long Island life…

CHAPTER ONE

DANTE DI SIONE FELT the adrenaline pumping through his body as he walked into the tiny airport terminal. His heart was pounding and his forehead was beaded with sweat. He felt like he'd been running. Or just rolled away from a woman after a bout of particularly energetic sex. Even though it was a long time since he could even remember *having* sex. He frowned. How long?

His mind raced back over the past few weeks spent chasing across continents and flitting in and out of different time zones. He'd visited a dizzying array of countries, been presented with a whole shoal of red herrings and wandered up against several dead ends before arriving here, in the Caribbean. All in pursuit of a priceless piece of jewellery which his grandfather wanted for reasons he'd declined to share. Dante felt the tight clench of his heart. A dying man's wish.

Yet wasn't the truth that he had been tantalised by the task he'd been given and which he had taken on as a favour to someone who had given him so much? That his usually jaded appetite had been sharpened by a taste of the unusual. Truth was, he was dreading going back to his high-octane world of big business and the slightly decadent glamour of his adopted Parisian home. He had enjoyed the unpredictability of the chase and the sense that he was stepping outside his highly privileged comfort zone.

His hand tightened around the handle of his bag which contained the precious tiara. All he needed to do now was to hang on to this and never let it go—at least, not until he had placed it at his grandfather's sickbed so that the old man could do what he wanted with it.

His mouth felt dry. He could use a drink, and… something else. Something to distract him from the fact that the adrenaline was beginning to trickle from his system, leaving him with that flat, empty feeling which he'd spent his whole life trying to avoid.

He looked around. The small terminal was filled with the usual suspects which this kind of upmarket Caribbean destination inevitably attracted. As well as the overtanned and ostentatiously wealthy, there seemed to have been some photo shoot taking place, because the place was full of models. He saw several giraffe-tall young women turn in his direction, their endless legs displayed in tiny denim shorts and their battered straw hats tilted at an angle so all you could see were their cute noses and full lips as they pouted at him. But he wasn't in the mood for anyone as predictable as a model. Maybe he'd just do a little work instead. Get on to René at his office in Paris and discover what had been going on in his busy and thriving company while he'd been away.

And then his gaze was drawn to a woman sitting on her own. The only pale person in a sea of tanned bodies. Her hair was blond and she looked as fragile as spun sugar—with one of those pashmina things wrapped around her narrow shoulders which seemed to swamp her. She looked *clean*. He narrowed his eyes. Like she'd spent most of her life underwater and had just been brought up to the surface. She was sitting at the bar with an untouched glass of pink champagne in front of her, and as their eyes met, she picked up her glass, flustered, and began to stare at it as if it contained the secret to the universe—though he noticed she didn't drink any.

Was it that which made him start walking towards her, bewitched by a sudden demonstration of shyness which was so rare in the world he inhabited? With a few sure strides he reached her and put his bag down on the floor, right next to a remarkably similar brown leather carry-on. But then she lifted her head and all he could think about was the fragile beauty of her features.

'Hi,' he said.

'Hi,' she said in a very English accent as she blinked up at him through thick lashes.

'Have we met before?' he questioned.

She looked startled. Like someone who had been caught in an unexpected spotlight. She dug her teeth into her lower lip and worried them across the smooth rosy surface.

'I don't think so,' she said, then shook her head so that the strands of fair hair shimmered over her narrow shoulders like a silky cascade of water. 'No, we haven't. I would have remembered.'

He leaned on the bar, and smiled. 'But you were staring at me as if you knew me.'

Willow didn't answer—not straight away—her

head was too full of confusion and embarrassment combined with a powerful tug of attraction which she wasn't quite sure how to handle. Yes, *of course* she had been staring at him because—quite honestly— who wouldn't?

Beneath the pashmina, she felt the shiver of goose bumps as she met his mocking gaze, acknowledging that he was probably the most perfect man she'd ever seen—and she worked in an industry which dealt almost exclusively with perfect men. Dressed with the carelessness only the truly wealthy could carry off, he looked as if he'd only just fallen out of bed— though probably not his own. Faded jeans clung to unbelievably muscular thighs, and although his silk shirt was slightly creased, he still managed to convey a sense of power and privilege. His eyes were bright blue, his black hair was tousled and the gleam of his golden olive skin hinted at a Mediterranean lineage. Yet behind the brooding good looks she could detect a definite touch of steel—a dangerous edge which only added to his allure.

And Willow was usually left cold by good-looking men, something she put down to a certain shyness around them. Years of being ill, followed by a spell in an all-girls school, had meant that she'd grown up in an exclusively female environment and the only men she'd ever really met had been doctors. She'd been cocooned in her own little world where she'd felt safe—and safety had been a big deal to her.

So what was it about this man with the intense blue eyes which had made her heart start slamming against her ribcage, as if it was fighting to get out of her chest?

He was still looking at her questioningly and she tried to imagine what her sisters would say in similar circumstances. They certainly wouldn't be struck dumb like this. They'd probably shrug their gym-honed shoulders and make some smart comment, and hold out their half-empty glasses for a refill.

Willow twisted the stem of the champagne glass in between her finger and thumb. *So act like they do. Pretend that gorgeous-looking men talk to you every day of the week.*

'I imagine you must be used to people staring at you,' she said truthfully, taking her first sip of champagne and then another, and feeling it rush straight to her head.

'True.' He gave a flicker of a smile as he slid onto the bar stool beside her. 'What are you drinking?'

'No, honestly.' She shook her head, because surely the champagne must be responsible for the sudden warmth which was making her cheeks grow hot. 'I mustn't have too much. I haven't eaten anything since breakfast.'

He raised his eyebrows. 'I was going to ask if it was any good.'

'Oh. Yes. Of course. Right. Silly of me. It's…' Feeling even more flustered, Willow stared at the fizzing bubbles and drank a little more, even though suddenly it tasted like medicine on her tongue. 'It's the best champagne I've ever had.'

'And you often drink champagne on your own at airports, do you?' he drawled.

She shook her head. 'No. Actually, I'm celebrating the end of a job.'

Dante nodded, knowing this was his cue to ask

her about her job, but the last thing he wanted was to have to listen to a résumé of her career. Instead, he asked the bartender for a beer, then leaned against the bar and began to study her.

He started with her hair—the kind of hair he'd like to see spread over his groin—because although he wouldn't kick a brunette or a redhead out of bed in a hurry, he was drawn to blondes like an ant to the honeypot. But up close he could see anomalies in her appearance which made her looks more interesting than beautiful. He noted the almost-translucent pallor of her skin which was stretched over the highest cheekbones he'd ever seen. Her eyes were grey—the soft, misty grey of an English winter sky. Grey like woodsmoke. And although her lips were plump, that was the only bit of her which was—because she was thin. Too thin. Her slim thighs were covered in jeans onto which tiny peacocks had been embroidered, but that was as much as he could see because the damned pashmina was wrapped around her like an oversize tablecloth.

He wondered what had drawn him towards her when there were other more beautiful women in the terminal who would have welcomed his company, rather than looking as if a tiger had suddenly taken the seat beside her. Was it the sense that she didn't really fit in here? That she appeared to be something of an outsider? And hadn't he always been one of those himself? *The man on the outside who was always looking in.*

Maybe he just wanted something to distract him from the thought of returning to the States with the tiara, and the realisation that there was still so much which had been left undone or unsaid in his troubled family. Dante felt as if his grandfather's illness had brought him to a sudden crossroads in his life and suddenly he couldn't imagine the world without the man who had always loved him, no matter what.

And in the meantime, this jumpy-looking blonde was making him have all kinds of carnal thoughts, even though she still had that wary look on her face. He smiled, because usually he let women do all the running, which meant that he could walk away with a relatively clear conscience when he ended the affair. Women who chased men had an inbuilt confidence which usually appealed to him and yet suddenly the novelty of someone who was all tongue-tied and flustered was really too delicious to resist.

'So what are you doing here?' he questioned, taking a sip of his beer. 'Apart from the obvious answer of waiting for a flight.'

Willow stared down at her fingernails and wondered how her sisters would have answered *this*. Her three clever, beautiful sisters who had never known a moment of doubt in their charmed lives. Who would each have doubtless murmured something clever or suggestive and had this gorgeous stranger tipping back his dark head and laughing in appreciation at their wit. They certainly wouldn't have been sitting there, tying themselves up in knots, wondering why he had come over here in the first place. Why was it only within the defining boundaries of the work situation that she was able to engage with a member of the opposite sex without wishing that the floor would open up and swallow her?

This close, he was even more spectacular, with

a raw and restless energy which fizzed off him like electricity. But it was his eyes which were truly remarkable. She'd never seen eyes like them. Bluer than the Caribbean sky outside. Bluer even than the wings of those tiny butterflies which used to flutter past on those long-ago summer evenings when she'd been allowed to lie outside. A bright blue, but a hard blue—sharp and clear and focused. They were sweeping over her now, their cerulean glint visible through their forest of dark lashes as he waited for her answer.

She supposed she should tell him about her first solo shoot as a stylist for one of the UK's biggest fashion magazines, and that the job had been a runaway success. But although she was trying very hard to feel happy about that, she couldn't seem to shake off the dread of what was waiting for her back in England. Another wedding. Another celebration of love and romance which she would be attending on her own. Going back to the house which had been both refuge and prison during her growing-up years. Back to her well-meaning sisters and overprotective parents. Back to the stark truth that her real life was nowhere near as glamorous as her working life.

So make it glamorous.

She'd never seen this man before and she was unlikely to see him again. But couldn't she—for once in her life—play the part which had always been denied to her? Couldn't she pretend to be passionate and powerful and *desirable*? She'd worked in the fashion industry for three years now and had watched professional models morph into someone else once the camera was turned on them. She'd seen them become coquettish or slutty or flirtatious with an ease which was breathtaking. Couldn't she pretend that this man was the camera? Couldn't she become the person she'd always secretly dreamed of being, instead of dull Willow Hamilton, who had never been allowed to do *anything* and as a consequence had never really learned how to live like other women her age?

She circled the rim of the champagne glass with her forefinger, the unfamiliar gesture implying—she *hoped*—that she was a sensual and tactile person.

'I've been working on a fashion shoot,' she said.

'Oh.' There was a pause. 'Are you a model?'

Willow wondered if she was imagining the brief sense of *disappointment* which had deepened his transatlantic accent. Didn't he like models? Because if that was the case, he really *was* an unusual man. She curved her lips into a smile and discovered that it was easier than she'd thought.

'Do I look like a model?'

He raised his dark eyebrows. 'I'm not sure you really want me to answer that question.'

Willow stopped stroking the glass. 'Oh?'

His blue eyes glinted. 'Well, if I say no, you'll pout and say, *Why not?* And if I say yes, you'll still pout, and then you'll sigh and say in a weary but very affected voice, *Is it that obvious?*'

Willow laughed—and wasn't it a damning indictment of her social life that she should find herself shocked by the sound? As if she wasn't the kind of person who should be giggling with a handsome stranger at some far-flung spot of the globe. And suddenly she felt a heady rush of freedom. And excitement. She looked into the mocking spark of his eyes and decided that she could play this game after all.

'Thank you for answering me so honestly,' she said gravely. 'Because now I know I don't need to say anything at all.'

His gaze became speculative. 'And why's that?'

She shrugged. 'If women are so unoriginal that you can predict every word they're going say, then you can have this conversation all by yourself, can't you? You certainly don't need me to join in!'

He leaned forward and slanted her a smile in response and Willow felt a sense of giddy triumph.

'And that would be my loss, I think,' he said softly, his hard blue eyes capturing hers. 'What's your name?'

'It's Willow. Willow Hamilton.'

'And is that your real name?'

She gave him an innocent look. 'You mean Hamilton?'

He smiled. 'I mean Willow.'

She nodded. 'It is—though I know it sounds like something which has been made up. But it's a bit of a tradition in our family. My sisters and I are all named after something in nature.'

'You mean like a mountain?'

She laughed—*again*—and shook her head. 'A bit more conventional than that. They're called Flora, Clover and Poppy. And they're all very beautiful,' she added, aware of the sudden defensiveness in her tone.

His gaze grew even more speculative. 'Now you expect me to say, *But you're very beautiful, too.*' His voice dipped. 'And you respond by...'

'And I told you,' interrupted Willow boldly, her heart now pounding so hard against her ribcage that she was having difficulty breathing, 'that if you're so astute, you really ought to be having this conversation with yourself.'

'Indeed I could.' His eyes glittered. 'But we both know there are plenty of things you can do on your own which are far more fun to do with someone else. Wouldn't you agree, Willow?'

Willow might not have been the most experienced person on the block where men were concerned and had never had what you'd call a *real* boyfriend. But although she'd been cosseted and protected, she hadn't spent her life in *total* seclusion. She now worked in an industry where people were almost embarrassingly frank about sex and she knew exactly what he meant. To her horror she felt a blush beginning. It started at the base of her neck and rose to slowly flood her cheeks with hot colour. And all she could think about was that when she was little and blushed like this, her sisters used to call her the Scarlet Pimpernel.

She reached for her glass, but the clamp of his hand over hers stopped her. Actually, it did more than stop her—it made her skin suddenly feel as if it had developed a million new nerve endings she hadn't realised existed. It made her glance down at his olive fingers which contrasted against the paleness of her own hand and to think how perfect their entwined flesh appeared. Dizzily, she lifted her gaze to his.

'Don't,' he said softly. 'A woman blushing is a rare and delightful sight and men like it. So don't hide it and don't be ashamed. And—just for the record—if you drink more alcohol to try to hide your embarrassment, you're only going to make it worse.'

'So you're an expert on blushing as well as being an authority on female conversation?' she said, aware that his hand was still lying on top of hers and that it was making her long for the kind of things she knew she was never going to get. But she made no attempt to move her own from underneath and wondered if he'd noticed.

'I'm an expert on a lot of things.'

'But not modesty, I suspect?'

'No,' he conceded. 'Modesty isn't my strong point.'

The silence which fell between them was broken by the sound of screaming on the other side of the terminal and Willow glanced across to see a child bashing his little fists against his mother's thighs. But the mother was completely ignoring him as she chatted on her cell phone and the little boy's hysteria grew and grew. *Just talk to him*, thought Willow fiercely, wondering why some people even bothered *having* children. Why they treated the gift of birth so lightly.

But then she noticed that Blue Eyes was glancing at his watch and suddenly she realised she was missing her opportunity to prolong this conversation for as long as possible. Because wouldn't it be great to go home with the feeling of having broken out of her perpetual shyness for once? To be able to answer the inevitable question, *So, any men in your life these days, Willow?* with something other than a bright, false smile while she tried to make light of her essentially lonely life, before changing the subject.

So ask him his name. Stop being so tongue-tied and awkward.

'What's your name?' asked Willow, almost as if it was an afterthought—but she forced herself to pull her hand away from his. To break that delicious contact before he did.

'Dante.'

'Just Dante?' she questioned when he didn't elaborate further.

'Di Sione,' he added, and Willow wondered if she'd imagined the faint note of reluctance as he told her.

Dante took a sip of his beer and waited. The world was small, yes—but it was also fractured. There were whole groups of people who lived parallel existences to him and it was possible that this well-spoken young Englishwoman who blushed like a maiden aunt wouldn't have heard of his notorious family. She'd probably never slept with his twin brother or bumped into any of his other screwed-up siblings along the way. His heart grew cold as he thought about his twin, but he pushed the feeling away with a ruthlessness which came easily to him. And still he waited, in case the soft grey eyes of his companion suddenly widened in recognition. But they didn't. She was just looking at him in a way which made him want to lean over and kiss her.

'I'm trying to imagine what you're expecting my response to be,' she said, a smile nudging the edges of her lips. 'So I'm not going to do the obvious thing of asking if your name is Italian when clearly it is. I'm just going to remark on what a lovely name it is. And it is. Di Sione. It makes me think of blue seas and terracotta roofs and those dark cypress trees which don't seem to grow anywhere else in the world except in Italy,' she said, her grey eyes filling with mischief. 'There. Is that a satisfactory response—or was it predictable?'

There was a heartbeat of a pause before Dante

answered. She was so *unexpected*, he thought. Like finding a shaded space in the middle of a sizzling courtyard. Like running cool water over your hot and dirty hands and seeing all the grime trickle away. 'No, not especially predictable,' he said. 'But not satisfactory either.'

He leaned forward and as he did he could smell the tang of salt on her skin and wondered if she'd been swimming earlier that morning. He wondered what her body looked like beneath that all-enveloping shawl. What that blond hair would look like if it fell down over her bare skin. 'The only satisfactory response I can think of right now is that I think you should lean forward and part your lips so that I can kiss you.'

Willow stared at him—shocked—as she felt the whisper of something unfamiliar sliding over her skin. Something which beckoned her with a tantalising finger. And before she had time to consider the wisdom of her action, she did exactly as he suggested. She extended her neck by a fraction and slowly parted her lips so that he could lean in to kiss her. She felt the brush of his mouth against hers as the tip of his tongue edged its way over her lips.

Was it the champagne she'd drunk, or just some bone-deep *yearning* which made her open her mouth a little wider? Or just the feeling of someone who'd been locked away from normal stuff for so long that she wanted to break free. She wanted to toss aside convention and not be treated like some delicate flower, as she had been all her life. She didn't want to be Willow Hamilton right then. She wanted the famous fairy godmother to blast into the Caribbean airport in a cloud of glitter and to wave her wand and transform her, just as Willow had been transforming models for the past week.

She wanted her hair to stream like buttery silk down her back and for her skin to be instantly tanned, shown to advantage by some feminine yet sexy little dress whose apparent simplicity would be confounded by its astronomical price tag. She wanted her feet to be crammed into sky-high stilettos which still wouldn't be enough to allow her to see eye to eye with this spectacular man, if they were both standing. But she didn't want to be standing—and she didn't want to be sitting on a bar stool either. She wanted to be lying on a big bed wearing very sexy underwear and for those olive fingers to be touching her flesh again—only this time in far more intimate spots as he slowly unclothed her.

All those thoughts rushed through her mind in just the time it took for her own tongue to flicker against his and Willow's eyes suddenly snapped open—less in horror at the public spectacle she was making of herself with a man she'd only just met than with the realisation of what was echoing over the loudspeaker. It took a full five seconds before her befuddled brain could take in what the robotic voice was actually saying, and when it did, her heart sank.

'That's me. They're calling my flight,' she said breathlessly, reluctantly drawing her mouth away from his, still hypnotised by the blazing blue of his eyes. With an effort she got off the stool, registering the momentary weakness of her knees as she automatically patted her shoulder bag to check her passport and purse. She screwed up her face, trying to act like what had happened was no big deal. Trying to pretend that her breasts weren't tingling beneath her pashmina and that she kissed total strangers in airports every day of the week. Trying not to hope that he'd spring to his feet and tell her he didn't want her to go. But he didn't.

'Oh, heck,' she croaked. 'It's the last call. I can't believe I didn't hear it.'

'I think we both know very well why you didn't hear it,' he drawled.

But although his eyes glinted, Willow sensed that already he was mentally taking his leave of her and she told herself it was better this way. He was just a gorgeous man she'd flirted with at the airport—and there was no reason why she couldn't do this kind of thing in the future, if she wanted to. It could be the springboard to a new and exciting life if she let it. That is, if she walked away now with her dignity and dreams intact. Better that than the inevitable alternative. The fumbled exchange of business cards and the insincere promises to call. Her waiting anxiously by the phone when she got back to England. Making excuses for why he hadn't rung but unable—for several weeks at least—to acknowledge the reason he hadn't. The reason she'd known all along—that he was way out of her league and had just been playing games with her.

Still flustered, she bent down to grab her carry-on and straightened up to drink in his stunning features and hard blue eyes one last time. She tried her best to keep her voice steady. To not give him any sense of the regret which was already sitting on the horizon, waiting to greet her. 'Goodbye, Dante. It was lovely meeting you. Not a very original thing to say, I know—but it's true. Safe journey—wherever you're going. I'd better dash.'

She nearly extended her hand to shake his before realising how stupid that would look and she turned away before she could make even more of a fool of herself. She ended up running for the plane but told herself that was a good thing, because it distracted her from her teeming thoughts. Her heart was pounding as she strapped herself into her seat, but she was determined not to allow her mind to start meandering down all those pointless *what if* paths. She knew that in life you had to concentrate on what you had, and not what you really wanted.

So every time she thought about those sensual features and amazing eyes, she forced herself to concentrate on the family wedding which was getting closer and the horrible bridesmaid dress she was being made to wear.

She read the in-flight magazines and slept soundly for most of the journey back to England, and it wasn't until she touched down at Heathrow and reached into the overhead locker that she realised the carry-on bag she'd placed in the overhead locker wasn't actually *her* bag at all. Yes, it was brown, and yes, it was made of leather—but there all similarities ended. Her hands began to tremble. Because this was of the softest leather imaginable and there were three glowing gold initials discreetly embossed against the expensive skin. She stared at it with a growing sense of disbelief as she matched the initials in her head to the only name they could stand for, and her heart began to pound with a mixture of excitement and fear.

D.D.S.

Dante Di Sione.

CHAPTER TWO

DANTE'S PLANE WAS halfway over northern Spain when he made the grim discovery which sent his already bad mood shooting into the stratosphere. He'd spent much of the journey with an erection he couldn't get rid of—snapping at the stewardesses who were fussing and flirting around him in such an outrageous way that he wondered whether they'd picked up on the fact that he was sexually excited, and some hormonal instinct was making them hit on him even more than usual.

But he wasn't interested in those women in too-tight uniforms with dollar signs flashing in their eyes when they looked at him. He kept thinking about the understated Englishwoman and wondered why he hadn't insisted she miss her flight, so that he could have taken her on board his plane and made love to her. Most women couldn't resist sex on a private jet, and there was no reason she would be any different.

His mouth dried as he remembered the way she had jumped up from the bar stool like a scalded cat and run off to catch her flight as if she couldn't wait to get away from him. Had that ever happened to him before? He thought not.

She hadn't even asked for his business card!

Pushing her stubbornly persistent image from his mind, he decided to check on his grandfather's precious tiara, reaching for his bag and wondering why the old man wanted the valuable and mysterious piece of jewellery so much. Because time was fast running out for him? Dante felt the sudden painful twist of his heart as he tried to imagine a future without Giovanni, but he couldn't get his head around it. It was almost impossible to envisage a life without the once strong but still powerful figure who had stepped in to look after him and his siblings after fate had dealt them all the cruellest of blows.

Distracted by the turbulent nature of his thoughts, he tugged at the zip of the bag and frowned. He couldn't remember it being so full because he liked to travel light. He tugged again and the zip slid open. But instead of a small leather case surrounded by boxer shorts, an unread novel and some photos of a Spanish castle he really needed to look at for a client before his next meeting—it was stuffed full of what looked suspiciously like...

Dante's brows knitted together in disbelief.

Swimwear?

He looked at the bag more closely and saw that instead of softest brown leather embossed with *his* initials, this carry-on was older and more battered and had clearly seen better days.

Disbelievingly, he began to burrow through the bikinis and swimsuits, throwing them aside with a growing sense of urgency, but instantly he knew he was just going through the motions and that his search was going to be fruitless. His heart gave a leap in his chest as a series of disastrous possibilities occurred to him. How ironic it would be if he'd flown halfway across the globe to purchase a piece of jewellery which had cost a king's ransom, only to find that he'd been hoodwinked by the man who had sold it to him.

But no. He remembered packing the tiara himself, and although he was no gem expert, Dante had bought enough trinkets as pay-offs for women over the years to know when something was genuine. And the tiara *had* been genuine—of that he'd been certain. A complex and intricate weaving of diamonds and emeralds which had dazzled even him—a man usually far too cynical to be dazzled.

So where the hell was it now?

And suddenly Dante realised what must have happened. Willow—*what the hell had been her surname?*—must have picked up his bag by mistake. The blonde he'd been so busy flirting with at the airport, that he'd completely forgotten that he was carrying hundreds of thousands of dollars' worth of precious stones in his hand luggage. He'd been distracted by her misty eyes. He'd read in them a strange kind of longing and he'd fed her fantasy— and his own—by kissing her. It had been one of those instant-chemistry moments, when the combustion of sexual attraction had been impossible to ignore, until the last call for her flight had sounded over the loudspeaker and broken the spell. She'd jumped up and grabbed her bag. Only she hadn't, had she? She'd grabbed *his* bag!

He drummed his fingers on the armrest as he considered his options. Should he ask his pilot to divert the plane to London? He thought about his meeting with the Italian billionaire scheduled for later that evening and knew it would be both insulting and damaging to cancel it.

He scowled as he rang for a stewardess, one of whom almost fell over herself in her eagerness to reach him first.

'What can I get for you, sir?' she questioned, her eyes nearly popping out of her head as she looked at the haphazard collection of swimwear piled in the centre of the table.

Dante quickly shoved all the bikinis back into the bag, but as he did so, his finger hooked on to a particularly tiny pair of bottoms. He felt his body grow hard as he felt the soft silk of the gusset and thought about Willow wearing it. His voice grew husky. 'I want you to get hold of my assistant and ask him to track down a woman for me.'

The stewardess did her best to conceal it, but the look of disappointment on her face was almost comical.

'Certainly, sir,' she said gamely. 'And the woman is?'

'Her name is Willow Hamilton,' Dante ground out. 'I need her number and her address. And I need that information by the time this plane lands.'

There were four missed calls on her phone by the time Willow left the Tube station in central London, blinking as she emerged into the bright July sunshine. She stepped into the shadow of a doorway and looked at the screen. All from the same unknown number and whoever it was hadn't bothered to leave a voicemail. But she knew who the caller must be. *The sexy stranger. The man she'd kissed. The blue-eyed man whose carry-on she had picked up by mistake.*

She felt the race of her heart. She would go home first and then she would ring him. She wasn't going to have a complicated conversation on a busy pavement on a hot day when she was tired and jet-lagged.

She had already made a tentative foray inside, but the bag contained no contact number, just some photos of an amazing Spanish castle, a book which had won a big literary prize last year and—rather distractingly—several pairs of silk boxer shorts which were wrapped around a leather box. She'd found her fingertips sliding over the slippery black material of the shorts and had imagined them clinging to Dante Di Sione's flesh and that's when her cheeks had started doing that Scarlet Pimpernel thing again, and she'd hastily stuffed them back before anyone on the Heathrow Express started wondering why she was ogling a pair of men's underpants.

She let herself into her apartment, which felt blessedly cool and quiet after the heat of the busy London day. She rented the basement from a friend of her father's—a diplomat in some far-flung region whose return visits to the UK were brief and infrequent. Unfortunately one of the conditions of Willow being there was that she wasn't allowed to change the decor, which meant she was stuck with lots of very masculine colour. The walls were painted bottle-green and dark red and there was lots of heavy-looking furniture dotted around the place. But it was affordable, close to work and—more importantly—it got her away from the cloying grip of her family.

She picked up some mail from the mat and went

straight over to the computer where she tapped in
Dante Di Sione's name, reeling a little to discover
that her search had yielded over two hundred thousand entries.

She squinted at the screen, her heart beginning to
pound as she stared into an image which showed his
haunting blue eyes to perfection. It seemed he was
some sort of mega entrepreneur, heading up a company which catered exclusively for the super-rich. She
looked at the company's website.

We don't believe in the word impossible.
Whatever it is you want—we can deliver.

Quite a big promise to make, she thought as she
stared dreamily at photos of a circus tent set up in
somebody's huge garden, and some flower-decked
gondolas which had been provided to celebrate a tenth
wedding anniversary party in Venice.

She scrolled down. There was quite a lot of stuff
about his family. Lots of siblings. *Snap*, she thought.
And there was money. Lots of that. A big estate somewhere in America. Property in Manhattan. Although
according to this, Dante Di Sione lived in Paris—
which might explain why his accent was an intrigu-
ing mix of transatlantic and Mediterranean. And yet
some of the detail about his life was vague—though
she couldn't quite put her finger on why. She hadn't
realised precisely what she'd been looking for until
the word *single* flashed up on the screen and a feeling of satisfaction washed over her.

She sat back and stared out at the pavement, where
from this basement-level window she could see the

bottom halves of people's legs as they walked by. A pair of stilettos tapped into view, followed by some bare feet in a pair of flip-flops. Was she really imagining that she was in with a chance with a sexy billionaire like Dante Di Sione, just because he'd briefly kissed her in a foreign airport terminal? Surely she couldn't be *that* naive?

She was startled from her daydream by the sound of her mobile phone and her heart started beating out a primitive tattoo as she saw it was the same number as before. She picked it up with fingers which were shaking so much that she almost declined the call instead of accepting it.

Stay calm, she told herself. *This is the new you. The person who kisses strangers at airports and is about to start embracing life, instead of letting it pass her by.*

'Hello?'

'Is that you, Willow?'

Her heart raced and her skin felt clammy. On the phone, his transatlantic/Mediterranean twang sounded even more sexy, if such a thing was possible. 'Yes,' she said, a little breathlessly. 'It's me.'

'You've got my bag,' he clipped out.

'I know.'

The tone of his voice seemed to change. 'So how the hell did that happen?'

'How do you think it happened?' Stung into defence by the note of irritation in his voice, Willow gripped the phone tightly. 'I picked it up by mistake... *obviously.*'

There was a split-second pause. 'So it wasn't deliberate?'

'Deliberate?' Willow frowned. 'Are you serious? Do you think I'm some sort of thief who hangs around airports targeting rich men?'

There was another pause and this time when he spoke the irritation had completely vanished and his voice sounded almost unnaturally composed. 'Have you opened it?'

A little uncomfortably, Willow rubbed her espadrille toe over the ancient Persian rug beneath the desk. 'Obviously I had to open it, to see if there was any address or phone number inside.'

His voice sounded strained now. 'And you found, what?'

Years of sparring with her sisters made Willow's response automatic. 'Don't you even remember what you were carrying in your own bag?'

'You found, *what*?' he repeated dangerously.

'A book. Some glossy photos of a Spanish castle. And some underpants,' she added on a mumble.

'But nothing else?'

'There's a leather case. But it's locked.'

At the other end of the phone, Dante stared at the imposing iron structure of the Eiffel Tower and breathed out a slow sigh of relief. Of course it was locked—and he doubted she would have had time to get someone to force it open for her even if she'd had the inclination, which he suspected she didn't. There had been something almost *otherworldly* about her... and she seemed the kind of woman who wouldn't be interested in possessions—even if the possession in question happened to be a stunning diadem, worth hundreds of thousands of dollars.

He could feel the strain bunching up the muscles

in his shoulders and he moved them slowly to release some of the tension, realising just how lucky he'd been. Or rather, how lucky *she* had been. Because he'd been travelling on a private jet with all the protection which came with owning your own plane, but Willow had not. He tried to imagine what could have happened if she'd been stopped going through customs, with an undeclared item like that in her possession.

Beads of sweat broke out on his forehead and for a moment he cursed this mission he'd been sent on—but it was too late to question its legitimacy now. He needed to retrieve the tiara as soon as possible and to get it to the old man, so that he could forget all about it.

'I need that bag back,' he said steadily.

'I'm sure you do.'

'And you probably want your swimwear.' He thought about the way his finger had trailed over the gusset of that tiny scarlet bikini bottom and was rewarded with another violent jerk of lust as he thought about her blond hair and grey eyes and the faint taste of champagne on her lips. 'So why don't I send someone round to swap bags?'

There was a pause. 'But you don't know where I live,' she said, and then, before he had a chance to reply, she started talking in the thoughtful tone of someone who had just missed a glaringly obvious fact. 'Come to think of it—how come you're ringing me? I didn't give you my phone number.'

Dante thought quickly. Was she naive enough not to realise that someone like him could find out pretty much anything he wanted? He injected a reassuring note into his voice. 'I had someone who works for me track you down,' he said smoothly. 'I was worried that you'd want your bag back.'

'Actually, you seem to be the one who's worried, Mr Di Sione.'

Her accurate tease stopped him in his tracks and Dante scowled, curling his free hand into a tight fist before slowly releasing his fingers, one by one. This wasn't going as he had intended. 'Am I missing something here?' he questioned coolly. 'Are you playing games with me, Willow, or are you prepared to do a bag-swap so that we can just forget all about it and move on?'

In the muted light of the basement apartment, Willow turned to catch a glimpse of her shadowed features in an antique oval mirror and was suddenly filled with a determination she hadn't felt for a long time. Not since she'd battled illness and defied all the doctors' gloomy expectations. Not since she'd fought to get herself a job, despite her family's reluctance to let her start living an independent life in London. She thought about her sister Clover's wedding, which was due to take place in a few days' time, when she would be kitted out in the hideous pale peach satin which had been chosen for the bridesmaids and which managed to make her look completely washed out and colourless.

But it wasn't just that which was bothering her. Her vanity could easily take a knock because she'd never really had the energy or the inclination to make her looks the main focus of her attention. It was all the questions which would inevitably come her way and which would get worse as the day progressed.

So when are we going to see you walking down the aisle, Willow?

And, of course, the old favourite: *Still no boyfriend, Willow?*

And because she would have been warned to be on her best behaviour, Willow would have to bite back the obvious logic that you couldn't have one without the other, and that since she'd never had a proper boyfriend, it was unlikely that she would be heading down the aisle any time soon.

Unless...

She stared at her computer screen, which was dominated by the rugged features of Dante Di Sione. And although he might have been toying with her—because perhaps kissing random women turned him on—he had managed to make it feel *convincing*. As if he'd really *wanted* to kiss her. And that was all she needed, wasn't it? A creditable performance from a man who would be perfectly capable of delivering one. Dante Di Sione didn't have to be her real boyfriend—he just had to look as if he was.

'Don't I get a reward for keeping your bag safe?' she questioned sweetly.

'I'll buy you a big bunch of flowers.'

'Flowers make me sneeze.'

'Chocolates, then.'

'I'm allergic to cocoa.'

'Stop playing games with me, Willow,' he snapped. 'And tell me what it is you're angling for.'

Willow stared at the piercing blue eyes on the computer screen. His thick black hair looked as if he had been running his fingers through it and she remembered how it had felt to have his lips brushing over hers. It was now or never. It was all about seizing the moment and doing something you wouldn't normally do. Because what was the point of sitting back and moaning about your fate as if it was set in stone, instead of trying to hammer out something new for yourself?

And here was a chance staring her straight in the face.

She drew in a deep breath. 'What I want won't cost you anything but your time. I'm being a bridesmaid at my sister's wedding next weekend and I'm fed up with people asking me why I don't have a boyfriend. All you have to do is pretend to be that man. For one day only, you will be my fictitious but very convincing boyfriend, Mr Di Sione. Do you think you could manage that?'

CHAPTER THREE

HE SHOULD HAVE told her no. Should have told her that he hated weddings. Because marriage stood for everything he despised and distrusted. Lies and deception and manipulation.

Dante straightened the silver-grey tie which complemented his formal charcoal suit and stared at his reflection in the hotel mirror.

So why *hadn't* he said no? Why *had* he agreed to accompany Willow Hamilton to her sister's wedding, where she was being a bridesmaid? It was true that she had his grandfather's tiara in her possession and she had been demonstrating a not-very-subtle form of blackmail to get him to be her plus one. But Dante was not a man who could be manipulated—and certainly not by a woman. If he'd really wanted that tiara back he would have gone straight round to her apartment and *taken* it—either by reason or seduction or quiet threat—because he nearly always got what he wanted.

So why hadn't he?

He gave his tie one final tug and watched as his reflected face gave a grim kind of smile.

Because he wanted her? Because she'd interested

and intrigued him and awoken in him a sexual hunger he'd been neglecting these past weeks?

The reflected smile intensified.

Well, why not?

He picked up his car keys and went outside to the front of the hotel, where the valet was opening the door of the car he'd hired for the weekend. It was an outrageously fast car—a completely over-the-top machine which would inevitably attract the attention of both men and women. And while it wouldn't have been Dante's first choice, if Willow wanted him to play the part of a very rich and super-keen lover, then it followed that he ought to drive something which looked like everyone's idea of a phallic substitute.

He drove through the streets of central London and tooted the horn as he drew up outside Willow's basement apartment. She appeared almost immediately and he watched her walk towards him, narrowing his eyes with instinctive appraisal—because she looked… He swallowed. She looked *incredible*. Gone was the big pashmina which had shielded her from the airport's overzealous air conditioning and hidden most of her body. In its place was a pale dress which skimmed the tiniest waist he'd ever seen, its flouncy skirt swirling provocatively around her narrow knees. Her blond hair was plaited and Dante felt his mouth dry. As she grew closer he could see that the collar of her dress was embroidered with tiny daisies, and it made her look as if she'd been picked fresh from a meadow that morning. She looked ethereal and fragile and he couldn't seem to tear his eyes away from her.

He shook his head slightly as once again he acknowledged her fey beauty and the realisation that she didn't seem quite part of this world. Certainly not *his* world. And then he noticed that she was carrying nothing but a small suitcase.

'Where's my carry-on?' he demanded as he got out of the car to take the case from her.

There was a pause as she met his gaze. 'It will be returned to you after the deal is done.'

'After the deal is done?' he echoed softly.

'When the wedding is over.'

He raised his eyebrows at her mockingly, but made no attempt to conceal the sudden flicker of irritation in his voice. 'And if I insist on taking it now? What then?'

He saw a momentary hesitation cross her fragile features, as if she had suddenly realised just who it was she was dealing with. But bravado won the day and she shot him an almost defiant look which made him want to pin her over the bonnet of the car and kiss her senseless.

'You're not in a position to insist, Dante,' she said, sliding inside with a graceful movement which made him wish she could do it again, in slow motion. 'I have something you want and you have to pay for it.'

He switched on the engine and wondered if she was aware that she had something else *he* wanted, and that by the end of the day he would have taken it… 'So where are we going?' he said.

'My family home. It's in Sussex. I'll direct you.'

'Women are notoriously bad at directions, Willow—we both know that. So why don't you just give me the postcode and I can program it into the satnav?'

She turned to look at him, a frown creasing her

brow. 'Are you for real, or did you just complete a crash course in being patronising? I think I can just about find my way to my family home without needing a robot to guide me.'

'Just don't fall asleep,' he warned.

'I'll do my best. But you're not exactly an aid to relaxation, are you?' Settling back in her seat, she gave him a clear list of instructions, then waited until he had negotiated his way out of London towards the south, before she asked, 'So what's in the bag which makes you want it so much?'

'Boxer shorts.' He shot her a look. 'But you already know that.'

Willow didn't react, even though the mention of his boxer shorts was threatening her with embarrassment, which she suspected was his intention. Because this was the new Willow, wasn't it? The woman who had decided to take control of her own destiny instead of having it decided by other people. The woman who was going to live dangerously. She studied his rugged profile as he stared at the road ahead. 'A few items of underwear wouldn't usually be enough to get a man like you to take a complete stranger to a family wedding and pretend to be her boyfriend.'

'Let's get a couple of things straight, shall we, Willow? Firstly, I have no intention of discussing the contents of that bag with you,' he said as he powered the car into the fast lane. 'And secondly, I intend to play your *lover*—not your damned *boyfriend*—unless your looks are deceiving and you happen to be fifteen.'

'I'm twenty-six,' she said stiffly.

'You look much younger.'

'That's what everyone says.'

There was a pause. 'Is that a roundabout way of telling me I'm unoriginal?'

She shrugged. 'Well, you know what they say… if the cap fits…'

A reluctant smile curved the edges of his lips. 'You need to tell me something about yourself before we get there,' he said. 'If you're hoping to convince people we're an item.'

Willow stared out of the car window as they drove through the sun-dappled lanes, and as more and more trees appeared, she thought about how much she loved the English countryside. The hedgerows were thick with greenery and in the fields she could see yellow and white ox-eye daisies and the purple of snake's head fritillary. And suddenly she found herself wishing that this was all for real and that Dante Di Sione was here because he wanted to be, not because she was holding him to ransom over some mystery package.

She wondered how much to tell him. She didn't want him getting scared. She didn't want him to start treating her as if she was made of glass. She was worried he'd suddenly start being *kind* to her if he learned the truth, and she couldn't stand that. He was rude and arrogant and judgemental, but she rather liked that. He wasn't bending over backwards to please her—or running as fast as he could in the opposite direction, which was the usual effect she had on people once they knew her history.

His words interrupted her silent reverie.

'We could start with you explaining why you need an escort like me in the first place,' he said. 'You're a pretty woman. Surely there must be other men who

could have been your date? Men who know you better than I do and could have carried off a far more
convincing performance.'

She shrugged, staring at the toenails which were
peeping through her open-toed sandals—toenails
which had been painted a hideous shade of peach to
match the equally hideous bridesmaid dresses, because Clover had said that she wanted her sisters to
look like 'a team.'

'Maybe I wanted to take someone who nobody
else knew,' she said.

'True,' he agreed. 'Or you could—and I know this
is controversial—you could always have chosen to
attend the wedding on your own. Don't they say that
weddings are notoriously fertile places for meeting
someone new? You might have got lucky. Or are you
one of those women who believes she isn't a complete
person unless she has a man in tow?'

Willow couldn't believe what he'd just said. Had
she really thought his rudeness was charming? Well,
scrub that. She found herself wishing she'd asked
around at the magazine to see if anyone there could
have been her guest. But most of the men she worked
with were gay—and the place was a hotbed of gossip.
It wouldn't have done her image much good if she'd
had to trawl around for a suitable escort, because the
biggest sin you could commit in the fashion industry
was to admit to being lonely.

She sneaked a glance at Dante. Whatever his short-
comings in the charm department he was certainly a
very suitable escort—in every sense of the word. The
formality of his pristine two-piece looked just as good
against his glowing olive skin as the faded denim

jeans had done. Perhaps even more so. The made-to-measure suit hugged his powerful body and emphasised its muscularity to perfection—making her shockingly aware of his broad shoulders and powerful thighs. The slightly too long black hair appeared more tamed than it had done the other day and suddenly she found herself longing to run her fingers through it and to muss it up.

She felt a rush of something molten tugging at the pit of her belly—something which was making her wriggle her bottom restlessly against the seat. Did she imagine the quick sideways glance he gave her, or the infuriatingly smug smile which followed—as if he was perfectly aware of the sudden aching deep inside her which was making it difficult for her to think straight.

She licked her lips. 'I'm not really like my sisters,' she began. 'You remember I'm one of four?'

'I remember.'

'They've always had millions of boyfriends, and I haven't.'

'Why not?'

He shot the question at her and Willow wondered if now was the time for the big reveal. To tell him how ill she'd been as a child. To tell him that there had been times when nobody had been sure if she would make it. Or to mention that there were residual aspects of that illness which made her a bad long-term choice as a girlfriend.

But suddenly her attention was distracted by the powerful interplay of muscles as he tensed one taut thigh in order to change gear and her mouth dried with longing. No, she was not going to tell him. Why peddle stories of her various woes and make herself look like an inevitable victim in his eyes? Today she was going to be a different Willow. The kind of Willow she'd always wanted to be. She was going to embrace the way he was making her feel, and the way he was making her feel was...*sexy*.

Carelessly, she wriggled her shoulders. 'I've been too wrapped up in my career. The fashion world can be very demanding—and competitive. I've been working at the magazine since I left uni, and they work you very hard. The swimwear shoot I was doing in the Caribbean was my first big break and everyone is very pleased with it. I guess that means I'll have more time to spend on my social life from now on. Take the next turning on the right. We're nearly there. Look. Only seven more miles.' She pointed at a signpost. 'So you'd better tell me a bit about you.'

Dante slowed the car down as he turned into a narrow lane and thought how differently he might have answered this question a few years back. The first thing he would have said was that he was a twin, because being a twin had felt like a fundamental part of his existence—like they were two parts of the same person. But not any more. He and Dario hadn't spoken in years. Six years, to be precise—after an episode when anger and resentment had exploded into misunderstanding and turned into a cold and unforgiving rift. He'd discovered that it was easier to act like his brother no longer existed, rather than acknowledge the fact that they no longer communicated. And that it hurt. It hurt like hell.

'But surely you must have looked me up on the internet,' he murmured.

She quickly turned her head to look at him, and for the first time, she seemed uncertain. 'Well, yes. I did.'

'And didn't that tell you everything you wanted to know?'

'Not really. Bits of it were very vague.'

'I pay people a lot of money to keep my profile vague.'

'Why?'

'To avoid the kind of questions you seem intent on asking.'

'It's just down that long drive. The entrance is just past that big tree on the right.' She leaned forward to point her finger, before settling back against the leather car seat. 'It said you had lots of siblings, and there was something about you having a twin brother and I was wondering what it was like to have a twin. If the two of you are psychic, like people say twins can be. And...'

'And what?' he shot out as her words trailed off.

She shrugged. 'There wasn't much information about your parents,' she said quietly.

Dante's fingers tightened around the steering wheel as he drew up outside a huge old house, whose beauty was slightly diminished by shabby paintwork and a general sense of tiredness. Bad enough that Willow Hamilton should have made breezy assumptions about his estranged twin, but worse that she had touched on the one fact which had ruthlessly been eliminated from his history. Didn't she realise that there was a good reason why there was scant mention of his parents in his personal profile?

He felt a slow anger begin to build inside him, and if it hadn't been for the damned tiara, he would have dropped her off there and then, and driven away so fast that you wouldn't have seen him for smoke. Because personal questions about his family were forbidden; it was one of the ground rules he laid down at the beginning of any date.

But this wasn't a normal date, was it? It was a means to an end. He stared down at her bare knees and felt a whisper of desire. And perhaps it was time he started taking advantage of some of the very obvious compensations available to drive these unwanted irritations from his head.

'I doubt whether knowing about my parentage or siblings is going to be particularly relevant in the circumstances,' he said coolly. 'Of far greater importance is finding out what turns each other on. Because, as lovers, we need to send out the vibe that we've had more than a little…*intimacy.* And in order to convey that to some degree of satisfaction, then I really need to explore you a little more, Willow.'

And before Willow could properly appreciate what was happening, he had undone their seat belts and was pulling her into his arms, as if it was something he had done countless times before. His cold blue eyes swept over her like a searchlight but there was something in their depths which disturbed her. Something which sent foreboding whispering over her spine. Was it the realisation that this man was way too complicated for her to handle and she shouldn't even try? Instinctively, she tried to pull away but he was having none of it, because he gave a silky laugh as he lowered his head to kiss her.

Willow sucked in a disbelieving breath as their lips met, because this wasn't like that lazy kiss at the airport. This was a completely different animal—an un-ashamed display of potent sensuality. This was Dante Di Sione being outrageously macho and showing her exactly who was in charge. It was a stamp and an unmistakable sexual boast and something told Willow that this emotionless kiss meant nothing to him.

But that didn't stop from her reacting, did it?

It didn't stop her from feeling as if she'd just stepped from the darkest shadows into the bright-est sunlight.

His seeking lips coaxed her own apart and she felt the tips of her breasts harden as he deepened the kiss with his tongue. Did he know she was helpless to re-sist from the moment he'd first touched her? Was that why he splayed his fingers over her dress and began to caress her aching breast? She gave a whimper of pleasure as she lifted her arms to curl them around his neck and felt a rush of heat between her legs—a honeyed throb of need which drove every other thought and feeling straight from her body. It felt so good. Unimaginably good. She felt exultant. Hungry for more. Hungry for him.

Softly, Willow moaned with pleasure and he drew his head away, his blue eyes smoky with desire and an unmistakeable trace of mockery glinting in their lapis lazuli depths.

'Do you want me to stop, Willow?' he taunted softly, his words a delicious caress which whispered over her skin, making her want him to talk to her that way all day long. 'Or do you want me to touch you a little more?'

His hand was now moving beneath the hem of her dress and she held her breath. She could feel the tiptoeing of his fingertips against the bare skin and the heat between her legs was increasing as he started to kiss her again. His words were muffled against her mouth as he repeated that same sensual, taunting question—and all the while he was inching his fingers further and further up her thigh.

'Do you?'

Her heart pounded as she opened her mouth to reply when the sound of footsteps crunching over gravel broke into the kiss like a rock smashing through a thin sheet of ice. Reluctantly Willow opened her eyes and pulled away from him, in time to see her sister's astonished face looking at them through the car window.

CHAPTER FOUR

'FLORA!' SOMEHOW WILLOW managed to stumble her
sister's name out through lips which were swollen by
the pressure of Dante's kiss. She tried to pull away
from him but he wasn't having any of it—keeping
his arm anchored tightly around her shoulders. Her
voice trembled a little as his fingertips started stroking at the base of her neck, as if he couldn't bear not
to be touching her. 'What…what are you doing here?'

But Flora wasn't looking at her. She was staring at
Dante as if she couldn't quite believe her eyes. Willow watched as her sister surreptitiously touched her
blond hair as if to check that it was pristine—which
naturally, it was—and then spread her fingers out
over her breastbone, as if to emphasise that at least
one of the Hamilton sisters had breasts.

'And just who is *this*, Willow?' she said in a voice
which didn't quite manage to hide her disbelief. 'You
really must introduce me.'

'He's…' Willow's voice faltered. *He's the man I've
bribed to be here. The man who made me feel I was
almost going to explode with pleasure, and that was
only from a single kiss.*

'My name is Dante Di Sione and I'm Willow's

guest for the wedding,' interjected Dante, and Willow saw Flora almost melt as his sensual lips curved into a lazy smile. 'Didn't she tell you I was coming?'

'No,' said Flora crisply. 'No, she did not. We weren't…well, we weren't expecting her to bring anyone—and as a consequence we've made no special allowances. Which means you'll be in Willow's old bedroom, I'm afraid.'

'And is there a problem with Willow's old bedroom?' he questioned.

'I would say there is, especially for a man of your dimensions.' Flora looked Dante up and down, as if shamelessly assessing his height. 'There's only a single bed.'

Willow wanted to curl up and die, and that was before Dante moved his hand from her neck to place it proprietarily over her thigh. He smiled up at her sister as he pressed his fingers into her flesh. 'Great,' he murmured. 'I do love a good squeeze.'

This clearly wasn't the reaction Flora had expected and the sight of Dante with his hand on her sister's leg must have confused the life out of her. But a lifetime of social training meant that her irritation didn't last long and she made an instant recovery. 'If you'd like to park over by the stables, Dante.' She flashed him a glossy smile. 'Once you've settled in we'll be serving coffee in the drawing room and you'll be able to meet my mother. Oh, and you'll have to try on your bridesmaid dress again, Willow—though I warn you that Clover is going to go ballistic if you've lost any more weight! And don't you think you ought to put a cardigan on? Your arms are covered in goose bumps.'

Dante started up the engine as they watched Flora walk into the main entrance of the grand house. Her blond hair swung down her back in a glossy curtain and she walked with the confident wiggle of a beautiful woman who knew she was being watched.

'So that's one of your sisters,' he said slowly as she disappeared through the open front door.

'Yes.' Willow nodded her head. *So get in first,* she thought. *Say all the stuff he must be thinking and that way you won't come over as vulnerable.* 'I told you my siblings were gorgeous, didn't I? And Flora especially so. Every man she meets falls in love with her. I...I think maybe she's single at the moment, though you can never be...'

'Willow.' He halted her flow of words by placing his finger firmly over her lips. 'Will you please shut up? I may have something of a reputation where women are concerned but even I would draw the line at going to a wedding with one sister, and then making out with another.'

'Not taking into account the fact that she might not be interested in you,' she said indignantly.

'No, of course not,' he murmured as he started up the engine. 'She was looking at me with nothing but cool indifference in her eyes.'

Willow couldn't decide whether to pull him up for his arrogance or simply acknowledge that he was telling the truth, because Flora *had* been looking at him as if she'd like to eat him up for breakfast, lunch and dinner and then maybe go back for a midnight snack. And yet he had been kissing *her*, hadn't he? Kissing her in a way she'd never been kissed before. She could still recall the fizzing excitement in her blood and the way she'd wanted to dissolve beneath his seeking fingers. She'd wanted him to carry on burrowing his fingers beneath her dress and to touch her where she was all hot and aching. Would he laugh or be horrified if he knew she'd never felt like that before? Would he be horrified to discover that she'd never actually had sex before?

They parked the car and she led Dante through the house by one of the back doors, beginning to realise what a big gamble she'd taken by bringing him here. Was he really a good enough actor to pretend to be interested in her when there was going to be so much Grade One crumpet sashaying around the place in their killer heels?

She pushed open the door of her old bedroom, the room where she had spent so much of her childhood—and immediately it felt like stepping back in time. It always did. It made her feel weird and it made her feel small. Little had changed since she'd left home, and whenever she came here, it felt as if her past had been preserved in aspic—and for the first time, she began to question why. Had her parents' refusal to redecorate been based on a longstanding wish not to tempt fate by changing things around?

Willow looked around. There was the portrait done of her when she was six—years before the illness had taken hold—with a blue sparkly clip in her blond hair. How innocent she looked. How totally oblivious to what lay ahead. Next to it was the first embroidery she'd ever done—a sweet, framed cross-stitch saying *Home Sweet Home*. And there were her books—row upon row of them—her beloved connection to the outside world and her only real escape from the sickroom, apart from her sewing. Later on, she'd discovered films—and the more slushy and happy-ever-after, the better. Because fantasy had been a whole lot better than reality.

Sometimes it had felt as if she'd been living in a gilded cage, even though she knew there had been good reasons for that—mainly to keep her away from any rogue infections. But her inevitable isolation and the corresponding protectiveness of her family had left her ill-equipped to deal with certain situations. Like now. She'd missed out on so much. Even at college she'd been watched over and protected by Flora and Clover, who had both been studying at the same university. For a long time she'd only had the energy to deal with maintaining her health and completing her studies and getting a decent degree—she hadn't had the confidence to add men into the mix, even if she'd found anyone attractive enough.

And she had never found anyone as attractive as Dante Di Sione.

She watched him put their bags down and walk over to the window to stare out at the wide green-grey sweep of the Sussex Downs, before turning to face her—his incredible lapis lazuli eyes narrowed. She waited for him to make some comment about the view, or to remark on the massive dimensions of her rather crumbling but beautiful old home, but to her surprise he did neither.

'So,' he said, beginning to walk towards her with stealthy grace. 'How long have we got?'

'Got?' she repeated blankly, not quite sure of his meaning even when he pulled her into his arms and started trailing his fingertips over her body so that she began to shiver beneath the filmy fabric of her delicate dress. 'For…for what?'

Dante smiled, but it was a smile edged with impatience and a danger that even Willow could recognise was sexual.

'That depends on you, and what you want.'

'What I want?' she said faintly.

'Forgive me if I'm mistaken, but I thought that you were as frustrated by your sister's interruption as I was. I was under the distinct impression that our fake relationship was about to get real, and in a very satisfying way. It would certainly be more convincing if we were properly intimate instead of just pretending to be. So are we going to play games with each other or are we going to give in to what we both clearly want?' he murmured as he began to stroke her breasts. 'And have sex?'

Willow quivered as her nipples tightened beneath his expert touch and even though his words were completely unromantic…even though they were the direct opposite of all those mushy rom-coms she used to watch—they were still making her *feel* something, weren't they? They were making her feel like a woman. A *real* woman—not some pale and bloodless creature who'd spent so much time being hooked up to an intravenous drip, while cocktails of drugs were pumped into her system.

Yet this hadn't been what she'd planned when she'd rashly demanded he accompany her here. She'd thought they were engaging in nothing more than an indifferent barter of things they both wanted. Unless she wasn't being honest with herself. *Face the truth, Willow.* And wasn't the truth that from the moment she'd seen him walk into the Caribbean airport terminal, her body had sprung into life with a feeling of lust like she'd never felt before? In which case—why was she hesitating? Wasn't this whole trip supposed to be about changing her life around? To start living like other women her age did.

She tipped up her face so that he could kiss her again. 'Have sex,' she said boldly, meeting the flicker of humour in his smoky blue gaze.

He smiled and then suddenly what was happening *did* feel like a fantasy. Like every one of those mushy films she'd watched. He picked her up and carried her across the room, placing her down on the bed and pausing only to remove the battered old teddy bear that used to accompany her everywhere. She felt a wave of embarrassment as he pushed the bear onto the floor, but then he was bending his lips to hers and suddenly he was kissing her.

It was everything a kiss ought to be. Passionate. Searching. Deep. It made Willow squirm restlessly beneath him, her fingers beginning to scrabble at his shirt as she felt the rush of molten heat between her legs. And maybe he had guessed what was happening—or maybe this was just the way he operated—but he slid his hand beneath her skirt and all the way up her leg, pushing aside the damp panel of her knickers and beginning to tease her there with his finger. Her eyes fluttered to a close and it felt so *perfect* that Willow wanted to cry out her pleasure—but maybe he anticipated that too, because he deepened the kiss. And suddenly it became different. It became hard and hungry and demanding and she was matching it with her own demands—arching her body up towards his, as if she couldn't get close enough.

She could feel the hardness at his groin—the unfamiliar rocky ridge nudging insistently against her—and to her surprise she wasn't daunted, or scared. Maybe it was just her poor starved body demanding what nature had intended it for, because suddenly she was writhing against him—moaning her eagerness and her impatience into his open mouth.

He reached for his belt and Willow heard the rasp of his zip as he began to lower it, when suddenly there was a loud knock on the door.

They both froze and Willow shrank back against the pillows, trying to get her ragged breath back, though it took several seconds before she could speak.

'Who is it?' she demanded in a strangled voice.

'Willow?'

Willow's heart sank. It was Clover's voice. Clover, the bride-to-be. Well-meaning and bossy Clover, the older sister who had protected her as fiercely as a lioness would protect one of her cubs. Just like the rest of her family.

'H-hi, Clover,' she said shakily.

'Can I come in?

Before Willow could answer, Dante shook his head and mouthed, *No*, but she knew what would happen if she didn't comply. There would be an outraged family discussion downstairs. There would be talk of rudeness. They would view Dante with even more suspicion than she suspected he was already going to encounter. The atmosphere would be spoiled before the wedding celebrations had even begun.

She shook her head as she tugged her dress back down, her cheeks flaming bright red as she readjusted her knickers. 'Hang on a minute,' she called, wriggling out of Dante's arms and off the bed, mouthing, *Don't say a word.*

His responding look indicated that he didn't really have much choice but there was no disguising the flicker of fury sparking in his blue eyes.

Willow scuttled over to the door and pulled it open by a crack to see Clover outside, her hair in rollers and an expression on her face which couldn't seem to make up its mind whether to be cross or curious.

'What the hell are you doing?' Clover asked sharply.

For a minute Willow was tempted to tell her to mind her own business, or at least to use her imagination. To snap back that she had just been enjoying a glorious initiation to the mysteries of sex when she had been so rudely interrupted. What was it with her sisters that they kept bursting in on her at the most inopportune moments? But then she reminded herself of everything that Clover had done for her. All those nights she'd sat beside her, holding her hand and helping her keep the nightmares at bay.

Telling herself that her sister was only acting with the best intentions, Willow gave a helpless kind of smile. 'I was just showing Dante the amazing view of the Sussex Downs.'

Clover slanted her a *who-do-you-think-you're-kidding?* look. 'Ah, yes,' she said, loud enough for the entire first floor corridor to hear. 'Dante. The mystery man who drove you here.'

'My guest,' said Willow indignantly.

'Why didn't you tell us you were bringing him?' said Clover.

'Maybe she wanted it to be a surprise,' came a drawling voice, and Willow didn't need to turn round to know that Dante had walked up behind her. She could tell from her sister's goggle-eyed expression even before he placed his hand on her shoulder and started massaging it, the way she'd seen people do in films when they were trying to help their partner relax. *So why did the tight tension inside her body suddenly feel as if it was spiralling out of control?*

'This is…this is Dante,' she said, hearing the hesitance of her words. 'Dante Di Sione.'

'I'm very pleased to meet you, Dante.' Clover's face took on the judgemental expression for which she was famous within the family. 'Perhaps Willow could bear to share you enough to bring you downstairs for coffee, so that everyone can meet you. My mother is particularly keen to make your acquaintance.'

'I can hardly wait,' murmured Dante, increasing the pressure of his impromptu massage by a fraction.

Willow had barely shut the door on her sister before Dante turned her round to face him, his hands on her upper arms, his lapis lazuli gaze boring into her.

'Why do you let her speak to you like that?' he demanded. 'Why didn't you just ignore her, or tell her you were busy? Surely she has enough imagination to realise we were making out?'

Willow gave a half-hearted shrug. 'She's very persistent. They all are.'

He frowned. 'What usually happens when you bring a man home with you?'

Willow licked her lips. Now they were on dangerous territory, and if she told him the truth, she suspected he'd run a mile. Instead, she shot him a challenging look. 'Why, are you afraid of my sisters, Dante?'

'I don't give a damn about your sisters.' He pulled her close against him. 'I'd just like to continue what we were doing a few minutes ago. Now...' His hand cupped her aching breast once more. 'Where were we, can you remember?'

For a minute Willow let him caress her nipple and her eyes fluttered to a close as he began to nuzzle at her neck. She could feel the renewed rush of heat to her body and she wondered how long it would take. Whether they would have time to do it properly. But what if it hurt? What if she *bled*? Pulling away from him, she met the frustration in his eyes.

Was she about to lose her mind? *Of course they wouldn't have time.* She'd waited a long time to have sex—years and years, to be precise—so why rush it and then have to go downstairs in an embarrassing walk of shame, to face her judgemental family who would be assembled in the drawing room like a circle of vultures?

'We've got to go downstairs,' she said. 'For...for coffee.'

'I don't want coffee,' he growled. 'I want you.'

There was a pause before she could summon up the courage to say it and when she did it came out in a breathless rush. 'And I want you.'

'So?'

'So I'm going to be a bridesmaid and I have to get my hair and make-up done before the ceremony.'

She swallowed. 'And there'll be plenty of time for that…later.'

Knowing he was fighting a losing battle—something he always went out of his way to avoid—Dante walked over to the window, trying to calm his acutely aroused body before having to go downstairs to face her frightful family.

He wondered what had made her so surprisingly compliant when her sister had come up here snooping around. He wondered what had happened to the woman who had flirted so boldly with him at the airport. The one who had demanded he be her escort as the price for returning his bag. He'd had her down as one of those independent free spirits who would give great sex—and her going-up-in-flames reaction every time he laid a finger on her had only reinforced that theory.

Yet from the moment he'd driven up the long drive to her impressive but rather faded country house, she had become ridiculously docile. He stared out at the breathtaking view. The magnificence of the distant landscape reminded him of his own family home, back in the States. Somewhere he'd left when he'd gone away to boarding school at the age of eight, and to which he had never really returned. Certainly not for any great length of time. His mouth twisted. Because wasn't it something of a travesty to call the Long Island place a *family home*? It was nothing but a grand house built on some very expensive real estate—with a magnificent facade which concealed all kinds of dirty secrets.

He turned back to find Willow watching him, her grey gaze wary and her manner slightly hesitant—

as if she expected him to say that he had changed his mind and was about to leave. He suddenly found himself thinking that she reminded him of a delicate gazelle.

'Why are you suddenly so uptight?' he questioned. 'Is something wrong?'

Willow stilled and if she hadn't fancied him so much she might have told him the whole story. But it was precisely *because* she fancied him so much that she couldn't. He'd start treating her differently. He'd be overcautious when he touched her. He might not even *want* to touch her. Because that was the thing with illness—it did more than affect the person it struck; it affected everyone around you. People who were mature and sensible might try to deny it, but didn't they sometimes behave as if the illness she'd once had was in some way contagious?

And why *shouldn't* she forget about that period in her life? She'd been given the all-clear ages ago and now was her chance to get something she'd wanted for a very long time. Something as powerful and as uncomplicated as sexual fulfilment, with a man she suspected would be perfect for the purpose, as long as she reminded herself not to read too much into it. For the first time in her life, she had to reach out for what she wanted. Not the things that other women wanted—because she wasn't asking for the impossible. She wasn't clamouring for marriage and babies—just a brief and heady sexual relationship with Dante Di Sione. But she had to be proactive.

She smiled into his hard blue eyes. 'I think it's because I'm the youngest, and they've always been a little protective of me. You know how it is.' She began to walk across the room towards him, plucking up the courage to put her arms around his neck. This close she could see into his eyes perfectly. And although she was short on experience, she recognised the desire which was making them grow so smoky.

And if she detected a flicker of suspicion lurking in their depths, then surely it was up to her to keep those suspicions at bay.

'I don't want to do it in a rush. I want to savour every single moment,' she whispered, trying to sound as if she made sexual assignations with men every day of the week. 'And don't they say that the best things in life are worth waiting for?'

He framed her face in his hands and there was a split second when she thought he was about to bend his head and kiss her, but he didn't. He just stared at her for a very long time, with the kind of look in his eyes which made a shiver trickle down her spine.

'I hear what you're saying and I am prepared to take it on board. But be very clear that I am not a patient man, Willow—and I have a very low boredom threshold. Better not keep me waiting too long,' he said roughly as he levered her away from him, in the direction of the door.

CHAPTER FIVE

Dante glanced around at the guests who were standing on the newly mown lawn drinking champagne. He risked another glance at his watch and wondered how soon this would be over and he could get Willow into bed—but like all weddings, this one seemed never-ending.

The place had been a hive of activity all afternoon. The faded grandeur of Willow's vast home had been transformed by legions of adoring locals, who had carried armfuls of flowers from the nearby village to decorate the house and gardens. Hedges had been trimmed and Chinese lanterns strung high in the trees. Rough wooden trestle tables had been covered with white cloths before being decked with grapes and roses and tiny flickering tealights.

It quickly dawned on him that the Hamiltons were the kind of aristocratic family with plenty of cachet but very little cash. The ceremony had taken place in *their own church*—he found that quite hard to believe—a small but freezing building situated within the extensive grounds. The bride looked okay—but then, all brides looked the same, in Dante's opinion. She wore a white dress and a veil and the service had been interminable. No change there. But he'd found himself unable to tear his eyes away from Willow as she'd made her way up the aisle. He thought how beautiful she looked, despite a deeply unflattering dress and a smile which suggested that, like him, she'd rather be somewhere else.

Before the ceremony he had endured a meet-and-greet with her family over some unspeakable coffee, drunk in a room hung with dusty old paintings. Flora and Clover he'd already met and the remaining sibling was called Poppy—a startlingly pretty girl with grey eyes like Willow's, who seemed as keen to question him as her sisters had been. Their attitude towards him had been one of unrestrained suspicion. They were curious about where he and Willow had met and how long they'd been an item. They seemed surprised to hear he lived in Paris and they wondered how often he was seeing their sister. And because Dante didn't like being interrogated and because he wasn't sure what Willow had told them, he was deliberately vague.

Her parents had appeared at one point. Her mother was tall and still beautiful, with cheekbones as high as Willow's own. She was wearing what looked like her husband's old smoking jacket over a dress and a pair of wellington boots and smiled rather distractedly when Dante shook her hand.

But her attitude changed the instant she caught sight of Willow, who had been over on the other side of the room, finding him a cup of coffee. 'Are you okay, darling? You're not tiring yourself out?'

Just what *was* it with these people? Dante wondered. Was that a warning look from Sister Number Three being slanted in his direction? He *got* that Willow prob-ably didn't bring a lot of men home and he *got* that as the youngest daughter she would be a little overpro-tected. But they seemed to be fussing around her as if she was some kind of teenager, rather than a woman in her mid-twenties. And she seemed to be letting them.

But now the wedding was over, the photo session was finished and he was standing on a warm sum-mer's evening with a growing sense of sexual antici-pation. He felt his mouth dry as he glanced across the lawn, to where Willow was listening to something her mother was saying, obediently nodding her blond head, which was woven with blooms and making her look even more ethereal than before. Her dress em-phasised the razor-sharp slant of her collarbones and the slenderness of her bare arms.

Maybe her intrinsic delicacy was the reason why everyone seemed to treat her with kid gloves. And why her gaggle of interfering sisters seemed to boss her around so much.

Her mother walked off and Dante put his untouched drink onto a table, walking through the growing dusk until he was standing in front of her. He watched as her expression underwent a series of changes. He saw shy-ness as well as that now-familiar wariness in her eyes, but he saw desire too—and that desire lit something inside him and made him want to touch her again.

'Dance with me,' he said.

With a quick bite of her lip, she shook her head. 'I'd better not. I have masses of things I need to do.'

'It wasn't a question, Willow,' he said, pulling her into his arms. 'It was a command and I won't toler-ate anyone who disobeys my commands.'

'That's an outrageous thing to say.'

'So outrageous it's made you shiver with desire?'

'I'm not.'

'Yes, you are.' Pulling her against his body, he breathed in the scent of flowers which made him long to remove that fussy dress and have her naked in his arms. He'd had enough of behaving like a teenager—only getting so far before another of her damned sisters interrupted them. He slid his hand over her ribcage, his heart thundering as his fingertips stroked the slippery satin. 'So how long does this damned wedding go on for?'

'Oh, ages,' she said, but the sudden breathlessness in her voice coincided with his thumb casually beginning to circle the area beneath her breast. 'We haven't even had the speeches yet.'

'That's what's worrying me,' he said, swinging her round and thinking how slight she was. He remembered how feather-light she'd felt when he'd carried her over to that ridiculously tiny bed and he wished he was on that bed right now with his mouth on her breast and his fingers between her legs. 'I don't know how much longer I can wait,' he said huskily.

'Wait?' She drew her head back and it was as if she had suddenly recognised her power over him, because her grey eyes were dancing with mischief. 'Yes, I suppose you must be hungry. Well, don't worry—supper won't be long. Just as soon as my father and the best man have spoken.'

In answer, he pressed his hardness against her with a sudden calculated stamp of sexual mastery and watched as her pupils dilated in response. 'I want you,' he said, very deliberately. 'And I'm tempted to take you by the hand and get us lost in these enormous grounds. I'd like to find somewhere sheltered, like the shade of a big tree, so that I could explore what you're wearing underneath that monstrosity of a dress. I'd like to make you come very quickly. In fact, I think I could make myself come right now, just by thinking about it.'

'Dante!'

'Yes, Willow?'

She drew away from him, trembling slightly, and once again he was confused, because wasn't she just a mass of contradictions? One minute she was so hot that he almost scorched his fingers when he touched her—and the next she was looking up at him with reproachful grey eyes, like some delicate flower he was in danger of crushing beneath the full force of his desire. And that was how her family treated her, wasn't it? Like she couldn't be trusted to make her own judgements and look after herself.

'You're very...'

'Very what?' He stalled her sentence with the brush of his lips against her cheek and felt her shiver again.

'D-demanding,' she managed.

'Don't you like me being demanding?'

Willow closed her eyes as he tightened his arms around her, distracted by the heat of his body and acutely aware that they were being watched. *Of course they were being watched.* Dante Di Sione was easily the most watchable man here—and hadn't that been one of the reasons she'd demanded his company? To show people that she was capable of attracting such a man? But suddenly it felt like much more than just *pretending* to be his lover; she wanted to *be* his lover. She wanted it to be real. She wanted to be like everyone else, but she couldn't. So she was just going to have to make the best of what she was capable of, wasn't she?

'Yes,' she whispered. 'I like it very much. It's just not very appropriate right now. We're in the middle of a crowd of people and there are things I'm supposed to be doing.'

'Like what?'

'Checking that everyone's got a drink so they can make a toast once the speeches start. And introducing people who don't know each other—that sort of thing.'

'All this hanging around and waiting is very dull,' he observed.

'Then circulate,' she said lightly. 'That's what people do.'

'I've done nothing *but* circulate,' he growled. 'I think I'll go crazy if I have to endure yet another society matron trying to calculate what my net worth is.'

She tilted her head back and studied him. 'So how do you usually cope with weddings?'

'By avoiding them whenever possible.'

'But you were unable to avoid this one?'

'It seems I was.'

She narrowed her eyes at him. 'There must be something very valuable in that bag to make you want it so much.'

'Right now, I want you far more than anything in that damned bag.'

Willow giggled, feeling a sudden heady rush of excitement which had more to do with the way he was making her feel than the glass of punch she'd drunk. 'Which was a very neat way of avoiding my question.'

'I don't remember you actually asking a question and it's the only answer you're going to get. So when can we leave?'

'After the cake has been cut,' she said breathlessly. 'Look, there are the main players getting ready to speak and I'm supposed to be up at the top table. I'll see you in a while.'

She tore herself away from his arms, aware of his gaze burning into her as she walked across the garden, but at that moment she was on such a high that she felt as if she could have floated over the candlelit lawn.

It didn't take Flora long to bring her right back down to earth as she joined her in the throng of Hamiltons at the top table.

'I've looked him up on the internet,' she said as soon as Willow was in earshot.

'Who?'

'Who do you think? The man who drove you here today in his flashy red sports car,' replied her sister. 'Mr Macho.'

Willow reached for a glass of champagne from a passing waitress and took a sip as her gaze drifted over towards Dante's statuesque form, which seemed to stand out from the milling crowd. 'He's gorgeous, isn't he?' she said, without really thinking.

'Nobody's denying that,' said Flora slowly. 'And I'm guessing that if you've brought him here, it must be serious?'

'Well, I suppose so,' said Willow evasively.

Flora lowered her voice. 'So you're aware that he's

an *international playboy* with lovers in every major city in the world who is also known as a complete maverick in the world of business?'

Willow took a mouthful of fizz. 'So what? I'm not planning some kind of corporate takeover with him.'

'He's way out of your league, love,' said Flora gently. 'He's a wolf and you're an innocent little lamb. You haven't exactly had a lot of experience with the opposite sex, have you?'

'Only because my family is too busy mounting an armed guard around me!'

Flora frowned. 'So what exactly is going on between you?'

There was a pause. 'I like him,' said Willow truthfully. 'I like him a lot.'

It was perhaps unfortunate that Great-aunt Maud should have chosen just that moment to drift past in a cloud of magenta chiffon and gardenia perfume, blinking rapidly as she caught the tail end of their conversation. 'So does that mean you're going to be next up the aisle, Willow?' She beamed, without waiting for an answer. 'I must say I'm not surprised. He is quite something, that young man of yours. Quite something.'

Dante listened to the formal speeches which always bored the hell out of him and steadfastly ignored the redhead who was flashing him an eager smile. But for once the sentiments expressed went beyond the usual gags about mothers-in-law and shotguns. The groom thanked all the bridesmaids and told them how beautiful they looked, but he left Willow until last, and suddenly his voice grew serious.

'I'd just like to say how much it meant to Clover, having Willow's support. But much more than that is having her here today, looking so lovely. It means... well, it means everything to us.'

Dante frowned as people began to cheer, wondering why the atmosphere had grown distinctly *poignant* and why Willow's mother was suddenly groping in her bag for a handkerchief.

But then Willow's father began speaking and after he had waxed long and lyrical about the bride, he paused before resuming—his eyes resting affectionately on the slender blonde in the bridesmaid dress who was twisting the peachy satin around her fingers and looking slightly awkward.

'I just want to echo Dominic's words and say how happy we are to see Willow here today looking, if I might add, positively radiant. We just want her to know how proud we are of her, and the way she handled her illness, when all her peers were running around without a care in the world. And how her recovery has made us all feel very, very grateful.'

The applause which followed was deafening and Dante's lips froze as suddenly it all made sense.

Of *course*.

That's why she looked so fragile and that's why her family fussed around her and were so protective of her.

She'd been ill.

How ill? It must have been bad for it to warrant a mention in not one but *two* of the wedding speeches.

He felt momentarily winded. Like that time when a tennis ball hit by his twin had slammed straight into his solar plexus. He had been itching to take Willow away from here as soon as the speeches were over, but suddenly he needed time. And distance. Because how could he now take her to bed in the light of what he had learned?

Did Willow sense where he was in the throng of people? Was that why her grey eyes suddenly turned to meet his? Only this time it was more than desire which pumped through his veins as his gaze connected with hers. It was a cocktail of emotions he was unfamiliar with. He felt sympathy and a flare of something which clenched his heart with a sensation close to pain. The sense that life was unfair. And yet why should that come as a surprise, when he'd learnt the lesson of life's unfairness at the age of eight, when his entire world had changed for ever?

Why the hell hadn't she told him?

He watched as the smile she was directing at him became slightly uncertain and she picked up her glass and took a mouthful of champagne. And part of him wanted to run. To get into his car and drive back to London. To fly on to Paris as soon as possible and put this whole incident behind him. Yet he couldn't do that—and not just because she still had his grandfather's precious tiara. He couldn't just turn his back on her and walk away. If she'd known real suffering, then she deserved his compassion and his respect.

He saw all the women lining up and giggling and wondered what was happening, when he realised that the bride was about to throw her bouquet. And he wondered why it came as no real sense of surprise when Willow caught it, to the accompaniment of more loud cheers.

He couldn't stay here. He could see some of her

relatives smiling at him, almost—*God forbid*—as if they were preparing to welcome him into the fold and he knew that he had to act. Ignoring the redhead with the cleavage who had been edging closer and closer, he walked straight up to Willow and took the empty champagne glass from her hand.

'Let's get out of here.'

He couldn't miss the look of relief on her face.

'I thought you'd never ask,' she said, sounding a little unsteady.

On her high-heeled shoes she was tottering as they walked across the darkening grass as if she'd had a little too much to drink—but for once Dante wasn't about to take the moral high ground.

He waited for her to mention the speeches, but she didn't. She was too busy weaving her fingers into his and squeezing them. He thought again about her father's words and how her experience had affected her. It meant she'd probably learnt in the hardest way possible about the fragility of life and the random way that trouble could strike. He wondered if she'd plumped for recklessness as a result of that. Was that why she would have had sex with him before the wedding had even started, if her damned sister hadn't interrupted them? He wondered if she was this free with everyone—an aristocratic wild child who'd learned to be liberal with her body. And he was unprepared for the sudden dark shaft of anger which slammed into him.

They reached her room without meeting anyone and the sounds of celebration drifted up through the open windows as she shut the bedroom door behind them and switched on a small lamp. He could hear music and laughter and the rising lull of snatched conversation, but there was no joy in Dante's heart right then.

She leaned against the door, her shiny ruffled dress gleaming and her grey eyes looking very bright. 'So,' she said, darting a rather embarrassed glance at the bride's bouquet she was still holding, before quickly putting it down on a nearby table. 'Now what?'

He wished he could wipe what he'd heard from his mind, leaving his conscience free to do what he really wanted—which was to walk over there and remove her dress. To take off her bra and her panties and strip himself bare, before entering that pale and slim body with one slow and exquisite thrust.

He went to stand by the window, with his back to the strings of Chinese lanterns which gleamed in the trees.

'Did you enjoy the wedding, Willow?' he asked carefully.

She walked across the room, pulling the wilting crown of flowers from her head and placing it on the dressing table, and a clip which clattered onto the wooden floor sounded unnaturally loud.

'It was okay,' she said, taking out another clip, and then another, before putting them down. She turned around then, her hair spilling over her shoulders, and there was a faint look of anxiety in her eyes, as if she had just picked up from his tone that something was different. She licked her lips. 'Did you?'

He shook his head. 'No, not really. But then, I'm not really a big fan of weddings.'

Her smile became a little brittle. 'Oh, well, at least

it's over now,' she said. 'So why don't we just take our minds off it?'

She began to walk unsteadily towards him and Dante knew he had to stop this before it went any further. Before he did something he might later regret. But it was hard to resist her when she looked so damned lovely. There was something so compelling about her. Something pure and untouched which contrasted with the hungry look in her eyes and the wanton spill of her half-pinned hair. She looked like a little girl playing the part of vamp.

He shook his head. 'No, Willow.'

But she kept on walking towards him until she was standing in front of him in her long dress. And now she was winding her arms around his neck and clinging on to him like a tender vine and the desire to kiss her was like a fever raging in his blood.

Briefly, he closed his eyes as if that would help him resist temptation, but it didn't—because the feel of her was just as distracting as the sight of her. And maybe she took that as an invitation—because she brushed her mouth over his with a tentative exploration which made him shiver. With an angry little groan he succumbed to the spiralling of desire as he deepened the kiss. He felt the kick of his heart as her hands began to move rather frantically over him, and what could he do but respond?

She was tugging at his tie as he started to caress the slender lines of her body, his fingers sliding helplessly over the slippery material. He felt her sway and picked her up, carrying her over to the bed, like a man acting on autopilot. She lay there, almost swamped by the silky folds of her bridesmaid dress, and as his hand reached out to stroke its way over her satin-covered breast, he felt a savage jerk of lust.

'Oh, Dante,' she breathed—and that heartfelt little note of wonder was almost his undoing.

Would it be so wrong to take her? To have her gasp out her pleasure and him do the same, especially when they both wanted it so badly? Surely it would be a *good* thing to end this rather bizarre day with some uncomplicated and mindless sex.

Except that it wouldn't be uncomplicated. Or mindless. Not in the light of what he'd learned. Because she was vulnerable. Of course she was. And he couldn't treat her as he would treat any other woman. He couldn't just strip her naked and pleasure her and take what he wanted for himself before walking away. She had gone through too much to be treated as something disposable.

With an effort which tore at him like a physical pain, he moved away from the bed and went to stand by the window, where the darkness of the garden was broken by the flickering gleam of candlelight. Tiny pinpricks of light glittered on every surface, like fallen stars. Beneath the open window he could hear a couple talking in low voices which then abruptly stopped and something told him they were kissing. Was that envy he felt? Envy that he couldn't just forget everything he knew and block out his reservations with a kiss?

It took several moments for the hunger to leave him, and when he had composed himself sufficiently, he turned back to find her sitting up on the bed looking at him—confusion alternating with the desire which was skating across her fine-boned features.

He drew in a deep breath. 'Why didn't you tell me you'd been so ill?'

Willow's first reaction was one of rage as his words fired into her skin like sharp little arrows. Rage that her father and Dominic should have seen fit to include the information *in their speeches* and rage that he should suddenly have started talking to her in that new and gentle voice. She didn't want him to be *gentle* with her—she wanted him hot and hungry. She wanted him tugging impatiently at her clothes like he'd been before, as if he couldn't wait to strip her bare.

'What does that have to do with anything?' she demanded. 'I had leukaemia as a child. What's the big deal?'

'It's a pretty big deal, Willow.'

'Only if people choose to make it one,' she gritted out. 'Especially since I've had the all-clear, which makes me as disease-free as you or the rest of the general population. What did you want me to do, Dante? Tell you all about the drugs and the side effects and the way my hair fell out, or how difficult it was to actually keep food down? When it comes to interacting with men, it's not exactly what they want to hear as a chat-up line. It doesn't really make you attractive towards the opposite sex.' She glared. 'Why the hell did Dom and my father have to say anything?'

'I think I might have worked it out for myself,' he said slowly. 'Because I'd had my suspicions ever since we arrived.'

'You had your *suspicions*?' she echoed angrily.

'Sure. I wondered why your sisters were acting as

if I was the big, bad ogre and I wondered why everyone was so protective of you. It took me a while to work out why that might be, but now I think I have.'

'So once I was very sick and now I'm not,' she said flippantly. 'End of subject, surely?'

'But it's a little bit more complicated than that, Willow?' he said slowly. 'Isn't it?'

For a minute she stiffened as she thought he might have learned about her biggest fear and secret, before she told herself he couldn't know. He wasn't *that* perceptive and she'd certainly never discussed it with anyone else. 'What are you talking about?' she questioned.

His eyes narrowed. 'Something tells me you've never brought a man back here before. Have you?'

Willow felt humiliation wash over her and in that moment she hated Dante Di Sione's perception and that concerned way he was looking at her. She didn't want him looking at her with *concern*—she wanted him looking at her with *lust*. *So brazen it out*, she told herself. *You've come this far. You've dismissed your illness, so deal with the rest.* She had him here with her—a captive audience—and judging by his body language, he still wanted her just as much as she wanted him.

'And how did you manage to work that out?' she questioned.

His eyes were boring into her, still with that horrible, unwanted perception.

'Just that every time I was introduced as your partner, people expressed a kind of barely concealed astonishment. I mean, I know I have something of a reputation where women are concerned, but they were acting like I was the devil incarnate.'

For a second Willow thought about lying to him. About telling him that his was just another anonymous face in a sea of men she'd brought here. But why tell him something she'd be unable to carry off? She didn't think she was *that* good a liar. And all she wanted was for that warm feeling to come back. She wanted him to kiss her again. She wasn't asking for commitment—she knew she could never be in a position to ask for that. All she wanted was to be in his arms again.

She thought about the person she'd been when he'd met her at the airport—that bold and flirtatious Willow she'd never dared be before—and Dante had seemed to like that Willow, hadn't he? She was certainly a more attractive proposition than the woman sitting huddled on the bed, meekly listening to him berate her.

'I thought you would be the kind of man who wouldn't particularly want a woman to burden you with every second of her past.'

'That much is true,' he conceded reluctantly.

'So, what's your beef?'

Rather unsteadily, she got off the bed, and before he could stop her she'd reached behind her to slide down the zip of her bridesmaid dress, so that it pooled around her ankles in a shimmering circle.

Willow had never stood in front of a man in her underwear before and she'd always wondered what it would feel like—whether she would feel shy or uninhibited or just plain self-conscious. But she could still feel the effect of the champagne she'd drunk and,

more than that, the look on his face was powerful
enough to drive every inhibition from her mind. Because Dante looked almost *tortured* as she stepped out
from the circle of satin and stood before him wearing nothing but her underwear and a pair of high-
heeled shoes.

And although people often told her she looked as if
she could do with a decent meal, Willow knew from
her time working in the fashion industry that slenderness worked in your favour when you were wearing nothing but a bra and a pair of pants. She could
see his gaze lingering on the swell of her breasts in
the ivory-coloured lace bra which was embroidered
with tiny roses. Reluctantly, it travelled down to her
bare stomach before seeming to caress the matching
thong, lingering longest on the flimsy triangle and
making her ache there.

Feeling as if she was playing out a part she'd seen
in a film, she lifted her fingers to her breast and
cupped the slight curve. As she ran her finger along
a twist of leaves, she thought she saw him move, as
if he was about to cross the room and take her in his
arms after all, and she held her breath in anticipation.

But he didn't.

Instead a little nerve began working furiously at
his temple as he patted his pocket, until he'd found
his car keys.

'And I think that's my cue to leave,' he said harshly.

'No!' The word came out in a rush. 'Please, Dante.
I don't want you to go.'

'I'm sorry. I'm out of here.'

'Dante…'

'No. Listen to me, Willow.' There was a pause

while he seemed to be composing himself, and when he started speaking, his words sounded very controlled. 'For what it's worth, I think you're lovely. Very lovely. A beautiful butterfly of a woman. But I'm not going to have sex with you.'

She swallowed. 'Because you don't want me?'

His voice grew rough. 'You know damned well I want you.'

She lifted her eyes to his. 'Then why?'

He seemed to hesitate and Willow got the distinct feeling that he was going to say something dismissive, or tell her that he didn't owe her any kind of explanation. But to her surprise, he didn't. His expression took on that almost gentle look again and she found herself wanting to hurl something at him...preferably herself. To tell him not to wrap her up in cotton wool the way everyone else did. To treat her like she was made of flesh and blood instead of something fragile and breakable. To make her feel like that passionate woman he'd brought to life in his arms.

'Because I'm the kind of man who brings women pain, and you've probably had enough of that in your life. Don't make yourself the willing recipient of any more.' He met the question in her eyes. 'I'm incapable of giving women what they want and I'm not talking about sex. I don't do emotion, or love, or commitment, because I don't really know how those things work. When people tell me that I'm cold and unfeeling, I don't get offended—because I know it's true. There's nothing deep about me, Willow—and there never will be.'

Willow drew in a breath. It was now or never. It was a huge risk—but so what? What did she have to lose when the alternative of not having him suddenly seemed unbearable? 'But that's all I want from you,' she whispered. 'Sex.'

His face hardened as he shook his head.

'And I certainly don't have sex with virgins,' he finished flatly.

She stared at him in disbelief. 'But…how on earth could you tell I was a virgin?' she whispered, her voice quivering with disappointment, before realising from his brief, hard smile that she had just walked into some sort of trap.

'Call it an informed guess,' he said drily. 'And it's the reason why I have to leave.'

The hurt and the rejection Willow was feeling was now replaced by a far more real concern as she realised he meant it. He was going to leave her there, aching and alone and having to face everyone in the morning.

Reaching down to the bed, she grabbed at the duvet which was lying on the bed and wrapped it around herself, so that it covered her in an unflattering white cloud. And then she looked into the icy glitter of his eyes, willing him not to walk away. 'If you go now, it will just cause a big scene. It will make people gossip and stir up all kinds of questions. And I don't think I can face them. Or rather, I don't want to face them. Please don't make me. Don't go,' she said urgently. 'At least, not tonight. Let's pretend that you're my lover, even if it's not true. Let me show my sisters and my family that I'm a grown-up woman who doesn't need their protection any more. I want to break free from their well-meaning intervention, and you're the person who can help me. So help me, Dante. Don't make me face them alone in the morning.'

Dante heard the raw appeal in her voice and realised how difficult that must have been for her to say.
She seemed so vulnerable that part of him wanted to
go over there and comfort her. To cradle her in his
arms and tell her everything was going to be all right.
But he couldn't do that with any degree of certainty,
could he? He didn't even trust himself to touch her
without going back on his word and it was vital he
kept to his self-imposed promise.

'This is a crazy situation,' he growled. 'Which
is going to get even crazier if I stay. I'm sorry, Willow—but I can't do it.'

In the distance, the music suddenly came to a halt
and the sound of clapping drifted in through the open
windows.

'But I still have your bag,' she said quietly. 'And I
thought you badly wanted it back.'

There was a pause.

'Are you...*threatening* me?' he questioned.

She shrugged. 'I thought we had a deal.'

He met her grey gaze and an unwilling feeling of
admiration flooded through him as he realised that
she meant it. And even though she wouldn't have
had a leg to stand on if he had decided to offer *real*
resistance, he knew he couldn't do it. Because there
were only so many setbacks a person could take—and
she'd had more than her fair share of them.

'Okay,' he said at last. 'The deal still stands,
though the terms have changed. And this is what
we're going to do. You are going to get ready for
bed in the bathroom and you're going to wear something—anything—I don't care what it is as long as
it covers you up. You are then going to get into bed

and I don't want to hear another word from you until morning, when we will leave for London before anyone else is awake, because I have no intention of facing your family first thing and having to continue with this ridiculous farce.'

'But…where will you sleep?'

With a faint feeling of disbelief that he should be consigning himself to a celibate night, he pointed to a faded velvet chaise longue on the opposite side of the room. 'Over there,' he said.

'Dante…'

'No,' he said, his patience dwindling as he moved away from her, because despite the fact that she was swaddled beneath that fat, white duvet, the image of her slender body wearing nothing but her bra and pants was seared into his memory. He swallowed. 'I want you to do that right now, or the deal is off— and if I have to drive myself back to London and break into your apartment in order to retrieve what is rightfully mine, then I will do it. Do you understand, Willow?'

She met his eyes and nodded with an obedience which somehow made his heart twist.

'Yes, Dante,' she said. 'I understand.'

CHAPTER SIX

THE STRONG SMELL of coffee filtered into her senses, waking Willow from her restless night. Slowly, her eyelids flickered open to see Dante standing by her bed with a steaming mug in his hand. He was already dressed, though looked as if he could do with a shave, because his jaw was dark and shadowed.

So were his eyes.

'Where did you find the coffee?' she asked.

'Where do you think I found it? In the kitchen. And before you ask, the answer is no. Everyone else in the house must be sleeping off their hangover because I didn't bump into anyone else along the way.'

Willow nodded. It was like a bad dream. Actually, it was more like a nightmare. She'd spent the night alone in her childhood bed, covered up in a baggy T-shirt and a pair of pants, while Dante slept on the chaise longue on the other side of the room.

Pushing her hair away from her face, she sat up and stared out of the windows. Neither of them had drawn the drapes last night and the pale blue of the morning sky was edged with puffy little white clouds. The birds were singing fit to burst and the powerful scent of roses drifted in on the still-cool air. It was

an English morning at its loveliest and yet its beauty
seemed to mock her. It reminded her of all the things
she didn't have. All the things she probably never
would have. It made her think about the disaster of
the wedding the day before. She thought about her
sister laughing up at her new husband with love shining from her eyes. About the youngest flower girl,
clutching her posy with dimpled fists. About the tiny
wail of a baby in the church, and the shushing noises
of her mother as she'd carried the crying infant outside, to the understanding smiles of the other women
present, like they were all members of that exclusive
club called *Mothers*.

A twist of pain like a knife in her heart momentarily caught Willow off-guard and it took a moment
before she had composed herself enough to turn to
look into Dante's bright blue eyes.

'What time is it?' she asked.

'Still early.' His iced gaze swept over her. 'How
long will it take you to get ready?'

'Not long.'

'Good,' he said, putting the coffee down on the
bedside table and then walking over to the other side
of the room to stare out of the window. 'Then just do
it, and let's get going as soon as possible, shall we?'

It was couched as a question but there was no disguising the fact that it was another command.

'What about my parents?'

'Leave them a note.'

She wanted to tell him that her mother would hit
the roof if she just slunk away without even having
breakfast, but she guessed what his response would
be. He would shrug and tell her she was welcome to

stay. And she didn't *want* to stay here, without him. She wanted to keep her pathetic fantasy alive for a while longer. She wanted people to see what wasn't really true. Willow with her boyfriend. Willow who'd just spent the night with a devastatingly attractive man. Lucky Willow.

Only she wasn't lucky at all, was she?

Sliding out of bed, she grabbed her clothes and took the quickest shower on record as she tried very hard not to think about the way she'd pleaded with Dante to have sex with her the night before. Or the way he'd turned her down. He'd told her it was because he was cold and sometimes cruel. He'd told her he didn't want to hurt her and maybe that was thoughtfulness on his part—how ironic, then, that he had ended up by hurting her anyway.

Dressing in jeans and a T-shirt and twisting her hair into a single plait, Willow returned to the bedroom, drank her cooled coffee and then walked with Dante through the blessedly quiet corridors towards the back of the house.

She should have realised it was too good to be true, because there, standing by the kitchen door wearing a silky dressing gown and a pair of flip-flops, stood her mother. Willow stared at her in dismay. Had she heard her and Dante creeping through the house, or was this yet another example of the finely tuned antennae her mother always seemed able to call upon whenever she was around?

'M-Mum,' stumbled Willow awkwardly.

A pair of eyebrows were arched in her direction. 'Going somewhere?'

Willow felt her cheeks grow pink and was racking her brains about what to say, when Dante intercepted.

'You must forgive us for slipping away so early after such a fabulous day yesterday, Mrs Hamilton—but I have a pile of work I need to get through before I go back to Paris and Willow has promised to help me.' He smiled. 'Haven't you?'

Willow had never seen her mother look quite so flustered—but how could she possibly object in the face of all that undeniable charm and charisma Dante was directing at her? She saw the quick flare of hope in her mother's eyes. Was she in danger of projecting into the future, just as Great-aunt Maud had done last night?

Kissing her mother goodbye she and Dante went outside, but during the short time she'd spent getting ready, the puffy white clouds had accumulated and spread across the sky like foam on a cup of macchiato. Suddenly, the air had a distinct chill and Willow shivered as Dante put the car roof up and she slid onto the passenger seat.

It wasn't like the outward journey, when the wind had rushed through their hair and the sun had shone and she had been filled with a distinct sensation of hope and excitement. Enclosed beneath the soft roof, the atmosphere felt claustrophobic and tense and the roar of his powerful car sounded loud as it broke the early-morning Sunday silence.

They drove for a little way without saying anything, and once out on the narrow, leafy lanes, Willow risked a glance at him. His dark hair curled very slightly over the collar of his shirt and his olive skin glowed. Despite his obvious lack of sleep and being in need of a shave, he looked healthy and glowing—like a man at the very peak of his powers, but his profile was set and unmoving.

She cleared her throat. 'Are you angry with me?'

Dante stared straight ahead as the hedgerows passed in a blur of green. He'd spent an unendurable night. Not just because his six-foot-plus frame had dwarfed the antique piece of furniture on which he'd been attempting to sleep, but because he'd felt bad. And it hadn't got any better. He'd been forced to listen to Willow tossing and turning while she slept. To imagine that pale and slender body moving restlessly against the sheet. He'd remembered how she'd felt. How she'd tasted. How she'd begged him to make love to her. He had been filled with a heady sexual hunger which had made him want to explode. He'd wanted her, and yet rejecting her had been his only honourable choice. Because what he'd said had been true. He *did* hurt women. He'd never found one who was capable of chipping her way through the stony walls he'd erected around his heart, and sometimes he didn't think he ever would. And in the meantime, Willow Hamilton needed protection from a man like him.

'I'm angry with myself,' he said.

'Because?'

'Because I should have chosen a less controversial way of getting my bag back. I shouldn't have agreed to be your plus one.' He gave a short laugh. 'But you were very persuasive.'

She didn't answer immediately. He could see her finger drawing little circles over one of the peacocks which adorned her denim-covered thigh.

'There must be something in that bag you want very badly.'

'There is.'

'But I don't suppose you're going to tell me what it is?'

The car had slowed down to allow a stray sheep to pick its way laboriously across the road, giving them a slightly dazed glance as it did so. Dante's instinct was to tell her that her guess was correct, but suddenly he found himself wanting to tell her. Was that because so far he hadn't discussed it with anyone? Because he and his twin brother were estranged and he wasn't particularly close to any of his other siblings? That all their dark secrets and their heartache seemed to have pushed them all apart, rather than bringing them closer together...

'The bag contains a diamond and emerald tiara,' he said. 'Worth hundreds of thousands of dollars.'

Her finger stopped moving. 'You're kidding?'

'No, I'm not. My grandfather specifically asked me to get it for him and it took me weeks to track the damned thing down. He calls it one of his Lost Mistresses, for reasons he's reluctant to explain. He sold it a long time ago and now he wants it back.'

'Do you know why?'

He shrugged. 'Maybe because he's dying.'

'I'm sorry,' she said softly, and he wondered if she'd heard the slight break in his voice.

'Yeah,' he said gruffly, his tightened lips intended to show her that the topic was now closed.

They drove for a while in silence and had just hit the outskirts of greater London, when her voice broke into his thoughts.

'Your name is Italian,' she commented quietly. 'But your accent isn't. Sometimes you sound American, but at other times your accent could almost be Italian, or French. How come?'

Dante thought how women always wanted to do things the wrong way round. Shouldn't she have made chatty little enquiries about his background *before* he'd had his hand inside her panties yesterday? And yet wasn't he grateful that she'd moved from the subject of his family?

'Because I was born in the States,' he said. 'And spent the first eight years of my life there—until I was sent away to boarding school in Europe.'

She nodded and he half expected the usual squeak of indignation. Because women invariably thought they were showcasing their caring side by professing horror at the thought of a little boy being sent away from home so young. But he remembered that the English were different and her aristocratic class in particular had always sent young boys away to school.

'And did you like it?' she questioned.

Dante nodded, knowing his reaction had been unusual—the supposition being that any child would hate being removed from the heart of their family. Except in his case there hadn't been a heart. That had been torn out one dark and drug-fuelled night— shattered and smashed—leaving behind nothing but emptiness, anger and guilt.

'As it happens, I liked it very much,' he drawled, deliberately pushing the bitter thoughts away. 'It was in the Swiss mountains—pure and white and unbelievably beautiful.' He paused as he remembered how the soft white flakes used to swarm down from the sky, blanketing the world in a pure silence—and how he had eagerly retreated into that cold space where nothing or nobody could touch him. 'We used to ski every day, which wore us out so much that there wasn't really time to think. And there were kids from all over the world, so it was kind of anonymous—and I liked that.'

'You must speak another language.'

'I speak three others,' he said. 'French, Italian and German.'

'And that's why you live in Paris?'

His mouth hardened. 'I don't remember mentioning that I lived in Paris.'

Out of the corner of his eye he saw her shoulders slump a little.

'I must have read that on the internet too. You can't blame me,' she said, her words leaving her mouth in a sudden rush.

'No, I don't blame you,' he said. Just as he couldn't blame her for the sudden sexual tension which seemed to have sprung up between them again, which was making it difficult for him to concentrate. Maybe that was inevitable. They were two people who'd been interrupted while making out, leaving them both aching and frustrated. And even though his head was telling him that was the best thing which could have happened, his body seemed to have other ideas.

Because right now all he could think about was how soft her skin had felt as he had skated his fingertips all the way up beneath that flouncy little dress she'd been wearing. He remembered the slenderness of her hips and breasts as she'd stood before him in her bra and panties—defiant yet innocent as she'd stripped off her bridesmaid dress and let it pool around her feet. He'd resisted her then, even though the scent of her arousal had called out to his hungry body on a primitive level which had made resistance almost unendurable. Was that what was happening now? Why he wanted to stop the car and take her somewhere—anywhere—so that he could be alone with her? Free to pull aside her clothes. To unzip her jeans and tease her until she was writhing in helpless appeal.

He wondered if he'd been out of his mind to say no. He could easily have introduced her to limitless pleasures in his arms—and what better initiation for a virgin than lovemaking with someone like him? But it wasn't his technique which was in question, but his inbuilt emotional distance. He couldn't connect. He didn't know how.

'So why Paris?' she was asking.

Make her get the message, he thought. *Make her realise that she's had a lucky escape from a man like you.*

'It's well placed for central Europe,' he said. 'I like the city and the food and the culture. And, of course, the women,' he added deliberately. 'French women are very easy to like.'

'I can imagine they must be,' she said, her voice sounding unnaturally bright.

The car was soon swallowed up by the heavier London traffic and he noticed she was staring fixedly out of the window.

'We're nearly here,' he said, forcing himself to make some conversational remark. To try to draw a line under this as neatly as possible. 'So…have you got any plans for the rest of the day?'

Willow gazed at the familiar wide streets close to her apartment and realised he was preparing to say goodbye to her. What she would like to do more than anything else was to rail against the unfairness of it all. Not only had he turned her down, but he'd deliberately started talking about other women—*French women*—as if to drive home just how forgettable she really was. And he had done it just as she'd been speculating about his fast, international lifestyle. Thinking that he didn't seem like the sort of man who would ever embrace the role of husband and father…the sort of man who really would have been a perfect lover for a woman like her.

Well, she was just going to have to forget her stupid daydreams. Just tick it off and put it down to experience. She would get over it, as she had got over so much else. No way was she going to leave him with an enduring memory of her behaving like a victim. *Remember how he moaned in your arms when he kissed you*, she reminded herself fiercely as she slanted him a smile. *Remember that* you *have some power here, too.*

'I'll probably go for a walk in Regent's Park,' she said. 'The flowers are gorgeous at this time of the year. And I might meet a friend later and catch a film. How about you?'

'I'll pick up my bag from you and then fly straight back to France.' He stifled a yawn. 'It's been an eventful few days.'

And that, thought Willow, was that.

She was glad of all the times when her mother

had drummed in the importance of posture because it meant that she was able to walk into her apartment with her head held very proud and her shoulders as stiff as a ramrod, as Dante followed her inside.

She pulled out the leather case from the bottom of her wardrobe, her fingers closing around it just before she handed it to him.

'I'd love to see the tiara,' she said.

He shook his head. 'Better not.'

'Even though I inadvertently carried a priceless piece of jewellery through customs without declaring it?'

'You shouldn't have picked up the wrong bag.'

You shouldn't have been distracting me. 'And I could now be languishing in some jail somewhere,' she continued.

He gave a slow smile. 'I would have bailed you out.'

'I only have your word for that,' she said.

'And you don't trust my word?'

She shrugged. 'I don't know you well enough to answer that. Besides, oughtn't you to check that the piece is intact? That I haven't substituted something fake in its place—or stolen one of the stones. That this Lost Mistress is in a decent state to give to your grandfather and...'

But her words died away as he began to unlock the leather case and slowly drew out a jewelled tiara—a glittering coronet of white diamonds and almond-size emeralds as green as new leaves. Against Dante's olive skin they sparked their bright fire and it was impossible for Willow to look anywhere else but at them.

'Oh, but they're beautiful,' she breathed. 'Just beautiful.'

Her eyes were shining as she said it and something about her unselfconscious appreciation touched something inside him. And Dante felt a funny twist of regret as he said goodbye. As if he was walking away from something unfinished. It seemed inappropriate to shake her hand, yet he didn't trust himself to kiss her cheek, for he suspected that even the lightest touch would rekindle his desire. He would send her flowers as a thank-you, he decided. Maybe even a diamond on a fine gold chain—you couldn't go wrong with something like that. She'd be able to show it off to her sisters and pretend that their relationship had been real. And one day she would be grateful to him for his restraint. She would accept the truth of what he'd said and realise that someone like him would bring her nothing but heartache. She would find herself some suitable English aristocrat and move to a big house in the country where she could live a life not unlike that of her parents.

He didn't turn on his phone until he was at the airfield because he despised people who allowed themselves to get distracted on the road. But he wished afterwards that he'd checked his messages while he was closer to Willow's apartment. Close enough to go back for a showdown.

As it was, he drove to the airfield in a state of blissful ignorance, and the first he knew about the disruption was when his assistant, René, rushed up to him brandishing a newspaper—a look of astonishment contorting his Gallic features.

'*C'est impossible!* Why didn't you tell me, boss?'

he accused. 'I have been trying to get hold of you all morning, wondering what you want me to say to the press…'

'Why should I want you to say anything to the press?' demanded Dante impatiently. 'When you know how much I hate them.'

His assistant gave a flamboyant shake of his head. 'I think their sudden interest is understandable, in the circumstances.'

Dante frowned. 'What the hell are you talking about?'

'It is everywhere!' declared René. 'Absolutely everywhere! All of Paris is buzzing with the news that the bad-boy American playboy has fallen in love at last—and that you are engaged to an English aristocrat called Willow Anoushka Hamilton.'

CHAPTER SEVEN

WILLOW FELT RESTLESS after Dante had left, unable to settle to anything. Distractedly, she wandered around her apartment—except that never had it felt more like living in someone else's space than it did right then. It seemed as if the charismatic American had invaded the quiet rooms and left something of himself behind. She couldn't seem to stop thinking about his bright blue eyes and hard body and the plummeting of her heart as he'd said goodbye.

She slipped on a pair of sneakers and let herself outside, but for once the bright colours of the immaculate flower beds in the nearby park were wasted on her. It was funny how your thoughts could keep buzzing and buzzing around your head, just like the pollen-laden bees which were clinging like crazy to stop themselves from toppling off the delicate blooms.

She thought about the chaste night she'd spent with Dante. She thought about the way he'd kissed her and the way she'd been kissed in the past. But up until now she'd always clammed up whenever a man touched her. She'd started to believe that she wasn't capable of real passion. That maybe she was incapable of reacting like a normal woman. But Dante Di Sione had awoken something in her the moment he'd touched her. *And then walked away just because she'd been ill as a kid.*

She bought a pint of milk on her way home from the park and was in the kitchen making coffee when the loud shrill of the doorbell penetrated the uncomfortable swirl of her thoughts. She wasn't really concentrating when she went into the hall to see who it was, startled to see Dante standing on her doorstep with a look on his face she couldn't quite work out.

She blinked at him, aware of the thunder of her heart and the need to keep her reaction hidden. To try to hide the sudden flash of hope inside her. Had he changed his mind? Did he realise that he only had to say the word and she would be sliding between the sheets with him—right now, if he wanted her?

'Did you forget something?' she said, but the dark expression on his face quickly put paid to any lingering hope. And then he was brushing past her, that brief contact only adding to her sense of disorientation. 'What do you think you're doing?'

'Shut the door,' he said tersely.

'You can't just walk in here and start telling me what to do.'

'Shut the door, Willow,' he repeated grimly. 'Unless you want your neighbours to hear what I have to say.'

Part of her wanted to challenge him. To tell him to go right ahead and that she didn't care what her neighbours thought. Because he didn't want her, did he? He'd rejected her—so what right did he have to start throwing his weight around like this?

Yet he looked so golden and gorgeous as he towered over her, dominating the shaded entrance hall of the basement apartment, that it was difficult for her to think straight. And suddenly she couldn't bear to be this close without wanting to reach out and touch him. To trace her finger along the dark graze of his jaw and drift it upwards to his lips. *So start taking control,* she told herself fiercely. *This is* your *home and* he's *the trespasser. Don't let him tell you what you should or shouldn't do.*

'I was just making coffee,' she said with an airiness which belied her pounding heart as she headed off towards the kitchen, aware that he was very close behind her. She willed her hand to stay steady as she poured herself a mug and then flicked him an enquiring gaze. 'Would you like one?'

'I haven't come for coffee.'

'Then why *have* you come here, with a look on your face which would turn the milk sour?'

His fists clenched by the faded denim of his powerful thighs and his features darkened. 'What did you hope to achieve by this, Willow?' he hissed. 'Did you imagine that your petulant display would be enough to get you what you wanted, and that I'd take you to bed despite my better judgement?'

She stared at him. 'I don't know what you're talking about.'

'Oh, really?'

'Yes. *Really.*'

'So you have no idea why it's all over the internet that you and I are engaged to be married?'

Willow could feel all the blood drain from her face.

'No, of course I didn't!' And then her hand flew to her lips. 'Unless…'

'So you do know?' he demanded, firing the words at her like bullets.

Please let me wake up, Willow thought. *Let me close my eyes, and when I open them again he will have disappeared and this will have been nothing but a bad dream.*

But it wasn't and he hadn't. He was still standing there glaring at her, only now his expression had changed from being a potential milk-curdler, to looking as if he would like to put his hands on her shoulders and throttle her.

'I may have…' She took a deep breath. 'I was talking to my sister about you—or rather, she was interrogating me about you. She asked if we were serious and I tried to be vague—and my aunt overheard us, and started getting carried away with talking about weddings and I didn't…well, I didn't bother to correct her.'

His eyes narrowed. 'And why would you do something like that?' he questioned dangerously.

Why?

Willow met his accusing gaze and something inside her flared like a small and painful flame. Couldn't he see? Didn't he realise that the reasons were heartbreakingly simple. Because for once she'd felt like she was part of the real world, instead of someone just watching from the sidelines. Because she'd allowed herself to start believing in her own fantasy.

'I didn't realise it was going to get out of hand like this,' she said. 'And I'm sorry.'

'You're *sorry*?' he repeated incredulously. 'You think a couple of mumbled words of apology and everything's going to go back to normal?' His face darkened again. 'My assistant has been fielding phone calls all morning and my Paris office has been inundated with reporters asking for a comment. I'm in the process of brokering a deal with a man who is fiercely private and yet it seems as if I am about to be surrounded by my own personal press pack. How do you think that's going to look?'

'Can't you just…issue a denial?'

Dante stared into her soft grey eyes and felt close to exploding. 'You think it's that simple?'

'We could say that I was…I don't know…' Helplessly, Willow shrugged. *'Joking?'*

His mouth hardened, and now there was something new in his eyes. Something dark. Something bleak.

'A denial might have worked, were it not for the fact that some enterprising journalist was alerted to the Di Sione name and decided to telephone my grandfather's house on Long Island to ask him for his reaction.' His blue eyes sparked with fury as they captured hers with their shuttered gaze. 'And despite the time difference between here and New York, it just so happened that my grandfather was suffering from insomnia and boredom and pain, and was more than willing to accept the call. Which is why…'

He paused, as if he was only just hanging on to his temper by a shred.

'Why I received a call from the old man, telling me how pleased he is that I'm settling down at last. Telling me how lovely you are—and what a good family you come from. I was trying to find the right moment to tell him that there is nothing going on between us, only the right moment didn't seem to come—or rather, my grandfather didn't give me a chance to say what I wanted to.'

'Dante…'

'Don't you *dare* interrupt me when I haven't finished,' he ground out. 'Because using the kind of shameless emotional blackmail he has always used to ensure he gets his own way, my grandfather then told me how much *better* he'd felt when he heard the news. He said he hadn't felt this good in a long time and that it was high time I took myself a wife.'

'I'm sorry.' She gave him a beseeching look. 'What else can I say?'

Dante felt a feeling of pure rage flood through him and wondered how he could have been stupid enough to take his eye off the ball. Or had he forgotten what women were really like—had he completely wiped Lucy from his memory? Had it conveniently slipped his mind that the so-called *fairer sex* were manipulative and devious and would stop at nothing to get what it was they wanted? How easy it was to forget the past when you had been bewitched by a supposedly shy blonde and a sob story about needing a temporary date which had convinced him to go to the damned wedding in the first place.

He stared at the slight quiver of Willow's lips and at that moment he understood for the first time in his life the meaning of the term *a punishing kiss*, because that was what he wanted to do to her right now. He wanted to punish her for screwing up his plans with her thoughtlessness and her careless tongue. He watched as a slow colour crept up to inject her creamy skin with a faint blush, and felt his body harden. Come to think of it, he'd like to punish her every which way. He'd like to lay her down and flatten her against the floor and…and…

'Are you one of those habitual fantasists?' he demanded hotly. 'One of those women who goes around pretending to be something she isn't, to make herself seem more interesting?'

She put her coffee cup down so suddenly that some of it slopped over the side, but she didn't even seem to notice. Her hands gripped the edge of the table, as if she needed its weathered wooden surface for support.

'That's an unfair thing to say,' she breathed.

'Why? Because you're so delicate and precious that I'm not allowed to tell the truth?' He gave a short laugh. 'I thought you despised being given special treatment just because you'd been ill. Well, you can't have it both ways, Willow. You can't play the shrinking violet whenever it suits you—and a feisty modern woman the next. You need to decide who you really are.'

She met his eyes in the silence which followed. 'You certainly don't pull your punches, do you?'

'I'm treating you the same as I would any other woman.'

'Oh, but that's where you're wrong, because you're not!' she said with a shake of her head. 'If I was any other woman, you would have had sex with me last night. You know you would.'

Dante felt the heavy beat of a pulse at his temple and silently cursed her for bringing that up again. Did she think she would wear him down with her persistence? That what Willow wanted, Willow would get. His mouth hardened, but unfortunately, so did his groin. 'Like I told you. I don't sleep with virgins.'

She turned away, but not before he noticed the dark flare of colour which washed over her cheekbones and he felt his anger morph inconveniently into lust. How easy it would be to vent his feelings by giving her what she wanted. What he wanted. Even now. Despite the accusations he'd hurled at her and the still-unsettled question of how her indiscretion was going to be resolved, it was sexual tension which dominated the air so powerfully that he couldn't hardly breathe without choking on it. He couldn't seem to tear his gaze away from her. She looked as brittle as glass as she held her shoulders stiffly, and although she was staring out of the small basement window, he was willing to lay a bet she didn't see a thing.

But he did. He saw plenty. He could see the slender swell of her bottom beneath the dark denim. He could see the silken cascade of her blond hair as it spilled down her back. Would it make him feel better if he went right over there and slid down her jeans, and laid her down on the kitchen table and straddled her, before feasting on her?

He swallowed as an aching image of her pale, parted thighs flashed vividly into his mind and he felt another powerful tug of desire. On one level, of *course* it would make them both feel better, but on another—what? He would be stirring up yet more consequences, and weren't there more than enough to be going on with?

She turned back again to face him and he saw that the flush had gone, as if her pale skin had absorbed it, like blotting paper. 'Like I said, I'm sorry, but there's nothing I can do about it now.'

He shook his head. 'But that's where you're wrong, little Miss Hamilton. There *is*.'

Did something alert her to the determination which had hardened his voice? Was that why her eyes had grown so wary?

'What? You want me to write to your grandfather and apologise? And then to give some kind of statement to the press, telling them that it was all a misunderstanding? I'll do all that, if that's what it takes.'

'No. That's not what's going to happen,' he said. 'It's a little more complicated than that. My grandfather wants to meet the woman he thinks I'm going to marry. And you, my dear Willow, are going to embrace that role.'

The grey of her eyes was darker now, as if someone had smudged them with charcoal and a faint frown was criss-crossing over her brow. 'I don't understand.'

'Then let me explain it clearly, so there can be no mistake,' he said. 'My grandfather is a sick man and anything which makes him feel better is fine with me. He wants me to bring you to the family home to meet him and that's exactly what's going to happen. You can play the fantasist for a little while longer because you are coming with me to Long Island. As my fiancée.'

CHAPTER EIGHT

A SOFT BREEZE wafted in through the open windows, making the filmy drapes at the window shiver like a bridal veil and the mocking significance of *that* didn't escape Willow. She drew her hand over her clammy brow and looked around the luxurious room. She could hardly believe she was here, on Dante's estate, or that he had persuaded her to come here for a long weekend, despite the many objections she'd raised.

But he'd made her feel guilty—and guilt was a powerful motivator. He'd said that her lies about being his fiancée had given his grandfather hope, and it was in her power to ensure that a dying man's hopes were not dashed.

'You seemed to want to let your family believe that you were going to be my bride,' were his exact, silken words. 'Well, now this is your chance to play the role for real.'

Except that it wasn't real, because a real bride-to-be would be cherished and caressed by her fiancé, wouldn't she? Not kept at a chilly distance as if she was something unwanted but necessary—like a bandage you might be forced to wrap around an injured arm.

They were installed in an unbelievably cute cottage in the extensive grounds, but in a way that was worse than staying in the main house. Because in here there was the illusion of intimacy, while in reality they were two people who couldn't have been further apart. She was closeted alone with a man who clearly despised her. And there was only one bed. Willow swallowed. This time it was a king-size bed, but the principle of where to sleep remained the same. Was he really willing to repeat what had happened at the wedding—sharing a bedroom, while keeping his distance from her?

Dante had telephoned ahead to tell the housekeeper that they wished to be guaranteed privacy. She remembered the look on his face as he'd finished the call. 'They'll think it's because we're crazy about each other and can't keep our hands off each other,' he'd said mockingly.

But Willow knew the real reason. It meant that they wouldn't be forced to continue with the farce for any longer than necessary. There would be no reason for Dante to hide his undeniable hostility towards her. When they were with other people they would be sweetness and light together, while in private...

She bit her lip, trying hard to block out the sound of the powerful shower jets from the en-suite bathroom and not to think about Dante standing naked beneath them, but it wasn't easy. Their enforced proximity had made her achingly aware of him—whether he was in the same room, or not.

They had flown in by helicopter an hour earlier and Willow's first sight of the Di Sione family home had taken her breath away. She'd grown up in a big

home, yes—but this was nothing like the crumbling
house in which she'd spent her own formative years.
This, she'd realised, was what real wealth looked like.
It was solid and real, and clearly money was no object. The white marble of the Long Island mansion
was gleaming and so pristine that she couldn't imagine anyone actually *living* in it. She had been aware
of the endless sweep of emerald lawns, the turquoise
flash of a swimming pool and the distant glitter of a
huge lake as their helicopter had landed.

A housekeeper named Alma had welcomed them
and told Dante that his grandfather was sleeping but
looking forward to seeing them both at dinner.

'And your sister is here, of course,' she said.

'Talia?' questioned Dante as the housekeeper nodded.

'That's right. She's out making sketches for a new
painting.' Alma had given Willow a friendly smile.
'You'll meet Miss Natalia at dinner.'

And Willow had nodded and tried to look as she
thought a newly engaged woman *should* look—and
not like someone who had recently been handed a diamond ring by Dante, with all the emotion of someone producing a cheap trinket from the remains of a
Christmas cracker.

'What's this?' she'd asked as he had deposited a
small velvet box on her lap.

'Your number one prop,' came his mocking response as their helicopter had hovered over the Di
Sione landing pad. 'The bling. That thing which
women love to flash as a symbol of success—the
outward sign that they've *got their man*.'

'What an unbelievably cynical thing to say.'

'You think it's cynical to tell the truth?' he'd demanded. 'Or are you denying that women view the acquisition of diamonds as if it's some new kind of competitive sport?'

The awful thing was that Willow secretly agreed with him. Her sisters were crazy about diamonds—and so were plenty of the women she worked with—yet she'd always found them a cold and emotionless stone. The giant solitaire winked at her now like some malevolent foe, splashing rainbow fire over her pale fingers as Dante emerged from the bathroom.

Quickly, she looked up, her heart beginning to pound. She'd been half expecting him to emerge wearing nothing but a towel slung around his hips, and guessed she should be pleased that he must have dressed in the bathroom. But her overriding sensation was one of disappointment. Had she secretly been hoping to catch a glimpse of that magnificent olive body as he patted himself dry? Was there some masochistic urge lurking inside her which wanted to taunt her with what she hadn't got?

Yet the dark trousers and silk shirt he wore did little to disguise his muscular physique and his fully dressed state did nothing to dim his powerful air of allure. His black hair was still damp and his eyes looked intensely blue, and suddenly Willow felt her heart lurch with a dizzying yet wasted sense of desire. Because since that interrupted seduction at her sister's wedding, he hadn't touched her. Not once. He had avoided all physical contact with the studied exaggeration of someone in the military walking through a field studded with landmines.

His gaze flickered to where she'd been studying

her hand and his eyes gleamed with mockery. As if he'd caught her gloating. 'Do you like your ring?'

'It looks way too big on my hand,' she said truthfully. 'And huge solitaire diamonds aren't really my thing.'

He raised his dark brows mockingly, as if he didn't quite believe her.

'But they have a much better resale value than something bespoke,' he drawled.

'Of course,' she said, and then a rush of nerves washed over her as she thought about the reality of going to dinner that evening and playing the part of his intended bride. 'You know, if we're planning to convince your grandfather that we really are a couple, then I'm going to need to know something about you. And if you could try being a little less hostile towards me that might help.'

He slipped a pair of heavy gold cufflinks in place and clipped them closed before answering. 'What exactly do you want to know?'

She wanted to know why he was so cynical. And why his face had darkened as soon as the helicopter had landed here today.

'You told me about being sent away to boarding school in Switzerland, but you didn't say why.'

'Does there have to be a reason?'

She hesitated. 'I'm thinking that maybe there was. And if there was, then I would probably know about it.'

Dante's instinct was to snap out some terse response—the familiar blocking technique he used whenever questions strayed into the territory of *personal*. Because he didn't trust personal. He didn't trust anyone or anything, and Willow Hamilton was no exception in the trust stakes, with her manipulation and evasion. But suddenly her face had become soft with what looked like genuine concern and he felt a tug of something unfamiliar deep inside him. An inexplicable urge to colour in some of the blank spaces of his past. Was that because he wanted his grandfather to die happy by convincing him that he'd found true love at last? Or because—despite her careless tongue landing them in this ridiculous situation—she possessed a curious sense of vulnerability which somehow managed to burrow beneath his defences.

His lips tightened as he reminded himself how clever Giovanni was. How he would see through a fake engagement in the blinking of an eye if he wasn't careful. So tell her, he thought. She was right. He should tell her the stuff which any fiancée would expect to know.

'I'm one of seven children,' he said, shooting out the facts like bullets. 'And my grandfather stepped in to care for us when my parents died very suddenly.'

'And…how did they die?'

'Violently,' he answered succinctly.

Her eyes clouded and Dante saw comprehension written in their soft, grey depths. As if she understood pain. And he didn't want her to *understand*. He wanted her to nod as he presented her with the bare facts—not look at him as if he was some kind of problem she could solve.

Yet there had been times when he'd longed for someone to work their magic on him. He stared out at the distant glitter of the lake. To find a woman he'd be happy to go to bed with, night after night—instead of suffering from chronic boredom as soon as anyone tried to get close to him. To find some kind of *peace* with another human being—the kind of peace which seemed almost unimaginable to him. Was that how his twin had felt about Anais? he wondered.

He thought about Dario and felt the bitter twist of remorse as he remembered what he had done to his brother.

'What exactly happened?' Willow was asking.

Her gentle tone threatened to undermine his resolve. Making him want to show her what his life had been like. To show her that she didn't have the monopoly on difficult childhoods. And suddenly, it was like a dam breaking through and flooding him.

'My father was a screwed-up hedonist,' he said bluntly. 'A kid with too much money who saw salvation in the bottom of a bottle, or in the little pile of white dust he snorted through a hundred dollar bill.' His lips tightened. 'He blamed his addictions on the fact that my grandfather had never been there for him when he was growing up—but plenty of people have absent parents and don't end up having to live their lives on a constant high.'

'And what about your mother?' she questioned as calmly as if he'd just been telling her that his father had been president of the Union.

He shook his head. 'She was cut from the same cloth. Or maybe he taught her to be that way—I don't know. All I do know is that she liked the feeling of being out of her head as well. Or maybe she needed to blot out the reality, because my father wasn't exactly known for his fidelity. Their parties were legendary. I remember I used to creep downstairs to find it looking like some kind of Roman orgy, with people lying around among the empty bottles and glasses and the sounds of women gasping in the pool house. And then one day my mother just stopped. She started seeing a therapist and went into rehab, and although she replaced the drink and the drugs with a shopping addiction, for a while everything was…' He shrugged as he struggled to find a word which would sum up the chaos of his family life.

'Normal?'

He gave a short and bitter laugh. 'No, Willow. It was never normal, but it was better. In fact, for a while it was great. We felt we'd got our mother back. And then…'

'Then?' she prompted again.

He wasn't even angry with her for her persistence because now it felt like some rank poison was throbbing beneath his skin and he needed to cut through the surface to let that poison out.

'One night there was some big row. I don't know what it was about—all I do know is that my father was completely loaded and my mother was shouting at him. I heard him yell back that he was going out and then I heard her going after him. I knew he was in no state to drive and I tried to stop her. I…'

He'd done more than try. He'd begged her not to go. He'd run over and clung to her with all the strength his eight-year-old body could muster, but she hadn't listened. She'd got in the car anyway and the next time he'd seen his mother was when she'd been laid out in her coffin, with white lilies in her hands and that waxy look on her cold, cold cheeks.

'She wouldn't listen to me,' he bit out. 'He crashed

the car and killed them both. And I didn't manage to stop her. Even though deep down I knew what a state my father was in, I let her go.'

He stared out at the grounds of the house he'd moved into soon afterwards when his grandfather had brought them all here. A place where he'd been unable to shake off his sorrow and his guilt. He'd run wild until his grandfather had sent him and Dario away to school. And he'd just kept on running, hadn't he? He wondered now if the failure of his attempt to stop his mother had been the beginning of his fierce need to control. The reason why he always felt compelled to step in and influence what was happening around him. Was that why he'd done what he'd done to his twin brother?

'But maybe you couldn't stop her.'

Willow's voice—suddenly so strong and sure—broke into his thoughts.

'What are you talking about?' he demanded.

'Children can't always make adults behave the way they want them to, Dante,' she said, her words washing over him like balm. 'No matter how hard they try.'

Dante turned round, still unable to believe how much she'd got out of him. She looked like some kind of angel sitting there, with her pale English skin and that waterfall of silky hair. In her simple cotton dress she looked so pure—hell, she *was* pure. But it was more than just about sex. She looked as if she could take all the darkness away from him and wash away the stain of guilt from his heart. And her grey eyes were fixed on him, quite calmly—as if she knew exactly what was going on inside his head and was silently urging him to go right ahead and do it.

He wasn't thinking as he walked across the room to where she sat at an antique writing desk with the oil painting of Sicily which hung on the wall behind it. The hot, scorched brushstrokes and cerulean blue of the sky contrasted vividly with her coolness. Her lips looked soft and inviting. Some warning bell was sounding inside his head, telling him that this was wrong. But some of the poison had left him now. Left him feeling empty and aching and wanting her. Wanting to lose himself in her.

She didn't object when he pulled her out of the chair and onto her feet. In fact, the sudden yearning in her eyes suggested that she'd wanted him to touch her just as badly as he needed to.

His hands were in her hair and his mouth was hovering over hers, their lips not quite touching, as if he'd had a last-minute moment of sanity and this was his chance to pull back from her. Was that why she stood up on tiptoe and anchored her hands to his shoulders? Why she flickered the tip of her tongue inside his mouth?

'Willow,' he whispered as his heart began to pound.

'Yes,' she whispered back. 'I'm right here.'

He groaned as he tasted her—his senses tantalised by the faint drift of her scent. Dropping his hands from her hair, he gripped her waist and he thought how incredibly *light* she felt. As light as those drifts of swansdown you sometimes saw floating across hazy summer lawns. He deepened the kiss, and as she sucked in a breath, it felt like she was sucking him right inside her. For a moment he thought about the very obvious place where he would like to *be* sucked and his hand reached down to cup her breast. He heard the urgent little sigh of delight she made. He felt the restless circle of her narrow hips, and he could feel control leaving him as she kissed him back. He tried to remember where he'd put his condoms and just how long they had before they were expected up at the main house. And all the time he could feel himself going under—as if he was being consumed by a tide of rich, dark honey.

But along with the sweet, sharp kick of desire came the reminder of all the things he'd told himself he wasn't going to do. He'd messed up enough in his life. He'd failed to save his mother. He'd ruptured his relationship with his twin brother. In business he'd achieved outstanding success, but his personal relationships were not the same. Everything he touched turned to dust. He was incapable of experiencing the emotions which other men seemed to feel. And even though Willow Hamilton had allowed her stupid fantasies to manipulate events... Even though she had dragged him into her fantasy and made it impossible for him to walk away from her—that gave him no right to hurt her.

It would be too easy to take her innocence. To be the first man to claim her body for his own. To introduce her to the powerful but ultimately fleeting pleasures of sex. He closed his eyes because imagining her sweet tightness encasing him was almost too much to bear. He thought about easing into her molten heat, with his mouth clamped to one of her tiny nipples. He thought about how good it would feel to be able to come inside her. To pump his seed into her

until he was empty and replete. To kiss her and kiss
her until she fell asleep in his arms.

But a woman's virginity was a big deal, and someone who had suffered as Willow had suffered deserved more than he could ever give her. Because
he was programmed not to trust and never to stay.
He would take pleasure and give pleasure and then
close the door and leave without a backwards glance.

Dragging his mouth away from hers and dropping his hand from her breast as if it was on fire, he
stepped away, trying to quieten down the fierce sexual hunger which was burning inside him. But when
he saw the confusion clouding her beautiful eyes, he
felt a moment of unfamiliar doubt which he couldn't
seem to block out.

His mouth twisted.

'I meant what I said back in England,' he gritted.
'You aren't somebody I intend to get intimate with,
Willow. Did you think that because I've just told you
something about my *deeply troubled* past...' His voice
took on a harsh and mocking tone. 'That I would want
you? Did you think any of this was for real? Because
if you do, you're making a big mistake. For the sake of
my grandfather and his romantic ideals, we will play
the part of the happily engaged couple whenever we
find ourselves in his company. But when we're alone,
the reality will be very different. Just so you know,
I'll be sleeping on the couch.' He gave a tight smile.
'And I'll do my best not to disturb you.'

CHAPTER NINE

THE DARK SHAPE was moving almost silently around the room but it was enough to disturb Willow from her troubled sleep. Pushing the hair back from her face, she sat up in bed and snapped on the light to see Dante standing fully dressed, his face shadowed and unfriendly.

'What are you doing?' she whispered.

'Going out for a drive.'

'But it's only...' She picked up her watch and blinked at it. 'Just after five in the morning!'

'I know what the time is,' he growled back as he grabbed a clutch of car keys.

'So...why?' Her voice was full of bewilderment as she looked at him. 'Why in heaven's name are you going out before the sun is even up?'

'Why do you think?' He turned to look at her properly and all his dark and restless energy seemed to wash over her. 'Because I can't sleep.'

Willow swallowed. 'That couch *does* look very uncomfortable,' she agreed carefully. 'It can't be doing your back any good.'

'It's got nothing to do with the damned couch, Willow, and we both know it.'

She leaned back against the pillows, wishing that

he would stop snapping at her, and just end this impasse. Wishing he'd just take off those jeans and that stupid jacket and come and get in bed with her and do what was almost driving her out of her mind with longing. How many nights had they spent here now? And still her virginity was intact. Nothing had changed—at least, not in him—though her desire for him was as strong as ever. She wanted to kiss him. She wanted to hold him. Yet he acted as if she was contaminated.

'It was a mistake to come to this damned cottage,' he bit out. 'And an even bigger mistake to agree to stay on until after Natalia's opening.'

'So why *did* you agree to it?'

'You know damned well why,' he growled. 'Because you managed to make yourself completely irresistible to my grandfather, didn't you? So that I could hardly refuse his suggestion that we hang around for a few more days.' His fingers tightened around his car keys as he glared at her. 'Was this just more of the same kind of behaviour you demonstrated so perfectly at your sister's wedding? Manipulating events so they'd turn out the way you wanted them to?'

'That is an outrageous thing to say,' she retorted, wrapping the duvet more tightly around herself and trying very hard to keep the sight of her tightening nipples away from his accusing eyes. 'Unless you're suggesting that I deliberately went out of my way to be nice to your grandfather, just because I had some sort of hidden agenda to trap you in this cottage?'

He gave an impatient shake of his head. 'That wasn't what I meant.'

'Because, believe me, no one would deliberately angle to have more time alone with you, when you're in *this* kind of mood!'

His eyes narrowed. 'I guess not,' he said.

'And to be honest, I don't know how much longer I can go on like this,' she said. 'Maintaining this crazy fiction of presenting ourselves as the happy couple whenever we're with Giovanni or Natalia—and yet the moment we're alone, we're…we're…'

Dante stilled as he heard the unmistakable break in her voice, which only added to his growing sense of confusion and frustration. Because he hated it when she acted vulnerable—something which was surprisingly rare. When her voice wobbled or she got that puppy-dog look in her eyes, it started making all kinds of unwanted ideas flood into his head. Was it possible that duplicity didn't come as easily to her as he'd originally thought? That the sweet and uncomplicated Willow he'd seen here in his Long Island home—being endlessly patient with his grandfather and lovely towards his sister—was actually the real Willow? His mouth hardened. Or was she trying and managing very successfully to twist him around her little finger?

'We what, Willow?' he questioned silkily.

'We circle each other like two wary animals whenever we're together!'

'Well, let me ease the burden by going out and making sure we're alone for as little time as possible,' he said. 'Like I said, I'm going out for a drive. I'll see you later.'

Walking across the room, he clicked the door shut behind him, and as Willow listened to the sound of his retreating footsteps, she slumped dejectedly back into the pillows.

A heavy sigh escaped from her lips. She was living in a prison. A gilded prison where everything she wanted was right in front of her. The only man she'd ever wanted was constantly within touching distance—only she wasn't allowed to touch. And the fiction of the happy front they presented to the outside world was cancelled out by the spiralling tension whenever they were alone together.

She'd thought she'd been getting close to him. She *had* been getting close to him. On the day they'd arrived, he'd dropped his formidable guard and told her things about his past—things about his childhood and his family which had made her want to reach out to him. She'd seen the bitter sadness distorting his features and had wanted more than anything else to comfort him.

And for a while he had let her. For a few moments he had held her tight and kissed her and something deep and strong had flickered into life as they'd stood, locked in each other's arms. Her experience of men was tiny, but she had *known* that kiss was about more than sexual desire. It had been about understanding and solace. She'd thought it had been about hope.

But then he had pushed her away almost coldly, and since then he hadn't come close. Only when they were being observed by other people did he soften his attitude towards her.

She'd met one of his sisters, Natalia—a talented artist who lived at the house. With her wavy brown hair tied back in a ponytail and tomboyish clothes, she wasn't a bit how Willow had imagined Dante's sister to be. She had recently returned from a trip to Greece, but her clear hazel eyes became shuttered whenever anyone asked about it.

And Willow had at last met the legendary Giovanni, Dante's grandfather. She'd felt a punch of painful recognition after being shown into his room and seeing the pills which the attendant nurse was tipping into a small plastic container. A sense of sadness had curled itself around her heart as she saw the unmistakable signs of sickness. She thought how the Di Sione family had so many of the things which society lusted after. With their lavish wealth and a sprawling mansion in one of the world's most expensive areas of real estate, they were a force to be reckoned with...but nobody could avoid the inevitability of death, no matter how rich they were. And Dante's grandfather's eyes held within them a pain which Willow suspected was caused by more than his illness. Was he trying to get his affairs in order before the end? Was that why he'd asked Dante to trace the costly tiara and bring it to him?

On the first of what became twice daily visits, Willow would perch on a chair beside the bed and chat to the old man. She told him all about her life in England, because she knew better than anyone how being housebound made the dimensions of your world shrink. She was less enthusiastic about her fictitious future with his beloved grandson, even though the old man's eyes softened with obvious emotion when he reached out to examine her sparkling engagement ring. And she hoped she'd done her best to hide her guilt and her pain—and to bite back the urge to confess to him that none of this was real.

After Dante had gone she lay in bed until the light came up, then walked over to the main house for breakfast. The dining room was empty but Alma must have heard her because she came in with a pot of camomile tea, just as Willow was helping herself to a slice of toast.

'Where is everyone?' asked Willow as she reached for a dish of jam.

'Signor Giovanni is resting and Miss Natalia's upstairs, trying on dresses for her exhibition,' replied Alma. 'Would you like Cook to fix you some eggs?'

Willow shook her head. 'I'm good, thanks, Alma. This jam is amazing.'

Alma smiled. 'Thank you. I made it myself.'

Slowly, Willow ate her breakfast and afterwards went for a wander around the house where there was always something new to discover. And it was a relief to be able to distract herself from her endless frustration about Dante by admiring the fabulous views over the Di Sione estate, and the priceless artwork which studded each and every wall of the mansion. She was lost in thought as she studied a beautiful oil painting of Venice when suddenly she heard a small crash on the first floor, followed by the unmistakable sound of Natalia's voice exclaiming something.

Curiosity getting the better of her, she walked up the curving staircase and along a wide corridor, past an open door where she could see Natalia standing in front of a mirror, a heavy silver hairbrush lying by her bare feet. She was wearing a green shift dress—one of the most shapeless garments Willow had ever seen—which did absolutely nothing for her athletic physique.

Instinctively, she winced and the words were out of her mouth before she could stop them. 'You're not wearing that, surely?'

'What?' Natalia looked down at the garment before glancing up again and blinking. 'This is one of my best dresses.'

'Okay,' said Willow doubtfully, going into the room and walking around behind Natalia to see if it looked any better from the back. It didn't.

'So what's wrong with this dress?' Natalia asked.

Willow shrugged as she looked at Dante's sister. 'Honestly? It looks like a green bin bag. Admittedly a very nice shade of green, but still…' She narrowed her eyes in assessment. 'Did Dante tell you that I work in fashion?'

Natalia shook her head. 'Nope. He's been characteristically cagey about you. If you want the truth, I was pretty surprised to meet you. He once told me that he didn't think that marriage was for him, and I believed him.' Her voice softened. 'That's why I'm so happy for him, Willow. Sometimes he seems so… alone…despite all the planes and the parties and the money he's made. I'm so glad he's found you.'

Willow's heart clenched with a guilt even though she felt a perverse kind of pride that their farce of togetherness was working so effectively. She turned her attention to Natalia again.

'You have a knockout figure and gorgeous hair and you don't do much with either.'

'I've never had to.'

'But today is different, isn't it?' persisted Willow. 'I mean, it's meant to be special.'

There was silence for a moment before Natalia answered. 'Yes.'

Willow glanced over at the clock on the mantelpiece. 'Look, we have plenty of time. I can see what you have in your wardrobe or we could raid mine. And I'm a dab hand with a needle and thread. Will you let me give you a bit of a makeover? Only if you want to, of course.'

There was a moment of hesitation before Natalia gave Willow the sweetest smile she'd ever seen. 'Sure,' she said. 'Why not?'

Dante parked the car and walked slowly to the house, his dark glasses shading his eyes against the bright golden glitter of the day. It was a beautiful day and he should have felt invigorated by the air and the drive he'd just had. He should have felt all kinds of things, but he didn't.

Because none of this was turning out the way it was supposed to. He'd thought that maintaining a fake relationship with Willow would be easy. He just hadn't anticipated the reality.

He hadn't thought through what it would be like, being with her day in and day out, because he had no experience of what it *would* be like. Because he didn't do *proximity*. He slept with women, yes. He *loved* sleeping with women and occasionally taking them out to dinner or the theatre—but any time he spent with them was doled out in very manageable slots and always on *his* terms. Yet now he found himself stuck with her in a cottage which seemed way too small and claustrophobic, and with no means of escape. His throat dried. She was there, but not there.

She was tantalisingly close, yet he had forbidden himself to touch her, for reasons which seemed less important as each day passed. And now a terrible sexual hunger raged somewhere deep inside him and it was driving him crazy.

For the first time in a long time, he found himself thinking about his twin. Was it being back here, and seeing the great sweep of lawns where they used to climb trees and throw balls, which had made the pain suddenly feel so raw again? He thought about what he'd done to Dario, and how he'd tried to make amends, and the taste in his mouth grew bitter. Because Dario hadn't wanted amends, had he? There was no forgiveness in his brother's heart.

Deciding to have some coffee before he faced Willow, Dante walked into the house to hear laughter floating down the curving staircase from one of the upstairs bedrooms. His eyes narrowed—the carefree quality of the sound impacting powerfully on his troubled thoughts. Frowning a little, he followed the unfamiliar sound until he reached his sister's bedroom, unprepared for the sight which awaited him.

Talia was standing on a chair, and Willow was kneeling on the floor beside it, with pins in her mouth as she tugged at the hem of a beautiful floaty dress quite unlike anything he'd ever seen his sister wear before. And it wasn't just the dress. He'd never seen Natalia with her hair like that either, or her eyes looking so big. He caught the milky lustre of pearls at her ears—they glowed gently against her skin—and suddenly felt a surge of protectiveness, because this was his baby sister, looking all grown up.

'What's going on?' he said.

Natalia looked up. 'Hi, Dante.' She smiled. 'I'm deciding what to wear to the exhibition of my work.'

He raised an eyebrow. 'But you never go to the exhibition.'

'Not in the past. But tomorrow night I do,' she said softly. 'And Willow has helped me choose what to wear. Isn't she clever?'

Willow.

For the first time, Dante allowed his gaze to linger on the slim blonde scrambling to her feet, her cheeks slightly pink as she removed a pin from her mouth and dropped it into a little pewter box. Her dress was creased and her legs were bare and he was hit by a wave of lust so powerful that he could feel all the blood drain from his head, to go straight to where his body was demanding it.

He'd left their suite early because he'd felt as if he would *explode* if he didn't touch her, and suddenly he began to wonder just what he was doing to himself. Whether pain was such an integral part of his life that he felt duty-bound to inflict it on himself, even when it wasn't necessary. Was he trying to punish himself by denying himself the pleasure which he knew could be his, if only he reached out and took it? Because Willow hungered for him, just as much as he did for her. He could read it in every movement of her body. The way her eyes darkened whenever she looked at him.

Her carelessness had led to that crazy announcement about them being engaged, but hadn't he committed far graver sins than that? Hadn't he once told the biggest lie in the world to his twin brother—a lie by omission. He had stood silent when Dario had accused him of sleeping with his wife, and hadn't their relationship been in tatters ever since?

Pushing away the regret which he'd buried so deep, he thought instead about what his grandfather had said, soon after he'd given him the tiara. That Willow was caring and thoughtful, and that he liked her. And Giovanni wouldn't say something like that unless he meant it. His sister seemed to like her too—and Talia could be notoriously prickly with new people, after all the bad stuff which had happened in *her* life.

He realised that Natalia was waiting for an answer to a question he'd forgotten. Something about Willow, he thought—which was kind of appropriate because it was difficult to concentrate on anything other than a pair of grey eyes and a soft pair of lips he badly needed to kiss.

'Yes, she is,' he said slowly. 'Very clever.'

A funny kind of silence descended as Willow's cheeks grew pink.

'Well, I think that's everything,' she said, brushing her hand down over the creases in her dress. 'You look gorgeous, Natalia.'

'Gorgeous,' Dante agreed steadily. 'And now I'd like to talk to you, Willow. That is, if Natalia has finished with you.'

'Sure.' Natalia gave a quick smile. 'We're all done here.'

In silence Dante followed Willow from Natalia's room, and once he had closed the door, she turned to him, her eyes filled with question.

'What is it?' she asked. 'Has something happened?'

But he shook his head. He didn't want whispered explanations in the corridors of this great house, with Natalia suddenly emerging from the bedroom or Alma or another member of staff stumbling upon them. He badly wanted to kiss her, and once he'd started, he wasn't sure that he'd be able to stop.

'I need to talk to you,' he said. 'In private.'

The journey to their cottage seemed to take for ever, and Willow's heart was pounding as she followed Dante through the grounds because she was aware that something about him was different. When he'd walked into the room and seen her and Natalia giggling together, there had been something in his eyes which had made her want to melt. He'd looked at her in a way which had made goose bumps whisper all over her skin and her heart start thumping with an urgent kind of hope. She'd seen a new tension in his body and hoped she hadn't imagined the hunger she'd seen in his blue eyes, but even if it was true, she wasn't sure she trusted it. Was he going to take her in his arms and run his hands over her body like he'd done before? Was he going to kiss her passionately—to the point where she was gasping with hunger and frustration—only to push her away again and add to that frustration?

In tense silence they walked down an avenue of tall trees, whose leaves were brushed with the first hints of gold, and when finally they reached the cottage, she turned to face him as he closed the door.

'What is it?' she questioned again. 'Why are you acting like this?'

'I'm not acting,' he said unsteadily. 'Up until now, maybe—but not any more. I've wanted you for so long and I've reached a point where I can't go on like this any longer because it's driving me insane. I've tried to resist you, but it seems I can't resist any more. And now I'm through with trying. I want you, Willow. I want you so badly I can hardly breathe.'

Her heart was performing somersaults as she looked at him, scarcely able to believe what she was hearing. 'You make it sound as if you're doing something you don't want to do.'

'Oh, I want to do it, all right,' he said simply. 'I can't remember ever wanting a woman as much as I do right now. Maybe because you've been off-limits for so long that it's stirred my appetite until I can think of little else but you. I don't know. All I know is that I don't want to hurt you.'

'Dante…' she said.

'No. Hear me out, because it's important that you do.' His gaze was very intense—his eyes like blue flames which burned right through her. 'I'm afraid your innocence will make you read too much into this and so I'm flagging it up before that happens. To make sure it doesn't happen. Because the act of sex can be deceptive, Willow. The words spoken during intimacy can often mimic the words of love and it's important you recognise that.'

She dug her teeth into her bottom lip. 'And you're afraid that if I have sex with you, I'll fall hopelessly in love with you?'

His face became shuttered. 'Will you?'

Willow wondered if it was arrogance which had made him ask that—or simply a remarkable honesty. She wondered if she should listen to the voice inside her head which was telling her to heed his warning.

That maybe she was setting herself up for a hurt bigger than any she'd ever known.

But it wasn't as easy as that. She wanted Dante in a way she'd never wanted anyone—a way she suspected she never would again. Even if she met someone else like him—which was doubtful—her fate was always going to be different from other women her age.

Because a normal life and marriage had never been on the cards for her and it never could.

But none of that was relevant now.

She wasn't asking the impossible. She wasn't demanding that he *love* her—all she needed to do was to keep her own emotions in check. *She had to.* Because anything else would frighten him away—instinct told her that. She gave a little shrug.

'I'll try my very hardest not to fall in love with you,' she said lightly.

'Good. Because there isn't going to be some fairytale ending to this. This fake engagement of ours isn't suddenly going to become real.'

'I don't care.'

And suddenly neither did he. He didn't care about anything except touching her like he'd wanted to do for so long.

Dante peeled the dress from her body and then couldn't stop staring—as if it was the first time he'd ever undressed a woman. She was all sweetness and delicacy. All blond hair and floral scent and pure white lingerie. He wrapped his arms around her. He wanted to ravish her and protect her. He wanted to spill his seed inside her—and yet surely a virgin of her stature could not take him when he was already this big and this hard.

He brushed a lock of hair away from the smoothness of her cheek. 'I'm afraid I might break you.'

'You won't break me, Dante. I'm a woman, not a piece of glass.' Her voice trembled a little as she lifted her chin and he saw the sudden light of determination in her eyes. 'Don't be different towards me just because I've never done this before, or because once I was sick. Be the same as you always are.'

'Be careful what you wish for.' With a little growl, he picked her up and carried her into the bedroom. Carefully, he laid her down on the bed before moving away and beginning to unbutton his shirt, telling himself that if she looked in any way daunted as he stripped off, then he would stop.

But she was watching him like a kid in a candy store and her widened eyes and parted lips were only adding to his desire—if such a thing was possible. He eased the zip down over his straining hardness and carefully watched her reaction as he stood before her naked—but her face was full of nothing but wonder, and hunger.

'Oh, Dante,' she said, very softly.

It was the sweetest thing he'd ever heard. He went over to the bed and bent over her, tracing the pad of his thumb over her trembling lips and following it with the slowest, deepest kiss imaginable. It made his heart kick and his groin throb, and when he drew back he could see she looked dazed. *You and me both, sweetheart*, he thought, his fingertip stroking along the delicate lace of the bra which edged her creamy skin, and he felt her tremble.

'Scared?' he said.

She gave a little shrug. 'Scared I might not meet your expectations.'

He unclipped the front clasp of her bra, so that her delicious little breasts sprang free and he smiled as he bent his head to trace each budding nipple with his tongue.

'You already have,' he murmured throatily. 'You're perfect.'

Willow didn't react to that because she knew she wasn't. Nobody was and in her time she had felt more imperfect than most. But the look on his face was making her feel pretty close to perfect and she would be grateful to him for ever for that.

And now his thumbs were hooking into the sides of her knickers and he was sliding them all the way down her legs.

'Mmm…' he said, his gaze pausing to linger on her groin. 'A natural blonde.'

And Willow did something she'd never imagined she'd do on her long-anticipated initiation into sex. She burst out laughing.

'You are outrageous,' she said as he dropped the discarded underwear over the edge of the bed.

'But you like me being outrageous, don't you, Willow?'

And that was the thing. She did. Dante Di Sione was both arrogant and outrageous, yes. She could understand why they called him a maverick. But he was a lot of other things too. Most men in his position, she suspected, would have bedded her before now—but Dante had not. He had tried to do the right thing, even though it had gone against all his macho instincts. He had resisted and resisted until he could resist no more. He was strong and masterful, yet he had a conscience which made her feel safe. And safety had always been a big deal for her.

'I think you know the answer to that question,' she murmured as she tipped her head back so that he could kiss her neck.

And Dante did know. He gave a groan of satisfaction as he explored her. He touched her wetness until she was trembling uncontrollably—until she had begun to make distracted little pleas beneath her breath. She was so ready, he thought, his heart giving a thunder of expectation as his hand groped blindly towards the bedside locker.

Thank God for condoms, he thought—though as he rolled the contraceptive on, it was the only time she seemed uncertain. He saw her biting down on her lip and he raised his eyebrows, forcing himself to ask the question, even though he could barely get the words out.

'It won't be easy and I can't promise that it won't half kill me to do it, but if you want to change your mind...'

'*No,*' she said fiercely, her eager kisses raining over his eyelids, his jaw and his mouth. 'Never! Never, never, never.'

Her eagerness made him smile and when finally he entered her there was only the briefest moment of hesitation as he broke through her hymen, and he was filled with a powerful sense of possession.

'Does it hurt?' he said indistinctly, fighting against every instinct in his body as he forced himself to grow still inside her.

But she shook her head. 'It feels like heaven,' she said simply.

Dante closed his eyes and finally gave himself up to the rhythm which both their bodies seemed to be crying out for, though already he could sense she was very close to the edge.

Gripping her narrow hips he brought himself deeper inside her, bending his head to let his tongue flicker over her peaking nipples while she twisted like some pale and beautiful flower beneath him.

'Dante,' she gasped, but she didn't need to tell him what he already knew.

He had watched with rapt fascination the build-up of tension in her slender frame. The darkening of those wintry eyes. The way her head moved distractedly from side to side so that her hair fanned the pillow like a silky blond cloud. Her back began to arch and her legs to stiffen, and just as her body began to convulse helplessly around him, he saw the rosy darkening of her skin above her tiny breasts.

'Dante,' she gasped again, and mumbled something else, but he didn't know what it was, and frankly, he didn't care. Because he'd been holding off for so long that he couldn't endure it for a second longer, so that when eventually his orgasm came, he felt the rush of blood and pleasure as his senses began to dissolve—and he felt like he was floating.

CHAPTER TEN

To WILLOW, IT felt like living in a dream.

Dante Di Sione was her lover and he couldn't seem to get enough of her. And the feeling was mutual.

But it wasn't a dream. It was real. She needed to remember that. To remind herself that this was temporary. That it meant nothing. It meant nothing but sex. *He'd told her that himself.*

She pulled the rumpled sheet over her and listened to the sound of running water coming from the en-suite bathroom.

The trouble was that when you really wanted something it was easy to start constructing fantasies—the kind of fantasies which had got her into trouble in the first place. She started thinking about Dante's lifestyle. About his dislike of weddings and expressed distaste of settling down and doing the 'normal' stuff. What would he say if she told him she didn't care about all that stuff either? And that they might actually be a lot more compatible than he thought.

But thinking that way could lead to madness. It could make you start hoping for the impossible— and hope was such a random and unfair emotion. Hadn't she watched her young friends die in hospital and vowed that she would never waste her time on useless hope?

So just enjoy what you have, she told herself fiercely. *Store it all up in your mind and your heart— so that you can pull it out and remember it when you're back in England and Dante Di Sione is nothing but a fast-fading memory.*

It started to feel like a real holiday as he showed her around his home territory and introduced her to places he'd grown up with. He took her to tiny restaurants in New York's Little Italy, where the maître d' would enquire after his grandfather's health and where Willow ate the best pasta of her life. They spent a day at a gorgeous place in Suffolk County called Water Mill, where a friend of Dante's had the most beautiful house, surrounded by trees. They visited Sag Harbor and spent the night having sex in a stunning hotel overlooking the water, and the following day took a trip out on the Di Sione boat, which was anchored offshore. But when she told him she wanted to see the guidebook stuff as well, he took her to Manhattan and Staten Island, to Greenwich Village and Gramercy Park—where the beautiful gardens reminded her of England. And when he teased her about being such a *tourist*, he couldn't seem to stop kissing her, even though the wind blowing off the Hudson River had felt icy cold that day.

'What are you smiling about?' questioned Dante as he came in from the shower, rubbing his hair dry.

Willow shifted a little on the bed. It was weird how your life could change so suddenly. One minute she'd been someone who knew practically nothing about men—and the next she was someone watching as one headed towards her, completely naked.

Don't get used to it, she thought. *Don't ever get used to it.*

'My thoughts are my own,' she said primly.

'I suspect you were thinking about me,' he drawled. 'Weren't you?'

'That's a very…' His shadow fell over the bed and she looked up into the glint of his blue eyes. 'A very arrogant assumption to make.'

He bent to trace a light fingertip from nipple to belly button, weaving a sensual path which made her shiver. 'But you like my arrogance,' he observed.

Willow shrugged as guilty pleasure washed over her. 'Sometimes,' she murmured. 'I know I shouldn't, but I do.'

I like pretty much everything about you.

He smiled as he sat down on the edge of the bed and slid his hand between her legs.

'What are you doing?' she said.

'I think you know the answer to that question very well, Willow Hamilton.'

She tried telling herself not to succumb as he began to move his fingers against her, because surely it would be good to turn him down once in a while? But she was fighting a losing battle. She couldn't resist him when he started to touch her like that. Or when he brushed his lips against her neck. And suddenly it was not enough. It was never enough. 'Come back to bed,' she whispered.

'I can't. I'm expecting a call from Paris. There isn't time.'

'Then make time.'

'And if I say no?'

'You'll say yes in the end, you know you will.'

Dante laughed softly as he lay down beside her, smoothing his hands over her body as he drew her close. He stroked her breasts and her belly. He brushed his lips over her thrusting nipples and the soft pelt of hair between her thighs. For a while the room was filled with the sounds of breathing and kissing and those disbelieving little gasps she always gave when she came and then in the background the sound of his work phone ringing.

'I'll call them back later,' he murmured.

Afterwards he fought sleep and dressed, though he had to resolutely turn his back on her, for fear she would delay him further. He pulled on a shirt and began to button it, but his thoughts were full of her and he didn't want them to be. He'd told himself time and time again that now Talia's show was over, he needed to finish this. To let Willow go as gently as possible and to move on. It would be better for her. Better for both of them. He frowned. So what was stopping him?

He kept trying to work out what her particular magic was, and suddenly the answer came to him. Why he couldn't seem to get enough of her.

It was because she made him feel special.

And he was not.

He was not the man she thought him to be.

He stared out of the window at the lake and felt the swell of something unfamiliar in his heart. Was this how his twin had felt when he'd met Anais—the sense of being poised on the brink of something sig-

nificant, something so big that it threatened to take
over your whole life?

'Dante, what is it?' Willow was whispering from
over on the bed, her brow creased. 'You look as if
you've seen a ghost.'

He turned around to face her. Perhaps he had. The
ghost of his stupid mistake, which had led to the sev-
ering of relations with his twin brother.

He shook his head. 'It's nothing.'

But she was rising from the rumpled sheets like
a very slender Venus, her blond hair tumbling all
the way down her back as she walked unselfcon-
sciously across the room and looped her arms around
his neck.

'It's clearly something,' she said.

And although she was naked and perfectly poised
for kissing, in that moment all Dante could see was
compassion in her eyes and his instinct was to turn
away from her. Because all his life he'd run from
compassion…a quality he'd always associated with
pity, and he was much too proud to tolerate *pity*—
he'd had enough of that to last a lifetime. He'd seen it
on the faces of those well-meaning psychologists his
grandfather had employed after the fatal crash which
had left them all orphaned. He'd seen it etched on the
features of those matrons at boarding school, where
they'd been sent when Giovanni had finally admitted
he couldn't cope any more. They'd all tried to get him
to *talk* about stuff and to tell them how he *felt*. But he
had clammed up, like those mussels he sometimes ate
with frites in France—the ones with the tight shells
you weren't supposed to touch.

Yet something about Willow made him want to talk. Made him want to tell her everything.

'You know I have a twin brother?' he said suddenly.

Cautiously, she nodded. 'But you don't talk about him.'

'That's because we are estranged. We haven't spoken in years.'

He untangled her arms from his neck and walked over to the bed, picking up a flimsy silk wrap and throwing it to her, disappointed yet relieved when she slipped it on because he couldn't really think straight when she was naked like that.

He drew in a deep breath as he met the unspoken question in her eyes. 'The two of us were sent away to a fancy boarding school in Europe,' he said slowly. 'And after we left, we started up a business together—catering for the desires of the super-rich. Our motto was *"Nothing's impossible,"* and for a while nothing was. It was successful beyond our wildest dreams…and then my brother met a woman called Anais and married her.'

There was a pause. 'And was that so bad?'

Dante looked into her clear grey eyes and it was as if he'd never really considered the matter dispassionately before. 'I thought it was,' he said slowly. 'I was convinced that she wanted Dario's ring on her finger for all the wrong reasons. Women have always been attracted to the Di Sione name in pursuit of power and privilege. But in Anais's case, I thought it was for the sake of a green card. More than that, I could see that she had her hooks into my brother. I could tell he really cared about her—and I'd never seen him that way before.'

'So what happened?' she said, breaking the brittle silence which followed.

Dante met her eyes. He had done what he had done for a reason and at the time it had seemed like a good reason, only now he was starting to see clearly the havoc he had wrought. He suddenly realised that his dislike of his twin's wife went much deeper than suspecting she just wanted a green card.

'I didn't trust her,' he said. 'But then, I didn't trust any woman.'

'Why not?'

'It's complicated.'

'Life is complicated, Dante.'

His mouth twisted. 'It's not a story I'm particularly proud of, but when we were at college, I was sleeping with a woman called Lucy. She was quite something. Or at least, so I thought—until I discovered she'd been sleeping with my twin brother as well.'

Willow stared at him. 'That's terrible,' she whispered.

He shrugged. 'I laughed it off and made out like it didn't matter. But it did. Maybe it turned her on to have sex with two men who looked identical. Or maybe she was just after the family name and didn't care which brother should be the one to give her that name.' He hesitated. 'All I know is that, afterwards, things were never quite the same between me and Dario. Something had come between us, though neither of us acknowledged it at the time. And after that, I always viewed women with suspicion.'

'I suppose so,' said Willow, and her hand reached up to touch his jaw. 'But after what had happened, it was natural you would be suspicious and examine the motives of the woman he eventually married. You were obviously looking out for him—you shouldn't beat yourself up about it.'

But Dante shook his head, forcing himself to look at the situation squarely for the first time. To see things as they were and not how he'd wanted them to be. And Willow needed to hear this. He didn't want her building up fantasies about him being the kind of caring brother who was just looking out for his twin. She needed to hear the truth.

'It wasn't just that,' he admitted slowly. 'The truth was that I wasn't crazy about Dario's new wife. I didn't like the power she had once she had his ring on her finger. She was so damned...*opinionated* and I hated the way Dario started listening to her, instead of me. Maybe I was just plain jealous.' He gave a ragged sigh. 'When he was out one morning I went round to confront Anais about her real motives in marrying him. I accused her of using him to get herself a green card and we had one hell of a row, which ended up with her throwing a glass of water over me. I guess I deserved it. We both backed down and that might have been the end of it—in fact, we'd both started talking—had Dario not walked in and found me walking out of *his* bedroom, buttoning up one of *his* shirts. He thought we'd been having sex.' He looked into Willow's widened eyes. 'He asked whether we'd been having sex.'

'And what...what did you say?'

'I didn't,' said Dante slowly. 'I didn't say anything. I used my silence to allow him come to his own conclusions, only they were the wrong conclusions. Because even though we'd both slept with Lucy, there was no way I would have ever touched his wife. But that didn't matter. All that mattered was that I felt this fierce kind of anger that he had accused me of such a thing. I thought that their relationship couldn't be so great if he thought his wife would jump straight into bed with his brother at the first opportunity. I thought the only way for things to get back to normal would be for them to break up—and they did. The marriage imploded and Dario cut all ties with me. He held me responsible and I couldn't blame him for that.'

'And did you…did you ever try to make amends?'

He nodded. 'At first I did. I was eaten up with guilt and remorse. But no matter how many times I tried to contact him, his mind was made up and he wouldn't see me, or speak to me. It was like trying to smash my way through a concrete wall with nothing but my bare hands, and in the end I gave up trying.'

He waited for her judgement. For the shock and outrage he would expect from a woman whose innocence he had taken and whose total tally of sexual partners was just one. Wouldn't she be disgusted by what he had done? Wouldn't she want to walk away from him, no matter how good he was between the sheets?

But there was no judgement there. The concern had not left her eyes. And for the first time in his life he was finding compassion tolerable.

'Why don't you go to him?' she asked.

'Because he won't see me.'

'Couldn't you at least…*try*? Because…' She sucked in a deep breath. 'The thing is, Dante…one thing I learnt when I was so ill was just how important family are. They should be the people you can depend on, no matter what. And you never, ever know what's around the corner. If something happened to Dario and you were still estranged, you'd never forgive yourself. Would you? And it's not too late to try again.' Her words became urgent. 'It's *never* too late.'

He shook his head, because hadn't he grown weary with being stonewalled? And all these years down the line, surely rejection would be all the harder to take. But as Dante looked into Willow's face, he realised he needed to be bigger than his pride and his ego. He thought about all the things she'd been through—things she hadn't wanted to tell him but which eventually he'd managed to prise from her. He thought about how she'd minimised her sickness with a few flippant sentences, making it sound no more inconvenient than a temporary power cut. Despite her slight frame and ethereal appearance, she was brave and resilient and he admired her for those strengths.

Walking over to the writing desk, he picked up his phone, but when he saw the name which had flashed onto the screen, he felt a sense of disbelief as he scrolled down to read the message. He looked up, to where Willow hadn't moved, a question darkening her grey eyes.

'What's wrong?'

'It's from Dario,' he said incredulously. 'And he wants to meet me.'

Her expression echoed his own disbelief. 'Just like that? Right out of the blue? Just after we'd been talking about him?'

'He says he heard I was at the house and decided to contact me.'

She gave a slightly nervous laugh. 'So it's just co-incidence.'

'Yeah. Just coincidence.' But Dante found himself thinking about something he hadn't allowed himself to think about for a long time. About the intuition which had always existed between Dario and him—that mythical twin intuition which used to drive everyone crazy with frustration. They'd used it to play tricks on people. They'd loved making their teachers guess which twin they were talking to. But there had been another side too. The internal side which had nothing to do with playacting. His pain had been his brother's pain. Their joy and dreams had been equally shared, until a woman had come between them.

And maybe that was how it was supposed to be. Maybe he had wasted all that energy fighting against the inevitable. For now he could see that not only had he been jealous of Anais, he'd been angry that for once in his life he'd been unable to control the outcome of something he wanted. Because the little boy who'd been unable to save his mother had grown into a man with a need to orchestrate the world and the way it worked. A man who wanted to control people and places and things. And life wasn't like that. It never could be.

He looked at Willow and once again felt that strange kick to his heart. And even though part of him wanted to act like it wasn't happening, something was stubbornly refusing to let him off the hook so easily. Was it so bad to acknowledge the truth? To admit that she made him feel stuff he'd never felt before—stuff he hadn't imagined himself *capable* of feeling. That she had given him a flicker of hope in a future which before had always seemed so un-remittingly dark?

'What does your brother say?' she was asking.

'That he wants to meet me.'

'When?'

'As soon as possible. He lives in New York. I could leave right away.'

'Then shouldn't you get going?'

The words were soft, and the way she said them curled over his skin, like warm smoke. Smoky like her eyes. He wanted to take her back to bed. To for-get all about the damned text and touch her until he was drowning in her body and feeling that strange kind of peace he felt whenever they were together, but he knew he couldn't. Because this meeting with Dario was long overdue. The rift was as deep as a canyon, and he needed to address it. To face it and accept the outcome, whatever that might be, and then go forward.

'I shouldn't be more than a few hours,' he said.

'Take as long as you like.'

His eyes narrowed. She was giving him a permis-sion he hadn't asked for and his default setting would usually have kicked against her interference. Because he hated the idea of a woman closing in on him...trap-ping him...trying to get her claws hooked right into him. Yet he would have welcomed Willow clawing him—raking those neatly filed fingernails all the way down his back and making him buck with pleasure.

He wondered when it was that his opinion of her had changed so radically. When he'd realised she wasn't some overprivileged aristocrat who wanted the world to jump whenever she snapped her pretty fingers—but someone who had quietly overcome her illness? Or when she'd offered him her body and her enduring comfort, despite his arrogance and his hard, black heart?

He walked across to her. The morning sun was gilding her skin and the silky nightgown she wore was that faded pink colour you sometimes found on the inside of a shell. She looked as pink and golden as a sunrise and he put his arms around her and drew her close.

'Have I told you that every time I look at you, I want you?' he said unevenly.

'I believe you said something along those lines last night.'

He tilted up her chin with the tip of his finger. 'Well, I'm telling you again, now—only this time it's not because I'm deep inside your body and about to explode with pleasure.'

Her lips parted. 'Dante…'

He nuzzled his mouth against her neck, before drawing back to stare into her clear eyes, knowing now of all the things he wanted to say to her. But not now. Not yet. Not with so much unfinished business to attend to. 'Now kiss me, Willow,' he said softly. 'Kiss me and give me strength, to help get me through what is going to be a difficult meeting.'

CHAPTER ELEVEN

AFTER DANTE HAD gone Willow tried to keep herself busy—because it was in those quiet moments when he wasn't around that doubts began to crowd into her mind like dark shadows. But she wasn't going to think about the future, or wonder how his Manhattan meeting with his twin brother was going. She was trying to do something she'd been taught a long time ago. To live in the day. To realise that this day was all any of them knew for sure they had.

She set off for a long walk around the grounds, watching the light bouncing off the smooth surface of the lake. The leaves were already on the turn and the whispering canopies above her head hinted at the glorious shades of gold and bronze to come. She watched a squirrel bounding along a path ahead of her and she listened to the sound of birdsong, thinking how incredibly peaceful it was here and how unbelievable it was to think that the buzzing metropolis of the city was only a short distance away.

Later she went to the library and studied row upon row of beautifully bound books, wondering just how many of them had actually been read. She found a copy of *The Adventures of Huckleberry Finn* and settled down to read it, soon finding herself engrossed in the famous story and unable to believe that she'd never read it before.

The hours slid by and she watched the slanting sunlight melt into dusk and shadows fall across the manicured lawns. As evening approached, Alma came to find Willow to tell her that Giovanni was feeling well enough to join her downstairs for dinner.

It was strangely peaceful with just her and Dante's grandfather sitting there in the candlelight, eating the delicious meal which had been brought to them. The old man ate very little, though he told Willow that the tagliatelle with truffle sauce was a meal he had enjoyed in his youth, long before he'd set foot on the shores of America.

They took coffee in one of the smaller reception rooms overlooking the darkened grounds, silhouetted with tall trees and plump bushes. Against the bruised darkness of the sky, the moon was high and it glittered a shining silver path over the surface of the lake. All around her, Willow could feel space and beauty— but she felt there was something unspoken simmering away too. Some deep sadness at Giovanni's core. She wondered what was it with these Di Sione men who, despite all their wealth and very obvious success, had souls which seemed so troubled.

Quietly drinking her espresso, Willow perched on a small stool beside his chair, listening to the sweet strains of the music which he'd requested Alma put on for them. The haunting sound of violins shimmered through the air and Willow felt a glorious sense of happiness. As if there was no place in the world she'd

rather be, though it would have been made perfect if
Dante had returned home in time to join them.

She thought about the way he'd kissed her goodbye that morning and she could do absolutely nothing about the sudden leap of her heart. Because you
could tell yourself over and over that nothing was
ever going to come of this strange affair of theirs,
but knowing something wasn't always enough to kill
off hope.

And once again she found herself wondering if she
came clean and told Dante the truth about *her* situation, whether this affair of theirs might last beyond
their flight back to Europe.

Giovanni's accented voice filtered into her
thoughts.

'You are not saying very much this evening, Willow,' he observed.

Willow looked up into his lined face, into eyes
which were dull with age and lined with the struggle of sickness, but which must once have burned as
brightly blue as Dante's own.

*And I will never know Dante as an old man like
this*, she thought. *I will never see the passage of time
leave its mark on his beautiful face.*

Briefly, she felt the painful clench of her heart
and it was a few seconds before she could bring herself to speak.

'I thought you might be enjoying the music,' she
said. 'And that you might prefer me not to chatter over
something so beautiful.'

'Indeed. Then I must applaud your consideration
as well as your taste in music.' He smiled as he put
down his delicate coffee cup with a little clatter. 'But

time is of the essence, and I suspect that mine is fast running out. I am delighted that my grandson has at last found someone he wishes to marry, but as yet I know little about the woman he has chosen to be his bride.'

Somehow Willow kept her smile intact, hoping her face didn't look clown-like as a result. She'd had been so busy having sex with Dante that she'd almost forgotten about the fake engagement which had brought them here in the first place. And while she didn't want to deceive Giovanni, how could she possibly tell him the truth? She opened her mouth to try to change the subject, but it seemed Giovanni hadn't finished.

'I am something of an expert in the twists and complexities of a relationship between a man and a woman and I know that things are rarely as they seem,' he continued, the slight waver in his voice taking on a stronger note of reflection. 'But I do know one thing...'

Willow felt the punch of fear to her heart as she looked at him. 'What?' she whispered.

He smiled. 'Which is to witness the way you are when you look at Dante or speak of him.' He paused. 'For I can see for myself that your heart is full of love.'

For a moment Willow felt so choked that she couldn't speak. Yes, she'd once told her sister that she liked Dante and that had been true. But love? She thought about his anguish as he'd recounted the story of his childhood and her desire to protect him—weak as she was—from any further pain. She thought about the way he made her laugh. The way he made her feel good about herself, so that she seemed to have a permanently warm glow about her. He made her feel complete—even though, for her, such a feeling could never be more than an illusion.

So could those feelings be defined as love? Could they?

Yes.

The knowledge hit her like a rogue wave which had suddenly raced up out of the sea. Yes, they could.

And even if Dante never loved her back, surely they could still be a couple until he tired of her.

Couldn't they?

'Your grandson is very difficult to resist,' she said with a smile. 'But he is a very complex man.'

Giovanni laughed. 'But of course he is. All Di Sione men are complex—it is written into our DNA. That complexity has been our attraction and our downfall—although pride has played a big part in our actions. Sometimes we make decisions which are the wrong decisions and that is part of life. We must accept the shadows in order to experience light.' His voice suddenly hardened. 'But I know as an old man who has seen much of the world that regret is one of the hardest things to live with. Don't ever risk regret, Willow.'

She nodded as she leaned forward to tuck a corner of the blanket around his knees. 'I'll try not to.'

'And let me tell you something else.' His voice had softened now, shot through with a trace of something which sounded like wistfulness. 'That I long to see the bloodline of my offspring continue before I die, and to know there is another generation of Di Siones on the way.' He smiled. 'I know deep down that Dante would make a wonderful father, even though he might not yet realise that himself. Don't wait too long before giving him a baby, my dear.'

It felt like a knife ripping through her heart as Giovanni's blessing brought all her secret fears bubbling to a head. Willow tried hard not to let her distress show, but she was grateful when the nurse came to help the patriarch to bed. And as she made her way back to the cottage, she couldn't stop Giovanni's unwittingly cruel words from echoing round and round in her head.

Don't wait too long before giving him a baby, my dear.

Stumbling inside, it took a few moments before she could compose herself enough to get ready for bed and to register from the quick glance at her cell phone that there was no missed call or text from Dante. With trembling fingers she put on her silk nightdress, slithering beneath the duvet and staring sightlessly up at the ceiling, as she reminded herself that he hadn't promised to ring.

She had to stop relying on him emotionally. She had to learn to separate from him.

This wasn't going anywhere.

It *couldn't* go anywhere, she reminded herself fiercely. And sooner or later she had to address that fact, instead of existing in la-la land.

She fell asleep—her sleep peppered with heartbreaking dreams of empty cribs—and when she awoke, the pale light of dawn was filtering through the windows, bringing Dante's still and silhouetted form into stark relief.

Brushing the hair from her eyes, Willow sat up.

'How long have you been there?' she questioned sleepily.

He turned round slowly. So slowly that for a minute she was scared of what she might see in his face. Distress, perhaps—if his reconciliation with Dario had come to nothing.

But she couldn't tell what he was thinking because his eyes gave nothing away. They were shadowed, yes, but there was no apparent joy or sorrow in their lapis lazuli depths.

'I got back about an hour ago.'

'You didn't come to bed?'

She could have kicked herself for coming out with something so trite. Obviously he hadn't come to bed, or he wouldn't be standing at the window fully dressed, would he?

But he didn't seem irritated as he walked towards her and sat down on the edge of the mattress.

'No,' he said. 'I thought if I came to bed, then I'd have sex with you, and...'

'And you don't want sex?'

He laughed. 'I always want sex with you, Willow, but it's very distracting and right now I don't want any form of distraction.'

She nodded, staring very hard at the needlepoint bedspread before lifting her eyes to his. 'Do you want to talk about what happened?'

Dante considered her question and thought that of all the women he'd ever known, no one else would have asked it in quite that way. It was curious, yes— but it wasn't intrusive. She was making it plain that she could take it or leave it—it was entirely up to him what he chose to tell her. She didn't want to give him a hard time, he realised. And wasn't her kindness one of the things which kept drawing him back to her, time after time?

He sighed and the sound seemed to come from somewhere very deep in his lungs. It hadn't been an easy meeting with his twin, but it had been necessary. And cathartic. The pain of his remorse had hurt, but not nearly as badly as the realisation of how badly he had hurt his brother. And now that it was over he was aware of feeling lighter as a result.

'Not really. I'm done with talking about it,' he said, taking her hand within the palm of his own and wrapping his fingers around it. 'Would it be enough to tell you that Dario and I are no longer estranged?'

Willow nodded. 'Of course it's enough.' Her fingertips strayed to his shadowed jaw, where she felt the rasp of new growth against her skin.

'Willow, I need to talk to you.'

'I thought you just said you were done with talking.'

'That was about family rifts. This is something else.'

She bit her lip because now he sounded like she'd never heard him sound before. All serious and…*different*. Did he want to end it now? *Already?* 'What is it?' she questioned nervously.

Almost reflectively he began to trace a little circle over her palm before lifting his gaze to hers. And Willow didn't know if it was the fact that the sun was higher in the sky, but suddenly his eyes seemed clearer and bluer than she'd ever seen them before, and that was saying something.

'I'm in love with you,' he said.

Willow froze.

'With me?' she whispered, her voice choking a little.

He reached out his other hand—the one which wasn't holding hers—and touched her hair, as if he was testing how slowly he could slide his fingers over it.

'Yes, with you,' he said. 'The woman who has me twisted up in knots. Who made me do what I told myself I didn't want to do. Who gave herself to me—the sweetest gift I've ever had, as well as the best sex of my life. Who taught me how to forgive myself and to seek forgiveness in others, because that has helped me repair the bitter rift with my brother. You are the strongest and bravest woman I've ever met.'

'Dante...'

'Shh. Who has withstood more than the average person will ever know,' he continued. 'And then just shrugged it off, like the average person would shrug off rain from a shower. But you are not an average person, Willow. You're the most extraordinary person I've ever met—and I want to marry you and have babies with you.'

Her voice was more urgent now. 'Dante...'

'No. Just let me finish, because I need to say this,' he said, his fingers moving from their slow exploration of her hair to alight on her lips, to silence her. And when he next spoke, his words seemed to have taken on a deeper significance and his face had grown thoughtful—as if he'd just discovered something which had taken him by surprise. 'I never thought I wanted marriage or a family because I didn't know what a happy family was, and I wasn't sure I could ever create one of my own. The only thing I did know was that I never wanted to exist in an unhappy family. Not ever again.' His mouth twisted. 'But somehow I believe I can do it with you, because I believe—with you—that anything is possible. And I want you by my side for the rest of my life, Miss Willow Anoushka Hamilton.'

Willow blinked her eyes, trying furiously to hold back the spring of tears as she tried to take in words she'd never expected to hear him say. Beautiful, heartfelt words which made her heart want to melt. Wasn't it funny how you could long for something— even though you tried to tell yourself that it was the wrong thing to long for—and then when it happened, it didn't feel quite real.

It seemed inconceivable that Dante Di Sione should be sitting there holding her hand, with all the restraint and decorum of an old-fashioned suitor and telling her he'd fallen in love with her and wanted her to have his babies. She should have been jumping up and down with excitement, like a child on Christmas morning. She should have been flinging her arms around his neck and whooping with joy, because wasn't this the culmination of all the hopes and dreams which had been building inside her, despite all her efforts to keep them under control?

So why was she sitting there, her heart sinking with dismay as she looked into his beautiful eyes and a feeling of dread making her skin grow cold and clammy?

Because she couldn't do it. She couldn't. She could never be the woman he wanted.

She thought about something else his grandfather

had said to her last night and the wistful expression on his face as he'd said them. *Regret is one of the hardest things to live with. Don't ever risk regret, Willow.*

He was right. She couldn't risk regret—not for her sake, but for Dante's. Because if he married her, he would have a lifetime of regret.

Yet how could she possibly convey that? She didn't want to disclose her own dark secret and have him kiss away her fears and tell her it didn't matter. Because it did. Maybe not now, when they were in the first flush of this powerful feeling which seemed to have crept up on them both—but later, almost certainly it would matter. When the gloss and the lust had worn off and they were faced with the reality of looking at the future. Would Dante still want her then? Wouldn't he long for his heart's desire, knowing she could never give it to him?

She couldn't give him the choice and have him decide to do something out of some misplaced sense of selflessness, or kindness. She had to make the choice for him, because it was easier this way. She drew in a deep breath and knew she had to dig deep into the past, to remember how best to do this. To recall the way she'd managed to convince her weeping parents that no, of course the treatment didn't hurt. She'd worked hard on her acting ability when she'd been sick and realised it was the people around her who needed comfort more than she did. Because in a funny way, what she had been going through had been all-consuming. It was the people who had to stand and watch helplessly from the sidelines who suffered the most.

So use some of that acting talent now. Play the big-

*gest part of your life by convincing Dante Di Sione
that you don't want to marry him.*

'I can't marry you, Dante,' she said, aware that
his blue eyes had narrowed. Was that in surprise, or
disbelief? Both, probably. He may have just made
the most romantic declaration in the world but that
hadn't eradicated the natural arrogance which was
so much a part of him.

He nodded, but not before she had seen that look
of darkness cross over his face, and Willow had to
concentrate very hard to tell herself it was better this
way. That it might hurt him a bit now—and it would
certainly wound his ego—but in the long run it would
be better. Much better.

She knew he was waiting for an explanation and
she knew she owed him one, but wouldn't all the explanations in the world sound flimsy? She couldn't
say that she thought their lifestyles were incompat-
ible, or that she'd never want to live in Paris, or even
New York—because she suspected he would be able
to talk her out of every single one.

There was only one way to guarantee Dante Di
Sione's permanent exit from her life and it was the
hardest thing to say. Hard to say it like she really
meant it, but she knew she had to try.

So she made her features grow wooden and her
voice quiet. Because, for some reason, quiet always
worked best. It made people strain towards you to
listen. It made them believe what you said.

'I can't marry you because I don't love you, Dante.'

CHAPTER TWELVE

DANTE'S EYES WERE shards of blue so cold that Willow could feel her skin freezing beneath that icy gaze. 'You don't love me?' he repeated slowly.

Willow nodded, hanging on to her composure only by a shred. 'No,' she said. 'I don't.'

She began to babble, as if adding speed to her words would somehow add conviction. 'It was just a part we were both playing for the sake of your grandfather,' she said. 'You know it was. It was the sex which made it start to seem real. Amazing and beautiful sex—although I've got nothing to compare it to, of course. But I'm guessing from your reaction that it was pretty special, and I guess that's what made us get carried away.'

He gave a short laugh. 'Made *me* get carried away, you mean?'

Keep going, she told herself. *Not much longer now. Make him think you're a cold hard bitch, if that helps.* 'Yes,' she said with a shrug of her shoulders. 'I guess.'

A strange note had entered his voice and now his eyes had grown more thoughtful. 'So it's only ever really been about sex, is that what you're saying, Willow? You decided early on that I was to be the man who took your virginity, and you were prepared to do pretty much anything to get that to happen, were you?'

All she had to do was agree with him and very soon it would be finished. Except that something in the way he was looking at her was making her throat grow dry. Because the softness had left his face and her breasts were beginning to prickle under that new, hard look in his eyes. Willow licked her lips. 'That's right.'

Dante stared at her, wondering how he could have got it so wrong. Had he been so bewitched by her proximity that he had started believing the fantasy which they'd both created? Had his reconciliation with his brother made him overly sentimental—making him want to grab at something which up until recently hadn't even been on his agenda? Perhaps his grandfather's illness had stirred up a primitive need inside him and he had made a bad judgement call. She didn't want him, or his babies. She didn't love him. She didn't care.

A smile twisted his lips. Ironic, really. He could think of a hundred women who would fight to wear his ring for real. Just not Willow Hamilton. And just because she'd never had sex with anyone before him didn't make her a saint, did it? He'd turned her on in a big way and it seemed he had liberated her enough to want to go out there and find her pleasure with other men. He felt a savage spear of something else which was new to him. Something he automatically despised because deep down he knew it would weaken him. Something he instinctively recognised as jealousy.

And suddenly he knew that in order to let her go,

he had to have her one last time. To remind himself
of how good she felt. To lick every inch of her soft,
pale skin and touch every sinew of her slender body.
To rid himself of this hateful need which was making his groin throb, even though he told himself he
should be fighting it. But he couldn't. For the first
time in his life, he couldn't. His sexual self-control
was legendary and he had walked away from women
when they'd been begging him to take them. Willow
was not begging—not any more. His bitter smile returned. But pretty soon she would be.

'Well, if it's only ever been about sex, then maybe
we ought to go out with a bang.' He smiled as her
head jerked back, her shock palpable. 'If you'll pardon the pun.'

Willow's heart pounded as she looked into his eyes
and saw the smoulder of intent there. She told herself
that this was dangerous. Very dangerous. That she
needed to get out of here before anything happened.

'Dante,' she whispered. But the words she'd been
about to say had died on her lips because he was
walking towards her with an expression on his face
which was making her blood alternatively grow hot
and cold. She could *see* the tension hardening his
powerful body as he reached her. She could *smell*
the raw scent of his arousal in the air. As he stroked
a finger down over her arm, she began to shiver uncontrollably. This was wrong. It was wrong and dangerous and would lead to nowhere but pain and she
knew she had to stop it. She *had* to. 'Dante,' she whispered again.

'One for the road,' he said in a cruel voice.

And then he kissed her in a way which shocked her

almost as much as it turned her on. It was hard and it was masterful—an unashamed assertion of sexual power. It was all about technique and dominance— but there was no affection there.

So why did she kiss him back with a hunger which was escalating by the second? Why didn't she just press her hands against that broad chest and push him away, instead of clinging on to him like some sort of limpet? He was strong enough and proud enough to accept her refusal. To just turn and walk away. They could end this strange relationship without stoking up any more emotional turmoil and then try to put the whole affair behind them.

But she couldn't. She wanted him too much. She always had and she always would. She wanted—how had he put it?—*one for the road.*

Did he see the sudden softening of her body, or did her face betray her change of feelings? Was that why he reached down to her delicate silk nightdress and ripped it open so that it flapped about her in tatters? His eyes were fixed on hers and she wanted to turn her head away, but she was like a starving dog sitting outside a butcher's shop as he swiftly bared his magnificent body and carelessly dropped his clothes to the floor.

Naked now, he was pressing her down against the mattress as he moved over her, his fingertips whispering expertly over her skin, making her writhe with hungry impatience. His big body was fiercely aroused, and even though his face looked dark and forbidding, Willow didn't care. Because how could she care about anything when he was making her feel like *this*?

She shuddered as he palmed her breasts and then bent his head to lick them in turn, his breath warm against her skin as she arched against his tongue. She could feel the rough rasp of his unshaved jaw rubbing against her skin and knew that it would be reddened by the time he had finished. And when he drew his head back she almost gasped when she saw the intense look of hunger on his face, his cheekbones flushed and his blue eyes smoky.

'Ride me,' he said deliberately.

She wanted to say no. She wanted him to kiss her deeply and passionately, the way he usually did— but she recognised that she had forfeited that luxury by telling him she didn't love him. All she had left was sex—and this was the very last time she would have even that. So make it raunchy, she told herself fiercely. Make him believe that this was what the whole thing had been about.

She slid out from underneath him to position herself on top, taking his moist and swollen tip and groping on the nearby bedside table for the condoms he always kept there. He had taught her to do this as he had taught her so much else, and she had worked on her condom application skills as diligently as a novice pianist practising her scales. So now she teased him with her fingertips as she slid the rubber over his erect shaft, enjoying his moan of satisfaction— even though it was breaking her heart to realise she would never hear it again. And when she took him deep inside her and began to move slowly up and down, he felt so big that she was certain he would split her in two. But he didn't. Her body quickly adapted to him, slickly tightening around him until she saw his fingers claw desperately at the rucked sheet on which they lay.

For a while she played the part expected of her and for a while it came so easily. Her fingers were tangled in her hair and her head was thrown back in mindless ecstasy as she rode him, glad she didn't have to stare into his beautiful face, scared that she might falter and give away her true feelings. Blurt out something stupid, and very loving. But suddenly he caught hold of her hips and levered her off him. Ignoring her murmur of protest, he laid her down flat against the mattress and moved over her again.

'No,' he said, his voice very intent as he made that first renewed thrust deep inside her. 'I want to dominate you, Willow. I want to remind myself that everything you know you have learned from me. I want to watch your face as you come, and I want you to realise that never again will you feel me doing this... and this...and *this*...'

She cried out then, because the pleasure was so intense it was close to pain. And if the first time they'd ever made love she had begged him not to be gentle with her—not to treat her as if she was made of glass—he certainly wasn't gentle now. It was as if he was determined to show her everything he was capable of, as he drove into her with a power which had her nails digging helplessly into his shoulders.

She almost didn't *want* to come—as if her orgasm would be a sign of weakness and by holding it back she could retain some control over what was happening— but already it was too late. Her back was beginning to arch, her body spasming around him as she opened her mouth to cry out her satisfaction.

But for once he didn't kiss the sound away and blot it into silence with his lips. Instead he just watched her as she screamed, as cold-bloodedly as a scientist might observe an experiment which was taking place in the laboratory. Only then did he give in to his own orgasm and she thought it seemed brief and almost perfunctory. He didn't collapse against her, whispering the soft words in French or Italian which turned her on so much. He simply pumped his seed efficiently into the condom before withdrawing from her and rolling away to the other side of the bed.

Several agonisingly long minutes passed before he turned to look at her and something about the coldness of his blue gaze made her want to shiver again.

'Time to get on that road,' he said softly.

And he walked straight towards the bathroom without a backward glance.

Willow's hands were trembling as she gathered up the tattered fragments of her torn nightdress and stuffed them into her suitcase, terrified that one of the staff would find them. She had composed herself a little by the time Dante emerged, freshly showered and shaved and wearing a dark and immaculate suit which made him seem even more distant than the look in his eyes suggested he was.

'Are you…are you going somewhere?' she said.

'I am.' He gave a cold smile. 'I'm leaving. And obviously, you'll be coming with me. We will drive to the airport—only we'll be going our separate ways from now on. You'll be heading for London, while my destination is Paris. But first, I need to speak to my grandfather.'

'Dante…'

'Save your breath, Willow,' he said coolly. 'I think we've said everything which needs to be said. I guess I should thank you for playing such a convincing fiancée. But I'm going to sit down with Giovanni and tell him that our relationship is over, and to remind him that he knows better than anyone that marriages simply don't work if there is no love involved.' His eyes glittered. 'If you're willing to sign a confidentiality clause, you can keep the ring. You should be able to get a decent amount of money for it.'

'I don't need to sign a confidentiality clause. And I won't talk about this to anyone. Why would I? It's not exactly something I'm very proud of.' Her voice was trembling as she stared at the huge diamond and thought about how much it must be worth. Shouldn't she keep it and sell it, and use the money to do some real good—for people who badly needed it? And wouldn't it help if he thought of her as greedy and grasping? If she could give him yet another reason to hate her? She curved her mouth into a speculative smile. 'But yes, I will keep the ring.'

The look of contempt on his lips was unmistakable as he turned away. 'Be my guest. And now pack your case and get dressed,' he said harshly. 'And let's get out of here.'

CHAPTER THIRTEEN

BEHIND THE FLASHING blue and gold illuminations of the Eiffel Tower, the Parisian sky was dark and star-less and the streets were quiet. Far below the windows of his offices, the river Seine looked cold and unin-viting and Dante was lost in thought when he heard the door open behind him and someone walk in. He swivelled round in his chair to see his assistant standing there, a pointed expression on his face.

'Yes, what is it, René?' he questioned impatiently.

'You are due at a drinks party at the Ritz…' René looked down at his watch. 'Ten minutes ago actually.'

Dante scowled. 'Ring them. Tell them that I've been held up and unlikely to make it in time.'

'I could do that, of course,' said René carefully. 'But it is the birthday party of the countess—and you know how much she wants you there.'

Dante leaned back. Yes, he knew. The whole world always wanted him, women especially. Except for one woman. His mouth hardened as he stared into space.

One woman. One infernal, infuriating woman who had made it clear that wanting him was the last thing on her particular wish list.

'Is there…is there something wrong, boss?'

Dante glanced across the room, tempted to confide in his loyal assistant—not something he ever did usually. But then, he didn't *usually* feel as if a heavy weight was pressing down hard on his heart, did he? Or his life seem as if there was something fundamental missing which made him feel only half complete. He shut his eyes. Had he imagined that the heartless way that the beautiful blonde had rejected him would have been enough to make him see sense? And that it would somehow be easy to forget her? Because if that was the case then it seemed that yet again he had been wrong, and he didn't like being wrong.

He thought about the contradiction she'd been. The tender and passionate woman in his arms who had rapturously embraced the joys of sex. He remembered her childlike delight when he'd taken her to Shelter Island for breakfast. The way she'd charmed his grandfather and made his tomboy sister look like a million dollars. He thought about the crazy hope she'd awoken in his heart, along with the realisation that, suddenly, all the things he'd never dared dream of felt as if they could be possible with her. He remembered the trembling expression on her face when he'd asked her to marry him. The way she'd tried to blink back the sudden tears of joy as she looked at him.

And then?

Then…nothing. In a voice which was deathly quiet and a face devoid of emotion, she had told him she couldn't marry him. She'd told him she didn't love him when those words belied her every action. It didn't make sense. He shook his head. None of it made sense. If she hadn't been so innocent, he might have suspected the presence of another man. Though maybe that wasn't such a crazy idea? She'd grabbed at the diamond ring quickly enough, hadn't she? So maybe she wasn't quite as naive as she seemed.

He watched as the lights on the tower turned to red, and then to gold. Perhaps he had been nothing but her *stud*—an alpha male chosen as the ideal candidate for her sexual initiation. Maybe the fact that he was a foreigner had allowed her to shed all her inhibitions—he knew some women were like that—when all along she'd intended to marry an English aristocrat of the same class as herself.

Once again, an unwanted streak of jealousy flooded through his veins like dark poison and he opened his eyes to find René looking at him with that same expression of concern. He thought about his assistant's question and he realised that yes, something was *very* wrong and it was more to do with his own behaviour. Because since when had he taken to asking himself questions, without bothering to seek out the answers?

'I need some information about a woman.'

'Same woman as before?' asked René innocently. 'It wouldn't happen to be a Miss Willow Hamilton, would it?'

'As quickly as possible,' said Dante impatiently.

'Bien sûr.' René's lips twitched. 'This is getting to be a bit of a habit if you don't mind my saying so, boss.'

'Well, I do mind.' Dante glowered as he stood up and pulled off his tie. 'I don't pay you to give your opinion when it isn't wanted. Have the car brought round and I will call at the countess's party for a while. And will you please wipe that smug expression from your face, because it is starting to infuriate me.'

Dante was driven to the first *arrondissement*, to the glittering cocktail party being held in one of the famous hotel's penthouse suites, but his heart wasn't in it—nor in any of the stellar guests who were present. The countess was delectable, but she left him cold—as did the other women who smiled at him with open invitation in their eyes. He endured it for a while, then slipped away—and when he arrived at work early the following morning, it was to find René already in the office, with a look of triumph on his face.

'I have the information you require,' he said.

'Go on.'

'She is living in London…'

'I already know that,' interrupted Dante impatiently.

'And she will be attending a fundraiser for the Leukaemia Society being held at the Granchester Hotel in London this Saturday.' René paused, his dark eyes hooded. 'You might also be interested to know that she has put her diamond engagement ring up for the charity auction.'

And for the first time in his life, Dante was speechless.

Willow looked up from behind the podium and for a moment there was complete silence in the large ballroom, before she spoke again. 'And that is why I consider it such an honour to be your new patron.'

An expectant hush fell over the assembled throng and she drew in a deep breath, knowing that she had to get this right. 'I wanted to give fellow sufferers hope, as well as supporting the fantastic new research which is taking place all over the world. I'm prepared to step out of the shadows and talk openly about what happened to me, instead of hiding it away. Because I'm better. And because, every day, there are more and more people like me, getting better. And I…'

Her words tailed off because, for a moment there, a trick of the light made her think she saw Dante standing at the back of the ballroom. She blinked, slightly impatient with herself. Was she now beginning to conjure him up from nowhere, so that he was about to become a constant presence in her daytime as well as her night-time thoughts?

'I…' She couldn't remember what she had been saying and someone held a glass of water towards her, but she shook her head. She stared to where the man stood, her eyes drinking him in—registering every pore of his sensual face. It *was* him. Very definitely him. Because nobody in the world looked quite like Dante Di Sione. Tall and broad and strong and magnificent and somehow managing to dominate the entire room.

And she couldn't allow herself to go to pieces at this point. Too many people were relying on her.

She fumbled around for the words which had been on the tip of her tongue and somehow managed to produce them. 'I just want to say that I think you are all wonderful, and I'm delighted to be able to tell you that the silent auction has raised almost half a million pounds.' She swallowed, and then smiled— a big smile which just grew and grew. 'So thank you

again from the bottom of my heart—for allowing me
to give something back.'

The sound of clapping began and swelled, echoing
loudly throughout the vast room as Willow stepped
carefully down from the stage, her narrow silver dress
not the easiest of garments to move around in. Now
what did she do? She risked a glance to where Dante
had stood, but he was no longer there and she felt her
heart plummet. Of course he wasn't there! She had
dreamt him up. It had been a fantasy—nothing more.
Why would he be here when he'd flown straight back
to Paris and they hadn't spoken since he had boarded
his jet in New York, all those weeks ago?

'Willow.'

The sound of his voice was unmistakable and her
knees buckled, but even though his hand was instantly on her elbow and his strength seemed to flow
straight into her, she shook herself free. Because she
had to learn to live without him. She had to.

'Dante,' she said, but her voice sounded faint.
'What are you doing here?'

His eyes were curious, but his tone was dry. 'No
ideas?'

She licked her lips. 'You were in London?'

'And happened to be passing? Yeah, you could say
that.' He gave a mirthless smile. 'Is there anywhere
quieter we can go to talk?'

She knew she should tell him that no, there wasn't.
She knew she ought to fetch her wrap and go outside
to find a cab. Go home and forget she'd ever seen
him. Her gaze travelled over his face and stayed fixed
on the features she'd missed so much. His blue eyes.
His sensual lips. The faint darkness which always

lingered around his jaw. 'There's the hotel's Garden Room,' she croaked.

In silence they walked to the plant-filled bar, with its white baby grand piano tucked away in the corner. Dante immediately managed to commandeer a quiet table at the back of the room but Willow knew instantly that she'd made a mistake in her choice of venue. A big mistake. Because the air was filled with the scent of jasmine and gardenia—heady scent which seemed unbearably romantic, as did the soft music which the pianist was playing. And the flickering candlelight didn't help. Maybe she could concentrate on her drink. Order some complicated cocktail with a cherry and an umbrella and give it her full attention.

But Dante waved the hovering waiter away and she guessed it was an indication of his charisma that he should be allowed to occupy the best table in the place without even ordering a drink.

She waited to hear what he would say and she tried to second-guess him, desperately trying to work out the right answers to whatever he was going to say. Trouble was, he asked the last question she wanted to hear. The one question she didn't want to answer. She'd lied about this once before, but she had been stronger then. She'd been so certain it had been the right thing to do and she hadn't been starved of his presence for almost five weeks, so that she could barely stop herself from reaching out to touch him.

'Do you love me, Willow?'

She looked into his eyes—which were the colour of midnight in this candlelit room—and she opened her mouth to tell him no. But a rush of stupid tears filled her own eyes and prevented her from saying anything, and mutely, she found herself shaking her head.

'Do you?' he said again. 'Just tell me, Willow. Say it out loud. That's all I'm asking. Tell me you don't love me and I'll walk out of here and you'll never see me again.'

She tried. For almost a minute she tried. Tried to force the words out of her mouth in the same way that you sometimes had to prise a stubborn Brazil nut from its shell. But the words wouldn't come. They just wouldn't come. At least, not the words she knew she should say. The other ones—the eager, greedy ones—they suddenly came pouring from her lips as if she had no control over them.

'Yes,' she burst out. 'Yes, I love you. Of course I do. I didn't want to. I still don't want to. And I'm sorry. I don't want to mess you around and I certainly don't want to send out mixed messages. So it's probably better if you forget everything I've just said. Because…because it can't lead anywhere, Dante— it just *can't.*'

His eyes narrowed, like someone who had just been presented with a locked room and was working out how best to open it without a key. 'Do you want to tell me why?'

'Because I can't give you what you want,' she whispered. 'You told me you wanted marriage. And babies. Your grandfather told me that he longed for nothing more than to see the next generation of Di Siones.'

'And?'

'And I can't promise you that. I had…' She swallowed and licked her lips. 'I had treatment for my

illness before I started my periods and they said it's
possible—even likely—that I may not be able to have
children.'

'But you didn't ever find out for sure?'

She shook her head. 'No. I know it's stupid, but
I preferred to live in a state of not knowing. I guess
I was too scared to confront it and I didn't want yet
another negative thing to define me. It seemed much
easier to just bury my head in the sand.' She shrugged
and bit her lip. 'But I suppose that's difficult for you
to understand.'

She didn't know what she had expected but it
hadn't been for Dante to pick up her hand—her left
hand—and to turn it over and study her palm as if
he was able to read her future, before lifting his sol-
emn gaze to hers.

'No,' he said. 'It's not difficult at all, because all of
us are sometimes guilty of not facing a truth which
is too hard to take. I did it with my own brother—
refused to accept that my reluctance to share him
was what lay at the root of our rift. But listen to me
very carefully, Willow—because you're not thinking logically.'

Her blurry gaze fixed on his stern features. 'What
do you mean?'

'There is *always* the chance that you or I can't have
a baby. That applies to every couple in the world until
they try themselves. Unless you're advocating putting
all prospective brides and grooms through some kind
of fertility test before they're allowed to marry?' He
raised his eyebrows. 'I don't think even royal families adopt that strategy any more.'

'Dante…'

'No,' he said. 'You've had your say and now I'm having mine. Understand?'

Pressing her lips in on themselves, she nodded.

'I love you,' he said simply. 'And the past few weeks have made me realise how much. Time spent away from you has only increased the certainty that I want to spend the rest of my life with you, and only you.' He placed a warning finger over her lips as they began to open. 'With or without children of our own. Because children aren't a deal-breaker. You not loving me would be the only deal-breaker. That's the only thing which would stop me from wanting to marry you, and I'm afraid you've just signed your own fate by telling me that you *do* love me.'

Dazed, she stared at him. 'Am I allowed to say anything yet?'

'Only if you're prepared to see sense and accept my proposal—unless you want me to go down on one knee in this very public place and ask you all over again, despite the fact that you've already auctioned off the first ring I gave you?'

'No! No, please don't do that. Don't you *dare* do that.'

'So you will marry me?'

'It seems I have no choice!'

She was laughing but somehow she seemed to be crying at the same time and Dante was standing up and pulling her into his arms and wiping her tears away with his fingers, before kissing her in a way that made the last of her reservations melt away.

And when the picture of that ecstatic kiss made its way into the gossip columns of next day's newspapers—with the headline *Society Girl to Wed No-*

torious Playboy—Willow didn't care. Because now she realised what mattered—the only thing which mattered. She was going to focus on what was truly important, and that was yet another thing Dante had taught her.

He'd taught her that love made you strong enough to overcome anything.

So she threw the newspaper down onto the carpet and turned to look at him, running her fingers over his olive skin and thinking how magnificent he looked in *her* bed.

Sleepily, he opened his eyes and gave a huge yawn as he glanced down at the bare hand which was currently inching its way up his thigh. 'I guess we'd better go out and buy you another ring. Would you like that?'

'I'd like that very much.'

'But not a diamond.' He smiled. 'A rare grey pearl, I think.'

'Mmm… That sounds perfect.' She moved over him, skin against skin, mouth against mouth—and ripples of desire shivered over her as she felt his hardness pressing against her. 'Just not now,' she whispered indistinctly. 'The ring can wait. But this can't.'

EPILOGUE

'COME AND SIT in the shade,' Dante said lazily. 'I don't want you getting burned.'

Willow pushed her straw hat back and smiled up into her husband's face. 'I'm unlikely to burn when you insist on applying factor fifty to my skin at every opportunity, am I?'

'True. In fact, I think you need another application right now,' he murmured, rising to his feet and standing over her. 'Come here.'

'That sounds like another excuse for you to start rubbing cream into my body.'

'You really think I need an excuse, Mrs Di Sione?' he growled, lifting her off the sun lounger and leading her inside to the air-conditioned cool of their beach-side house.

Willow bit her lip with sheer pleasure as she felt his lips whisper over her throat, thinking she couldn't remember ever feeling so happy. Or lucky. So very lucky. For the past month they'd been honeymooning in a Caribbean beach house, while nearby the crystal waters lapped contentedly against sugar-fine sands. They swam in the mornings, napped in the after-noons and took lazy days out on the Di Sione boat, which had been sailed from New York and was now anchored off the island.

They had married quietly in the small church built in the grounds of her parents' house and the building had been transformed for the occasion, discreetly bankrolled by her future husband. The badly repaired hole in the ceiling had been miraculously fixed and the air was scented with gardenias and jasmine similar to those which had perfumed the Garden Room at the Granchester on the night Dante had asked her to marry him.

'Did you like our wedding?' she questioned softly.

'I loved it. Every second.'

'You didn't think it was too quiet?'

'No. It was perfect. Just like you.' Dante unclipped her bikini top and began to skate his fingertips over her nipples. He had wanted a quiet wedding. There had still been so much *stuff* going on about Giovanni's Lost Mistresses—with his brothers and his sisters all over the place trying to find random pieces of jewellery and other stuff which had once belonged to his grandfather, and nothing completely resolved. The uncertainty about who would be able to attend and who wouldn't had made Dante decide to have the smallest of weddings, with only his brother Dario in attendance as his best man. He told Willow he planned for them to visit the Long Island estate during the forthcoming holidays, where they would have a big post-wedding party.

But he'd known all along that he didn't need pomp, or ceremony. If it could have been just him and Willow, he wouldn't have complained. In the end, he was the one who badly wanted to place a gold ring on her finger and make her his. He'd wanted to marry her more than he could ever remember wanting anything. Because she gave him everything he needed—and more.

And if she'd questioned him over and over about his need for children, he had reassured her with a certainty which went bone-deep. He'd told her that there were lots of possibilities open to them if they couldn't conceive. Like he'd said, it wasn't a deal-breaker. Until one day she'd started believing him and never mentioned it again. And if either of them had been able to see into the future, they would have seen Willow Di Sione holding two baby girls—beautiful, blue-eyed twins, just like their daddy.

Dante gave a contented sigh as he remembered back to their wedding day. Without a doubt she had made the most exquisite bride in the history of the world—with a veil which had been worn by her grandmother, held in place with the glittering tiara of white diamonds and emeralds as green as new leaves. Dario had offered her use of the matching earrings, but although Willow had been very grateful, she had declined the offer. 'A woman can wear *too* much jewellery, you know,' she'd whispered to her prospective husband—and Dante had laughed with a feeling of pure pleasure.

Her slender figure had been showcased by a pale, gauzy dress, beneath which she'd sported a garter embroidered with dramatic flames of yellow and red. And when slowly he'd been removing it on their wedding night, his hand had lingered on the raised surface of vibrant hues, which she'd so lovingly stitched.

'Flames?' he questioned with a frown.

'As a kind of homage to an earlier Dante and his famous inferno.' She smiled. 'But mainly because my life would be hell without you.'

He smiled back. 'Interesting. But I thought brides were traditionally supposed to have something blue?'

And that was when her fingertips reached up to trace over his cheeks with the most gentle touch he had ever known. A touch which had made him shiver with pleasure and count his blessings.

'Your eyes are the bluest thing I've ever seen, Dante Di Sione.' Her voice had been low and trembling. 'I'll settle for those.'

* * * * *

If you enjoyed this book,
look out for the next instalment of
THE BILLIONAIRE'S LEGACY:
A DI SIONE FOR THE GREEK'S PLEASURE
by Kate Hewitt.
Coming next month.

'I think we should get married.'

Xavier's eyes widened. 'I beg your pardon?' he said faintly. 'Am I imagining things, or did you just propose marriage?'

'That's exactly what I said,' Rosie confirmed.

He looked incredulous.

'It would solve all our problems,' she said. 'Yours especially,' she hurried on. 'So it seems to me to be the sensible thing to do—'

'Sensible?' He raked his hair with exasperated fingers.

'You need an heir, or you'll lose your half of the island to me, and unless you've got someone in mind—'

'I don't.'

'Then…'

'Better the devil I know?' he suggested grimly.

'You can't buy me out—you should know that by now— and if we marry you get to keep your share.'

'What's in it for you?'

'Everything,' she said bluntly. *And nothing*, she thought. 'A secure future for the islanders and the island,' she insisted, ignoring the chill in his eyes. 'So, will you consider my suggestion?'

She had no idea what Xavier was thinking as he stared into the fire. Her best guess was that this was Xavier the businessman, weighing up the odds.

'I can't believe you're serious about this,' he said, looking round at last.

'You'd have my full cooperation,' she stressed, sensing the faintest of possibilities that he might say yes.

'I would certainly expect your cooperation in bed.'

Wedlocked!

Conveniently wedded, passionately bedded!

Whether there's a debt to be paid,
a will to be obeyed or a business to be saved…
She's got no choice but to say, 'I do!'

But these billionaire bridegrooms have got another
think coming if they think marriage will be easy…

Soon their convenient brides become the object
of an *inconvenient* desire!

Find out what happens after the vows in

The Billionaire's Defiant Acquisition
by Sharon Kendrick

One Night to Wedding Vows
by Kim Lawrence

Wedded, Bedded, Betrayed
by Michelle Smart

Expecting a Royal Scandal
by Caitlin Crews

Trapped by Vialli's Vows
by Chantelle Shaw

Baby of His Revenge
by Jennie Lucas

Look out for more *Wedlocked!* stories
coming soon!

A DIAMOND
FOR DEL RIO'S
HOUSEKEEPER

BY
SUSAN STEPHENS

First Published in Great Britain 2016
By Mills & Boon, an imprint of HarperCollins*Publishers*
1 London Bridge Street, London, SE1 9GF

© 2016 Susan Stephens

ISBN: 978-0-263-92135-9

Printed and bound in Spain
by CPI, Barcelona

Susan Stephens was a professional singer before meeting her husband on the Mediterranean island of Malta. In true Modern Romance style they met on Monday, became engaged on Friday and married three months later. Susan enjoys entertaining, travel and going to the theatre. To relax she reads, cooks and plays the piano, and when she's had enough of relaxing she throws herself off mountains on skis, or gallops through the countryside singing loudly.

Books by Susan Stephens

Mills & Boon Modern Romance

In the Sheikh's Service
Master of the Desert

One Night With Consequences

Bound to the Tuscan Billionaire

Hot Brazilian Nights!

In the Brazilian's Debt
At the Brazilian's Command
Brazilian's Nine Months' Notice
Back in the Brazilian's Bed

The Skavanga Diamonds

Diamond in the Desert
The Flaw in His Diamond
The Purest of Diamonds?
His Forbidden Diamond

The Acostas!

The Untamed Argentinian
The Shameless Life of Ruiz Acosta
The Argentinian's Solace
A Taste of the Untamed
The Man from Her Wayward Past
Taming the Last Acosta

Visit the Author Profile page
at millsandboon.co.uk for more titles.

For my wonderful readers, who give me licence to dream.
You're always at the forefront of my mind,
and this is for you.

CHAPTER ONE

'THIS IS A private beach...'

Rosie had to raise her voice to reach the big, brutal-looking man lowering the anchor on his sleek black launch off shore. He'd stilled, so she was sure he'd heard her, but for some reason he'd chosen to ignore her. Waving her arms made no impact at all.

'Damned invaders,' Rosie's late elderly employer, Doña Anna, would have said as she waved her walking stick at any sailors bold enough to drop anchor near her private island. *'You can't swim here! This is my island!'* Standing belligerently, with her crab-like hands planted firmly on her bony hips, Doña Anna would continue to berate visitors—whom Rosie had always thought couldn't do much harm if all they wanted to do was enjoy the crystalline waters and sugar-sand beach for an hour or so—until they took the hint that they weren't welcome and left for kinder waters.

Rosie tensed as the man stared straight at her. With maybe fifty yards between them, his penetrating assessment stabbed her like an arrow.

Her body reacted in the craziest way, softening and yearning as the force of his personality washed over her. The effect was as powerful as if they were standing toe to toe.

She was instantly in 'fight or flight' mode. Her brain sharpened to make that call. Only what they'd called her pure, damned stubbornness at the orphanage was keeping her rooted to the spot. She might not have had the best of starts in life, but she wasn't a victim and never would be.

And a promise was a promise, Rosie vowed. Her promise to Doña Anna, that she would keep the island safe, was sacrosanct. However intimidating the man seemed, until she knew what he wanted, he wasn't getting any further than the shore.

The man had other ideas.

Her heart thundered as he sprang lightly onto the bow rail, preparing to dive into the sea. Keeping the island safe would take more than good intentions, she suspected. He was twice her size and built like a gladiator.

His dive made barely a ripple in the water. Surfacing, he powered towards the shore. There was something hard and ruthless about him that stole away her earlier confidence, replacing it with apprehension. Crew of a mother yacht generally wore some sort of uniform with the name of their boat emblazoned on it. He wore no identifying clothing. Stripped to the waist in cut-off shorts, he was maybe thirty...older than she was, anyway.

Rosie was in her early twenties. She couldn't even be sure of her date of birth. There was no record of it. A fire at the orphanage had destroyed all evidence of her history shortly after she arrived. Her life experience was limited to the strange, isolated world inside an institution, and now a small island off the southern tip of Spain.

She'd been lucky enough to be offered a job on Isla Del Rey by a charity that ran a scheme for disadvantaged young people. The post involved working on a trial basis as a companion/housekeeper for an elderly lady who had driven six previous companion/housekeepers away. On the face of it, not the most promising opportunity, but Rosie would have jumped at anything to escape the oppressive surroundings of the institution, and the island had seemed to offer sanctuary from the harsh realities of the outside world.

That world was back with a vengeance now, she thought as the man drew close to shore.

She took up position, ready to send him on his way. Doña Anna had given her so much more than a roof over her head, and she owed it to the old lady to keep her island safe.

Against all the odds, Rosie had become close to her employer, but in her wildest dreams she could never have predicted that in one last act of quite astonishing generosity Doña Anna would leave orphan Rosie Clifton half of Isla Del Rey in her will.

Rosie's inheritance became an international scandal. She hadn't been exactly welcomed into the land-owning classes, more shunned by them. Even Doña Anna's lawyer had made some excuse not to meet her. His formal letter had seemed impregnated with his scorn. How could she, a lowly housekeeper and an orphan to boot, step into the shoes of generations of Spanish aristocracy? No one had seemed to understand that what Rosie had inherited was an old lady's trust, and her love.

Doña Anna's generous bequest had turned out to be a double-edged sword. Rosie had come to love the island, but without a penny to her name, and no wage coming in, she could barely afford to support herself, let alone help the islanders to market their organic produce on the mainland, as she had promised them she would.

The man had reached the shallows, and was wading to the shore. Naked to the waist and muscular, his deeply tanned frame dripping with seawater, he was a spectacular sight. She couldn't imagine a man like that going cap in hand for a loan.

Rosie had failed spectacularly in that direction. Every letter she'd sent to possible investors for the island had been met with silence, or scorn: *Who was she but a lowly housekeeper whose life experience was confined to an orphanage?* She couldn't even argue with that view, when it was right.

He speared her with a glance. She guessed he could open any door. But not this door. She would keep her deathbed promise to Doña Anna, and continue the fight to keep the island unspoiled. Which, in Doña Anna's language, meant no visitors—especially not a man who was looking at Rosie as if she were a piece of flotsam that had washed up on the beach. She would despatch him exactly as Doña Anna would have done, Rosie determined, standing her ground. Well, perhaps not quite the same way. She was more of a firm persuader than a shouter.

Her heart pounded with uneasiness as he strode towards her across the sand. She was alone and vulnerable. He'd chosen the best time of day to spring his surprise. Rosie had never made any secret of the fact that she liked to swim early in the morning before anyone was up. When she was alive, Doña Anna had encouraged this habit, saying Rosie should get some fresh air before spending all day in the house.

Snatching up her towel from the rock where she'd spread it out to dry, she covered herself modestly. Even so, she was hardly dressed for receiving visitors. The house was half a mile away up a steep cliff path, and no one would hear her cry for help—

She wouldn't be calling for help. She owned fifty per cent of this island, with the other fifty per cent belonging to some absentee Spanish Grandee.

Don Xavier Del Rio was Doña Anna's nephew, but as he hadn't troubled to visit his aunt during Rosie's time on the island, not even attending her funeral, Rosie doubted he would inconvenience himself now. According to Doña Anna, he was a playboy who lived life on the edge. As far as Rosie was concerned, he was a hard-hearted brute, who didn't deserve such a lovely aunt.

Admittedly, when it came to his business, he seemed to be successful. But, billionaire or not, in Rosie's view, he should have made some effort to visit Doña Anna— or perhaps he was just too important to care.

He couldn't believe what he was seeing. The girl had set herself up on the beach as if he were the intruder. 'You're right,' he barked at her. 'This *is* a private beach. So what the hell are you doing here?'

'I own—I mean, I live on the island,' she said, tipping her chin a little higher in what he supposed was an attempt to stare him in the eyes.

He towered over her. She was small and young and lithe, with long, striking red hair, and an expression that appeared candid, but was most definitely defiant and determined. She was pale, but outwardly composed. He knew who she was. The lawyer had warned him she might be difficult and not to be deceived by her innocent looks.

'Did the lawyer send you?' she challenged, seeming to have no guard on her tongue.

'No one *sent* me,' he replied, all the time assessing her keenly.

'Then why are you here?'

Her clenched fists were the only sign that she was nervous. She had courage to stand up to him, but he wasn't a bully and she was a young girl alone on the beach. He ordered his muscles to stand down. 'I'm here to see you.'

'Me?'

She put one small hand on the swell of plump breasts peeping above the towel. And then a stiff breeze caught hold of her hair and lifted it, tossing it about. The urge to fist a hank of it, so he could ease her head back and kiss her throat, was overwhelming.

She might hold appeal, but anyone who could persuade his crotchety aunt to leave them such a sizeable bequest had to be more conniving than she looked.

'We have business to discuss.' He glanced up the cliff towards the house.

'You can only be one person,' she said, levelling her cool amethyst gaze on him. 'The lawyers have shown no interest in me, or in the island. They're happy to let Isla Del Rey go to hell, and me with it. Every door in the city's been slammed in my face. But I suppose you already know that... Don Xavier.'

He remained impassive. The day the contents of his aunt's will had become known her lawyers had been in touch with him to profess their undying loyalty. The firm had worked for the Del Rio family for years, the head of the firm was at pains to remind him, and every associate was squarely behind Don Xavier in this most *regrettable* situation. There was a good case to challenge the will, the lawyer had assured him, no doubt rubbing his hands with glee at the thought of more fees to come. Xavier had dismissed the man's suggestion out of hand. He would deal with the situation, as he would deal with this girl.

'Are you responsible for me being ignored in the city?' the girl now challenged him, firming her jaw with affront.

'No,' he said honestly. His aunt had always been mischievous, and never more so than when she had drawn up her will. Now he'd met the girl with whom he shared the bequest, he suspected Doña Anna must have taken much pleasure in putting as many obstacles in his way as she could before he could lay claim to an island that was rightfully his. 'No doubt the money men think as I do, that the responsibility of Isla Del Rey cannot rest in the hands of one young girl.'

'Well, I don't suppose you're interested in my opinion,' she flashed back.

She was going to give it to him anyway, he suspected.

She proved him right. 'Anyone lucky enough to have relatives should cherish them, not abandon them, however difficult they might be.'

'Was that a dig at me?' he asked with mild amusement. 'Are you suggesting that I have as little claim to the island as you?'

'You have the name,' she conceded. 'You also have the reputation. Why would your aunt leave the island she loved above all things to a man as notorious as you?'

The bluntness of this statement silenced him for a moment, and he had to admit to some grudging respect. Her boldness was shocking, but it was also refreshing. He guessed her blunt character had been forged on the anvil of a difficult childhood. She'd had to find ways to survive, and had chosen logic and stubbornness over compliance and self-pity. She was brave. He'd give her that. Not many people would take him on.

'No argument, Don Xavier?'

He raised a brow, but what she'd said was true. His reputation hung by a thread. He lived hard and fast, funded by the lifestyle his highly successful business ventures provided. He wasn't interested in love and caring. They had only brought him disappointment in the past. He had no time for such things now. That was why he had avoided both the island and his aunt. He wasn't proud to admit that the thought of rekindling the feelings he'd had for the old lady when he was a boy had made it easier for him to stay away. His parents had knocked all thoughts of love out of him. More grief? More regret? Why would he invite them in? He'd done what Doña Anna had asked him to do, which was to make more money to fund those schemes she would have been proud of, and that had to be enough.

But his mischievous aunt was asking more of him in her will. He could only imagine she had been playing games with him when she had added a particular caveat that stood in the way of him claiming his inheritance.

'I imagine it's the terms of your aunt's will that brought you here,' the girl commented forthrightly.

What business was it of hers?

Against his better judgement, his senses stirred as she continued to interrogate him with her astonishingly beautiful amethyst eyes.

'We're both here for the same reason, I imagine,' he countered evenly. 'To sort out the terms of the bequest.'

'I live here, you don't,' she said, smiling a faint challenge at him.

Was she staking her claim? If she'd read the will, and he presumed she had, she would know he could forfeit his half of the island if he didn't provide the estate with an heir within two years. It must have amused his aunt to put his infamous reputation to the test.

'You're under some pressure, I imagine,' the girl said.

Seeing the glint of amusement in her eyes, he guessed she was enjoying this as much as his aunt must have done. He could imagine them getting on together. And of course the girl could afford to laugh, as her fifty per cent of the island was safe. All she had to do was wait him out, hope he didn't produce an heir, and she would own the island outright. His trump card was the fact that she didn't have any money to support herself, so nothing was certain. Not yet.

'So you're familiar with the terms of my aunt's will?' he confirmed as they stood facing each other, weighing each other up.

'Yes,' she said frankly. 'Your aunt's lawyer was difficult to begin with. He didn't want to show me anything, but I insisted.'

I bet you did, he thought.

'He couldn't deny my request,' she explained. 'To be honest, I just wanted to see your aunt's will with my own eyes to confirm that I really had inherited half of Isla Del Rey, but then...' Biting down on her lip, she looked away.

'Yes?' he prompted, sensing serious thoughts beneath her calm exterior. The worst mistake he could make would be to take this woman lightly.

'But then I read that bit about you,' she said, refocusing her luminous stare on his face. 'So I understand the pressure you're under.' She couldn't resist a little smile as she added, 'I always knew Doña Anna had a strange sense of humour, but I have to admit she excelled herself this time. Maybe if you hadn't ignored her for so long—'

'I stand reprimanded,' he said curtly. He didn't want to discuss his aunt with anyone, let alone this young woman.

'The thing I find confusing,' she said, 'is this. I always thought Doña Anna believed in family. At least, that was the impression she gave me, but now it seems she was hell-bent on punishment.' She screwed her eyes up as she thought about it.

And they were still beautiful.

'Punishing me, not you,' he said.

'But still…' She stared at him with interest for a good few moments. 'You must have really rattled her cage. But you did, by staying away so long.'

She wasn't frightened of speaking her mind. The more he saw of her, the more she intrigued him. His original intention had been to send her sailing away from the island on a raft made of money. He doubted now he'd met her that she'd stand for that. She was intelligent and defiant, and also extremely attractive.

That sort of interest could get in his way. He couldn't allow distractions like this girl to knock him off course. She was right about the will throwing everything into chaos. Doña Anna, of all people, should have known his limitations. He could make money hand over fist, but he'd make a lousy parent. Why try to saddle some poor child with a father who was incapable of feeling?

'We'd better go to the house,' he said, turning to the main point of his visit.

'What? No,' she said.

'I beg your pardon?' He swung around to see her digging her little toes into the sand.

'You should have contacted me in the usual way—to

arrange a meeting that didn't involve a confrontation on the beach at dawn,' she explained, frowning at him.

He dipped his head to hide a smile. People had been known to try and bribe his PA to secure a few minutes of his time. Rosie Clifton, on the other hand, was only short of his aunt's walking stick to wave in his face as she did her best to drive him away. But her time was up now. However appealing he might find her, he was a busy man.

'I said, no!'

He gazed at her with incredulity as she took the few steps necessary to dodge in front of him and block his way. 'It's not convenient,' she explained, holding her ground.

Not convenient for him to tour *his* house, his island? An astonishing number of doors might have opened in the recent past for orphaned Rosie Clifton, but no door had ever closed in his face. He would visit his house, and he would tour his island. And then he would decide what to do about the girl.

'Perhaps another time?' she tempered, reacting to his thunderous expression no doubt. 'Some time soon?' she offered with the hint of a smile.

Her charm was wasted on him. 'Some time now,' he insisted, moving past her.

CHAPTER TWO

HE SHOULD HAVE known she'd race after him. When she grabbed hold of his arm, he felt the power of those tiny fingers as clearly as if they were stroking his groin. The thought of those hands clutching him in the throes of passion was enough to stop him dead in his tracks. Her touch was electrifying. And then there was her spirit. Rosie Clifton might not possess a fraction of his wealth or power, but she knew no fear. It was impossible for him not to admire her just a little.

'You can come up to the house another time,' she said, still hanging on to his arm as she stared up into his face. 'We'll make a proper appointment. I promise.'

'Will we?' he demanded with irony.

As he stared down her amethyst eyes darkened, confirming his growing suspicion that the attraction between them was mutual. And inconvenient, he reminded himself firmly. He wasn't here for seduction. He had business with Rosie Clifton.

'Neither of us is dressed for a formal meeting,' she pointed out. 'We won't feel comfortable. And when there are such important things to discuss…'

He awarded her a point for a good, persuasive argument.

'So…?' Her beautifully drawn lips parted as she waited for his answer.

'So I'll come back,' he agreed.

'Thank you,' she exclaimed with relief.

It was an error on his part. He had given her chance to prepare for *the next time*. His aunt must be laughing in her grave. Doña Anna couldn't have planned this better, placing two people with the same aim—one an idealist, and the other a business mogul—in direct conflict with each other. Inwardly, he huffed a smile of admiration. He had to admit, this sort of mischief was right up her street.

'Before you go…' She nibbled on her lip.

'Yes?'

'I want you to know that I really loved your aunt.'

He shrugged. Should he care? Was she waiting for him to make some comment to echo this? He examined his feelings scrupulously and came up with nothing. The numbness inside him had been there since childhood, he supposed. He didn't know how he felt about his aunt, though he might have known that nothing short of a dynasty would satisfy Doña Anna.

'Your aunt brought you up, didn't she?' Rosie pressed.

'Only because my parents preferred the fleshpots of Monte Carlo,' he said with an impatient gesture that told her to leave the subject alone.

'That must have hurt you,' she said gently, as if she cared.

'It was a long time ago.' He frowned, hoping that would put her off.

It seemed to. She didn't say anything more on the subject, but she looked at him with something close to pity, which annoyed him even more.

'Your aunt said she threw you out when you were a teenager.' She laughed, seeming to find this amusing. 'She said it was the best thing she ever did for you—but then she was always teaching people lessons, including me.'

'But not the type of lesson that would include holding your tongue,' he murmured dryly.

She ignored him and continued. 'Doña Anna said old money doesn't last for ever, and that it's up to each new generation to make its own luck in life. Which you've done in shedloads.' Her eyes widened with admiration.

Only her innocence and complete lack of sophistication could allow for this, he thought as she went on to list his credentials. 'First you made a fortune in the tech world, and then you made a second fortune building six-star hotels across the world with state-of-the-art golf courses attached.' She frowned. 'I imagine that's why your aunt left me half the island—to stop you rampaging over here. Rumour says you're a billionaire,' she added with startling candour.

'I don't much care about that.'

'She told me that too,' she called after him as he began to stroll away from her towards the sea.

'Was there anything she didn't tell you?' he said, stopping in his tracks.

'Oh, I'm sure there were lots of things she left out...'

He could only hope.

'Did she speak about me often?' he asked. He was suddenly filled with a need to know. He felt a pang of regret as he asked the question, which was a first for him.

'She did talk about you—quite a lot,' Rosie revealed brightly, and with no malice he could detect. 'I'm sorry if I've upset you,' she said as he turned away.

'You haven't upset me.' Pausing beside one of the gargantuan rocks on the beach, he leaned back against its smooth surface. Like it or not, the girl had brought the past back into clear focus.

'I should get back,' she said.

'Do you swim here every day?' he said, turning to look at her. Suddenly, he wasn't so keen for her to go.

'Every morning—I have done ever since I arrived on the island. Such a luxury,' she said. Rolling her head back, she closed her eyes as if she was reliving each and every moment she'd spent in the surf.

The island must have been a revelation to her after the orphanage. He couldn't imagine being brought up in an institution with no personal interest lavished on a person at all. At least he'd had Doña Anna. He was almost glad now that fate had intervened for Rosie Clifton. He would have had to be a heartless monster not to.

A visit to the orphanage by the royal patron of one of the charities he sponsored had led to Rosie being singled out. The prince had told Xavier that this particular girl had caught his attention because of her calm and resilient manner. He wondered now if Rosie's luminous appearance had attracted the prince's attention. That, and her obvious innocence. When the prince had first mentioned Rosie, he had thought immediately of his aunt and the possibility that a young girl might succeed where so many older, professional carers had failed. Never in his wildest dreams had he imagined that Rosie Clifton would be quite so successful. He searched now for guile beneath the frankness of her stare, and found none. 'Do you swim on your own in the sea?'

'Why not?' she countered pertly. 'You did.'

When she cocked her head to issue the challenge, she

somehow managed to look more appealing than ever. It was time to rein in his feelings before they started to cloud his judgement. 'Do you think that's wise?' he said, turning stern. 'What if you got into trouble in the water?'

'I can get into trouble on the land just as easily,' she said.

As she masked her smile it was hard not to like her, which was everything he had vowed not to do. When she shrugged, drawing his attention to the womanly frame beneath the tightly bound towel, and to her slender shoulders with their sprinkling of freckles like gold dust on her skin, he knew he was in trouble.

'One thing I learned as a child,' she added frankly, 'was how to keep my head above water.'

'I have no doubt of that,' he agreed as she tossed her hair back, sending the glistening waves cascading in a fiery cloud almost to her waist. 'But you're taking a big risk with your safety,' he warned.

'It's not such a big deal if you know the seas around the island, is it, Don Xavier…?'

'Touché,' he murmured to himself. 'You're right,' he admitted. 'I swam here many times as a boy, but that doesn't make it safe for you.'

'Are you saying you're a better swimmer than I am?' There was both challenge and humour in her eyes now.

'Enough!' he insisted, knowing it was time to end this before she won him over completely. 'Allow me to introduce myself formally. Don Xavier Del Rio, at your service…'

'I doubt that somehow.' She laughed. 'And I don't want you to be at my service. But I am pleased to *formally* meet you at last,' she teased him. 'Perhaps we can start over?' She suggested this hopefully, extending a hand for him to shake. 'Rosie Clifton,' she declared, 'at no one's service.'

He laughed. 'There's never been the slightest doubt of that.'

As he brushed his lips against the back of her hand he felt her tremble. When he let her go, she quickly put her hands behind her back, as if to keep them out of mischief. She wasn't so good at hiding her feelings, after all. He didn't intimidate her. She didn't feel particularly antagonistic towards him. She was naturally wary and inquisitive, but when he touched her, she was aroused. He wondered what new discoveries he would make about Rosie Clifton. Compliance must have been her best defence at the orphanage, and she would have had to be accommodating to keep her job with his aunt. She must have worked out by now that half an island was of no use to either of them, and he was curious as to where she thought they'd go from here. 'What do you know about me, Rosie?'

'Probably as much as you know about me,' she said frankly. 'I know you by reputation, of course. Who doesn't? But as that's only hearsay and I like to draw my own conclusions about people, I'm keeping an open mind right now.'

'Should I thank you for that?'

'Do as you like,' she said easily. 'I do know that everything you've achieved in life, you've done without anyone's help. Doña Anna told me that too,' she explained, unintentionally twisting the knife in the wound she'd inadvertently opened. He'd had enough of this. She was getting under his skin, making him feel too much. He couldn't have that. 'But that doesn't tell me who you are, or if I can trust you—'

He sidestepped her and made for the house.

'Hey!' She chased after him as he headed for the cliff path. And, *Dios*, now she was standing in front of him.

'Get out of my way, please,' he instructed quietly.

'No.' Folding her arms, she said loud and clear, 'You're not going a step further. I told you already, it's not convenient for you to visit the house.'

He could swing her over his shoulder and carry her there, but that would lead to nowhere good for Rosie Clifton, and maybe life had beat up on her enough. She was far too young and too innocent for him, with his sophisticated tastes in the bedroom. She featured nowhere on his agenda, other than to buy her off.

'I said no,' she warned again, when he went to move past her.

He stopped. She amused him. Her lips might be kissable, but they were currently set in such a firm, determined line. And now another question occurred to him: Was Rosie Clifton really as innocent as she looked? Had she been swept along by circumstances beyond her control, or was she a consummate actress who had managed to fool his aunt? Tricksters didn't tend to have *swindler* tattooed on their brow. Either way, he would deal with Ms Clifton. If nothing more than good fortune and happy fate shone on Rosie Clifton, then a financial settlement to make her eyes water would soon get rid of her. If she was an idealist who believed she was saving the island from a ruthless playboy entrepreneur, namely him, then his cantankerous aunt had indeed met her match, and there would be trouble ahead—but not for him.

'If you don't get out of my way, I shall have to move you.'

Just the thought of taking that lithe, rebellious body in his arms was enough to whip his senses into an agony of lust, but she just laughed. 'I'd like to see you try,' she said.

He held up his hands, palms flat. He could wait. Except for the issue of the heir—he held all the cards and she held none. She couldn't fight him through the courts. She lacked the money to do so. She was at his mercy. Even if he failed to produce an heir and his half reverted to her, she'd never have the money to continue to manage the island. Whichever way she turned, there was no future for Rosie Clifton on the island. The only fight she could put up was with words. They both knew the outcome was inevitable. He would own one hundred per cent of Isla Del Rey. It was just a matter of time. But there was no mileage in making her miserable.

'Try to be reasonable,' he suggested. 'It's important that I see the house as soon as possible to make an initial assessment of the changes that need to be made.'

'What changes?' she retorted. 'The hacienda is perfectly serviceable as it stands.'

Rosie doubted anything had been refurbished or rearranged since the man who was making her body yearn for things it could hardly imagine had lived there as a boy. She had always thought the old house perfect. It wore the patina of age and regular use with such comfortable ease, reflecting everything that was cosy and special about the home Doña Anna had made for them both. What right did he have to come storming in, talking about change?

'The sooner the better,' he repeated, in what she gathered was his best attempt at a pleasant tone. He failed to charm her.

'I'm afraid that won't be possible,' she stated firmly. He moved past her, but she caught up with him again.

If it was possible for a man to grow taller and become more intimidating, he'd just done that.

'You can't keep me away for ever.' His stern eyes heated every part of her, and, instead of resenting him, she found to her bemusement that she was excited. 'Or had you forgotten I also own fifty per cent of this island?' he demanded.

'I haven't forgotten anything,' she said, especially the bizarre terms of Doña Anna's will. No wonder he was so angry. Those terms had left her flailing for the necessary finance to remain living on the island, and him needing an heir. She might be at her wits' end, but his buccaneering lifestyle had been cut off at the root. 'All I'm suggesting is a rain check. When we've both calmed down and we're properly dressed for the occasion, I'd be pleased to show you around.'

Reason had always worked best for Rosie when she had encountered difficult situations at the orphanage. If there was one thing that living in an institution had taught her, it was the basic rules of survival. The most important rule of all was to make no ripples, and if she did, to smooth them over fast.

She shivered involuntarily as Don Xavier's black stare licked over her. Her almost naked body was eager for more of his attention. Thankfully, she had more sense.

'My PA will be in touch,' he said coolly. 'Once I've had a chance to inspect both the island and the hacienda, you will be invited to the mainland for a meeting, where we will discuss terms.'

What terms? When did she agree to this?

His dismissive gesture now suggested that it would be more convenient still if he could brush her under the table along with everything else he found superfluous in his life. She had no intention of going to the mainland for a meeting. His terms? His territory? She might be young, but she wasn't stupid.

'I'm not sure that will be convenient for me,' she said bluntly. 'And, as far as I'm aware, we have nothing to discuss. The terms of the will are quite clear.'

His expression blackened to a frightening degree. This was a man who wasn't used to anyone disagreeing with him, she gathered.

'Are you marooned on the island?' he thundered.

'No, but I have a lot on.'

'Such as?' he derided. 'You've no funds—no income.'

'I can accomplish a lot with hard work and no money,' she argued. 'And just because I've been turned down by lenders to date, doesn't mean I'm giving up. I don't think your aunt would give up. And I don't think Doña Anna would leave me half this island unless she was confident I could sort things out.'

'Your intention is to help the islanders market their organic produce, I believe?'

He was well informed. 'Why not?' She might as well put her stake in the ground now.

Maybe it would be better to soften her attitude and try to engage his support? Her main goal was to help the islanders, not herself, and if she didn't control her feelings—feelings she usually had no trouble controlling—the next deputation to the island might include Don Xavier's legal team.

Correct. And she couldn't risk that. She had no funds to fight him. It was time to swallow her pride and make him feel welcome. Maybe if they worked at it they could find a solution together. She was no good at dressing things up, so she just said the first thing that came into her head. 'If you come back tomorrow I'll make you some ice cream.'

The look he gave her suggested she might as well have invited him to join her in a bondage session, complete with whips and masks.

'Three o'clock tomorrow,' he rapped. 'And no ice cream.'

CHAPTER THREE

THE FOLLOWING DAY, Rosie's heart was pounding with anticipation as she waited for Don Xavier to arrive. He might be cold and arrogant, but she was thrilled at the thought of seeing him again. She didn't have much excitement in her life, but she'd always been a dreamer. And today Don Xavier was playing the starring role. Maybe it was his need for an heir that had stirred her imagination. How was he going to get one? The usual way, obviously—but with whom? He probably had hordes of glamorous girlfriends, but she couldn't imagine him settling down.

In honour of his visit she was wearing her one good dress. She'd bought it in a thrift shop with the small allowance she'd received from the prince's charity. The money was supposed to help her to prepare for her first placement. She'd spent most of it on books to help her understand the needs of the elderly, and the rest on ice cream as she worried about whether or not she'd be up to the job.

The dress was yellow, with a floating cotton skirt and fitted top. The colour didn't do much for her freckled complexion and it clashed with her flaming red hair, but there hadn't been much choice in her size. It was old-fashioned, but had seemed to Rosie's untrained eye to be the type of dress that wouldn't alarm an elderly lady searching for a discreet companion. Predictably, Doña Anna had hated it, calling it Rosie's custard dress, but Rosie still thought it was pretty and low-key.

She stared out of the kitchen window, wondering if Don Xavier had changed his mind. Maybe his people would arrive instead, and try to drive her away. Her pulse raced with anger at the thought. He'd better come back and face her.

So far the sea was placid blue, and decidedly empty. There was no sleek black launch approaching, and no impossibly good-looking Spanish visitor powering through the waves towards her. But she was ready for whatever came next. She had cleaned the house from top to bottom, and was satisfied that it had never looked better. He couldn't fail to be impressed. She had always longed for a house of her own to care for, and saw the work as a privilege rather than drudgery. And she would gladly kick her pride into touch if she could persuade him to give her a loan to help the islanders launch their plan to market their produce worldwide.

The more she reflected on this, the more she wondered about Doña Anna's intentions when she drew up her will. Was this one last attempt to save Don Xavier from his empty, meaningless life? Or was that Rosie being romantic again? In her view, all the money in the world couldn't buy the love and support of a family, and, if Don Xavier had only known it, Doña Anna had been waiting to welcome him back into her family home with open arms.

Brushing her hair away from her face, Rosie pulled away from the window. It looked as if he wasn't coming. Her gaze lingered on the flowers she'd cut fresh from the garden that morning... Iceberg roses: pure white and lightly scented. The full, fat blooms thrived in clusters, just like the best families, she mused, smiling at the analogy. Not that she was an expert on either families or roses. The reason she loved the roses was for the way they thrust their scented heads so proudly above the weeds she hadn't got round to pulling out yet. There were so many things on the island worth preserving.

Isla Del Rey had bewitched Rosie from the moment she'd stepped onshore. She had been instantly dazzled by the island's beauty. It was so warm and sunny after the dreary cold of the city-centre orphanage where she'd grown up. There were sugar-sand beaches and vibrant colours everywhere, instead of unrelieved grey. And so much space and clean air to breathe. She had left a grimy city behind, and with it the restrictions of the orphanage. On the island, for the very first time in her life, she'd felt free. Best of all, she loved the people for the way they smiled and waved at her, as if they wanted to welcome her to their beautiful island home. Their cause had been her cause ever since.

Perhaps the biggest treat of all when she'd arrived had been the discovery that she would have a room to herself. And it was such a beautiful room. Light and spacious, Rosie's new bedroom overlooked the ocean, which was like a dream come true. Another favourite place in the hacienda was the library, where Doña Anna had encouraged Rosie to read any book she liked. That was when Rosie had suggested reading to the old lady. From that day on they had shared many adventures together, and, even if those adventures were confined to the pages of a book, Rosie credited storytelling with bringing them closer.

The varying tales had prompted Doña Anna to reveal so many episodes from her life. Rosie's experience of love and life had been practically zero up to then, but reading to Doña Anna had awoken in her a love for family, and a longing for the type of romance she was reading about in books. Love grew between the two of them during these regular sessions in the library. It made Rosie long for children of her own, so she could tell them about Doña Anna, and keep the memory of a very special woman alive. Her dream was that her children would pass on that memory to their children, so they would understand how lives could be turned around if just one person cared enough to make a difference.

When Doña Anna asked Rosie to stay on, making what was originally supposed to be a temporary position as housekeeper/companion permanent, it was the happiest day of her life. And the easiest decision she'd ever had to make, Rosie remembered. Doña Anna was the mother figure she'd never known. She loved the old lady for her prickly kindness, and for her generous heart.

She would always love her, Rosie reflected as she glanced at her wristwatch and frowned for the umpteenth time.

He glanced at the clock and ground his jaw. He had never been so impatient to get away from a meeting before, but he was itching to get back to the island.

And whose fault was that?

A pale, determined face, framed by a fiery cloud of shimmering red hair, came to mind. He resolutely blanked it. The last thing he needed was for the basest form of primal instinct to colour his renowned detachment.

And then there was Isla Del Rey, and his conflicting memories of the island, to further muddy the water.

While ideas were batted between his team, he thought back. As a youth he had loathed the island for its restrictions. As a boy, he had associated the place with loneliness and disappointment, which was only made bearable thanks to the intervention of his aunt.

In fairness to his parents, they had never professed to love him. They never tired of telling him that he was both an accident and an inconvenience. Hope that they would one day learn to love him had taken a long time to die. He'd come home from school full of excitement at the thought of seeing them again, only to find them ready to leave as he arrived. Or they would promise to come and not turn up at all.

One day his mother told him to his face that everything he touched turned to dust. She'd been a beauty before he was born, loved by his father and feted by the world, but now, thanks to her son, Xavier, she was nothing. He had destroyed her. And when his seven-year-old self had begged her not to say such things, clinging to her hand as she left the room, she had shaken him off with disgust, and then laughed in his face when he'd started crying. No wonder he'd steered clear of romantic entanglements. He'd seen where they led.

Doña Anna had stepped into the breach, raising him, and encouraging him to make the best of the island—to swim around it, and to sail around it—and he'd enjoyed his first love affair on the beach. But though his aunt had told him on numerous occasions that his mother's words were just the emotional outpourings of a troubled woman, those ugly words still rang in his head. He wasn't capable of love. He was a jinx, a misfortune. He destroyed love—

He turned as Margaret, his second in command,

coughed discreetly to attract his attention. 'You want these plans acted upon right away, Xavier?'

'That's right,' he confirmed.

She knew he'd been remembering. Margaret had an uncanny knack of sensing when he was wrestling the demons from the past.

'And you want that done *before* you attempt a satisfactory settlement with Rosie Clifton?'

'Do you doubt I'll reach a settlement with the girl?'

Everyone but Margaret laughed at his remark. Margaret had read the will, so she knew he had to produce an heir. Two years was no time at all, she'd told him with concern written all over her face. What was he supposed to do? Pluck one out of thin air? The thought of breeding with one of the women he customarily dated held no appeal at all.

'I think this is a tricky situation of a type we haven't encountered before,' Margaret now commented thoughtfully.

Tricky was the understatement of the year.

'If you mean Ms Clifton fires on emotion, while I work solely with the facts, then you're probably right,' he conceded. 'But surely, that guarantees a satisfactory outcome for our side?'

Whether Margaret agreed or not, he would go ahead with his plans. Who was going to stand in his way? Not Rosie Clifton, that was for sure—

Rosie Clifton...

He couldn't get her out of his head. Just her name was enough to set his senses raging. He suspected that beneath her composure Señorita Clifton could whip up quite a storm...

'I've never known you to be so distracted at a meeting,' Margaret commented discreetly.

He noticed everyone was leaving the room, while he had been thinking about Rosie Clifton. He was glad there was an air of excitement. His team was like a pack of greyhounds in the traps, eager to chase up every detail in his plan.

'You're right,' he agreed, standing to hold Margaret's chair. 'I've got a lot on my mind.'

Women had always been ornaments in the past, to be enjoyed and briefly admired. He had never thought of them as potential mothers to any children he might have. He'd never thought of having children, or settling down. Life had kicked that notion out of him. His best plan was to make Rosie Clifton an offer for her half of the island that she couldn't possibly refuse.

She might refuse.

There was that possibility, he conceded now he'd met her. The figure he had in mind was substantial, but would she take it? She was an idealist with her own plans for the island. She knew his reputation for taking wasteland and transforming it into a site of unparalleled luxury, but to Rosie every inch of that island held magic and potential—and not for a six-star hotel.

'Xavier...'

'Yes, Margaret?' He would trust this woman with his life. She was the only woman he would trust with his fortune. Margaret was his fifty-four-year-old financial director, an accountant with a steel-trap mind who could run circles around every bean counter he knew. It was thanks to Margaret that he could take time away from the business. As a judge of people she had no equal. What would Margaret make of Señorita Clifton? he wondered.

'I knew the meeting might run over,' she said as he held the door for her, 'and so I took the liberty of ordering the chopper to be fuelled and ready for you. You can leave at once.'

Margaret's second talent was for reading his mind. His mood lifted, and he smiled at her decadent English vowels. Years of drilling in a strict UK boarding school accounted for the precision of her accent, Margaret had once told him. He didn't care. He'd forgive her anything. She was the one woman in his life who had never disappointed him. Nodding briefly, he smiled his thanks and then they both went their separate ways.

It was late afternoon. Rosie was sitting on the beach, staring out to sea as she dabbled her feet in the water. She kept telling herself she knew Don Xavier wouldn't come.

She should be relieved he wasn't coming. She wasn't relieved. Part of her wanted to get their business over with as fast as she could, while another, far less worthy part of her just wanted to see him again. Her best guess was that he couldn't admit—not even to himself—that the island still meant something to him, and so he had decided to stay away. She got that. She had difficulty with emotions, having hidden hers for years. She would have been laughed at when she lived at the orphanage if she had given away even a hint of her romantic dreams, but that had never stopped her dreaming. In fact, sometimes, she thought she was overburdened with dreams, but they had never turned her into a block of ice like Don Xavier.

Almost six o'clock! The day was flying away. It was time to go back to the house. The glaring light of a sultry Spanish afternoon was fast burning out to burnished gold. The sunset promised to be spectacular, which was the only thing holding her on the beach. The sky was an intense, almost metallic blue, while the first signs of dusk were appearing on the horizon in random drifts of fluffy pink clouds. The sea was so smooth it looked like a skating rink, as if the waves, having exerted themselves all day, couldn't be bothered to crash on the shore, so they were creeping up it instead. She scrunched her toes in the wet sand, loving the sensation as she allowed the rhythmical sound of the waves to flitter across her eardrums. Even that wasn't soothing. Her irritation about the missing guest was stronger. Don Xavier seemed to find it easy to walk away from things and she'd been looking forward to another verbal sparring match with him. They had to get together if they were going to sort out the future of the island, and they should do that as soon as possible. They had a duty to the islanders.

She had wanted a chance to make him understand how much she cared for the island, and how lucky she felt to have been given the chance to live here. Helping the islanders was just her way of thanking them for their kindness towards her. Her dream was to share the island one day with other young people who'd had no advantages in life. She guessed that would have to wait, as her tiny pot of money would run out soon—

A sound distracted her. She couldn't identify it at first. Then she realised it was the sound of rotor blades approaching fast. As she sprang to her feet a gleaming black craft appeared over the cliff at the far end of the bay. She remained motionless as it wheeled onto its side, at what appeared to her to be an impossibly acute angle.

She exhaled with relief when it levelled off to skim the surface of the sea, driving up spumes of water in glittering clouds. It kept on coming towards her, and only wheeled away at the very last minute. Rising rapidly, it banked steeply before turning inland. The pilot seemed to be flying on the edge of what was possible.

So it could only be one man, Rosie reasoned. Who else would take such risks with his life and company property?

And she shouldn't be here on the beach daydreaming, but up at the house ready to greet him—or to hold him off!

To hell with greeting him! She should be up at the house to establish her right to call the hacienda home— the only home she'd ever known. More importantly, the hacienda had meant everything to Doña Anna, and no patronising, nose-in-the-air grandee was going to bulldoze it, to build yet another of his glitzy hotels. Kicking off her flip-flops, she began to run.

Rosie scrambled up the cliff path as if the hounds of hell were after her, and she didn't stop until she reached the boundary to the property—a fence she hadn't realised was quite so broken down. She picked her way carefully through the broken struts of a barrier that was supposed to divide a once beautiful formal garden from the glorious wilderness. As of now, it was all glorious wilderness, she saw with concern.

Imagining Don Xavier seeing the same thing made Rosie wince. She'd known things were bad, but not this bad. She'd meant to do something about the garden, but had no money to pay a gardener, and there was so much to do inside the house. Any spare time she had was spent researching grants and subsidies for the islanders, to help them get their plans for marketing their organic produce off the ground.

She glanced up to see the helicopter hovering over the hacienda. It looked like a giant black hand come to claim its rightful property. Its shadow was like an omen.

Descending slowly from the sky, it looked like a malevolent locust as it settled on its widespread skids. It seemed to Rosie to be the clearest signal yet that she had no money, no power, no influence, while Don Xavier Del Rio had a cash register for a heart. What was going to happen to the island if she didn't stand firm? Why had Doña Anna set them against each other like this? She couldn't have expected them to work together. Don Xavier would never consider it. Doña Anna hadn't been exactly noted for her willingness to compromise, and yet that was what she expected them to do.

So was she going to disappoint the woman who had given her a fresh chance in life?

Drawing a deep steadying breath, Rosie smoothed her hair and straightened her dress, ready for her second meeting with Don Xavier.

CHAPTER FOUR

THE KITCHEN DOOR was open so he walked straight in. It smelled clean, but looked shabby. He leaned over the pristine sink to see if the window really was in as much danger of falling out as he'd first thought. He heard a faint noise behind him—just a breath, a slight shift in the air. He turned and she was there.

His good intentions counted for nothing. His body responded instantly to the sight of Rosie Clifton, his groin tightening as blood ripped through his veins. She was so young, so innocent—and so not his type, but it seemed that no argument he could put up could take anything away from her appeal. The low-slanting sun was shining straight into her face. She looked like an angel waiting to fall, in shades of white and gold—and yellow? As she came deeper into the kitchen he took more notice of the dress. It was a hideous dress that must have hung unloved in a thrift shop for years, but on Señorita Clifton it served a very definite purpose, which was to cling to her shapely form with loving attention to detail.

'Don Xavier,' she exclaimed in a calm, clear voice, walking forward to greet him.

'Señorita Clifton.' His tone was cool.

'Rosie, please,' she insisted, forming the words

with the kissable lips he hadn't been able to get out of his mind.

'Rosie.' He inclined his head slightly in acknowledgement of her arrival, and then he remained still, waiting for her to come to him.

He could try every trick in the book, but she was never dismayed. The power of her easy-going personality was undeniable. As she extended her tiny hand for him to shake, she tipped up her chin to look him in the eyes, and he felt the force of that stare in his groin, which didn't just tighten now, but ached with the most urgent need.

'Welcome to Hacienda de Rio,' she said with a smile, as if he were the interloper. And then, having realised her mistake, instead of blushing or showing how awkward she surely must feel at the blunder, she put her hand over her mouth and giggled before exclaiming, 'That was a bit of a clanger, wasn't it?'

He stared coolly into her eyes, trying to read her. He could read every woman he'd ever met, from the mother who had barely made eye contact with him, to Doña Anna's scathing and ironic stare, and, after them, the legions of women who knew very well how to flirt with their eyes; they were all transparent to him, but Rosie Clifton was an enigma, and she intrigued him. She was also extremely self-possessed for a girl from nowhere, who had owned nothing but the clothes she stood up in until a few weeks ago.

Seeing the cold suspicion in his eyes, she had taken a step back. Feeling the table behind her legs, she reached behind her to rest her palms on the scrubbed pine surface, making her breasts appear more prominent than ever. Had any other woman done the same thing, he might have wondered if it was an invitation, but Rosie

Clifton only succeeded in making herself look younger and more vulnerable than ever. Perhaps that too was a ploy of sorts, he reflected.

'So, you got here at last?' she challenged him lightly.

He shrugged. 'I came as soon as I could.'

She pressed her lips together in a wry, accepting smile. 'Your aunt mentioned that you're a workaholic.'

He had forgotten how self-possessed she was. But now there was a faint blush on her face, and her amethyst eyes had darkened. He watched her breathing quicken, displaying the shape of her full breasts quite graphically in the close-fitting dress.

'This is, of course, as much your home as mine,' she said candidly.

'How kind of you to say so.' He resisted the temptation to state the obvious: that his claim went back a thousand years.

'You haven't forgotten the ice cream I promised, have you? I made two flavours.'

Rosie wasn't sure when she had decided to treat Don Xavier as a normal human being, rather than as an aristocrat with centuries of breeding behind him. They were wildly unequal in every sense, but, as nothing could change that, she had decided to be herself.

Maybe it was the Doña Anna effect, Rosie reflected as she reached for two bowls. In this one precious inheritance Doña Anna had made sure they were equals. The Spanish Grandee and the orphan housekeeper shared a huge responsibility thanks to the way that Doña Anna had drafted her will, but the more Rosie thought about it, the more it seemed to her that Don Xavier's need for an heir gave her some leverage over him. She had no other power to wield, but he had a schedule to meet, or he would forfeit his fifty per cent of the island to her. Of course, she could just wait him out and hope he couldn't produce an heir in the time specified, but she had no intention of wasting two years of her life hanging around for that. She wanted to get things moving on the island for the sake of the islanders as soon as she could.

Which, ideally, would mean working together, she thought, deflating somewhat when she caught sight of Don Xavier's unsmiling face.

Dipping down, she reached into the freezer to pull out the boxes of ice cream. The air in the kitchen seemed to have frozen harder than the ice cream in the tub.

Whatever happened next, she wasn't going to be railroaded into making any decision that didn't feel right. She might have everything to learn about being a landowner, but Doña Anna had taught her not to be silent and accepting, but to question everything.

'Vanilla,' she announced, prising the lid off the tub. 'And Doña Anna's favourite—fresh strawberry. I picked the fruit from the garden this morning—'

'I haven't come here to eat ice cream,' the towering monument to privilege and wealth currently occupying her kitchen coldly stated.

He hadn't expected Rosie to be so relaxed on this second meeting, Xavier realised. She'd had time to think about things, and must surely realise the hopelessness of her situation. He was stationed at one end of the kitchen table, while she was at the other, and she didn't seem concerned at all. As she opened a drawer to reach for a serving spoon he put the documents he'd brought with him very prominently on the table.

She didn't look at them once—or didn't appear to, but then she baited him with a level stare. 'These look official,' she said, moving them out of the way so she could arrange her dishes. 'They look like the type of papers that won't bring anyone any happiness. "Beware of lawyers, " Doña Anna used to tell me. "Trust no one but yourself, Rosie." So...what flavour would you like?'

He was taken aback for a moment. He had dealt with many difficult situations in business, but nothing like this. 'What else did Doña Anna warn you about?'

'Honestly?' she said, pulling an attractive face as she thought about it for two seconds. 'Nothing. Not you. Not anything. I think she must have trusted me to get on with things. And at the end, when she was dying, and I knew I was about to lose the best friend I'd ever had, the last thing on my mind was lawyers, or wills.'

He believed her.

'I'll look at the documents later,' she said, 'if that's all right with you?'

And if it wasn't all right with him, she would still look at the documents later, he guessed. In fairness, nothing would bounce him into doing anything in a hurry, so he couldn't argue with that.

'There *is* one thing I feel compelled to do,' she said, 'and I hope you'll go along with me in this one little thing...'

'That depends what it is,' he said.

If they never did anything else together, they would do this, Rosie determined. The ceremony she had in mind held as much significance for her as toasting the life of a loved one in champagne at a wake. Taking a moment to celebrate the life of a very special woman, who had done so much for both of them, before normal hostilities were resumed shouldn't be too much to ask. It was time to find out.

'No ice cream for me, thank you.' Don Xavier put up his hand as if to ward off the scoop of ice cream she was offering him.

Her stomach was clenching with apprehension, but she'd started so she'd finish. 'I'm afraid I must insist.'

'You must *insist*?' he said, scanning her face as if he thought she'd gone mad.

'I don't have any champagne to toast your aunt,' Rosie explained, 'and as Doña Anna loved ice cream, I thought we could both take a moment to remember her.'

Her throat was so tight by the time she'd finished this little speech she couldn't have argued with him if she'd tried, so it was a relief when he reached for the bowl. Lifting her own bowl, she proposed huskily, 'To Doña Anna...'

A muscle flexed in Don Xavier's jaw, and then—and she was sure she wasn't mistaken—the faintest hint of amusement sparked in his eyes. So he was human after all. 'I'm sure if we do this together, we can do more things together,' she prompted as she waited for him to start eating. She had to stop herself exclaiming with relief when his firm mouth closed around the spoon.

'Doña Anna,' he murmured, holding her gaze until heat flared inside her.

'Doña Anna,' she repeated, trying not to meet his eyes as she wondered what else he could do with that sexy mouth. He was just so unreasonably hot. She had never been alone with such a good-looking man before, let alone so close to him. Her ideal was based on the heroes in the books she used to read to Doña Anna, and they were all big and dark and dangerous too.

And that was quite enough rambling off-track for one day, Rosie warned herself firmly. If Don Xavier had made the slightest move she'd have run a mile.

'Are we done here?' he asked, dipping his head to bait her with his piercing stare.

'Yes, I think so. Thank you for that.' Her body thanked him very much. She was tingling with awareness.

He wanted to smear her with ice cream and lick it off slowly. He wanted to lay her down on the kitchen table and attend quite thoroughly to Señorita Clifton's every need. He wanted to explore every hungry part of her body slowly. He could certainly see some use for the ice cream. The contrast of heat and cold would be a torment to her—to him too, but that torment would end with pleasure so extreme, they would never forget it.

'The tour?' he prompted, shaking himself around.

'Of course.' She smiled primly into his eyes, but he couldn't help wondering what was going on behind that lambent gaze.

Why did the one woman in the world he needed to eject from his life as efficiently and quickly as possible have to be so desirable, and so ready for seduction?

Why did she have to be so infuriatingly in his way?

It was vital to keep his mind on his goal, which was to own one hundred per cent of the island. He had to leave all thoughts of seducing Rosie Clifton out of it.

'When we've completed the tour, you can sign the documents...' He glanced at them.

Her gaze followed his to the table. 'I'll have to read them first,' she said. 'That's another lesson Doña Anna taught me,' she explained blithely. 'Never write anything down that you're not happy for the whole world to read—and never sign anything until you know what you're putting your name to.'

Striding to the kitchen door to hide the impatience on his face, he opened it. 'Don't you trust me?'

'Should I?' She looked up candidly as he closed the door behind them both.

He should be used to her directness by now. She'd never had the chance to develop social niceties, he allowed. What you saw was what you got with Rosie Clifton. She had to be the most straightforward woman he'd ever met. 'Those documents concern the future of the island,' he informed her. 'Something I thought you cared deeply about.'

'I do,' she assured him, 'but I care for Doña Anna's last wishes equally.'

'In that case, you'll read them and sign them.'

'When I've read them, I'll decide what to do,' she said in a pleasant tone that made it hard to argue.

'We'll discuss it later,' he snapped. 'It's getting dark.'

Later? She kept her cool, but inwardly she quailed. How long did Don Xavier plan to stay? As for reading the documents later, she got the distinct impression that it didn't matter whether she did or not, as his decision regarding the island was already made.

'Do I have your attention, Señorita Clifton?'

'You have all of it,' she said honestly, running to catch up with him. She would have to be made of wood not to be impressed by his staggering good looks and his physique, but even they couldn't compete with the force of his personality. 'Shall I lead the way?' she suggested pleasantly.

'Would you?' he murmured, mocking her, she was sure.

'I'd love to,' she parried, guessing this might be the one and only time she got one step ahead of Don Xavier.

CHAPTER FIVE

THIS WAS WORSE than he'd thought. The tour took far longer than he'd expected. So long, it was almost dark by the time they had finished with the house. How long had he been away from the island? He hadn't thought it long enough for everything to fall into ruin. His expression had remained carefully neutral throughout, but both he and Rosie knew that if he'd spared his aunt some time he could have stopped the rot in its tracks. Things were so bad it would be better to demolish the hacienda and then rebuild it. Even here on the deck in the shadows of dusk he could see the timbers were rotting beneath his feet.

Rosie watched him as he walked, brooding. Buying her out and then keeping her on to act as a link between his team and the islanders had been one possibility, but that possibility was gone now. She might be well respected on the island, but the work required was way beyond her scope to direct. He had tried telling himself that this was just one more business negotiation amongst many, but the agony on Rosie's face when he uncovered each new flaw had found a way past his defences. His expression alone must have told her that the house was beyond repair. It should be demolished before there was an accident.

At least he understood why Doña Anna had been so keen to keep him away. She had hated change, and must have closed her eyes to the deterioration. She had been fiercely proud, refusing all his offers of help. He had begged her to accept professional care when her health had begun to fail, and money for the island as well, but she had turned him down on both counts, insisting that the island was doing very well, thank you, and she would source her next companion from one of the many charities he funded. With the prince's prompting, Rosie Clifton had seemed the obvious choice. If he'd only known then how things would work out—

'Something wrong?' he called after Rosie, who was heading back inside the house at speed.

'I'm cold. I need a cardigan. Please…make yourself at—'

He heard the break in her voice, and guessed the blinkers were well and truly off. Seeing everything through his eyes had been an unwelcome wake-up call. Only a matter of days ago, he would have thought her tears a good thing. Of course she would cry. Of course the helpless little orphan would look to him to save the day, but the situation had turned out to be far more complicated than that. He understood property, and could take a realistic view. Rosie only knew that this was Doña Anna's home, and as such she thought the hacienda was inviolable.

At least she understood the enormity of the task now. She had no option but to sign the documents. She couldn't raise the money. She'd already tried, and failed. She had to accept that only his wealth could save the island. He was offering far more than her share was worth in recognition of her care of his aunt. But Rosie's job was done now, and it was time for her to move on.

If she proved foolish and refused to take his money, his lawyers would take over. Whatever Rosie decided, the outcome would be the same. He wouldn't allow his judgement to be clouded by his growing interest in some young girl, and he had never entered into a negotiation without it ending in success for him. The only difference this time was some slight regret that Rosie's sunny optimism would move on, out of his life. That, and the thought of some other man putting his hands on her, which made his hackles rise. It was time to remind himself once and for all that Señorita Clifton had no place in his life.

She'd done the one thing she had vowed not to do, Rosie fretted, tense with frustration and anger because she'd shown her feelings; something she had learned not to do in the orphanage. Don Xavier had undone her control in a couple of hours. And now she had run away from a problem—several problems: the house, the island, her inheritance, and him. She was currently locked down in the sanctuary of her bedroom, trying to work out what to do next. It wasn't as if she had any experience in high level negotiations. During the tour, he'd found fault with everything. That hurt when this was the only home she'd ever known. But it didn't mean she was going to roll over and sell out. She had to find a way out of this, or squads of men in steel-capped boots would be marching over the islanders' carefully tended fields in no time flat. And, yes, the house was dilapidated. She was even prepared to believe it was as dangerous as he'd said, but both house and island deserved a second chance.

'What doesn't kill you makes you stronger,' Doña Anna used to say. She had to keep on with the regular meetings she'd set up with the islanders, and lobbying the big food chains until one of them came on board with her ideas. She wouldn't give up until the very last hope was extinguished. And when that light went out, she'd think of something else.

Sitting bolt upright on the bed, she stared up stubbornly at the damp patches on the ceiling to make a vow that Isla Del Rey would never become another of Don Xavier's flashy hotel schemes. She would fight on, as Doña Anna had done all her life. 'Whatever it takes,' the old lady used to say, 'we must keep the island authentic, Rosie.' And if Rosie had to keep Don Xavier in a headlock until he backed off, she'd somehow find the strength to do it.

She was gone so long he decided to go upstairs to choose a bedroom.

Preferably one with Señorita Clifton in it—

He killed that thought stone dead. He could afford no distractions. The work here couldn't wait. He'd brought an overnight bag, guessing his inspection might take some time—

'Señorita Clifton!' He had almost barged into her as she came bowling out of her room. 'Are you all right?' he asked, steadying her. He could feel her tension as well as her fire beneath his hands. Her eyes were black with passion as she stared up at him.

'Don Xavier!' she flashed as if riding the crest of a wave of anger.

'What's eating you?' he said.

'Your plans to wreck the island, if you must know,' she flared.

Too many hormones; too few avenues for them to

escape, he concluded as he huffed a short laugh. 'You obviously know more about my plans than I do.'

'So you deny that you're going to level the land and build another of your hotel schemes on the island?'

Her breasts were rising and falling rapidly as she sucked in air. She was a wild little animal, he thought as he stared down into her impassioned face. Curled up close in her burrow most of the time, she was a tigress when she set herself free.

'Nothing is decided yet, so may I suggest you calm down?'

'Don't patronise me. Calm down?' she derided. 'You'd better let me go,' she warned.

Yes. He better had. He'd been hanging on to her all this time, and she hadn't exactly been fighting him off.

'I know you must be upset by what I've shown you today,' he said, trying for a reasoned tone, 'but I have a duty to point out the dangers when you're living in the house.'

Her eyes filled with tears. He didn't know what was worse, seeing her angry, or seeing her miserable.

Proud to the last, she whipped her face away from his.

'You've nothing to worry about,' he said, somehow overcome by a sense of how alone she was. It had to be because he was back in the old house, he reasoned as he continued to reassure her. 'I'll stay on until I've made a full inventory of the remedial work that needs to be done here.'

'What?' She turned a shocked face on his.

'You must have expected me to stay the night?'

'Actually, no.' Her stare was levelled on his. 'I'm surprised you're prepared to risk the danger.'

He tried so hard not to smile. 'I think I'm equal to the dangers here, Señorita Clifton.'

She stared at him defiantly as she braced her angry fists against his chest.

Lifting his hands, he let her go.

It took her a moment, but she was right back in the game within a couple of heartbeats. 'Of course you must stay the night,' she told him in a pleasant tone. 'This is as much your house as mine.'

He inclined his head, wondering how long her warmth would remain imprinted on his hands. The memory of that small, soft body straining against his would stay with him for a long time.

He took the torture like a man. 'There are six or seven bedrooms, as I recall,' he observed in a matter-of-fact tone. 'Which means I can sleep at one end of the house, while you sleep at the other.'

'You won't trouble me,' she assured him.

He disagreed. He imagined that even with their doors locked and bolted, and at opposite ends of the house, they would trouble each other all through the night.

'I'll be right back with some clean linen for you,' she offered, hurrying away.

She could feel the heat of Xavier's stare on her back, and the moment she was out of sight she leaned back against the wall to grab some down time from the tension. What was happening to her? He was like a magnet drawing her into danger, and she had no more sense than to go with it. Worse, she didn't want to fend him off. His touch was light and unthreatening—she could still feel it on her arm. Closing her eyes, she enjoyed the sensation for a moment, but that only made her want more.

Her feelings were all over the place. She should hate him for what he represented, and for the danger he posed to the island with his schemes, but while hungry fire was surging through her veins that wasn't easy. And now he was going to stay the night. It was too intimate, too disturbing in every way. She would have preferred to keep him at arm's length—preferably with an arm as long as a continent.

Opening the door, she rifled through the linen closet, choosing the best of a bad lot in a pile of threadbare sheets. But at least they were clean and smelled of sunshine, she reassured herself, bringing the bedding to her face as she walked down the corridor. She could hear Don Xavier banging about in one of the rooms. She stopped outside the door, drew a deep breath, and then knocked politely.

'Come...'

His imperious tone made her blood boil. She was being hospitable, while he was treating her like a...like a housekeeper, Rosie thought, fighting back a laugh. That was exactly what she was—or what she had been. The humour in the situation soon restored her high spirits. Entering the room, she took in everything at a glance: his expensive leather bag and the crisp clean clothes arranged neatly on the bed...

And *him*.

So much *him* her heart was thundering like a jackhammer. Even now she couldn't get used to the sight of so much man.

'Señorita Clifton?'

Adopting a polite, yet remote expression, she laid the folded sheets on the bed.

'My apologies, *señorita*, I will move these things away, and then you can make up the bed for me.'

Judging by his raised brow, her jaw must have dropped to the floor.

'Do you have a problem with that?' he asked with surprise.

Yes. She did. She was going to start as she meant to go on. He had two hands just as she did. Even a little thing like making up his bed could give Don Xavier the wrong idea. As far as this inheritance went, they were equals. If she gave him the impression that nothing had changed and gave in to his every whim, how was she supposed to stand up against his plans for the island?

'You'd make the bed for a friend, or for a welcome visitor, wouldn't you?' he probed, identifying the problem right away.

'Gladly,' Rosie admitted, 'but as you have yet to prove that you're either of those things...'

His laugh cut her off. 'You're a source of constant amusement to me,' he admitted. 'I never know what to expect from you next.'

'Goodnight?' she suggested. Turning on her heels, she headed for the door.

'We'll continue our tour at six o'clock sharp.'

'It's barely light then—'

'It's light enough,' he ruled. 'I have many other things to do. I'm a very busy man, *señorita*. I can't hang around here for ever.'

Thank goodness.

'Goodnight,' he said.

As his firm mouth tugged in the suspicion of a smile, she shrugged. She'd been dismissed, Rosie gathered. She was careful to close the door behind her with barely a click, when the urge to slam it in Don Xavier's mocking face was overwhelming.

He was up well before dawn the next morning. He hadn't slept. He hoped Señorita Clifton had enjoyed a similarly disturbed night. He stared at his reflection in the mirror, furious to have her intrude on his thoughts first thing. All night, he conceded. She had been in his head all night.

If things had been different between them, their differences could have been settled in bed, but that wasn't an option with Rosie Clifton, who was so obviously enjoying giving him the runaround. She was testing her female power; something new to her, he suspected. When they'd first met she was uncertain, yet controlled, but now those amethyst eyes flashed fire at him on a regular basis. He liked that. He liked her. She was as fiercely determined as he was to see her plans through. She would make a worthy opponent in any dispute, which would make the pleasure, when she finally admitted defeat and accepted a settlement for her half of the island, all the sweeter. It would certainly please him to escape the parent trap his aunt had laid.

Okay. Stay cool, Rosie directed herself as Don Xavier came out of the house. If he'd been stunning in those cut-off shorts, he looked even better in banged-up denim that fitted snugly on his hips and, um, lower body…desert boots, and a close-fitting top that hinted at the muscular torso her memory could so readily supply. His inky-black hair was thick and tousled. His stubble was dense and sharp. He was dark and powerful, threatening and sexy in an immediate and very potent way. He looked as if someone had lit his blue touch paper this morning. But would she have the sense to stand back from the explosion?

'Good morning,' he called out.

Even his voice was virile.

'Good morning!' she responded brightly with what

she hoped he would accept was an innocent smile. Did he remember how it felt to accidentally touch each other, or to hold her as he steadied her on her feet? Did he remember those glances between them that had held for several dangerous beats too long? Had he tossed and turned all night as she had? She could only hope—

'Ready for the tour?' he demanded, striding up to her.

'Absolutely,' she confirmed briskly. 'Shall we go?'

'Lead the way.'

As he drew alongside, her gaze brushed appreciatively over him again; once was never enough. It would have been so much safer to share her inheritance with a wizened old man, or even a pipe-and-slippers man, rather than this wild-haired brigand, who managed to look even more disreputable this morning than he had when he strode out of the sea. She wished she'd tried a little harder with her own appearance, but lack of sleep and determination not to be late for the tour had led to her grabbing the first thing that came to hand, which happened to be an ancient top and even older shorts.

This isn't a fashion show, Rosie reminded herself, but just the start of some cold-blooded negotiations.

Really? Then, why was it so hard to concentrate?

Because she kept thinking back to Don Xavier taking his shower this morning. She'd been making coffee in the kitchen just a few feet below him when she heard the water running. She'd stilled, picturing him naked, his swarthy face turned up to the spray, eyes closed as he raked back his thick black hair. And then his lean, tanned hands moved on...slowly, down the length of his body, only pausing to map his iron buttocks, and a few other interesting landmarks on the way—

'Señorita Clifton?'

'I'm sorry...did I miss something?'

Blinking the erotic daydream away, she stared up into Xavier's shockingly handsome face. That didn't help her concentration either. 'Did you find the coffee I left on the stove?'

He frowned. 'I did. Thank you.'

'Good.' She was reluctant to leave those images in the shower behind, especially when he'd starred in her erotic fantasies all night.

'Is something wrong?' he asked when she bit her lip and frowned.

Only that it was time for her to get real. Don Xavier had only shown an interest in Rosie and the island when Doña Anna had given him no option.

'Nothing,' she said, knowing she must concentrate on the task in hand with a brain that had turned to mush from lack of sleep.

'I'd like to start with the path down to the beach.'

Xavier shot everything into sharp focus with just those few words. The path was narrow, and dangerously steep. There were loose rocks and shale where you could slip.

'This looks dangerous,' he said when they reached the top of the path.

If only he could see the island through her eyes—

'Hang on to me,' he insisted, offering her a steadying hand.

'It's fine. I go down here every day,' she said blithely, ignoring his help.

'If you come down here on your own, and you fall, you could lie here for hours,' he said. 'There should be a handrail, at least—'

She took big, reckless steps, just to prove a point.

'Wait!' he commanded, catching up with her. 'I don't

want to be clearing up your mess if you fall onto the rocks.'

'I don't imagine you do,' she yelled back, slithering on regardless. 'How would that look in court?'

And then, somehow, he got in front of her. If she'd taken chances descending, he'd taken more. 'Take my hand,' he insisted coldly.

She ground her jaw and did as he asked. He showed no sign of moving otherwise. There was nothing cold about his hand; his grip was warm and firm, and left her breathless with mounting excitement. Until she remembered where they were and who he was.

'Watch where you put your feet,' he rapped.

Keeping them out of her mouth was her biggest problem.

'Tired already?' he demanded when she stopped halfway down.

'No. I'm admiring the view,' she said, refusing to make eye contact with a man who made her feel all sorts of unwanted things.

'You must have been impressed when you saw the coastline for the first time?' he observed in the most relaxed piece of conversation they'd shared.

'Seeing the beauty of the island after the city?' she said, feeling she should respond. 'You've got no idea.'

'I have some,' he argued, staring out to sea. 'I'm seeing things all over again.'

Thanks to her? Rosie wondered, watching the breeze ruffle Xavier's hair. No. She didn't flatter herself to that extent. Still, at least they were relaxing a little with each other, and that couldn't be a bad thing. 'After living in the orphanage, coming here was like visiting heaven on a day pass,' she admitted. 'I was startled by the island's beauty. Everywhere I turned, the vistas, the wide-open spaces, the freedom…' She stretched out her arms as if she could touch it. 'I couldn't see a single flaw—'

'And now?' he asked.

Her smile died. She hadn't seen a single flaw on the island until Xavier arrived.

'There really needs to be a proper handrail here,' he said as she continued her descent.

'There's no money for a handrail, not even for a rope.' She remembered how she'd begged Doña Anna to have something put in place, so the old lady could reach her beloved beach in safety. She could have kicked herself now, for not realising there was so little money in the pot. And guilty that she'd been given a wage at all, when that money would have been better spent on repairs.

'Did my aunt come down this path?' Xavier asked, frowning.

'Oh, yes,' Rosie confirmed, smiling as she remembered. 'She used to say she could slide down on her bottom, and climb up again on her hands and knees. "What's wrong with that, missy?" she would ask me. Or, "Do you think I'm too old for that?"'

'And what did you say?' Xavier flashed her a look of genuine interest.

'I gave the expected reply, of course,' Rosie admitted wryly. 'I'd tell her that she certainly wasn't too old. But if I dared to venture an opinion—something like, "I just think—" she would cut me off mercilessly. "Don't think," she'd snap. "It's my job to think. Not yours."'

Xavier laughed. 'I guess we've both felt the sharp edge of her tongue.'

'I never took offence,' Rosie explained, enjoying the new warmth between them in spite of her wariness regarding Xavier's intentions towards the island. 'I just accepted that, however close we were, when it came to the Isla Del Rey, there was never any doubt that Doña Anna was in charge.'

And always had been until she died, but now the future of the island was up for grabs.

CHAPTER SIX

HE WAS DISAPPOINTED. Not because the island held any
surprises for him, but because he hadn't expected it to
be quite so run-down. The state of everything stirred
his nagging sense of guilt. He should have come back
long before now. He should have overruled his aunt and
done everything he could to make her more comfortable, and see the island thrive. He'd always been too
busy, and she'd been adamant that he must remain so.
And now he knew why. She hadn't wanted him to see
that she'd lost her grip.

'The house has always been shabby,' he admitted
when he and Rosie reached the beach. Why he felt the
need to reassure her, he had no idea. 'Not that a bit of
peeling paint would have mattered to me when I was a
boy—I doubt I even noticed it.'

Slipping off her sandals, Rosie started to paddle in
the surf. She looked so young and so appealing it was
hard to remember that she was just another hurdle in
his way.

'You must have been glad of a home to come to, after
school,' she remarked, kicking the water so the spray
caught the light.

'Doña Anna always made me welcome,' he agreed.

'And your parents?'

She had her back to him as she asked the question. She must have heard the rumours like everyone else. What Doña Anna hadn't told her, the islanders would have supplied. 'Best not mention them,' he said.

She turned to look at him and her mouth slanted attractively as she admitted, 'I have the same problem.'

He huffed a wry smile, but a spike of guilt stabbed him when he thought how much worse her childhood had been than his.

'So, what did you do on the island?' she asked, maybe trying to smooth over the awkward moment.

'I made a raft once out of driftwood just like this. Sadly, it disintegrated once I got out to sea.'

'Well, at least you didn't drown.' She laughed.

'Almost.'

'You should have made dens onshore. It's a lot safer.'

'Safety was never a consideration for me.'

'I guess that's why Doña Anna drove you out.'

'I don't blame her.' He laughed. He'd been a rebel through and through, but when he'd left the island he had tried to be a credit to his aunt. He'd thought that meant working as hard as he could to be the best, but even that wouldn't satisfy Doña Anna. She'd wanted an heir, a dynasty—

'What the—?' Rosie had splashed water at him, and now she was running away.

Choice: he could stand on his dignity, or he could give her a soaking.

As he caught up with Rosie and swung her into his arms he asked himself why his aunt had brought him back to the island and put a girl at his side like this—had she been determined to torment him from the grave?

As Rosie shrieked he dumped her in the sea. She shrieked even louder.

She recovered fast. Scooping up armfuls of seawater, she chucked it at him. He fought back. She gave as good as she got. She was so different from the sophisticated women he knew that he started to laugh, and laughing wasn't helpful when it came to winning water fights.

'How about I hold you under the waves for half an hour?' he threatened.

'How about you catch me first?' she countered.

And then she was off, like a dolphin, swimming effortlessly in her shorts and top. She could certainly swim. She might have grown up in the inner city, but she'd made up for it since coming to the island. Clambering out of the water, she stood dripping wet in front of him. Her outfit of choice was soaked through, the shorts so ragged, and the top so worn, he doubted even she knew what colour they had been originally. He thought he'd never seen anyone more beautiful.

This was really getting out of hand. 'We should go,' he said, bringing the high jinks to an abrupt end by turning his back on her.

He felt her disappointment follow him across the beach, and knew without doubt that he wanted her. Which was more than inconvenient. Lust was roaring through him, making nonsense of his agenda for the day.

Appointments could be postponed, he reasoned. He was under no pressure to leave the island right away. He could send for his people and have them come to him. It would be better for his team to see the island for themselves. He would set up his headquarters at the hacienda. It made perfect sense.

So much for keeping everything on a professional footing! Playing in the sea? Coming out of the water, looking like a contestant in a wet T-shirt contest with a see-through top clinging to her breasts? What was wrong with her? Was she crazy?

Xavier had kept his gaze confined to her face, but that smile playing around his sexy mouth said she believed he'd got the upper hand. She guessed he hadn't dumped too many of his sophisticated girlfriends in the sea—not that she was a girlfriend, or even close. At best, she was an irritation. So maybe the island had infected them both with *joie de vivre*—something else she guessed he wasn't used to.

When they got back to the house she had to admit he was right about the improvements. Paint was peeling on the front door, and the timber around the windows was rotten. She supposed she should thank him for opening her eyes before the entire house fell on her head.

'After you,' he said, holding the front door open for her.

'Coffee?' she asked on impulse. 'Or are you in a hurry to get away?'

'You still have the documents to read.'

Trust him to remember. But she would take a look. He'd started to open up and so had she. It was the least she could do.

'But I'd love a coffee,' he added with a smile that warmed her through.

Was it too much to hope this ease between them could continue, and that maybe they could find some common ground that would enable them to work together for the good of the island? When they brushed against each other as they walked into the kitchen, it was just the lightest touch, but it might as well have been a lightning bolt to her overly responsive body. It was a reminder of how it had felt when he closed his arms around her to steady her. She had liked that feeling. A lot.

She made the coffee, and picked up the documents. 'I need to look at these alone,' she explained. Life and fantasy were becoming dangerously entangled. She'd lived on hope for most of her life, and was determined to be realistic now she had responsibilities. 'I'll call you when I'm ready. Why don't you take your coffee into the library?' she suggested. 'You'll be more comfortable in there.'

Was he listening? Xavier was staring at the kitchen ceiling, no doubt chalking up how many cracks there were, before moving on to assess the damp in the corners.

'Don't take too long,' he said, without sparing her a glance.

'I'll take as long as I need.' She meant it. He might exert a magical power over her body, but when it came to her promise to Doña Anna, nothing, not even Don Xavier Del Rio, could swerve her from her course.

'No,' Rosie announced from the doorway to the library where he was sitting. 'I'm sorry, but I can't accept this.'

He swung around in the library chair to stare at her. He'd been waiting in the library for over an hour. From the look on Rosie's face, they wouldn't be having a pleasant chat over coffee any time soon regarding money transfers from his bank to hers.

'I can't sign this. I'm sorry.' Walking deeper into the room, she put the documents on the library table in front of him.

'Then, what will you sign?' He stood to face her. He could understand her reluctance to accept so much money. She wouldn't know what to do with it. But he had advisors who could help her with that. Unless… 'If you don't think my offer's enough…'

'Your offer is an insult to someone who loved your aunt,' she argued quietly. 'If you had offered Doña Anna a fraction of that amount, she could have put everything to rights and you'd have no complaints about the island.'

'Are you asking for more?' He hadn't expected this, but Rosie had him over a barrel.

'I hope you're joking?' she flared. 'What you're offering is a ridiculous amount. You could buy a country for that. You've obviously got far too much money—'

He cut across her with an angry gesture. 'Then, what *do* you want?'

He hadn't achieved his level of success without taking every element of a deal into account. He'd seen other people fail when emotion was involved, which was yet another reason for him to remain exactly as he was. He would accept that there was no way of accurately calculating nostalgia in a monetary sense, but he'd done his very best.

'I want a say in the future of this island, and you're asking me to sell my right to that.'

'Correct,' he agreed. 'And my offer's fair.'

'No.' Rosie shook her head. 'I won't do it. I'm not thinking of me, but—'

'Doña Anna and the islanders?' he interrupted. 'Yes. I know your passion where they're concerned. But if you really want the best for them, you should leave the island to me.'

She huffed incredulously. 'Do you think there's even the slimmest chance of that?'

He shrugged. He'd up his offer if he had to. He did so, naming an amount that would make most people reach for a chair. Rosie didn't even blink. But then, it was as if all the emotion she had so successfully suppressed in life broke free. Snatching up the documents, she ripped them to shreds in front of his eyes.

'That's what I think of your offer!' she blazed.

Enraged, she was magnificent, but he remained focused on the deal. 'Everything has its price,' he said calmly.

'You still don't get it, do you?' she exclaimed, frowning with frustration. 'Even you don't have enough money to tempt me to sell my share of the island. You can't calculate everything in terms of money. When we were on the beach and you told me how much Doña Anna had done for you, and I told you I understood, because she'd done the same for me, I thought we were beginning to understand each other. But we're further apart than ever, because it's all about money for you. You don't care about the island. The only thing you care about is your bottom line. And winning,' she raged.

'That's easy for you to say—you don't have people depending on you for their jobs.'

'There's plenty of work on the island,' she argued.

'Growing vegetables?'

'Why not?' she blazed. 'What's more important— another golf club, or more food, good organic food?'

'Another of your little fantasies,' he suggested.

'If you would only agree to help the islanders with your connections, instead of driving on with your plan, I believe this island could be successful in every way.'

'Just as you believe you can live here with no visible means of support.'

'If I have to, I will.'

'But you don't have to,' he roared.

His tone shocked her. She had shocked herself. She was facing Xavier, braced for battle, when they were both usually so controlled. Somehow, combined, they were combustible. And now she couldn't stop. 'You can't buy the island, and you can't buy me!'

'Actually. I can,' he said with infuriating confidence.

She huffed incredulously 'You seriously think you can put a price on me?'

'I'm a businessman. That's what I do,' he countered.

'You're only a businessman thanks to the aunt you neglected—the aunt who gave you everything to help you become the man you are today. Do you think she'd be proud of you now?'

'I would think so, yes,' he said calmly, though niggling at the back of his mind was his aunt's unreasonable demand for him to provide an heir. What on earth had caused her to put that in her will?

His apparent composure rattled Rosie. It was as if a dam had been breached and now a lifetime of suppressed passion came flooding out.

'I don't agree,' she snapped. 'Doña Anna expected more of you than this. I'm guessing that's why she gave me a say in her will.'

He could have told her that he'd sent regular payments to his aunt for years, but that she had distributed the money to the islanders, rather than keeping anything back for herself, but he was done trying to reason with Rosie Clifton.

Passion roared between them as she whirled around to stalk away. Catching hold of her, he brought her back. Cupping her face, he made her look at him, and then he finished the kiss he wished he'd started the night before. Rosie made angry sounds deep in her throat. He countered these with a lifetime of experience in seduction that only succeeded in making her madder still, but her lips were soft and warm, and he could be very persuasive. He had never felt such a desire to kiss a woman before, and within a few moments she was fighting to keep him close as animal instinct took over.

He wanted her. That was all he knew. He wanted her now—here on the library table. No waiting. No thought. Just sensation. Need and passion combined inside him, driving the primal urge to mate. His hands claimed her buttocks. He pressed her hard against his straining erection. She responded by throwing her head back, and groaning with need as she thrust her hips hungrily against his.

Fortunately for both of them, an alarm bell went off in some part of his brain. One of them had to show restraint. Unfortunately, as Rosie showed no sign of letting him go, that had to be him.

Her face was flushed with passion as he held her at a safe distance. Her eyes were as black as jet. She wiped the back of her hand across kiss-swollen lips, as if she couldn't believe what she'd done. 'My answer's still no,' she said.

He laughed. He couldn't help himself.

'You think this is funny?' she demanded in fury.

'Not in the least,' he admitted. He was impressed.

'I'm leaving,' she said.

'For good?'

'This isn't a joke, Xavier.'

He cut her off at the door. Planting his fist on the smooth wood above her head, he kept her trapped in front of him. 'My office will send the documents through again. May I suggest you sign them next time?'

'You're not listening to me,' she gritted out, meeting his unblinking stare fearlessly. 'I've no intention of signing your wretched documents.'

For just an instant he wanted to kiss her again. Then

the wall he lived behind snapped back into place. It was time for Señorita Clifton to hear some hard truths. 'Your job here is done,' he said evenly. 'You need an income to live on, and that has to come from somewhere.'

'But not from you,' she said. 'Or do you think I'm incapable of earning a living?'

Pulling his fist from the wood, he stood clear of the door as she straightened her clothes and walked out.

Leaning back against the wall, he closed his eyes. Rosie Clifton was the most infuriating woman he'd ever met, but at least he now understood why his aunt had liked her—loved her, he amended. It had to be love that prompted such a generous bequest, unless his aunt's sole aim had been to torment him.

He decided not. His aunt had been spiky, but never vengeful. And Rosie Clifton's spirit had been forged under circumstances of extreme difficulty, which was why she had no trouble standing up to him. She might be naïve in many ways, but she was courageous and resilient. He guessed his aunt had seen something of herself as a young girl in Rosie.

'Xavier...'

He turned at the sound of Rosie's voice. She stood framed in the doorway. She had brushed her hair and washed her face. She looked a lot calmer.

'I came to say I'm sorry.' She lifted her chin. 'I haven't been very businesslike.'

'Neither of us has been very businesslike.'

'We were a little overheated,' she admitted carefully.

Putting it mildly, he thought. Even now he wanted her. He wanted to see that furious fire light again in his arms.

'I've been thinking how this place could look,' she

said, glancing around, 'if I could persuade you to restore things, rather than to knock them down and rebuild. Maybe we could work together? I was angry before, after reading those documents, but I can't let my pride stand in the way of improvements.'

'And?' he prompted.

'And I've got a proposition for you.'

It had taken courage for her to come back and confront him. There was nothing to be gained by frightening her away—if anything could frighten Rosie Clifton. 'I'm listening,' he encouraged.

'It's not a long-term plan,' she explained, frowning as if the words wouldn't come easily. 'We'd have to see how it progressed year by year.'

'Not long term, then?' he observed dryly.

'I mean not permanent,' she said, refusing to be diverted from her thoughts with humour. 'With your money, and my understanding of the island and the people who live here, you could fund improvements, while I undertake the project management for you. I'd draw up proper accounts—'

As if that were all it entailed, he thought as she went on. Her intentions were good, but the island needed more than a few light touches, it required major renovation work, both to the house, and to the infrastructure. Architects and engineers—a whole raft of specialisms would have to be employed. 'All my projects are money-making schemes.'

'Then, you can afford one that isn't.'

'This sounds like a vanity project to me. You're asking me to pour my money into a house and island so that you can live here in comfort.'

'That's not it at all,' she argued, but her cheeks blazed

red as it dawned on her that it must have sounded exactly like that to him.

'This island has to pay its way,' he said bluntly.

'I'm trying—and with your help and influence, maybe investors would listen to me.'

'As I have no previous experience or interest in farming, why would they?'

'So you'd stand in my way—when you weren't busy trying to find someone to give you an heir, that is.'

He was shocked that she would throw that in his face.

Xavier thought he held all the cards, but she wasn't even close to admitting defeat. She would find a solution to this. She had to.

'You should consider my proposal, Rosie. More money. You'd be secure for life. For the good of the island alone, you should accept it.'

But then she'd have all the money in the world to help the island, and no right to do so. 'My answer has to be no.'

There had to be a way out of the impasse. Doña Anna must have anticipated this situation, but what had she wanted Rosie to do? It was as if there was an unwritten message in the will, and she just wasn't getting it.

CHAPTER SEVEN

HIS TEAM ARRIVED that same afternoon. The dining room would serve as his boardroom for now. No one would stay overnight, so accommodation wasn't a problem, and the launch would take everyone back to the mainland.

Rosie was baking in the kitchen. She was up to her elbows in flour when he looked in. She had white smudges on her nose and cheeks, and added more with the back of her hand when she saw him.

'Ah, good, thank you,' he said, surprised and pleased at the effort she was going to on his behalf.

She frowned. 'Why?'

'Why what?' he asked, halfway out of the door.

'Why are you thanking me?'

'You anticipated my request,' he suggested with a shrug.

'Your request?' she queried, putting even more smudges of flour on her face.

He moved to one side as she moved past him to put her baking tray into the oven. She looked perfect for her role in the day ahead: casual, low-key, and efficient. His aunt would have tolerated nothing less. He found her very sexy in form-fitting jeans that clung lovingly to her curves. He lingered a moment as her simple white T-shirt rode up when she bent down, drawing his gaze to her soft, silky skin and the swell of her buttocks. 'Beautiful,' he murmured, temporarily distracted.

'The muffins?' she declared, straightening up. 'I'm using one of my all-time favourite recipes.'

The look she gave him when she planted flour-covered hands on her hips shot straight to his groin.

'Excuse me, please...' She drew herself in as she went to move past him, presumably so they didn't touch.

He stepped in her way. 'It's good of you to go to so much trouble for my team.'

'*Your* team?'

'The people in my team will really appreciate it.'

She frowned at him, confused. 'May I go now?' she murmured, still frowning.

'Of course.' He smiled as he stood back. 'Coffee would have been enough, though.'

'But cake's always nice, don't you think?'

His lips pressed down as he shrugged. 'If you insist.'

Remembering his colleagues in the next room, he turned to leave, but paused at the door to remind her to bring cream and milk when she served refreshments, and also decaf coffee for Margaret. 'A plate of biscuits on the side for those who don't like cake would be nice,' he added. 'Oh, and maybe a cheese sandwich to bridge the gap between meals. What are you serving later, by the way?'

There was a long moment of silence, and then she said, 'There must be some mistake. The muffins aren't for you. I can manage a packet of biscuits—'

'I'm sorry?'

'And I won't be serving meals, either, as I'll be busy later.'

'Busy? But you're the housekeeper.'

'I used to be the housekeeper,' she said. 'As you made

clear, my job here is done. It ended when your aunt died. Only the bequest in Doña Anna's will allows me to stay on—that and my tiny pot of savings. As I promised your aunt, I'm not going anywhere. I'll be holding one of my regular meetings with the islanders today, so I can update them with where we are with applications and so forth. The cakes are for them. I'm sorry if you thought otherwise. If you'd asked, I'd have been happy to bake a double batch, but you didn't let me into your plans. That's why we need to work together.' She added, tongue in cheek, 'Perhaps we could cut them in half?'

'I take it that making coffee won't be beyond you?' he asked coolly.

'I'll leave everything you'll need ready on a tray, but I do have some chores I must do while the cakes are baking. Oh, and I'll need the dining room by four o'clock.' Seeing his expression, she added, 'Now you're back, we have to cooperate on certain things. I'm sure you don't want the islanders upset any more than I do, thinking everything's going to change overnight. They miss your aunt too. We owe it to them to keep things as smooth as possible. Cake will help,' she finished with a smile.

She might be young, and owning anything might be new to her, but she was learning fast. She was also sending him a message. This was not the young girl the lawyer had described to him, or the uncertain girl he had first met on the beach. This was a woman who was slowly becoming aware of the power she had been given, and who wasn't afraid to use it. He would have to rethink his plans where Rosie Clifton was concerned.

She had no complaints where Don Xavier was concerned. At least, not today. He and his team behaved perfectly, vacating the dining room at three-thirty prompt. They were to continue their discussions during a walking tour of the island, apparently. One of his team had even offered to stay behind to help Rosie in the kitchen.

'It won't take me long, honestly,' she told the kindly older woman called Margaret, who was a bit like a city version of Doña Anna, that was, a bit more put together, but with the same shrewd, wise air. 'I know you have to get away.'

Margaret wouldn't take no for an answer and picked up a clean linen cloth to dry the dishes. 'Don Xavier is an impatient man. I take it you've noticed?'

'I have,' Rosie confirmed as they shared a smile.

There was something in Margaret's eyes that said she was very fond of Xavier, and that any criticism she made was made with the warmth of a friend who knew him well. 'There'll be some changes here,' she said, glancing keenly at Rosie. 'You are prepared for that?'

'If I agree with them, yes.'

'You wouldn't want to see this place falling down, I imagine?' Margaret looked at her.

'Of course not, but I wouldn't like to see it bulldozed, either.'

They cleared the kitchen together in silence for a while, then, folding her cloth, Margaret said, 'I know things seem black now, but remember you're still grieving. Both of you are. It should be possible to bend a little in time.'

'Really?' Rosie raised an amused brow. 'You see Xavier bending?'

'Give him a chance.' Margaret's soft tone held Rosie's attention. 'More importantly,' she said, 'give yourself a chance, Rosie.'

The rest of the afternoon was taken up with Rosie's meeting with the islanders, so she didn't have the time to think much about what Margaret had said. Her meetings were happy events, casual, but purposeful. Everyone brought something to eat in the break, and there was quite a feast laid out on the dining-room table. Don Xavier's team had left on the launch, so she thought it the ideal opportunity to ask him to join them. The islanders remembered him well, and she thought they'd be pleased to see him.

She was surprised by just how pleased. And this wasn't the aloof and arrogant man who had emerged from the surf like an invader come to claim his territory, but the man she had played with on the beach, a warm and engaging man amongst his friends. She doubted there'd be much time left for more formal discussion while so many reunions were under way, but that was okay. This was all she could have asked for.

Everything was going swimmingly until one of the elders of the village asked outright about changes that might be coming to the island.

'You have nothing to worry about,' Xavier told him before Rosie had chance to speak. 'My project will bring more jobs. Nothing will change for you. It will only get better.'

'That's not very specific,' Rosie tried to point out, but everyone was too busy smiling at Xavier and patting him on the back, telling him they knew he'd come back, and that he would never let them down.

He turned to look at her eventually, but it was the briefest glance. 'And you will have the reassurance of knowing that Señorita Clifton is here amongst you. You already know she has your best interests at heart.'

So everything was decided without a single word

from her. But at least he'd accepted her staying on, Rosie reasoned, so she'd hold back on confronting him right away. 'You still haven't told us about your plans,' she reminded him. 'Wouldn't this be a good time to share?'

'When the architect's scheme is finished, everyone here will be the first to see it,' he assured the room with a charming smile and an expansive gesture.

That went down well, but Rosie wasn't reassured. 'By that time whatever you decide to build on the island will be a *fait accompli*,' she pointed out.

She hated being railroaded, and as the conversation turned to dredging the bay to build a fabulous marina, and clearing vast swathes of land for the luxury hotel and golf course, she could feel her tension growing. Xavier could turn on the charisma, and had won everyone over. He could have suggested erecting a launch pad for moon rockets and she guessed the result would have been the same. Everyone was so pleased to see him, they would have agreed to anything he cared to suggest, and he would push these plans through, regardless of her opinion.

She waited until everyone had left before confronting him with her concerns. 'A six-star hotel? A golf course and marina? Do you think that's what Doña Anna intended?'

'Doña Anna isn't here to guard her island any more,' he said, easing onto one taut hip. 'We have to do that for her.'

She shook her head and laughed. 'You'll spoil the island. You'll tear it apart.'

'And you'd see it crumble into the sea,' he countered, straightening up. 'Improvements have to be made.'

'I agree,' she exclaimed with frustration. 'But why can't they happen slowly, and develop naturally?'

'You might have time for that—the islanders don't. I'm offering jobs today, not uncertainty tomorrow.'

And Margaret had said they could compromise?

'You only see what you want to see, Rosie,' Xavier insisted. 'And I understand why. You had a difficult life before you met Doña Anna. The contrast between here and the orphanage must have been extreme, so now you only see the good things and blank the rest. But that's no good to the islanders. They need progress now.'

'I'd do anything for them...*anything*.'

'I know that. So take my money. Make a good life for yourself,' he said quietly and intently, 'somewhere else.'

For a moment she was lost for words. The island was her home, the only home she wanted. It was everything she had ever dreamed of; that and a family of her own. The islanders and Doña Anna had given her that family, welcoming her to their beautiful island with open arms. Now it was her turn to do everything in her power to help them. She was getting better at writing to companies she'd found on the Internet, and she had sourced a huge number of charities to approach for grants. It was all work in progress, but she couldn't walk away from it now. Just because she hadn't received any positive replies yet, didn't mean she was ready to give up.

'Who is more likely to make things right for the islanders?' Xavier pressed. 'You, or me?'

His words stung her, because they were too dangerously close to the truth. But she couldn't back down now. She remembered the orphanage, and the matron deriding her. Rosie had wanted to stay on at school and go to college, but had been told that she could put that out of her head, as there were no funds for that sort of thing, and she didn't have the brains for it, anyway.

What if the matron was right?

Never mind that. Was she being selfish? Would Xavier's plans be better for the island?

No. Shaking her head, she remembered her promise. 'If you would only help me a little—maybe introduce me to some of your contacts, I could put the islanders' scheme in front of them, and try to get the business off the ground. Surely, there could be room for your scheme and theirs if everything was coordinated properly?'

'Are you backing down?'

'No,' she said firmly.

'In that case, I can only assume that you're asking me to help you fund your dream of Utopia.'

'All I'm asking is that you act as a go-between in this one small thing.'

'It isn't a small thing to invite my contacts to invest in you. Exactly how much experience of running a business shall I tell them you have? And make no mistake, Rosie, doing what you're suggesting—turning small-holders into commercial farmers—will be one hell of a business. You'd have to replace the infrastructure of the island, just for a start.'

'You'll need to do the same thing,' she protested. 'Why can't we work together?'

The sensible thing, Xavier reasoned, was to pay her off and send her packing, but so far they hadn't found a price. And though Rosie Clifton was the biggest risk to clear thinking he'd ever met, he was loath to send her away.

'If you're serious about this, you have to start thinking commercially. You need to meet the right people—'

'Exactly,' she interrupted, her eyes firing with passion. 'But how am I supposed to do that, unless you help me?'

'My money, your heart?' he mocked lightly.

'Why not?' She didn't even blink.

'All right,' he agreed, accepting her challenge. 'I'm holding a cocktail party at my apartment on the mainland. The guests will be exactly the type of people you need to meet.'

'Are you inviting me?' she asked him with suppressed excitement.

It was hardly fair of him to do so. His guests were hard-driven business professionals who would eat her alive.

'Are you?' she pressed.

'I'm not sure,' he admitted honestly.

'Why not?' she exclaimed.

'Because it might be said that every party needs a novelty item, an engaging piece of gossip to make it fly, and I'm not sure I'm ready to see you humiliated.'

'Only "not sure"?' she asked, starting to smile.

'I wouldn't stand for it,' he spelled out.

'I accept,' she said brightly.

Closing his eyes for a moment, he groaned inwardly at the thought of what Rosie's attendance at the drinks party would do to his precious clear thinking.

'All right,' he said. 'Decision made. You'll come to the mainland with me, and I'll do my best to make sure you don't feel out of place.'

She tipped her head to one side to stare at him with laughing eyes. 'You don't have much confidence in me, do you?'

The truth was, he didn't know what to expect from the redoubtable Rosie Clifton. But then she frowned. 'I don't know what I'm going to wear for this party of yours.'

'I'll buy you a dress,' he offered.

'I can't accept money from you—'

'*Dios*, Rosie! When are you going to stop being so

proud? What are we talking about here—a dress and a pair of shoes? When you've sorted yourself out, you can pay me back.'

'When I've accepted your pay-off, do you mean?' she asked him suspiciously.

That was exactly what he meant. 'We'll think of something,' he said.

She had to accept. She was getting nowhere on her own, Rosie thought. And unless she could come up with funding for the islanders' scheme, Xavier and his team would steamroller his plans through.

'You think too much,' he said, reading her preoccupation. 'You want it—you've got it. Now, leave it alone.'

He was right. Building bridges between them was more important than worrying about her entry into high society. But...

'A cocktail party.' Her throat tightened on the unaccustomed phrase. 'I've never been to one of those before.'

'You've never owned half an island before,' Xavier pointed out, 'but you seem to be handling it.'

'Handling you, do you mean?'

He almost smiled. She did too. It was time for new beginnings. She had to take the next step, or he would leave her in his wake. She had to find the courage to finish what she'd started.

CHAPTER EIGHT

WHEN THE MASSIVE marble and gilt hotel where she was to stay on the mainland loomed into sight, Rosie thought it even more terrifying than the flight over from the island, and that had been something. She had never travelled in a private jet before. They used the bus at the orphanage, and she had caught the ferry to the island after flying there on a commercial jet with the comfort of hundreds of people around her. There had been no one to talk to or distract her in the hushed luxury of Xavier's private jet, as he had gone on ahead, and her nerves were shredded by the time the plane landed. The hotel was her second hurdle. The limousine that had brought her directly from the tarmac outside the jet had stopped outside the grand entrance. Her luggage would be brought up directly, the driver told her stiffly as she stepped out of the car.

Her throat dried as she mounted the marble steps and glanced up at the towering façade. Doors were opened before she had a chance to touch the handle, and once inside the lobby she found it bustling with elegant, beautifully dressed people, who seemed to smell of money; everything smelled of money to Rosie's untutored nose. There were huge floral displays, and such a mix of scents, sounds and new impressions they made her dizzy as she wove her way through the throng.

Having been given her instructions at the desk—where she'd stood in line for ages, only to discover she should have used another desk where they only handled those privileged individuals whose rooms were located on the higher floors—she crossed to the bank of elevators. Having tried frantically to operate the lift, she now discovered there was a man to do that for her. And the elevator cabin wasn't just a functional steel-and-glass method of moving between floors, but an elegant affair with a velvet banquette and gilt-framed mirrors. She was careful to stand well away from the walls in case she marked them.

'This is your floor,' the lift operator informed her.

'Thank you.' She'd had a chance to study her reflection. She looked so out of place it was almost funny. Except it wasn't, because she wanted to make the right impression, and, judging from the man's manner towards her, she hadn't made a very good start. He was probably wondering why Security had allowed her upstairs in the first place in her thrift-shop dress and worn canvas sneakers. She might have wondered the same thing, if she hadn't known by now that the name Don Xavier Del Rio opened any door. But whatever was waiting for her beyond the elevator doors, she would remember her promise to Doña Anna and hold her head up high.

She walked slowly down the subtly lit corridor, trying to take everything in. She felt as if she were wrapped in money, cosseted and protected from the outside world, which was obviously the hotel's objective. Even the air smelled expensive. And it was so quiet. The carpet was so thick it absorbed the sound of footsteps, while the walls were covered with silk rather than paper, which would muffle any sound. The décor was the type of tasteful opulence Rosie had only seen in magazines before. It must have taken a lot of putting together, she guessed, but it was certainly effective. Even the muted colours had been chosen to soothe the harried guests, providing them with a haven from their busy lives.

So what was she doing here?

It was time to put thoughts like that out of her mind. She had to think positively now. She was here to attend a cocktail party, whatever that might entail.

Her door was at the end of the corridor. After several failed attempts, she managed to get her key card to work. Standing on the threshold, she stared around. The room was so vast she couldn't take it in. Catching sight of her bedazzled expression in one of the mirrors on the wall, she quickly closed her mouth, closed the door—and then she saw the dress. It was spread out on the sofa with a soft cream wrap next to it. She loved the wrap, but her heart picked up pace when she took a closer look at the dress. It looked like something a starlet would wear. Cut to fit like a second skin, it had a plunging neckline, and a split up the side that would leave nothing to the imagination. No way could she wear underwear beneath it.

Picking it up, she walked over to the mirror and held it against her. The dress was obviously expensive and very beautiful, in its way, but if anyone had asked her honest opinion she would have said it was a bit flashy, and definitely not something she would have chosen for herself. She preferred to blend into the background, rather than stand out, and there was no hope of blending in a dress like this. With her shabby shoes and custard dress, she looked like a child about to dress up in her big sister's clothes. And then she saw the shoes lined up neatly on top of their box. But were they shoes, or instruments of torture? She'd never worn high-heeled shoes before. 'Pride must bear a pinch,' Doña Anna would have said. And she was being ungrateful, Rosie concluded, pulling a face. Putting her concerns to one side, she headed for the bathroom to shower and change.

'Do you want me to give you a hand?' Xavier's driver enquired politely when they had arrived outside what had to be the most impressive office building in the city.

'Would you mind?' Rosie had got herself stuck halfway between the car seat and the pavement. The dress was so tight, and her heels were so high, that she couldn't find a way of propelling herself forward, short of pulling her skirt above her knickers to free her legs.

'Just put your hand on my arm and trust me,' the chauffeur advised, 'and I'll get you out, somehow...'

He'd been quite stuffy up to that point, but now, when they shared a look at his suggestion, they both started to laugh. 'I'll take you inside,' he offered when he'd got her out in one piece and had steadied her on the pavement.

'Thanks for the offer, but I'll be fine.' She was terrified, but she had to do this on her own. She had to learn how big business and society worked if she was going to be any use to the islanders.

Did she want to learn how society worked?

Not particularly, Rosie concluded, when she was left on the wrong side of the revolving doors, while everyone else pushed past her, but Doña Anna had insisted that part of Rosie's development as a person must include broadening her horizons, so here she was, broadening them.

'Excuse me, please…' Pinning a confident smile to her face, she made sure that the next group approaching the entrance didn't brush her aside so easily, and finally she was inside the building.

The party was on the forty-fourth floor. She felt like a flamingo on stilts as she exited the elevator and followed the noise down the corridor. The double doors were open wide in welcome, while the room beyond was packed with elegantly dressed people, all of whom seemed to know each other. Breathing in, she begged pardon politely, and wove her way through the crowd towards Xavier. She had spotted him immediately. He was at the hub of everything. He was like a magnet that drew people to him. He was also the tallest and easily the best-looking man in the room, and her heart went crazy, though she determinedly blanked the fantasy of him turning to see her, and holding out his arms to embrace her, as if she were the only woman in the world.

He was busy talking and hadn't seen her arrive. She hovered in the background, listening. He was chatting about the island, saying he was keen to get started on his new scheme there, but there were one or two problems still standing in his way. The glances that passed between his guests made Rosie wonder if they thought she was the problem. A couple of the men turned round to look at her. Whether they recognised her from the newspapers, she couldn't be sure, but she felt uncomfortable when they started murmuring to their companions.

'Ah,' Xavier said, swinging around. 'Allow me to introduce Señorita Clifton.'

It was as if the entire room drew a collective breath. Everyone stilled and turned to look at her. She felt like a curiosity at a museum. Then, a man who was obviously important, judging by the way the crowd had parted for him, took hold of Xavier's arm and led him away, and the same people who had feigned interest in her only moments before now turned their backs on her and ignored her.

She stood for a moment, not knowing what to do. Her feet were killing her, and she was surrounded by a wall of backs. Kicking off the heels, she hung them from her wrist like a clumsy bracelet. She could probably have taken her clothes off too. No one would have noticed, but at least her feet were happy now.

She set off on a tour of the room, trying to engage people in conversation. They either ignored her or moved away. Determined that she would not be shut out, she grabbed a plate of canapés from the bar and started to offer them around. The plate was almost empty by the time she reached Xavier, and not one word of thanks had come her way. She had joined the ranks of invisible people, and vowed in that moment that she would never take anyone for granted, let alone ignore them.

Waiting politely until Xavier had finished his conversation, she waved the plate under his nose. 'Canapé, sir?'

'What on earth are you doing?' he said, frowning with surprise. 'And what on earth are you wearing?' he murmured.

'Well, you chose it.'

'I certainly did not.' He removed the plate from her hand and handed it to a waiter with a few words of thanks. 'One of the secretaries picked it up for you.'

How comforting to think she was like a file that could be passed around the office for someone else to deal with.

Taking hold of her arm, Xavier steered her through

the press of people to a cooler spot beside the door. 'Let's get out of here,' he said.

He took her to his private office. It was stylish, yet plain, with every gizmo known to man. She was impressed. She tensed as he closed the door, suspecting she'd let him down. She'd fallen at the first hurdle, making a hash of her so-called entry into society.

'Why didn't you introduce yourself around?' he said, frowning.

She had to laugh. 'You only have to enter a room and you're the centre of attention. I didn't know anyone here. More importantly, they didn't want to know me.'

Xavier's frown deepened. 'You should have said if you were having difficulties.'

'I wasn't *having difficulties*. I didn't want to interrupt your conversation, that's all. And these are your guests, not mine. I don't expect you to devote every waking minute to me.'

'Just a few of those minutes?' he suggested, slanting a smile.

She didn't like to think what that smile could do to her. And it was too late to blank it out. It had already warmed her, and reminded her of her favourite fantasy, that involved happy-ever-after with the man of her dreams. 'A few minutes would probably be enough,' she said.

Xavier sighed, and turned away as his smile broadened. 'I suppose I owe you an apology. I should have been a better host.'

'But it suits your purpose better if I leave empty-handed,' she said shrewdly.

He swung around. 'You're determined to think the worst of me.'

'Then give me a reason not to.'

The crease was back in his cheek. 'Maybe I will,' he said with a flash of his sexy dark eyes.

A few long moments, and then he laughed as he spotted the shoes hanging from her wrist. 'They didn't suit you?'

'They hurt,' she confessed.

'And you hate the dress—not a great result, clothes-wise.'

She plucked at the dress and frowned. 'I know it sounds ungrateful, but I have to agree, this is not my favourite outfit.'

Pulling his head back to stare at her, Xavier narrowed his eyes in speculation. 'How much do you hate the dress?'

'Well…' she tried to be objective '…it's obviously been designed for someone with far more sophistication than me.'

'That's very tactful. I think it was designed for someone who likes to be noticed.'

Well, he was right in thinking she had no desire to stand out.

'I don't like it much, either,' he said.

She shrugged. There wasn't much she could do about that.

But Xavier had an answer to just about everything. Taking hold of the dress at the neckline, he ripped it apart.

'How do you feel about it now?' he said.

CHAPTER NINE

THE BRUSH OF his hands against her breasts was a scintillating distraction, but it didn't take Rosie long to find her voice. 'There's a party going on outside this room,' she protested as she tried frantically to gather the ripped fabric together. She glared at Xavier. 'You're mad! There are people laughing and chatting on the other side of that door. Your guests!' she reminded him. 'Guests who could walk in here at any time and see us together! Like *this*!' she added, her voice rising at least another octave. 'You haven't even locked the door!'

Xavier's powerful shoulders eased in a relaxed shrug. 'That's half the fun.' His voice was low and confident.

'For you,' she argued. 'Who dares to criticise Don Xavier Del Rio? You can do what you want, when you want.' *And with whom you want*, Rosie silently added. Even she had fallen victim to his spell. She'd get nowhere until she woke up and seized back some control. 'The dress is ruined, and I don't have a spare tucked away in my evening bag, in case you were wondering.'

'I wasn't.'

He couldn't care less. She needed to work out how to walk back into the party with a dress hanging off her shoulders. It was time to man up and take control.

Well, that should be easy, she thought, fuming when she saw his mocking face.

Think—think... She wasn't going to allow him to pull her strings like a puppet all night, was she? It might not feel like it at the moment, but it was Xavier who was on the back foot. Her inheritance was safe. She could fight for the islanders for the rest of her life, and there wasn't a damn thing he could do about it. But he had to produce an heir. If she didn't make something of her advantage now, then she deserved to lose the island. Her mind raced through the limited possibilities. First on the agenda was sorting out her current predicament. Maybe there was a spare waitress's uniform she could borrow?

'So, Señorita Resourceful?' Xavier prompted with amusement. 'What are you going to do now?'

'More than you suppose,' she tossed back at him.

'Oh?' There was amusement in his eyes, but also a new wariness had crept in.

'You think you've got it all covered, don't you?' she said. 'You can walk out of here with a knowing smile, while I'm left to do the walk of shame into a party where I'm already unwelcome. I'm guessing you think this introduction to high society will put me off for good, and that I'll be only too pleased—grateful, even—to accept your pay-off, and go to live quietly, while you move your bulldozers in.'

'You have an extremely vivid imagination, Señorita Clifton.'

'Do I? I think you see this as the start of returning things to how you imagine they should be,' she said, still busily tucking and folding.

Xavier frowned. 'What do you mean by that?'

'You might even give me a job as a housekeeper on

the island, if I'm lucky,' Rosie said. Raising her head, satisfied she had done the best she could with the dress, she saw Xavier's jaw clench, suggesting she was right. 'The Del Rio family will reign supreme once again, and everything in your world will have returned to how it should be—in your eyes,' she finished grimly.

'You know nothing about my family.' His tone was ominously quiet.

'I can hardly believe you've got one. My theory is that you were raised in a petri dish and then planted on top of the gold at the end of the rainbow.'

'I have as much a family as you do,' he said.

'We both had Doña Anna,' she argued.

He was quiet for a moment, and then he shrugged. 'If you're upset about the dress, I'll buy you another.'

'The dress is the least of my worries. We can't go on like this—you trying subtly, or not so subtly, to drive me away. I'm. Not. Going. Anywhere,' she spelled out. 'That's the last time I'm going to say it, so what are you going to do about that?'

Actually, Rosie thought, what was *she* going to do about it? Seizing control took more than good intentions. If she didn't like Xavier's suggestions regarding the future of the island, it was up to her to come up with something new.

'Take the dress off,' he murmured. 'It's ruined.'

'You're not listening to me, are you?' she demanded with frustration.

He smiled, and, though she knew she should stick rigidly to the point, those dark eyes held such danger they excited her. She wasn't used to flirting, and, though she knew this wasn't the time for it, the tension between them was threatening to snap. And then he made a big mistake. Putting a hand on her cheek, Xavier dipped his head as if to kiss her—as if it were his right! Don Xavier Del Rio had to learn that she could be dangerous too—

'*Que diablos*—'

Buttons bounced across the floor as she reached up and ripped his shirt apart.

She was filled with an unreasonable passion, born of the desire to assert herself. Why shouldn't she enjoy the heat of his hard, hot flesh beneath her fingers? Why shouldn't she lock her hands around what remained of his shirt and yank it apart? She was on fire. There was no chance of stopping her until both his shirt and jacket were on the floor. The fight was on. Xavier gave her no chance to enjoy her triumph. Seizing what was left of her dress, he ripped it from neck to hem.

'What are you going to do about that?' he challenged as it fell to the floor.

Her answer was to launch herself at him. Pummelling her fists against his chest, she gave vent to her passion in animal sounds of anger that all too soon turned to sounds of need. When she had finally exhausted herself, and her blows had slowed, she looked up to find, to her frustration, that Xavier was still smiling. So much for seizing control!

'Why, Señorita Clifton,' he murmured, 'I would never have credited you with quite so much passion.'

She was breathing so heavily it was hard to argue, and the next thing she knew she was in his arms. Holding her firmly in place, Xavier cradled her breasts, and then chafed her nipples remorselessly until pleasure consumed her, wiping every sensible thought from her head. Dipping his head, he claimed her mouth, and with a thoroughness and skill that obliterated the world as she knew it. His kisses were addictive and he felt so unbelievably good. He tasted minty and hot, and, when she pressed her body against his, she loved the feel of his steel against her curves.

'Do you hate me as much as the dress?' he queried with amusement. 'I think you must,' he said, staring down. 'You lived such a quiet life on the island until I arrived.'

'I lived such a safe life,' she argued, but that only made him laugh all the more. 'Don't,' she said, in between kisses. 'Don't make fun of me.'

'Is that what I'm doing?' he whispered, staring deep into her eyes. 'I thought I was making love to you.'

Cupping her face, he made her look at him, and, though she knew she should resist, she couldn't see anything but good humour and desire in his eyes. The first was unreasonably attractive, while the desire both terrified and excited her. He was tempting her to kiss him back. She didn't hate Xavier. She wanted him. She hadn't even known she was capable of feelings as strong as this. He nuzzled the exposed skin below her ear. The lightest touch of his sharp black stubble made her shiver with helpless need. Her body melted against his, while her breasts felt so full and heavy, and all she could think about was having him touch them again. He didn't disappoint her. Dipping his head, he lightly abraded the tip of each nipple with his teeth and with his tongue, until she couldn't deny him anything, and went willingly as he backed her towards the desk.

'It's the first time I've known you lost for words,' he commented with amusement as she gave a shaking groan.

'It's not my words I've lost, it's my dress. Aren't you even going to apologise?'

Xavier shrugged and his lips pressed down as he thought about it. 'I'm sorry,' he said, slipping his hand between her legs. 'Could you possibly ease your thighs apart?'

'That is not what I meant, and you know it,' she exclaimed on a gasp of shock.

'No, but it's what you want,' he said. 'So relax. Forget about the party and leave everything to me—'

She woke up like a shot. This encounter meant nothing to Xavier, but if she let him steamroller this too, her cause would be out of the window. She'd seen first-hand at the orphanage how destructive casual sex could be; someone always got hurt.

'Rosie? Rosie, what's wrong?'

Xavier's concern broke through to her. In his favour, he backed off the moment he felt her resistance, but now she was trapped in the past. Wiping a hand across her face, she tried to shake the ugliness out of her head. She must learn to move forward, and not become a victim of circumstance, which meant not doing something now she might live to regret.

The cocktail party was still in full swing outside the door. A tense silence had fallen inside the room. Then, an exuberant partygoer crashed into the door and the noise brought Rosie to her senses. 'What am I going to do about the dress?'

'There's a solution to every problem,' Xavier assured her.

'Even this one?' she queried sceptically.

'Of course.' Picking up the phone on his desk, he held her gaze as he pressed speed dial. 'Margaret? I'm in my study. I need you to do something for me.'

Margaret was a genius. She handed a shirt through the door, and made no comment when Xavier left the room to join his guests.

'I brought some dresses for you,' she called out to Rosie.

'Come in,' Rosie invited warmly, having kicked her ruined clothes beneath the desk. Luckily, some interior decorator had thought a fine cashmere throw would look amazing on one of the sofas and she was using it as a cover-up, so there was no embarrassment—well, not much on her side, and even less on the unshockable Margaret's side.

Once the door was safely closed behind her, Margaret held up the selection of dresses for Rosie to choose from.

'I can't thank you enough,' Rosie exclaimed with relief.

'I'm only sorry it took so long. Problems are my speciality, but miracles take a little longer.' Margaret eyed Rosie keenly. 'Xavier said you spilt something down the front of your dress?' She didn't wait for an answer. 'So I took the liberty of bringing underwear along as well.' She plonked down the boxes she had stuffed beneath her arm. 'Hope I got your size right. All I had to go on was our meeting on the island, and again tonight when you walked into the room.'

'I'm just so grateful, I'd grovel for a hessian sack tied with a piece of rope, but these are amazing. Thank you. It saves sneaking away wrapped in a throw.'

'I can't imagine you sneaking anywhere,' Margaret said frankly.

'I don't know what I'd have done without you.'

'Nonsense,' Margaret insisted. 'You would have walked through that door with your head held high, and to hell with what anyone thought.'

Rosie grinned. 'You're probably right.'

'That little red number hit the bin, I imagine?' Margaret said, looking at her shrewdly.

'You saw it?'

They both laughed.

'I would have come to your rescue sooner at the party,' Margaret explained with a rueful grimace. 'I could see how rude people were being to you, but I was talking to the ambassador at the time, and he's one person I can't ditch.'

'Please don't apologise. You've done enough for me as it is.'

'Of course I must apologise,' Margaret insisted. 'One of us should. Xavier's guests have behaved appallingly tonight, and he shouldn't have allowed it to happen. And I shall tell him so—'

'Please don't.'

'Well, at least let me make up for your rocky start to the evening,' Margaret insisted. 'When you're ready, I'll be only too happy to introduce you around.'

'You're very kind.'

'I'm very practical,' Margaret argued. 'As are you, Rosie Clifton. Ten minutes? Don't worry. I'll come back,' she said, heading for the door. 'Just call me when you're ready.' She glanced at the phone on the desk.

'Now I understand why Xavier has you on speed dial,' Rosie said, smiling at her new friend.

'I do have my uses,' Margaret agreed, shooting Rosie a brief, ironic look.

CHAPTER TEN

AFTER AN INTERESTING start to the evening, his party was deemed an unqualified success. Rosie had impressed him. She had moved with increasing confidence amongst his guests since Margaret had introduced her around. She looked stunning in an ice-blue dress cut on remarkably similar lines to her old yellow dress, though in some expensive designer fabric. Margaret had excelled herself as usual. The expression on Margaret's face at this moment, however, did not bode well. She was sailing towards him like a galleon in full sail. Taking hold of his elbow, she ushered him out of hearing of the other guests. He didn't complain. So long as he could still see Rosie, whatever Margaret wanted to say was fine by him.

'She's a diamond, that one.'

'You like Rosie Clifton?'

'Yes, I do. And you've treated her abominably tonight.'

'Is that what she told you?'

'Far from it,' Margaret admitted. 'She thinks you're wonderful, which just goes to show how mistaken a person can be.'

'I didn't ask you here to give me a lecture,' he chastised Margaret warmly, delighted to hear Rosie's opinion of him.

'You invited that poor girl, and then you left her stranded with people she didn't know. That's not good, Xavier. It's not worthy of you, and you know I'll speak my mind if I think you've done something wrong.'

'That's why I hired you,' he commented dryly.

'Then make it up to her. I've told her you'll see her safely home tonight. She wasn't happy about that, either,' Margaret conceded, avoiding his interested stare. 'But I'm sure you'll find a way to make amends.'

He was too.

'Use your powers of persuasion, if you want her to cooperate when it comes to the island,' Margaret suggested, as if he needed a prompt. 'Don't try and pressure her, or she'll fight back. She deserves better than that,' she added, directing a level stare into his eyes.

Having delivered her rebuke, Margaret sailed off in search of more wrongs to right.

'Who's taking you home tonight?' he asked, walking up to Rosie as she stood waiting to collect her wrap from the temporary cloakroom.

'You are, apparently,' she said, giving him one of her looks. She reserved her smile for the man who'd found her wrap, he noticed.

'You're very forward, Ms Clifton.'

'I'm very forward? You have a lot of ground to make up for tonight. If Margaret hadn't intervened, I'd be calling a cab back to the hotel right now.'

'It would be my pleasure to take you home.'

'Thank you,' she said coolly. 'Margaret said I must be sure not to leave without you.'

'She makes me sound like an umbrella.'

'Slightly more ornamental,' Rosie commented as she turned to thank the cloakroom attendant.

'Thank you,' she said primly as he stepped forward to help with her wrap. His only reward was the way she trembled when his hand touched her naked skin as he lifted her hair out of the way.

He stood back to watch as she walked to the exit. A couple of his guests stopped her to say goodnight, and to press business cards into her hands, and one of them was the ambassador. She'd been a hit tonight.

He arrived at her side in time to hear the elderly statesman purring over her hand, 'It's been a pleasure meeting you, Señorita Clifton.'

He guided her away from the ambassador with a few polite words, as well as all the other men standing in line to say one last goodnight to the very attractive Rosie Clifton.

'I think he's nice,' she said as he led her away. 'Are you jealous, Don Xavier?'

He huffed a dismissive laugh. 'I have to agree, you do look rather young and innocent in that dress.'

'Because I am young and innocent,' she reminded him with no smile. 'But that doesn't make me naïve, except where business is concerned, and there I'm happy to admit that I have everything to learn—with your help,' she added, with a flash of her astonishing eyes.

'So I'm on board with *your* plans now, am I?' he queried with a quirk of his brow.

'I don't know. Are you?' she said.

He chose not to answer and called for the lift. Rosie wasn't afraid to speak her mind, and in that she had joined a very exclusive group of women, consisting only of Margaret, and his late aunt, Doña Anna.

He drove her home. To his home. One of several he owned in the city.

'This isn't the hotel,' she commented.

'Well spotted,' he said dryly, noting the fact that her bravado was fast leaching away. He drove in through the gates. The mansion overlooked the park, and was both vast and beautiful. He was very proud of it, and found himself hoping that she liked it too.

'So why have you brought me here?' she demanded.

'For a nightcap?'

That half-serious suggestion was met by another piercing Rosie look. 'A nightcap?' she repeated sceptically. 'You know I hardly drink.'

'Neither do I, but I thought it would be a chance for us to get to know each other better.'

'Something Margaret suggested you should do?'

He pulled his luxury sports car alongside the steps. 'I do have some original thoughts. Let's call it a peace mission. One drink,' he said.

'And then I'm leaving,' she confirmed.

He helped her out of the car, and took her straight inside to the library, where his staff had lit a blazing fire. She looked around with interest. This was his favourite room in the house, and, for some reason, it really mattered to him that she liked it. The furnishings were comfortable and the walls were lined with books. Just the smell of old paper and worn leather bindings soothed him, and he definitely needed something to soothe his raging libido. Their clashes at the drinks party had taught him a lot about Rosie Clifton, and had confirmed his belief that fierce fires raged beneath her cool exterior, which wasn't helping his sexual hunger at all.

She might be out of her depth and sinking fast, but Rosie had to rally and stand up to him. Why had Xavier brought her to his fabulous home? Did he think he was going to seduce her? No chance. Still, this introduction to his luxury lifestyle told her more about his huge wealth and impeccable taste than the media could ever hope to with a few photographs and a lot of hysterical guff. She'd had so many new experiences tonight, her head was reeling, but she would sort it out. It didn't help that her body was on full alert after that encounter with Xavier's erotic expertise, but she would tame that too.

'You like the books,' Xavier commented as she allowed her fingertip to drift across a row of what were almost certainly first editions.

Discussing such a harmless shared interest gave her calm time, thinking time. 'I love them.' She had never seen so many leather-bound volumes gathered together in one place before. 'How can you ever bear to leave this house?'

He shrugged. 'I have books in all my houses.'

'Lucky you,' she murmured as she walked along the line of books. So many of the stories she'd read to Doña Anna had involved an unequal partnership, but that hadn't stopped the heroine succeeding—sometimes with audacity, but always with courage. An idea had been banging around in Rosie's head since their encounter in his office. It was radical, but might just work. 'Reading was the first thing that brought me close to your aunt.'

As he hummed she sensed she'd struck a nerve. It was perhaps better not to mention anything about her relationship with Doña Anna while things between them were still strained. 'Why did you ask me here?' she said instead, moving away from the books to face him.

'I'm trying to make amends.'

She didn't believe him for a minute, especially as he was opening a bottle of champagne.

'You do drink champagne, I take it?' he said, catching her look.

'I don't know,' she admitted honestly. 'I've never drunk champagne, but I'd love to try a small glass.'

A flash of surprise crossed Xavier's face. She guessed there were a lot of things he took for granted that she had never tried. 'But there's never been a better time for champagne.' Her heart started thumping as she got ready to spring her surprise.

'Oh?' he pressed with interest as he poured the foaming liquid into matching crystal flutes.

'Yes.' The prospect of voicing her solution to their problems was alarming, and if there had been any other way she would have taken it. But she had to be both courageous and bold, or she might as well pack her bags and leave the islanders to fend for themselves.

Xavier handed her a flute, which she eyed curiously. 'Would you prefer something else?'

'No. This is perfect. Thank you.'

This had to be what Doña Anna had intended all along, Rosie concluded as she reviewed her plan. She would be in charge of her own destiny, and she would have an equal say over the future of the island. Xavier had tried to buy her off, and when that failed he was trying his best to charm her, but she was the one with the leverage, not him. He was the one in need of an heir, and all the champagne and blarney in the world couldn't change that.

'Would you mind if I proposed the toast?' she suggested.

He frowned a little, as well he might—he would have run for the hills if he'd known what she had in mind. And she wasn't in a much better state. Her breathing had sped up. Her heart was beating so fast and loud she was sure he could hear it. This was huge, and once she spoke the words out loud—if, *if* he agreed, the die was set.

'Of course—go ahead,' he said indulgently, not suspecting for a moment what she had in mind. 'You've had a bit of practice, after all—the ice cream,' he reminded her. 'Well? What's your toast?'

She took a deep breath and then just spat it out. 'I think we should get married.'

Xavier's eyes widened. 'I beg your pardon?' he said faintly. 'Am I imagining things, or did you just propose marriage?'

'That's exactly what I said,' she confirmed.

He looked incredulous.

'It would solve all our problems,' she said. 'Yours especially,' she hurried on, 'so it seems to me to be the sensible thing to do—'

'Sensible?' His expression was incredulous as he raked his hair.

'Yes—shall we sit down?' she suggested. 'There are quite a lot of things to discuss.'

'You don't say?'

The look on Xavier's face suggested the world and everything in it had gone mad. He must be shocked, Rosie reasoned as she crossed the room to sit on the sofa.

'Please,' she said, injecting her voice with what she hoped was the correct amount of supplication. 'Won't you join me?'

Xavier's face was a grim mask when he came to sit across from her. 'Go on,' he prompted with a wave of his hand.

'You need an heir or you'll lose your half of the island to me, and unless you've got someone in mind—'

'I don't.'

'Then...'

'Better the devil I know?' he suggested grimly.

'You can't buy me out, you should know that by now, and if we marry you get to keep your share.'

'What's in it for you?'

'Everything,' she said bluntly. And nothing, she thought. 'A secure future for the island,' she went on. 'We can't leave the islanders wondering if they have a future with you, or with me. They need certainty, as I think you pointed out. And how can you risk your investment without that same guarantee?'

This wasn't the romantic marriage proposal she had imagined as a child. This was a cold-blooded transaction of a type that was Xavier's speciality. She hoped it would appeal to his logical mind. She had no hope at all that it would appeal to his romantic nature, as he didn't have one.

'Marriage would put us on equal footing,' she explained, 'and it would open doors that have been slammed in my face. I'd be able to help the islanders—really help them. You've seen how people react to me. No one wanted to speak to me at the party unless you were at my side, or Margaret was introducing me around. This would give me credibility, an equal say in what happens to the island, and it would give you the heir you need to keep the island.' Her stomach tightened on the words. The thought of sex with Xavier was the most terrifying prospect, but as she had so far failed to find an alternative—

'I can see that it would help you,' he said coldly.

'And you,' she insisted, ignoring the chill in his eyes. 'So, will you consider my suggestion?'

She had no idea what Xavier was thinking as he stared into the fire. Her best guess was that this was Xavier the businessman, weighing up the odds.

'I can't believe you're serious about this,' he said, looking round at last.

'You'd have my full cooperation,' she stressed, sensing the faintest of possibilities that he might say yes.

'I would certainly expect your cooperation in bed.'

Her heart clenched tight.

'I have a rather tight schedule to meet.'

It lurched, but she held her nerve. 'I hope we'd work together in every way.'

'I'd make sure of it,' he said without a scrap of warmth.

It was time to close the deal. She knew nothing about such things, and was firing on instinct. She surprised herself with how unemotional she could be when so much was at stake. 'This is for both of us,' she said levelly. 'Without marriage to me, the risk of losing your inheritance is very real for you, and I know the island means a lot to you, in spite of what you say. Isla Del Rey is as special to you as it is to me. You might have all the power and influence in the world, but without my cooperation in this one thing, your plans are stalled.'

'What do you know of marriage? Very little, I think,' he went on without waiting for her to answer. 'Marriage brings nothing but unhappiness. Wedlock is well named, in case you didn't know. People enter into marriage with expectations—or, in your case, dreams—and when they find it can never match up to these fictions, what follows is misery for all concerned.'

'In your case, maybe,' she protested.

'Can you quote a single instance where I'm wrong?' Xavier demanded. 'No. I didn't think so. You don't have a clue. And as for this heir Doña Anna has insisted I must provide. My aunt has gone down in my estimation. I would have thought that she, of all people, would understand that having a child in the middle of a love-less marriage denies that child the right to happiness, and that it colours the rest of their life.'

'Only if they allow it to,' she said, sensing Xavier was talking about himself.

'And what would you know about it, when you have no experience of relationships—none at all.'

'Except with your aunt,' she said steadily. 'And what-ever you think of me, or Doña Anna, I will not break my promise to keep her island safe. And, yes, you're right in saying I don't have any experience of marriage, or happy-ever-after. I didn't have any experience of love until I came to the island and met Doña Anna, but one thing you must know with absolute certainty is that if I have a child I will love that child with all my heart, and I will never abandon it as you were abandoned. You need an heir, but you're sure you'll fail as a father, as you were failed by your parents, but why would that happen?'

'You're so sure of everything,' he said.

'Yes, I am. I have to be. I've had to be positive, or I'd still be back in the institution. Just think how you're loved on the island, and the love that's waiting for that child. Everyone hopes you'll return to Isla Del Rey one day, and that hope has no strings attached, or documents to sign, and nothing to be gained by the islanders, other than the rightness of you being back amongst people who love you. And I'll tell you something else—'

'I'm sure you will,' he said.

'You won't deny me my dreams, because I won't let you.'

'The hearts and flowers you imagine are not a given,' he said. 'I think you have a very naïve view of things.'

'Maybe,' Rosie agreed, 'but better that than I remain bitter about a past I cannot change. If we work together we could achieve a lot on the island. That's what I think Doña Anna wanted when she drew up her will. My heart, your business acumen,' she said, smiling encouragement. 'And, who knows? I'm sure we'll annoy the heck out of each other, but we might even start enjoying it.'

His cynical expression didn't promise that, but everything was on the line now: her heart, her fears, her future. 'This really matters to me, Xavier.'

'I'm sure it does,' he said, staring at her without warmth. 'Dipping a hand into my bank account would matter to most people.'

Shaking her head, she laughed, but it was a sad sound, totally lacking in humour. 'You haven't listened to a word I've said. This isn't about money.' *You infuriating, damaged man*, she thought. Xavier didn't think he needed help from anyone. He didn't need an island. He *was* the island, isolated and alone.

'One minute you're working in the orphanage,' he said, his eyes dark with suspicion, 'and the next you're inheriting half an island. And now you seem to think you can marry the other half.' With a shake of his head, he gave her a cutting look. 'Your idea of marriage might catch on. It seems like a very good bargain to me—for you, and for every other penniless woman in the world.'

'Then refuse me,' she challenged. 'I'm sure you'll find someone to oblige you with an heir, with all that money at your disposal.'

Xavier's expression darkened. 'What did you imagine when you were offered the position of housekeeper to an elderly woman? Did you think it would give you the chance to charm my aunt into leaving you something in her will?'

'I think all you see is bad in people,' she countered, 'and I think that's sad. You're the loser,' she added heatedly. 'No wonder you're still alone. I'm doing this for the good of the island, and that's my only reason. Do you think that anyone would want to marry a man who can't feel anything, without a very good reason for it? And as for playing your aunt? I was stunned by Doña Anna's generosity. I still am. And I'm determined to do everything she expected of me. I will never forget how much I owe her—and I'm not talking about the bequest now, but the home she gave me, and the love we shared. I don't think my plan's naïve. It's not as if we're talking about a love match. Ours will be more of a business deal.' Her heart sagged as she said this, but it was done now, and she had to get through to him somehow.

'I think I know a little more about business deals than you.'

She shrugged. 'Then you must see the good sense in this. Work with me to put the island right.'

'Turn it into a vegetable plot?' he suggested.

She ignored that comment. 'Once everything is on an even keel, we can arrange a discreet divorce.'

'No stone left unturned,' Xavier observed. 'I'm impressed.'

And patronising, she thought. 'It's said your success rests on your ability to put plans into action right away—'

'Sensible plans,' he interrupted, 'plans that have been thoroughly researched, and will work. I can see what you have to gain from this—'

'And you,' she countered firmly.

'You're quite a hard little piece, aren't you?' he remarked with an accusing stare.

Not at all. Not even slightly, and she wilted inwardly

at Xavier's description, though not a jot of that showed on her face. Living in an institution was a strange and enclosed experience. She couldn't have survived it without a little steel in her backbone—

Without a lot of steel in her backbone, Rosie amended.

'So, what's your answer?' she pressed.

CHAPTER ELEVEN

DOÑA ANNA HAD TIED him up in knots, ensuring he came back to the island, met Rosie, and then fulfilled his aunt's request to provide an heir. How neat. Doña Anna was the only woman in the world who had ever been able to put a curb on him. She'd done it once before when he was a youth, and she was doing it again from the grave. That Rosie Clifton had chosen to make this proposal, shocking him with her accusations, only endorsed his aunt's opinion of the girl. Whatever his answer, he had to admit his aunt had made a good choice in her lieutenant. He supposed he owed Rosie some grudging respect for the fact that she never gave up. Nothing would deter her from following his aunt's wishes to the letter.

'Marriage to you will give me the power to help the island,' she told him now, her face shining with good intentions.

'I'm expected to fund your ideas?'

'Only if you agree.' Her eyes were full of hope.

'This marriage to me will certainly allow you to continue your meteoric rise in the world.'

'Please don't talk like that when there's a child involved,' she begged him.

'*You* should remember that there's a child involved,'

he fired back. He'd seen the effect of a marriage and a child on his parents. 'You do realise this would have to be a marriage in the fullest sense.' With consequences he dreaded more than Rosie, he suspected. Everything was fantasy and theory to Rosie, but now she must face the truth.

'Of course,' she assured him, but her face was ashen. He guessed she was thinking about their wedding night and all the nights after that.

'And if you expect me to consult with you concerning my plans for the island—'

'I do expect consultation between us,' she stated firmly.

Even as she spoke the words Rosie knew they were wasted on Xavier. He'd probably never consulted with anyone in his life. So maybe that was one thing she was better at than him, she reasoned. Her life had been one long series of negotiations, with compromise the only way to survive the system she'd grown up in. 'You might find it stimulating to hear new ideas,' she suggested.

'I have a team for that,' he said. 'But if we do run out of ideas, I'll be sure to call on you.'

'So your answer's no?' It was a struggle to read him as he stared into the middle distance.

'Not necessarily.'

Rosie had given him everything he needed on a plate. He was sorry she'd be hurt—and she would get hurt—but it couldn't be helped. His aunt should have known that this would have a bad ending. He'd never made any secret of the fact that the chains of domesticity were not for him. 'Yours is a very unusual proposition.'

'It's bold,' she argued.

'It's a marriage of convenience.'

'Yes,' she agreed. 'That's what's so good about it—both sides benefit.'

Was she being so businesslike because she thought it was the only way to communicate with him, or did she have that hard streak beneath her vulnerable shell? Looking at her face, he decided she was certainly gritty and determined. She was a survivor, like him, he concluded. 'Isn't a marriage of convenience a little outdated?'

'In this instance, it will be perfectly in tune with our needs.'

'Then I agree,' he said.

'You do?' She looked at him with surprise.

'Pay attention, Ms Clifton. I just agreed to marry you. As you so rightly say, my aunt has faced us both with a problem, and the best way to solve that problem is with a straightforward business deal. I agree that we should be married—and as soon as possible.'

Triumph came in many forms, Rosie now discovered. She felt light-headed in victory, and frightened at what she'd done. Her erotic fantasies involving Xavier belonged in her fantasy world, where he was everything she wanted him to be, and he made no unreasonable demands on her. In reality, he was too much of what she wanted, and his demands would probably be many and vigorous, but, with everything at stake, what choice did she have?

'Okay,' she said, extending her hand for him to shake on the deal. 'Let's do it.'

'You do know that in those few words your world has changed for ever?' he asked as he closed his hand around hers.

'I know it,' she whispered, sensation streaming through her at his touch. 'And I'd hoped my world would change,' she added levelly. 'It would have to, to embrace yours.'

'Good.' He seemed pleased. 'I'll have my people make a formal announcement. We'll have to celebrate. I'll hold a ball.'

'A ball?' Rosie was aghast. The drinks party had been bad enough. This was all moving too fast.

'It's usual to make a formal announcement,' Xavier assured her. 'We must give everyone chance to congratulate the happy couple.'

What happy couple? Rosie thought, shivering inwardly.

'Is something wrong?' Xavier asked her.

He knew very well what was wrong. She needed reassurance that she was doing the right thing, and there was no one, absolutely no one, who could give her that. 'I'm surprised you care what the world thinks about our forthcoming marriage.'

'I don't, but I thought you might,' he said.

She appreciated his concern. 'Thank you.'

'Don't mention it.' His stare was dark and triumphant, and it stripped away her brief moment of confidence, but she had to do this. It was the only way she could stop the island being torn apart. And, yes, the eyes of the world would be on them the instant this went public; and yes, cruel comments would be made, but this wasn't about her feelings, but about the island and her promise to Doña Anna to keep it safe. 'How will you explain away the suddenness of our marriage? Coming so soon after the reading of the will, won't it seem odd?'

'I don't have to explain anything,' Xavier assured her.

Of course he didn't. Don Xavier Del Rio didn't play by the rules; he never had. No explanations were necessary.

'I expect the press to report it as a *coup de foudre*, love at first sight, our first meeting having been engineered by my aunt, your employer, Doña Anna. That will get us through for the duration of our marriage.'

'You make our marriage sound more like a prison sentence.' She felt a pang that it couldn't be more, and had to remind herself that a road bridge between fantasy and fact had never existed.

'It will be what you make of it,' Xavier stated. 'It's your idea.'

From the frying pan into the fire, she thought. 'Where will the ball be held?'

'Here, of course.'

Of course. She could forget having a happy, relaxed party amongst friends on the island. The announcement of their impending marriage would be made amongst people she didn't know at a stiff, formal ball.

'Do you have a problem with that?' Xavier probed when she bit down on her lip.

'No. Of course not.'

'In two weeks' time.'

'So soon?' Her heart flipped over. 'Will that be enough time to arrange everything?'

Xavier gave her an amused look. Anything was possible for Don Xavier Del Rio. She'd better get used to it, though a second encounter with high society was not the best start to the plan that she had so boldly put in motion. She could tell he was pleased, because he'd take over now. Their marriage of convenience would be over and done with at breakneck speed.

The night of the ball had arrived. He stared at his stern, formally dressed reflection in the mirror, wondering if Rosie was ready for this. Their last meeting had been here, and when she'd left her face had brightened as if she'd expected him to take her in his arms and seal their bargain with a tender kiss. For her sake, he had resisted any show of affection. It would be wrong to pretend that this wedding was anything more than a convenience for both of them. He admired Rosie for the strength and grace with which she came through the problems she faced, but his cold nature, forged in the bitter past, always triumphed in the end.

He felt nothing for Rosie. So why was he still thinking about her?

His only interest was in seeing how the evening played out, he told himself firmly. Rosie had guts. She would get through it. She had elected to play hardball, and now she had to prove that she could.

Members of so-called high society were already arriving at his gates. The cathedral would be crammed for their wedding. His scandalous match with his late aunt's housekeeper must have kept dinner tables alive with gossip since the invitations went out. Even the ambassador had changed his schedule in order to attend both the wedding and the ball, and the cream of Spanish society would join his guests tonight, together with several members of the royal family. This would not be a low-key affair. Margaret was in charge of arrangements, so he had every confidence that it would all go smoothly. Rosie would not be allowed to put a foot wrong. It remained to be seen what his guests thought of her, but it was what he thought when he saw her after several days apart that intrigued him. His mind was a blank canvas where that was concerned. Would he feel anything more than some fleeting lust when Señorita Clifton arrived at the ball?

* * *

She couldn't have done this without Margaret's help, Rosie reflected, wishing her heart would calm down. It had been thundering for most of the day as she contemplated the evening ahead. Seeing Xavier again was even more daunting than facing his guests at the ball. She'd know at once what he was thinking. She would be able to read his thoughts in his eyes. He might be resigned, or impatient, or… No. Hoping he'd be pleased to see her was too much to ask.

Ball gowns weren't exactly her area of expertise, Rosie fretted as she stared at her reflection in the mirror. 'Do I look all right?'

'You look beautiful,' Margaret assured her as she bustled about, tweaking Rosie's ankle-length gown.

When Margaret had knocked on the door of her suite at the hotel, Rosie had welcomed the friendly older woman with open arms. Finding a ball gown *and* a wedding dress in the time available was way beyond her scope. She had been busily scouring the pages of a magazine, wondering which of the grand boutiques would be likely to let her through the door in her custard dress, when Margaret arrived. She was more a jeans and T-shirt girl, and after the fiasco of the red dress she couldn't risk another disaster. Margaret's down-to-earth encouragement turned out to be just what she'd needed.

Margaret's approval meant a lot to Rosie. She believed she could trust her to give her an honest opinion. That was what she was waiting for now as Margaret walked a full circle around her.

'I love the gown,' Margaret said as she stared critically at Rosie from every angle. 'It's really stylish, and I've never seen you looking more beautiful.'

'I wouldn't have had a clue what to choose for the

ball without you,' Rosie admitted, 'and I certainly wouldn't have known where to shop for it.'

Margaret laughed at this. 'But now you know that when Xavier is involved the designers come to you.'

'And work through the night to get the dresses ready in time,' Rosie added, still marvelling at what was possible for the rich and famous. The designers must have thought it was a love match to rush about as they had. If they'd known the truth, perhaps they wouldn't have been quite so enthusiastic about it, though the scandal alone would make them famous.

'Are you happy, Rosie?' Margaret asked with genuine concern in her voice.

Was she happy? Rosie stared at her face in the mirror, wishing with all her heart that she could confide her fears about the future to Margaret. 'Of course I'm happy,' she said brightly in an attempt to reassure the older woman.

'Then, let's go,' Margaret prompted.

It was too late to change her mind now. Sucking in a deep, steadying breath, she held her head up high as they left the suite together.

He had expected Margaret and Rosie to arrive long before now. What was keeping them? Surely it was just a matter of picking a dress that fitted and putting it on?

He shifted position impatiently, his stare fixed on the door. All his guests had arrived, and were waiting, as he was, for the most important guest of the night. The evening couldn't have been more perfect. All the doors into the garden had been opened and the sky was littered with stars. The moon was suspended like a silver crescent, resting back on a velvet bed. The orchestra was playing, candles were lit, and chandeliers glittered.

Champagne and conversation flowed freely. The ball was already deemed a success. 'And with the additional treat of your special announcement,' one elderly lady had just cooed in his ear. 'None of us can wait for that.'

He could imagine. He disliked being on everyone's tongue and the sooner this was over, the better, as far as he was concerned. The scandal sheets were full of it with incendiary comments about the unsuitability of his marriage. He expected rumbles to go on for quite a while, until some new *cause célèbre* burst upon the public consciousness and everyone forgot about him. He could only hope Margaret had steered Rosie in the right direction. After the unfortunate red dress, a mistake now would attract derision, which would in turn keep the gossip running. Most of his guests were good people, but they did love to talk, and there were piranhas amongst them who loved nothing more than to see a person fall. He could take their scorn, but beneath her bravado Rosie was vulnerable to attack, and, whatever else this match promised, he would not stand by and see her bullied.

He tensed as the room fell silent. Even the musicians had put down their instruments as everyone turned to stare at the door.

Rosie had entered the ballroom.

Standing at the top of the steps, she was framed in light. Her presence coursed through him like a light-ning bolt. She was dressed in an exquisite gown of soft, clear blue. The colour was a perfect foil for her glorious red-gold hair. She looked quite astonishingly beautiful. The impact was so staggering it was as if he were seeing her for the very first time. The gown was slim-fitting, and subtly styled with a modest neckline. Beautifully beaded in the same colour as the dress, the fabric sparkled discreetly as she moved. It drew his attention from the loveliness of her face to the perfection of her womanly form. She was the only woman in the room, as far as he was concerned, and his senses soared as she glanced around. Looking for him, he hoped.

Her chin lifted when she saw him and a faint smile touched her lips. The connection between them was immediate, and obvious to everyone else. He didn't care about anyone else, and watched entranced as she walked down the stairs towards him. She'd left her hair loose, the way he liked it, and she was so surprisingly elegant, and yet so painfully vulnerable. He wanted to shield her from all the hungry eyes, but sensed that this walk through the lines of the great and good was something Rosie wanted to do on her own.

Her beauty transfixed every man in the room. His hackles rose as they stared at her. But it was more than Rosie's physical perfection that held him. She was luminous. She had an inner serenity that no other woman could match. She might have been a lost soul from the orphanage when she had first arrived on Isla Del Rey, but Rosie Clifton had found herself tonight, and she was magnificent.

The conductor lifted his baton when she reached the middle of the dance floor, and struck up an elegant Viennese waltz. Some alchemy dictated that Rosie didn't walk towards him, but appeared to float in time to the music as the crowd fell back to let her pass. A collective sigh went up when she reached his side. All thoughts of crude gossip were instantly forgotten. She had silenced the chatterers with nothing more than her poise and innocent appeal.

'Good evening, Xavier.'

'Margaret's done a good job,' he replied dryly, and with maximum understatement.

'I did have some say in it,' she reprimanded him with the hint of a smile.

His groin tightened as she continued to stare levelly into his eyes. 'I'm sure you did,' he agreed, 'and I have to say, you look very beautiful.'

'Do I?' She seemed stunned by his comment.

'Of course you do,' he confirmed, as if this were obvious. 'You're easily the most beautiful woman in the room.'

His senses were in overload. He was in an agony of lust, but something more was happening to him. For all that he boasted of having no feelings, he felt something now, and it was a feeling far more powerful than lust; a feeling that made him want to lead her out of here to somewhere private and quiet. Everything about her: the scent she was wearing, her warmth, her gaze on his face, and her body within inches of his; he could only think she had bewitched him. Remaining cool and detached, as he had intended, was no longer a certainty. His body was like that of a youth with no control.

'I was hoping you'd approve,' she said.

He could see the vulnerability in her eyes. She was so bold, and yet so fragile. Physically, she was small and soft and desirable, and he would have to be made of stone not to want her. 'Do *you* approve?' he murmured. 'I mean, your engagement ball,' he explained, glancing around. He suddenly realised that her answer really mattered to him.

'It's such a beautiful evening. I only hope I don't spoil it for you.'

'I shall have to keep you close all night, to make sure you don't,' he said.

The intimacy between them grew rapidly after that. It was almost as if they were enclosed in a private bubble that excluded all his guests, leaving them on the outside looking in. Rosie laughed and relaxed as he drew her into his arms for the first dance. He would have liked that moment, that very first moment of contact between them, to last for the rest of the night. Her skin felt so warm and soft beneath his touch, and when she closed her hand around his, the desire to protect her overwhelmed him. All thoughts of bargains between them vanished instantly. He was seriously interested in this woman. He wanted her like no other. Judging by the hectic rise and fall of her breasts, she wanted him too. It didn't take long for his thoughts to stray onto the dark side as he contemplated all that innocence aching for his experience to lead the way. It was a feeling that would remain with him for the rest of the night.

His guests applauded politely as he led Rosie in the dance. They were eager to catch their first glimpse of the innocent young housekeeper in the arms of the Spanish Grandee, and had formed a tight circle around them. If they knew Rosie had proposed to him, they wouldn't believe it. That was enough to make him smile. There was the added satisfaction of feeling Rosie tremble when he placed his hand in the small of her back. By the end of the night, his guests would be saying theirs was a love-match. He laughed inwardly at the thought, and almost wished it were true.

CHAPTER TWELVE

MARGARET SMILED ENCOURAGEMENT as Rosie danced with Xavier. If being this close to him hadn't reminded Rosie so vividly of her loss of control at the cocktail party, she might have relaxed, and enjoyed being in his arms. As it was, she felt overwhelmed by what she'd done, and deeply worried for the future of her waning control. Just being this close to him, dancing with him, being in his arms, was enough to cloud her judgement. Being married to him was no guarantee she could handle him. Xavier was so much more experienced than she was. And yet she felt he was right for her in every way. Or was that just this romantic setting and her romantic nature combining? The expression in his eyes was warmer than she'd ever seen it, but—

'Relax,' he said, sensing her tension.

She must relax. She had to hide her feelings. Keeping them under wraps was what had always kept her safe. Xavier was super-intuitive. She had to remember that at all times.

One dance led to another, and then the ambassador cut in. Xavier yielded to the older man gracefully, but when a young royal prince tried to do the same he wasn't so accommodating. Seeing how tense he'd become, she politely declined the prince, pleading tiredness as she allowed Xavier to lead her away.

'You have a very beautiful home,' she said as he escorted her outside. 'You have great taste.'

'My decorators have great taste,' he corrected her.

'The floral displays are exquisite.'

'I'm glad you like them,' he said with a smile that suggested he'd softened a little.

She thought he'd probably guessed that she was trying to distract herself from the purpose of the ball. 'Roses are my favourite flowers…'

She wasn't sure he heard her as he led her through the French doors and onto the veranda overlooking the exquisite formal gardens. 'I can only imagine growing up in a place like this.' Resting her forearms on the marble balustrade, she leaned over to glance around.

'I didn't grow up here.'

She was instantly alert at his tone, which was tinged with old hurt.

'I went away to school,' he revealed.

'And then you lived with your aunt?'

'In the holidays, yes,' he confirmed in the same stilted tone.

'You didn't see a lot of your parents.'

She'd struck a nerve, Rosie thought as a muscle flexed in Xavier's jaw.

'I bought this house with my first fortune,' he said.

'Your first fortune?' she teased, wanting to reach out to him, and not really knowing how.

'I won't deny I've been successful.'

'And why should you? You should be proud of what you've achieved.' Especially after surviving the legacy of bitterness created by his parents' self-indulgent lifestyle, she wanted to add.

'And so should you,' he said, surprising her. 'In some ways, we're not so different, you and I.'

She laughed. 'Just a billion or so apart, and then, of course, there's your title—'

'Which doesn't mean a thing,' he said. 'Come on—' He indicated that she should go ahead of him. 'It's time to go inside so I can make the announcement.'

Her heart banged in her chest at the thought, and she had to remind herself that this was her idea. She knew the moment had to come, but just to hear it said in public would make it real. She had dreamed of this moment since she was a little girl, but had never thought it would be like this. Her dreams had been hazy, involving a handsome lover, and Rosie smiling happily and trustingly into the face of the man she would spend the rest of her life with. Instead, she'd got an arrangement; a marriage of convenience, as Xavier had called it. No one must guess they were faking their emotions, or they would both become figures of ridicule, and her chance to raise support for the island amongst people who mattered would be dust. That didn't stop her wishing the fantasy could come true, and Xavier's announcement would mark the beginning of something wonderful, rather than the beginning of the end.

'Before we go in,' he said, drawing her to one side, 'I want to show you the ring—so there are no surprises,' he explained.

'You've already surprised me,' Rose admitted. 'I didn't expect a ring.'

Xavier frowned as he asked, 'Do you think so little of me?'

'Not at all,' she admitted frankly. 'It's just that I didn't expect anything beyond an announcement of our engagement.'

'Of course there must be a ring,' he said.

'Of course,' she agreed, realising that her comment

was further proof of her naivety. The assembled guests would expect her to have an engagement ring. This was Don Xavier Del Rio's fabulously lavish engagement party, after all.

She got another shock, and not a good one, when Xavier flipped the lid on a night-blue velvet box. 'I can't accept that,' she protested, looking at the huge jewel sideways as if it were a snake. To Rosie's eyes, it seemed to be an unnecessarily large stone.

'Why?' he demanded, seeming bemused.

'Because I don't need such a valuable diamond.'

'What did you imagine I would give you?' Xavier demanded, scrutinising the enormous diamond solitaire as if he were seeing it for the first time. 'I can't see anything wrong with this ring.'

'There's nothing wrong with it,' Rosie admitted. 'It's absolutely stunning. It's just not for me.'

Anyone would have been dazzled by the rainbow sparkle thrown off by the magnificent stone. It was a beautiful and obviously priceless gem, but it belonged in a crown, or a sceptre.

And now she had offended him.

'What *do* you want?' he asked, frowning.

'Something smaller and more discreet?'

'Small?' he repeated, as if she had suggested something obscene.

'Small*er*,' she said, knowing they couldn't keep their guests waiting much longer.

'Well, it's too late for that,' he said, 'and, under the circumstances, I think everyone should be left in no doubt that I am fully committed to this match.'

'I'm sorry. You must think me ungrateful.' She only wished there were no barriers between them, and she could really explain how she felt, but she was as much to blame for the distance between them as Xavier. Rosie's childhood had taught her to feel that she wasn't worthy of love, and she guessed that his had taught him pretty much the same. 'I'd rather not wear this,' she said honestly as she handed back the ring. 'Wearing it would feel dishonest to me.'

'Nonsense,' Xavier insisted, but something in his eyes suggested he might just understand. He confirmed her suspicion when he said, 'I do know you a little. That's why I took you aside. I anticipated some reluctance on your part, but we can't disappoint our guests now. We'll go back into the ballroom, where you will smile when I make the formal announcement of our engagement, and gasp with pleasure when I show you the ring.'

It was only the understanding in his eyes that made her agree. 'All right, I'll do it,' she said. Her heart squeezed tight when she saw the relief on his face. 'Of course I'll do it,' she repeated, suddenly filled with the most urgent need to reassure him.

The next day every newspaper carried the story of the fabulous engagement ball at Don Xavier Del Rio's palatial mansion, which had taken yet another eligible bachelor off the scene. Everyone seemed to have been persuaded by their play-acting, Rosie read with relief. She was back at the hotel, and had ordered every newspaper she could think of, so she could check that no one suspected their engagement was a fake, and their subsequent marriage would be a sham. They'd made the headlines, of course, and there were endless shots of Rosie staring lovingly at Xavier, and Xavier smiling down at his fiancée. There were even more shots of the ring, and from every possible angle. *'The ring of the century'* some were saying, as if the fabulous jewel were a weather condition that had blown everyone away.

As far as Rosie was concerned the ring was a monstrous billboard, reminding her of her mistake in ever thinking this plan made sense. How could she play-act a marriage to Xavier, when she was fast developing feelings for him? And to make matters worse, they were feelings that would only be dismissed and discarded by Xavier, who wasn't capable of feeling anything.

The ring was also a huge responsibility, Rosie reflected, tossing the newspaper aside, and one she had no interest in keeping. The diamond was so big and heavy it kept swinging around her finger, and she didn't dare to take it off in case she lost it. She knew she was being ungrateful, but the ring seemed to represent everything that was wrong with their match. She held the ring up to the light. It was so big it looked unreal. So, perhaps it was the perfect ring, after all…

She was going to keep her promise to Doña Anna but at a far higher price than she'd imagined. If she and Xavier were lucky enough to have a child, she would love that baby with every fibre of her being, and defend it fiercely from hurt, but would Xavier do the same, or was the idea of an heir just a figure of speech to him?

One of the worst parts of the ball had been speaking to the islanders after the announcement of their engagement. Xavier had invited a group of them to the ball. Trying to join in their excitement at the news of their engagement had torn her in two. She hated the pretence, and wondered if Xavier had noticed that she'd left the ball almost immediately after talking to them. Seeing she was upset, Margaret had stepped in, calling for the driver to take Rosie back to the hotel. Rosie had slipped away while Xavier had been talking to the ambassador. She hadn't wanted to interrupt him, or give him the chance to try to stop her leaving. She'd played her part. She had been charming to all his guests, and they'd been charming back, now that she was to marry such a prominent member of the aristocracy. Safely back at the hotel, she'd stared at herself in the mirror, hardly recognising the woman in the exquisite dress. She'd washed her face, put on her cotton PJ's, and had fallen into bed exhausted, sleeping fitfully as she dreamed about an impossibly handsome man, dancing the night away with an impossibly naïve woman, who didn't have a clue what tomorrow held.

She sprang alert at the sound of a knock on the door. Breakfast. Thank goodness! She was starving. She'd been too nervous to eat before the ball, and during it she had been with—

'Xavier?'

She stood back from the door as he strode in. 'Are you all right? If I'd known you were coming…' Smoothing her hair, she tightened the belt on the hotel's towelling robe. He looked as if he hadn't slept for a week. His stubble was thick. His hair was tangled. He had obviously tugged on the first jeans he'd found.

'Everyone wondered where you got to last night,' he said, swinging around to face her.

Was he angry, or was he concerned about her? She couldn't tell. His eyes were ravaged with exhaustion, and his body looked unbearably tense.

'I stayed at the ball until almost midnight.'

'I know when you left,' he said. 'And you left without a word to your host.' He angled his chin, his black eyes firing questions at her.

'My fiancé,' she corrected him in a timely reminder

that they had both made a pledge last night in front of hundreds of witnesses.

'You should have stayed. We have a lot to talk through.'

'Like…?' she prompted, unconsciously twisting the belt on her robe until it started to cut into her hand.

Like how he felt about fathering a child, Xavier thought, when there was no possibility of him developing a talent for empathy, or learning parenting skills in the time available. 'Like your views on becoming a mother,' he said. 'Are you ready for it? You're very young.'

'But I feel as if I've been preparing for this all my life. Surely you must know how I feel? I've dreamed of nothing but having a family of my own for as long as I can remember.'

'But not forming that family like this, surely?'

'If your heir means nothing more to you than securing the island, then, yes, I do have doubts,' she admitted.

'For the child,' he said, nodding agreement. 'So you can only hope I'll feel differently once the child is born?'

'Maybe you never will,' she said, her eyes searching his. 'Or, maybe you're worried that you won't be able to feel any different when you're a father.'

'I'm supposed to experiment on a child? I'm supposed to wait to see how I feel when it's born?' he exclaimed, growing increasingly heated.

'I hope you know that's not what I meant,' Rosie said with real concern. She'd never seen him like this before. 'Both of us knew this would never be easy.'

'Easy?' He huffed an ugly laugh. 'That's an understatement. Are you saying you want to pull out?'

He sounded almost hopeful. 'You should know me better than that,' she said firmly.

'Maybe you want me to slow down—give you more time?' Xavier suggested.

'What difference would waiting make?'

He seemed to be the one needing reassurance, and so she admitted quietly, 'My only concern is for the baby.' She couldn't help but smile. Her heart was full to overflowing at the thought of a child. 'A child needs security and a proper home—'

Xavier cut her off with an impatient gesture. 'A Del Rio child will have everything it needs. And the ring?' he prompted, moving on from one subject to the next as if they held equal importance. He looked for it on her hand.

'Here—' The diamond had swung around again. She righted it, and put out her hand so he could see it. 'Take it and put it away somewhere safe. Return it to the jeweller, if you can. It's served its purpose.' She tried to pull the ring off her finger, but the band was so tight she couldn't get it over her knuckle.

'Leave it where it is,' he said. 'There's no going back. You made a promise.'

'And I will keep that promise, with or without this ring.'

Leaving him, she went to the bathroom to find some shampoo to ease the ring off her finger.

'Here,' she said, going back into the room and holding it out to him.

'You're sure about this?' he said, hesitating before taking it back.

'I'm absolutely certain.' What purpose would a flashy ring serve on the island? She wouldn't wear anything that might put distance between her and the people she cared about.

As he took the ring their hands touched, and she felt

the same heat and the same longing she always felt when he was close. Her gaze flew to his, and, of course, he was watching her. His grip on her hand slowly moved to her wrist, and from there to her sensitive upper arm, until he was bringing her close and dipping his head and kissing her, and she was clinging to him, with need and want, and tears were stinging the backs of her eyes.

This was insane. She was asking to be hurt.

'I haven't slept all night, thanks to you,' he growled.

'You must have a guilty conscience,' she said, burying her growing feelings for him beneath another joke. 'I slept like a baby.'

'Liar,' he murmured against her kiss-bruised mouth. He caged her against the wall with one hand planted above her head and his other caressing her cheek. 'I know this isn't easy for you—'

'But it's the best—the only solution,' she insisted, trying to convince herself. She'd come up with the solution out of sheer desperation, and now it was up to her to shut her mind to the hurt waiting in the wings.

'I've never made allowances for another person's feelings before,' Xavier admitted, his dark stare blazing into hers. 'Maybe I'm clumsy at it.'

'You're terrible at it,' she assured him, curving a smile. 'But that's only because you've never allowed yourself to care for anyone.'

'Are you calling me a coward?' he challenged softly.

'Where feelings are concerned? Yes. I am.'

'You have the same problem,' he argued. 'You've never risked your heart.'

'Which is why I understand you.' She met the challenge in his eyes with a level stare.

'Do you understand me?' Xavier queried. He looped his arms around her waist and stared down at her. 'If you do, you must know that the ring was a showstopper, designed for that purpose. I asked for something striking and I got it.'

'You didn't go to a store, then?'

He frowned. 'I commissioned it from the royal jewellers, of course.'

'Of course you did.' She began to laugh.

'What's so funny?' he queried, but warmth was beginning to glow in his eyes.

'You,' she said. 'You're funny.'

He stared at her for a moment, and then brushed a gentle kiss across her lips. He always made her heart ache for so much more and that was dangerous. Understanding what made someone tick was the first step to growing close.

'I always knew billionaires didn't shop on the High Street like everyone else,' she said, trying to avoid the risk to her heart with some humour.

CHAPTER THIRTEEN

'I'M SORRY YOU don't like the ring, but, as ours was never supposed to be a genuine engagement, I thought it didn't matter.'

He was right, but each of his words was like a stab to her heart. 'Even if ours had been a real engagement, I don't need jewellery like that,' she said. 'I'd have no use for it,' she added with a shrug. 'I'm just as happy threading daisies for a crown.'

'You can't make a ring out of daisies,' Xavier pointed out.

'A piece of string, then.' She laughed. 'But, please, no more diamonds the size of duck eggs. Okay?'

'The ring was just a prop for the drama we're engaged in,' Xavier said, shrugging it off. 'It had to make an impact, and look convincing in print, and I think it did that.'

'My piece of string would have caused more of a stir,' Rosie argued, slanting one of her grins at him.

'And been far more you,' Xavier agreed, his dark eyes dancing with laughter. 'But that wasn't what last night was about,' he said, turning serious. 'It was about convincing everyone that this is real, so you get the credibility you want, and I get the one thing money can't buy.'

A child. Xavier's heir.

'But now I'm afraid I've got some bad news for you.'

Her heart lurched with dread.

'I'm going away on business for a few days.'

'Is that all?' Her relief was obvious. 'That's good news for me, surely?' she teased, determined to keep things light between them. 'So, what have you come here for? To get the ring and make sure I don't bolt while you're away?' She could see she had hit the mark from the expression in his eyes. 'Don't worry. I'll be here when you get back, and I'll be at your side for the wedding. We will be married, and we will see this through.'

'And I promise you won't have anything to worry about.'

She wanted to laugh hysterically at that comment.

'Everything's in hand,' Xavier assured her. 'Our wedding will be held in the cathedral, with a reception at my mansion afterwards. Transport has been organised, so all you have to do is put on the dress and turn up.'

'Right.' She nodded her head as if she were accepting directions to a café in town, and had to remind herself that theirs was a marriage of convenience, and that that was how such things played out. Theirs was not a meeting of two hearts.

She might have thought up this idea, but she couldn't help wishing their wedding day could be something more than this meticulously planned arrangement.

'It will be a grand affair,' Xavier told her without apology.

Fabulously lavish, she translated.

'I hope you're all right with that?'

And if she wasn't?

'I'm fine with that,' she lied.

'No expense will be spared. I'll make it a day for you to remember.'

Was that a promise or a threat? She had no doubt their wedding would be a spectacularly extravagant day. Without intimacy. Without meaning. Without love.

'You will stay on at the hotel,' Xavier went on, as if she had any choice. 'The designer will return for a last fitting of the dress, while make-up artists and hairdressers will attend you on the day. It will be easier for you to stay here than to go back to the island. Don't look so worried. I guarantee I'll be back for the wedding.'

'It would be a half-hearted affair without you,' she joked weakly.

'Does nothing get you down, Rosie Clifton?'

Plenty. The lack of love in their arrangement got her down. She had never expected any, and so she couldn't admit to being disappointed in that direction. Her concern for a child not yet born got her down even more. She had done what she had thought was for the best, and was now left with the growing suspicion that she'd only made things worse. Was this what Doña Anna had intended?

'If anything gets me down, I'll bounce back up again,' she said in an attempt to convince herself as much as Xavier. Exactly how she was going to do that, she didn't have a clue.

'This is a difficult situation for both of us,' Xavier remarked. 'Doña Anna was always tricky to handle, but her swan song takes some beating. And you definitely don't want the ring? You can keep it if you want to,' he offered.

'I definitely don't want it,' Rosie confirmed with a wry smile. 'Honestly, it's absolutely unnecessary.'

Something like admiration crossed Xavier's face,

and then he stowed the ring away in the back pocket of his jeans as if it were a penny sweet. 'What are you thinking about now?' he prompted with interest when she frowned and chewed her lip.

'I was thinking back to the orphanage,' she admitted.

'Look forward instead,' Xavier advised.

Rosie had been remembering when she used to sit on a scraggy patch of grass with her chin on her knees, dreaming about her wedding day. The day would be all misty white, and she would be dressed in a billowing gown. There would be crowds of guests and loads of flowers, and a fabulously handsome husband would be waiting to take her away from the colourless institution.

'I was just dreaming about happily-ever-after,' she admitted recklessly. 'I know it won't come to that for us, because ours is an arrangement, but maybe it won't be all bad?'

'I hope not,' he said with feeling. 'And dreams are free, Rosie Clifton, so you can dream all you like.'

In less than a week her dream would be dust.

'Your life has changed now,' Xavier told her, 'so no more talk of the orphanage.'

She still felt as if she were on the outside looking in.

'Rosie?' Xavier prompted, seeing her abstraction. 'I think we should lay this ghost once and for all,' he said in a voice she couldn't ignore. 'I want you to tell me about your worst time in the orphanage.'

'Do you really want to know?'

'I really do,' he said.

She wouldn't tell him about her wedding day fantasy. He'd think her soft. 'Christmas was the worst time,' she said after a moment's thought.

'Why?' He frowned.

'Because well-intentioned people arrived with gifts,

and that gave us children a tantalising glimpse of the outside world.'

'But surely you'd rather have those people come to visit at Christmas than not?'

'Of course, and I don't mean to sound ungrateful.' But she had felt like an animal in the zoo, to be cooed over, petted and fed a titbit before the visitors went away again. She had always imagined the visitors returning to their warm and cosy homes to open their presents beneath a massive Christmas tree, before stuffing themselves with food until they couldn't stand up. But what had given her the biggest pang of all was the thought of them sharing the happiness of a family united over the holiday season. How she'd envied that, until she'd found the same warmth and welcome waiting for her on the island. 'I'm frightened our wedding's going to be like that,' she admitted.

'Like what?' Xavier pulled back his head with surprise. 'What's wrong with Christmas?'

'Absolutely nothing. I'm just afraid that I'll be put on show at our wedding, and then whisked away to be impregnated with the Del Rio heir.'

'For goodness' sake,' Xavier exclaimed. 'What a thing to say. And now you're shivering.' He drew her close. 'I didn't realise you were so upset about it. Why didn't you say?'

'I'm dreading it,' she admitted.

'The impregnation, or the wedding?'

His delivery was so deadpan she couldn't help but laugh.

'That's better,' Xavier said softly.

Rosie's laugh sounded brittle to him. It made him want to take her in his arms and reassure her, and only his desire to keep her safe from him was stopping him.

'What has my aunt done?' he murmured, speaking his thoughts out loud.

'Brought us together to torment us, I think,' Rosie observed in her usual down-to-earth way. 'And for better or for worse, this time.'

'My thoughts exactly,' he agreed. Bringing her into his arms, he gave her a hug. What harm could one hug do? 'Whatever this is or isn't between us,' he said, pulling his head back to stare at her, 'I promise I'll make it easy for you. You don't have anything to be frightened of—in bed, or out of it. And as for the rest, you'll have Margaret's support all the way. Better?' he murmured when she seemed to relax.

Worse. Far, far worse. She wanted the fantasy she'd dreamed of so much it hurt. She didn't need Xavier's money, or his name, but she did need this warm, caring man, the man who lay deep beneath the armour Xavier had built so successfully around his heart.

Seducing Rosie would be all too easy. She had a touching eagerness to experience everything life had to offer. She had shocked him disappearing at midnight without warning, but her unpredictability was one of the qualities he liked best about her. Yes, it annoyed the hell out of him, but doormats bored him, and gold-diggers were ten a penny. He doubted anyone could cage this wild bird. The thought that anyone might try to do so enraged him. No one would take away Rosie Clifton's freedom, if he had anything to say about it, not even him.

'You look grim,' she said, pulling back to stare at him.

'Do I?' He shrugged. He should be smiling at the thought that Rosie had proved he had some small shred of humanity left. She had made him care what happened to her, when he'd thought he was incapable of feeling, and she'd made him care for the island all over again.

'I hope you're not looking grim because you're thinking about our wedding,' she said.

He had been thinking about their wedding, but not in the way Rosie imagined. They would marry, and he hoped an heir would follow, but instead of him breaking it off then, he would set her free as she deserved, and with her bright face right in front of him he was suddenly dreading the thought of doing that. 'I've got a plane to catch,' he said, reluctantly easing away from her. 'So I'll see you at the altar—'

'With a modest ring, I hope,' she teased.

They shared a smile. His was cynical, hers was guileless. 'I'll see what I can do,' he promised.

'Safe journey,' she called out as he made for the door.

He turned around. She was still smiling, still employing the eternal optimism that had kept her upbeat throughout her years in the orphanage. He hoped it would continue to help her now.

Rosie's wedding day dawned as every bride hoped it would, with sunshine and birdsong outside the window.

But every bride hoped for company to share her happy day, and she didn't expect to face the start of that day alone in her hotel room.

She'd always been alone, and she'd always got through, Rosie reassured herself. Margaret had been with her for most of the week and Margaret couldn't be expected to be around 24/7. She would have her own preparations to make. Margaret was a guest of honour at the ceremony; the ceremony the press was calling the wedding of the year.

This wasn't a marriage in the real sense, Rosie told herself firmly as she jumped out of bed, so she had nothing to worry about.

Their wedding night would be real enough.

Yes, well, she'd handle that too. She didn't have time to think about it now. She had other things to do—a shower to take, and her courage to buckle on, along with the blue garter the designer had insisted she must wear high up on her thigh under her dress…where only Rosie's husband would see it.

What did the woman imagine? That theirs was a love match?

Why wouldn't she, when the whole world thought that was exactly what it was?

Pausing on her way to take a shower, she trailed her fingertips reverently across the exquisite Swiss lace skirt of her gown. Her wedding dress was everything a fantasy wedding dress should be. An entire workroom had spent the limited time available working through the night to make sure it was ready in time, and Rosie couldn't have loved it more. She had promised herself that at least for the few short hours of the ceremony, she would believe in the dream. It wouldn't hurt anyone if she did so.

Her heart began to flutter as she thought about Xavier, and what he would be doing now. She was missing him. She hadn't seen him since he went away, and, however much of a charade this was, she was certain they were drawing closer. If she teased him he took it well, instead of standing on his dignity. She only wished they could both unwind the past and start over, with no hang-ups standing in their way, but she suspected no one entered a marriage completely clean in that sense.

She turned at a knock on the door. Breakfast. She raced to open the door to her suite, not wanting to keep the server waiting.

'Margaret!' She'd never been more relieved to see anyone in her life.

'I thought I should pop in.' Margaret darted a quick glance around the room. 'I'm not intruding, am I?'

'Not at all—I'm alone. Please come in! It's good of you to spare the time when I know you must be busy.'

'Nonsense,' Margaret declared. 'Who's busier than the bride? All I need to do is to put on a dab of lipstick and a suit that isn't tweed, and I'm done. I was wondering if you'd got something old to wear,' Margaret continued on as she shrugged off her sensible mac and cast it aside on a chair. 'You know the old saying, Something old, something new, something borrowed, something blue— Ah, I see you have that.' Margaret's shrewd eyes twinkled as she surveyed the dress and the garter hanging around the neck of the padded hanger. 'The dress is new, the garter is blue, and I've brought my tiny beaded reticule for you to *borrow* for the reception, and I've brought something that belonged to my mother for you—a small gift from me to wish you well. They can be your something old,' she said.

'I can't possibly accept a gift like this,' Rosie breathed as Margaret showed her the small pearl stud earrings. They were the perfect finishing touch for the dress, but she was overwhelmed by the gift, by the thought, and by the kindness behind it.

'Of course you can accept them,' Margaret insisted with a warm smile as she closed Rosie's hand around her present. 'Now, come on,' she chivvied. 'We don't want to be anything more than fashionably late. We'll have breakfast together, and then I'll help you to dress.'

* * *

The moment Rosie saw the cathedral with its tall spires and intricate carvings she made a promise to make her vows sincerely. Whatever her situation, she would show respect for the church, and for everyone who had entered the same portals with their hearts full of emotion. As she stepped out of the limousine she reminded herself that she'd always been resilient. She would go through with this, and she would make it work. Margaret was waiting to organise the billowing silk chiffon train, with its liberal scattering of diamanté and seed pearls. The dress was so beautiful that the assembled onlookers gasped when they caught their first sight of it.

Lifting her chin, Rosie mounted the steps slowly and alone. She had explained to Margaret that she wanted to do this, as this was her journey, and her decision, and she was determined that she wouldn't fail in any part of it. Margaret didn't know the whole story; she'd never asked, but she respected Rosie's decision. Having given the organist the prearranged signal when the bride arrived, Margaret followed Rosie into the church.

As the crashing chords of the organ rang out, the voices of the choir soared in a triumphal anthem. *Was all this for her?* For a split second, Rosie couldn't move. Her feet simply refused to obey her brain's instructions, and her throat was so very tight, she doubted she'd be able to say her vows. The cathedral was packed. There didn't seem to be a single free seat. The scent of incense was so heavy she could hardly breathe. She looked for Xavier, but it was like looking down the wrong end of a telescope, and she had a legion of curious guests to walk through before she could reach his side. Then he turned and his dark stare blazed into hers. An unbreakable bond seemed to connect them, drawing her towards him, and now she noticed the roses: Arctic roses, the same roses that grew so bravely in the garden at the hacienda.

She took the flowers as a signal. Even if they were just coincidence, rather than a loving gesture from Xavier, his promise to make this a happy and special day looked as if it might come true.

The roses kept her on track. She thought of them as emergency lights in the cabin of a jet, leading her towards him, and almost laughed at the thought. She quickly governed her face in front of the dignitaries present. She didn't want them thinking she was nervous, or over-faced by the occasion. It was a relief to reach Xavier's side. He looked stunning, every bit the Spanish Grandee. She responded to him with yearning as she came to a halt at his side. She sucked in a shaking breath as he lifted her veil, and was surprised by the warmth in his eyes. He was thanking her, she told herself sensibly. He was probably relieved she'd turned up.

'And now you may kiss the bride...'

Is it really over?

Up to that point, everything had been dreamy and virginal, white, but now the world shot into vivid colour. Xavier's blood-red sash of office, which he wore over his dark, formal suit, made Rosie remember their wedding night. The voices of the choir soared even higher in celebration as Xavier dipped his head to chastely kiss her on both cheeks. She closed her eyes, but all she could think about was what lay ahead of her when they were finally alone. But she smiled when she looked at the wedding ring on her finger.

'Do you like it?' Xavier asked.

'I love it,' she said honestly. 'It's the perfect ring for

me.' It was a plain band, with no stones or ornamentation. If they'd been a proper couple and had gone shopping for rings together, she couldn't have found anything to please her more.

'It's time, Rosie,' Xavier prompted.

She turned with him to face the congregation, and, linking her arm through his, she allowed Xavier to lead her forward to greet the world as his wife.

CHAPTER FOURTEEN

THE RECEPTION SEEMED ENDLESS. Rosie ate little and tried not to think too much, while the hours passed in a haze of good wishes and congratulations. She was only just coming to terms with the yawning gap between an idea and an accomplished fact. Her throat tightened as she gazed at Xavier. His expression was governed for the public and it was impossible to read his thoughts. An encouraging smile from Margaret put her back on track. She was no longer the bemused orphan, revelling in the simple pleasures of freedom on a beautiful island, but a wife and property owner, with huge responsibilities. She had married a Spanish Grandee, who had centuries of tradition behind him, but as well as all her duties she had to be true to herself.

When the Master of Ceremonies indicated that the guests must be silent and Xavier rose to his feet to speak she knew the end of the celebration was in sight. Xavier was as commanding as ever, and she was pleased that he remembered to acknowledge his debt to Doña Anna.

'For bringing me a wife,' he said, turning to look at Rosie. That look sent sparks flying through her. 'And now you must excuse us,' he added when the applause had died down. 'My bride and I are leaving.'

Her stomach flipped when he turned to look at her

again. She only wished she could thrill as she had the first time, but now she was facing the thought of being alone with him, and that meant confronting the greatest demon of all: her fear that sex brought pain, and disaster followed. That was the legend in the orphanage, and she'd seen nothing since then to change her mind.

'We have an appointment with the tide,' Xavier explained genially to their guests. He reached out a hand to help her from her chair. 'And the tide waits for no man,' he added in an intimate murmur, staring deep into her eyes.

'Not even you?' she challenged, demanding a last burst of energy from the spirit that had kept her going throughout the day.

'Not even me,' he confirmed in the same low, husky whisper. 'Please stay for as long as you like,' he added to their guests. 'There will be fireworks at midnight.'

Maybe even before that, Rosie thought dryly, recognising impending hysteria when it came knocking.

Xavier took hold of her hand in a firm grip, flashing awareness through her veins as he led her from the table.

'What about my things?' she said, pulling back. Everything she owned was still at the hotel.

'You can have your things sent on,' he told her. 'And you'll have new things where we're going.'

He'd waited long enough, she guessed, and no more stops would be made along the way.

A helicopter was waiting for them on the lawn outside. Xavier was the pilot.

'Where are we going?' she asked through the mic attached to her headphones when she was safely strapped into the passenger seat beside him.

'It's a surprise.'

Xavier's voice sounded metallic and distant in her ears as they lifted off. They flew over the twinkling lights of the city and headed out to sea. Now there was only blackness surrounding them, and overhead the moon, until she saw the great white ship, looming out of the darkness, impossibly large and impossibly sleek. She'd heard about super-yachts, but had never seen one before.

'Is it yours?' Of course it was his, she thought as Xavier started talking through his mic in preparation for landing. Don Xavier Del Rio's wealth was incalculable, and this was just one more symbol of his power.

As the helicopter sank lower she recognised the sleek black launch on which Xavier had first arrived on Isla Del Rey. It was just one toy amongst many on board this billionaire's ocean-going yacht. 'How big is it?' she asked when he'd ended his call.

'The length of twelve of your London double-decker buses,' he said, settling the helicopter smoothly on its skids.

'Not that big, then,' she teased, hoping to reclaim some of the warmth they'd shared at their wedding reception. For some reason, Xavier seemed all business now—distant and preoccupied.

Switching off the engine, he removed her headphones. When his fingertips brushed her face she wanted him to kiss her, and like a fool closed her eyes. When nothing happened she opened them again to find he'd moved away.

'Wait there,' he said. 'I'll lift you down so you don't trip over your dress. Welcome to my world,' he added dryly.

Would she ever be ready for his world? Rosie wondered as Xavier opened her door and the clean fresh scent of ozone replaced the warm air inside the cabin. She couldn't imagine a time when she would ever get used to this billionaire lifestyle, and had to hide her apprehension when he helped her out, before escorting her down a seemingly endless line of crew waiting to welcome them.

Everyone seemed so happy to see her, and that almost made it worse. She hated deceiving the crew— like the islanders before them—and almost wished their marriage could be what it seemed.

Xavier insisted on carrying her over the threshold into their suite of rooms. The moment he closed the door and set her down in the middle of a huge and very opulent bedroom, she felt small and insignificant, and smothered by huge wealth and privilege.

What on earth had possessed her to think this would work? Rosie agonised for the umpteenth time. She'd have plenty of opportunity to find out. They were quite alone. No one would disturb them here. She was fast discovering how many layers of insulation lay between the super-rich and the rest of the world.

She still grouped herself very firmly with *the rest*, Rosie determined as Xavier loosened the neck of his shirt. Shrugging off his jacket, he tossed it on a chair.

He looked at her properly for the first time since the reception. 'You'd better turn around so I can help you out of that dress.'

Her mouth dried. She'd known this was coming, but still…

She turned and tried to concentrate on the thick rugs beneath her feet, and how beautifully they were woven in the most amazing multitude of jewel colours, but, however hard she tried to distract herself from what was happening, her gaze kept flashing to the crisp white linen sheets on the huge, teak-framed bed. Xavier had brought her straight into the bedroom. No time to lose when it came to making an heir—

'Forgive me,' he said, maybe sensing something of her apprehension. 'Would you like a drink first?'

She swallowed deep. 'Water, please.'

She seized the chance to take in her surroundings when he went to pour a glass from the crystal jug placed ready for him beside the bed. Polished wood and burnished brass provided a suitably classy setting for artefacts from all over the world. Crystal lights illuminated exquisite works of art, paintings that told stories as eloquent as the books they both loved. She glanced at Xavier's back, and thought again how attractive he was. If only there had been more time to get to know him better. Maybe it was all business for him now they were married, and they wouldn't have a proper conversation again. *Outside bed.*

There were several low brass tables, laden with food and drink, suggesting he planned to remain in the bedroom for quite some time. Her pulse went crazy at the thought, while her mouth turned drier than ever.

'Your water,' he said, handing her the glass.

'Thank you.'

She took a great gulp, and when he moved behind her she almost took a bite out of the glass rim. When his warm hands touched her naked back, her body quivered with awareness. The sound of the laces on her gown sliding through silk and snapping free made her start to shiver all over again. She wasn't wearing a bra, as support was built into the dress. Xavier brushed the gown from her shoulders in one smooth move. It pooled on the rug at her feet. He removed her veil and smoothed her hair. Brushing her hair aside, he kissed the nape of her neck until she shivered with arousal, and then he encouraged her to turn around, so she was standing in front of him naked.

'No stockings?' he murmured, his mouth tugging with the humour she had so desperately hoped would return.

'No shoes, either,' she confessed.

'How long have you been barefoot?' He frowned, pretending to be stern.

'Since you met me?' She slanted a rueful smile.

'You were wearing flip-flops when I first met you.' His husky voice was warm with humour. 'So now you're my wife, you're determined to go barefoot?'

'Only because my wedding shoes pinched.'

He laughed, a rumble low in his chest. 'Of course, you took your shoes off,' he said with an accepting shrug. 'You're Rosie.'

'I was a bride with sore feet,' she argued softly, wondering if she dared hope that Xavier was trying to put her at her ease. She wasn't embarrassed standing in front of him naked. She was like an open book, waiting to see what would fill the next chapter. Something about her manner must have touched him, because he took her face very gently in his hands to kiss her as she'd always dreamed her husband would kiss her on her wedding night. It was a gentle and undemanding kiss, and when she responded, softening and sighing, he pushed his fingers through her hair to cradle her scalp, holding her with extreme tenderness, as if she were very precious to him. This was not the fiery passion that had consumed them once before, but the start of a very thorough seduction, she suspected. Xavier could make love to her with nothing more than teasing kisses that made her want so much more. His lips were warm and persuasive, and when his tongue demanded possession of her mouth, she couldn't refuse him anything.

Lifting her into his arms, he carried her to the bed. Laying her down, he stood back and undressed. He was like a statue cast in bronze, deeply tanned, and brutally beautiful. She stared at him in awe.

'Touch me,' he said, joining her on the bed.

When she hesitated he took hold of her hands and guided her fingers across his muscular chest, and on over the ridged muscles of his belly. 'Hold me,' he commanded softly.

Her anxious gaze flew to his face and she shook her head.

'Why not?' he whispered, his stare dark and long.

'Because I've never done anything like this before, and I'll probably get it horribly wrong.'

He smiled. 'What's to get wrong?' Drawing her into his arms, he guided her, and when she gasped, he asked, 'Did I scorch you?'

Only her heart.

'Do I frighten you, Rosie?'

Lifting her head, she stared steadily into his eyes. 'No. You don't frighten me, Xavier.'

He kissed her, and within moments he deepened the kiss. He could soothe and arouse her all at the same time, and explore her body until she was whimpering with need. Lacing her fingers through his hair, she closed her eyes and basked in pleasure.

Nudging one hard-muscled thigh between her legs, he worked some magic with his hands that made her forget her fears. Arching her body towards him, she searched for more contact, more pleasure, and when he cupped her buttocks in his big, strong hands to hold her in place as he pleasured her, cries of need poured from her throat. She needed this—needed him.

'Not enough?' he murmured.

'No,' she exclaimed.

'And now?' he whispered.

She was beyond speech by this time, and could only exhale raggedly and shake her head.

'Enough?' he said as he caught just the tip of his erection inside her.

'No—' The word was torn from her throat.

Pinning her wrists above her head, he brought his face close to ask, 'Do you trust me?'

'Yes... I trust you.'

And so he stroked and dipped and pulled away again, until she was writhing beneath him, helpless with frustration. She needed so much more than he seemed prepared to give her. But then, very slowly, and all the time holding her gaze, he sank deep.

There was a moment, the very briefest of moments, when her body yielded to him and she felt a pinprick of discomfort. It was enough for her to briefly forget the erotic trance into which he'd placed her, but he had expected this, and now he soothed her with tender words and gentle kisses, until all she could think about was him.

Xavier took her slowly and carefully until he was lodged deep inside her, where he rested for a moment, giving her a chance to become used to the sensation. And then he worked his hips until she was clinging to the edge of the precipice with her fingertips. One deep, firm thrust, and she fell, gratefully claiming her release with shocked and greedy cries of pleasure, and when she finally quietened there was only one word on her lips, and that was, 'More.'

Xavier withdrew almost completely before taking her again, and this time he wasn't so gentle, or so considerate and slow. And she loved it even more than the first time.

'More?' he suggested, his mouth tugging in a wicked smile as she groaned rhythmically in time with the subsiding waves of pleasure. He didn't wait for her answer, and plunged deep. She was more than ready for him when he commanded. 'Now!'

'Let me ride you,' she insisted when she was calm enough to speak. 'I want to do more than lie here and be pleasured.'

'You'll find no argument from me,' he agreed. Lifting her into position, he said, 'Take me.'

She needed no encouragement, especially when Xavier thrust his hips towards her to a dependable beat, applying pressure exactly where she needed it.

Throwing her head back, she allowed him to hold her and guide her. She loved the way he liked to watch. She wanted to make it last for as long as she could, but Xavier made that impossible. Taking a firm hold of her hips, he upped both pressure and speed until her mounting cries of excitement became wails of release.

And that release was so fierce for both of them she didn't have the strength to do more than collapse exhausted onto his chest when it was done. And even then the pleasure continued to pulse through her, until finally she drew a deep, contented breath and fell asleep.

CHAPTER FIFTEEN

SHE WOKE TO find Xavier making love to her. He was behind her, moving slowly, but steadily, rhythmically, lazily thrusting, so that her pleasure level on waking was exquisitely extreme. Leaning forward, she raised her hips, making herself even more available for him. She knew he liked to watch. Every action has a reaction, she thought, smiling to herself as he groaned with pleasure and upped the pace. He couldn't wait and neither could she, and very soon both of them were driven by a fierce hunger that could only have one ending.

'You're insatiable,' he murmured with approval when her cries of pleasure had finally died down.

'And you are very good at what you do,' Rosie admitted, groaning with satisfaction as she rested back.

Xavier raised himself on one elbow to stare down at her. Dawn was peeping through the drapes, illuminating his face. He looked more disreputable than ever. Morning was kind to him. His wild hair was dishevelled, while his stubble was thicker, sharper, blacker, and, best of all, he was smiling lazily at her with that rare smile that meant so much to her. She leaned forward to plant a kiss on his lips.

Xavier's answer to that was to turn her beneath him. He had no need to prepare her. She was ready and groaned with contentment when he sank deep. He made no pretence of drawing things out this time, and they moved urgently towards the longed-for goal. When his warmth flooded her, she felt a great, almost primal sense of completion. She had never been so happy in all her life. Resting back on the pillows, she turned her wedding ring round and round, making it glitter in the growing light.

'I think you like that ring,' Xavier commented huskily.

'I love it,' Rosie admitted. The simple gold band seemed to represent everything that was right about them. The circle was complete—almost. It would be complete when they went back to the island and started to work there together.

She turned with surprise as Xavier swung off the bed. Reaching out, she tried to catch hold of him, but he eluded her. 'I have to work,' he said. 'Nothing's changed where that's concerned.'

'What happened to the time you could always take off?' she argued.

'I can't take time off today,' he said, seeming preoccupied. 'There's plenty for you to do on board,' he added, as if she were a child in need of entertainment.

Was that it? He'd made efforts to impregnate her, not once, but many times. Did he consider the job done now? A wave of cold dread washed over her. She couldn't pretend she wasn't bewildered as she watched him stroll naked across the room, and she wasn't sure how to respond.

'Take a shower and then a swim, if you like,' he added. 'There are two pools, a cinema, and a gym— or a reading room, if you prefer. I'll see you later—'

'Later?' She sat bolt upright in the bed. 'When, later? Will I see you at lunch?'

'I thought the idea was that we make no demands on each other,' Xavier commented as he closed the door on his dressing room.

True. But that didn't make it any easier to accept.

It was only later when she came out of the shower and heard the helicopter taking off, she realised that Xavier wasn't just leaving her to go to his study, or to some other room on the vessel, he was actually taking a trip. She had no idea how long he'd be gone. He hadn't given her an agenda. And this was supposed to be their honeymoon—

Get over it, Rosie told herself impatiently as she towelled down after her shower. She hadn't married a pipe-and-slippers man, and this wasn't one of her fantasies that she could tailor to suit herself. She had to accept every facet of Xavier's complicated life. But that didn't mean she had to sit around on her backside, waiting to see what he might do next. She had a super-yacht to explore, and plans of her own to make, now that she had the means to do so.

But this time the instruction from her can-do spirit had a very hollow ring to it.

Gathering up her wedding dress from the floor, she spread it out carefully on the sofa. Her gaze lingered on the beautiful workmanship. Hours of work had gone into the exquisite dress. *And for what?*

Stop that! She might be naïve in some things, but she had never been pathetic. She had to get used to the idea of being Xavier's convenient wife.

Her biggest problem now was what to wear. There were so many clothes in her dressing room. The rails were packed and the drawers were full. There was every accessory money could buy, and swimwear better suited to a supermodel. She chose one of the plainer costumes, and a sundress to wear over it. She was exploring the inside of a drawer when she came across a beautiful enamelled casket, decorated in shades of turquoise, jade green and violet, and gasped when she opened it to find a treasure trove of jewels. Rubies glistened against her skin like drops of blood, while sapphires sparkled as she held them up to the light. Emeralds flared and opals flashed fire, but for some reason they made her feel lonelier than ever. She didn't need all this extravagance, and would have traded every jewel in the world to have breakfast with her husband on this, the first morning of their married life.

Silence surrounded her as she ran the chains and bracelets through her fingers. The jewels were fabulous, but they couldn't satisfy the practical woman she had become. Like the clothes and all the facilities on board, she felt, they were just toys to keep her happy. She looked at her simple wedding ring again, and turned it around her finger, knowing she would always love that best of all.

But she wasn't going to sit around feeling sorry for herself while Xavier was away. A sun hat and bare feet later, and she was ready to explore the ship.

He wasn't flying to the mainland on business as Rosie probably thought. Xavier was flying to the coast, and from there, out to the island. She was right in saying he didn't need to work on any particular day. His worldwide business was a well-oiled machine that allowed him to take time off whenever it suited him. What suited him now was space from Rosie. She'd really thrown him with the way she'd made him feel. He had shocked himself by wondering, when she'd stood beside him at the altar, if he loved her. It sure as hell wasn't indigestion digging away at his heart, then or now.

He landed the helicopter on the beach and then went for a walk, and after that a swim. He'd forgotten how good it felt to be on the island, free from the concerns of the outside world. It was therapeutic just sitting on the rocks, gazing out to sea. He rarely slowed down his pace of life these days, but the island demanded that he must.

He was beginning to see Isla Del Rey as Rosie must have seen it on her first day here, though he guessed that after the orphanage her experience must have been magnified tenfold. The island was startlingly beautiful; something else he'd forgotten over the years. There were deep ravines and rushing rivers, placid lakes and thick forest. Yes, the old house and grounds were badly run-down, but it was definitely worth saving. Old friends from the island, whom he hadn't seen for years, had opened his eyes at the wedding, clapping him on the back and complimenting him on his choice of bride. They told him that they had faith in Señorita Clifton, or Doña Rosa, as they had taken to calling Rosie on the island.

He stood and turned his face to the sun. The island's lush bounty was boundless. It was the perfect place to bring up a child. He had closed his mind to that possibility because of his own experience with parents who didn't want him. He accepted now that that had left a bitter mark, but not an indelible mark, thanks to Rosie. He could see the island afresh because of her. Even the ocean was a contradiction that reminded him of her. The water was a clear, tranquil blue today, but it could so quickly turn to furious grey—

He spun around as one of the elders of the island called to him.

'Va a comer con nosotros, Xavier?'

Would he care to eat with the family? He certainly would. It would be a great honour, he called back, pleased to think they still cared about him.

He hadn't wanted to come back to Isla Del Rey, but he had. He hadn't wanted to care for the island, but he did. He hadn't wanted to care for anyone, because his experience of love had been so negative, but he cared for Rosie. He smiled as he thought about her as he fell into step with his elderly host. He didn't just care for Rosie Clifton—what was the point in denying it any longer? He loved her.

Time passed quickly on the balcony of his old friend's family home. Several generations had insisted on joining them, and they had laid out a feast to thank Xavier for inviting them to his wedding. He could hardly refuse their hospitality, and stayed until the screeching seagulls overhead in search of their supper reminded him that Rosie was still waiting for him on the ship.

She'd dressed for dinner. She'd never dressed for dinner in her life. She'd had no call to, but on one of her many exploratory missions around the ship she had spotted the stewards laying out a dining table beneath the stars. They were unfolding the finest white linen and adding a last polish to gleaming silver cutlery. Candles glowed in tall silver sconces, while beautiful flower arrangements had materialised seemingly out of nowhere, so she could hardly rock up in her jeans. The dress she had chosen from the vast selection in her dressing room was really beautiful. Made of soft ivory chiffon, it finished around knee length and had a nipped-in waist with quite a low neck. But the style was lovely, rather than obvious, and she had left her hair loose, as Xavier preferred it. She was still barefoot. He liked that too. She'd had a good day at sea, but had missed him, and however many times she told herself that she understood why he'd had to go, she really didn't, though something told her they would both have to compromise in this most unusual marriage.

She sat down to dinner. The stewards acknowledged her with polite smiles.

One asked what she would like to drink, and then stood back in the shadows as another poured her a glass of water. She couldn't think what else to say. She didn't want to start eating in case Xavier arrived, so she had to ignore her stomach's growls of complaint.

As time wore on and the sky grew inky black, she began to feel embarrassed. The stewards were still standing motionless, waiting for their next instruction. She was a new bride, barely one day married. They must be wondering if Xavier had had enough of her already. He probably had, Rosie thought, her stomach clenching with concern. She was young, broke, and unsophisticated. She brought nothing but her passion to the marriage. Though Xavier hadn't seemed disappointed last night, she reassured herself. He'd been so caring and sexy.

She tapped her fingers on the table as more doubts set in. The candles were slowly burning down as she strained her ears for signs of the helicopter returning, and she almost jumped out of her skin when she heard the buzz of rotor blades approaching. Now she was angry with herself for being so self-obsessed. What if Xavier had had a problem, and that was why he was late?

The stewards rushed to move her chair as she bolted from the table.

'I'll be back,' she called out happily. One good thing that had resulted from her in-depth study of the vessel was that she could find her way to the helipad blind-folded.

He landed and saw Rosie at once. He wanted her with a madness that consumed him. He wanted to tell her about the things he'd been planning on his way back. 'You waited for me,' he said, embracing her.

'Xavier, I—'

Taking hold of her arm, he led her straight across the deck and down to their stateroom.

'Xavier—'

He slammed the door behind them. Pressing her back with the weight of his body, he silenced her with a hungry kiss.

'Xavier, you can't—'

'What can't I do?' he demanded, brushing the wisp of a dress from her shoulders. There was no need to rip it, as it fell off at a touch. Her skin felt so smooth and warm beneath his hands. The memory of her body was still so fresh in his mind. She was so beautiful and desirable, and he was so painfully erect.

'Xavier!'

Something in her tone stopped him dead.

'What's wrong with you?' she demanded in a tight, angry voice. 'You left me alone all day, and now this? You have to work. I get it. I understand that your work might take longer than you thought, but couldn't you have let me know you were safe? I was worried about you.' She searched his face with frustration. 'You could have contacted the ship,' she insisted. 'I'm not angry for myself, but your stewards have been hanging around all night, waiting for you.' When he didn't answer she got angry. 'Don't you care for anyone but yourself? This is the first full day of our honeymoon—'

On top of his frustration, tension, and his monumental decision to turn both his plans and his life upside down, Rosie's accusations were the straw that broke the camel's back. 'Ours is an arrangement—*an arrangement*!' he roared. 'I don't have to explain my every move to you.'

And now she had tears in her eyes, and he wasn't proud of that. 'I'm sorry.' He had never asked another human being to forgive him in his life. There had never been any call for him to do so, and now he'd upset the one person he should protect to his last breath.

Rosie was in no mood to forgive him. She was firing on all cylinders, chin raised, eyes blazing, 'An arrangement to suit you,' she accused him, 'because a man as unfeeling as you could never get an heir any other way.'

She hated saying words like that. The expression in Xavier's eyes wounded her as much as she'd wounded him, but she had to get through to him somehow. Leaving her so soon after their passionate wedding night, with no proper explanation, had cut her to the bone. 'Was that just part of our bargain when you made love to me last night?' she asked him. 'You did make love to me. Please tell me I'm not mistaken about that.' She hated the note of desperation in her voice. 'So, what am I to think?' she demanded when Xavier said nothing. 'You love having sex with me, and you love having me around for the challenge and the banter, but you'll never be able to love me in the way I need to be loved.'

'What way is that, Rosie?' he asked quietly.

She sucked in a breath as she searched her mind for the right words to express her feelings. 'I want to be loved fiercely, wildly, passionately—I don't even know,' she admitted, raking her hair with frustration.

'Do you think I'm so different from you?' Xavier demanded. 'Do I have different needs? Are you asking me to believe you entered into our agreement for anything less than one hundred per cent of the island? Or was it my finer qualities that tipped the balance for you? Perhaps the truth is, you would stop at nothing to get your share increased—and enjoy my lifestyle while you're at it?'

'That's not fair,' she exclaimed.

'So I'm not entitled to have the same doubts as you? You dream because it's safe—

'That's right, leave!' he stormed as she turned for the door.

Like his mother before her, Rosie thought, halting abruptly. 'I'm not going anywhere,' she said. 'I don't run away from anything. I never have. You have to bloom where you're planted, I was told at the orphanage, and that's what I'm going to do here.'

Her heart ached for both of them. Xavier was right in saying that neither of them was prepared to risk expressing their feelings, but there was one thing she had to get straight. 'I've never been interested in your money, or your lifestyle. From what I've seen, you've got everything and nothing. It doesn't matter if you drink out of crystal glasses on your super-yacht, or a plastic beaker at the orphanage. Life is empty, if you shun love and go through it alone.'

'You're an expert on feelings now?' he said, with a lift of his brow.

'I only know what I feel in here.' She touched her chest. 'And you can say what you like about Doña Anna, but I think she threw us together in one last attempt to jolt both of us onto a better track.'

'My aunt didn't have a romantic bone in her body.'

'That shows how little you knew her.'

'Are you saying you knew her better than me?' Xavier demanded with disbelief.

'I did,' she said bluntly. 'Did you never wonder why Doña Anna lived alone?'

'I was her nephew, not her agony aunt. Of course I didn't know.'

'Did it never occur to you that your aunt had a lot of love to give, or did you just see her as a grouchy old lady who brought you up because there was no one else who was prepared to step up and do that?'

'Maybe,' Xavier admitted, frowning. 'But how does that change anything?'

'Did you know that her fiancé was killed just before they were due to be married, or that he was the love of her life?'

'I didn't know.' And he was shocked to learn that his aunt had been left alone and lonely, until Rosie had arrived on the island.

'We grew close when I read to your aunt in the library—that was when she told me that books were her escape. She went on to explain why she felt the need to escape.'

'Dios,' Xavier murmured beneath his breath. 'I had no idea.'

'And no reason why you should. I doubt Doña Anna would have confided in her nephew, even if you had never left her side.'

'So, what are you saying?'

'She could only put the pieces into play. She couldn't direct us from the grave.'

'Couldn't she?' He huffed a humourless laugh. 'This seems typical of her mischief to me.'

'Was she ever malicious, as far as you know?'

'Never,' he admitted. 'Not in all the time I knew her.'

'Then why would she do this if she hadn't wanted us to be together?'

And now she'd said too much. Or maybe not...

Rosie's heart lifted as Xavier pulled away from the wall, but then it clenched with despair as he turned without another word and left the room.

CHAPTER SIXTEEN

HE STOOD ON the deck, staring out to sea, wondering where they'd be now if their life experiences had been different. His best guess was that his aunt and Rosie would have found each other somehow, and that Rosie would be on the island right now, doing everything she could to help the islanders even with zero funds and only her eternal optimism driving her forward.

He certainly wouldn't have come up with the plan that he had. If his childhood had been different, he would have visited the island regularly and felt comfortable there, instead of harking back to the bitter memories of childhood disappointment. Rosie had made him confront things he hadn't thought about for years, which was ironic when her childhood made his seem idyllic by comparison, and the wounds he lived with nothing more than an indulgence.

He had to put the past to good purpose now, as she had, and use those lessons to move forward. She was right in saying that wealth meant nothing unless it could do some good, and life was certainly diminished without someone to share it with.

He hadn't intended to make her unhappy. He hadn't even realised how unhappy she was, but now he felt her pain as keenly as his own. All that mattered to him, he had discovered, was Rosie's happiness. His ring was on her finger, and Rosie was in his bed, but what would it take to win her heart?

Doubt was still hammering down on her the next morning. She'd slept alone. Xavier hadn't been near their stateroom, which left her with the growing suspicion that she had damaged something precious, like a green shoot she'd carelessly trodden down beneath the heel of her shoe. As she stood beneath the shower, she felt the loss of him keenly. She wanted the comfort of his arms, the thrill of his body, and the caring individual she'd increasingly seen emerge in him. The one thing she had never once considered was giving up—not on her relationship with Xavier, and not on her commitment to the island. So it was time to swallow her pride, get dressed, and go to find him.

Don Xavier was in his study, one of the stewards told her.

'Rosie.' Xavier stood as she opened the door. 'Please. Come in…'

She felt his warmth reaching out to her. He was standing behind the desk at the far end of the room. Even in shadow, he was the most compelling man she'd *ever* met, Rosie concluded wistfully.

'Is something wrong?' he asked.

'Just that I wish I knew you better,' she admitted. 'I wish I knew what made you tick.'

'That's easy,' he said.

'Is it?' She stood by the door, knowing that if she came any closer her feelings would overwhelm her.

'We're the same, you and I,' he said.

She shook her head ruefully. 'I don't think so. You're frightened of feeling.'

'Whereas you have no difficulty in expressing yourself,' he countered with a wry look.

She knew one thing for certain. She would rather spend the rest of her life getting over Xavier than another night on the ship without him. She wanted to be close to him, to be one with him in every way there was.

'You came here to say something?' he prompted.

Yes, and the air was so still, it seemed as if the whole world were listening in. She didn't know where to begin. Xavier was impossible to know, and impossible to live without.

'Rosie?' he prompted.

'I want to understand you,' she said.

'Then take a look in the mirror,' he suggested.

She frowned. 'We couldn't be more different, you and I. Parental love and family solidarity might seem like Shangri-La to me, but I'm not ready to give up on my dreams yet.'

'What do you mean?' His voice was soft, his stare intent. 'Are you saying I'm not capable of loving a child?'

'Are you?'

Coming around the desk, he stood in front of her. 'We should give it a chance—give us a chance. You're as bad as me. You shut out feelings too, and if they creep up on you you tell yourself it's another of your fantasies, and that makes them easier to deal with.'

'Maybe,' she accepted. 'But how can we give this a chance? How can it work between us? You and your six-star hotels, and your lavish marinas, and me with my vegetable plots?'

Xavier's face warmed. 'You don't know my plans.'

'Then why don't you tell me? We should work together.'

'Do you think that's what my aunt intended all along?'

Hope was a fragile thing, and she wasn't ready to commit fully yet. 'Maybe Doña Anna expected more of me than I can give.'

'No.' Xavier shook his head decisively. 'I don't believe that for a moment. Everyone has doubts. It's what drives us forward. You're stronger than you know, Rosie.'

'So you believe in me?'

'Isn't that obvious?' Cupping her chin, Xavier made her look at him. His eyes were warm and full of everything she needed to see. 'You're the strongest woman I've ever met. Don't let the past bring you down, Rosie. Isn't that what you'd like to tell me? I know you love the island—everyone knows it—but what about something for you? You don't have to give all the time. Sometimes people want to do things for you, and sometimes you have to let them.'

'Forgive me,' she whispered, closing her eyes. 'I know you had a lousy childhood, just as I know what we both owe Doña Anna.'

'Do you trust me, Rosie? On our wedding night you said you did.'

'I did. I do,' she said, staring that trust into Xavier's eyes.

'Tell me what you want—what you really want.'

I want you, she thought. *I want you to love me. I want you to put your arms around me. I want to believe you, if you tell me that you want me to stay. I want to have a child we both love and care for, not a child that's been manufactured just to continue a family line.*

'Say it, Rosie. Don't just think it. Say it out loud.'

He was asking her to risk her heart, and the words

she so desperately wanted to say stalled on her lips. She just couldn't get them out. And then she had a light-bulb moment, and she realised what Xavier was trying to get her to do. They were both locked up on their individual islands, and it was up to each of them to break free.

She began haltingly. Tiny steps towards sharing her feelings, something she'd never done before. 'I want this to be real between us,' she admitted. 'I want to say what I think, instead of hiding my feelings from you all the time—' It was almost a relief, she discovered, this letting go, and as she gained in confidence her words gathered pace. 'I want to tell you how you make me feel, and not have you laugh at me—'

'Laugh at you?' Xavier interrupted, frowning.

'Yes,' Rosie admitted. She was quiet for quite some time, and then she added softly, 'I want to tell you that I love you.'

'Say that again,' Xavier insisted.

'I want to tell you that I love you,' she repeated in a louder, clearer voice.

'And?' he prompted.

'And why am I the only one doing this?' she protested, only half teasing him.

'My turn will come?' he suggested with a smile.

'I want to tell you that I know what you're trying to do, and that I agree that until each of us can free ourselves from the past, neither of us is going anywhere, as individuals, or as a couple, however temporary our marriage might be, or even as joint owners of Isla Del Rey. The past will always hold us back, hold us down— we both have to change, and maybe we've got a long way to go before we can do that. I want us both to speak openly, for good and for bad, and without editing every comment first. I want to share everything with you, but I can't, because I get frightened—'

'You? Frightened?' Xavier's look was disbelieving.

'Frightened you'll think I'm stupid,' Rosie admitted.

'Never.' Slanting his sexy smile, Xavier shook his head. 'You're like a light shining so bright you almost blinded me. And it was definitely a light I didn't want to see. You blinded me with your honesty, and left me questioning what I've been doing with my life. 'So, why don't you ask me about my plans for the island?'

She hardly dared to ask. 'What have you done?'

'We're sailing there now,' he said, 'so you'll see for yourself. The islanders are planning a fiesta in our honour to celebrate our marriage. They want us to have a proper celebration, amongst friends.'

'Tell me about your plans first,' Rosie insisted.

'Okay. I'm going to create a kids' centre on the island in honour of my aunt. She always wanted me to do something useful with my money. At the time I was too busy amassing a fortune to work out what she meant. I was so desperate not to end up like my parents—always with their hands in someone else's pocket—so money meant everything to me then. But this is going to be a non-profit-making scheme. It will be the perfect tribute to a woman I neglected in life, and am determined to honour in death. How do you feel about going in with me on that?'

'Are you serious?' Rosie was stunned. 'I'd love to. What changed your mind?'

'You did,' Xavier admitted. 'When I went back to the island yesterday, I saw everything through your eyes, and then I understood what the island really needed, and what I could bring to it.'

Reaching out, he drew her close. Her face and her

body tingled. Staring into her eyes, he dipped his head and kissed her long and slow. When he pulled back, he said, 'I love you, Rosie. I'd do anything to make you happy. I've loved you from the moment I first saw you on that beach—I just didn't know what those feelings were.'

'You only knew I annoyed the hell out of you?' she suggested, starting to smile.

Xavier laughed. A bolt of sheer happiness lit up his face. 'No one had ever held me at bay before,' he admitted. 'I hadn't felt that angry for years. I hadn't felt anything for years. I was furious at being dragged back to an island that made me remember my childhood and my parents, and all my mixed-up feelings. And then there was the indignity of having to share the island with my aunt's housekeeper. How ridiculous,' he said, embracing her warmly. 'How arrogant I was. My only thought was to drive you away as fast as I could.'

'And now?' she whispered.

'And now I have to keep you by any means possible. What would it take to do that, Rosie? What would it take to make ours a real marriage?'

She looked at him. 'Just love me.'

As they arrived at Isla Del Rey a crowd was waiting for them on the dock. It was entirely different from the formal gathering of dignitaries who had attended their wedding in the cathedral. These were people Rosie knew and loved. Everyone had dressed up for the occasion. It was party night on Isla Del Rey. There was nothing the islanders loved more than a celebration, and they must have pooled their limited resources to give them a welcome like this. She was touched by the effort they'd gone to, and so very happy to be back on the island she loved. This was special, she thought as she walked down the gangplank hand in hand with Xavier.

An even bigger surprise awaited her as Xavier had organised a blessing of their vows. Taking hold of both her hands in his, he searched her eyes. A yearning grew inside him as they stared at each other, and he knew in that moment that his life and everything in it depended on the answer Rosie would give him.

'Are you happy to renew your vows?' Xavier asked.

'Oh, yes,' she said, smiling deep into his eyes.

A happy grin spread across his face.

'Are *you* sure about this?' she asked him discreetly. 'Are you sure you want me to renew our vows with me barefoot in a sundress with a rose in my hair?'

'I've never seen you looking more beautiful, or more Rosie-like.' He squeezed her hand to reassure her as a notary halted in front of them.

'Do you have the ring you spoke of?' the notary asked him.

'I have it,' Xavier confirmed, pulling the piece of string out of his pocket. 'Will this do?'

'Very nicely,' the man agreed with a warm smile for Rosie.

The simple renewal of their wedding vows meant so much to Rosie, it was her dream come true: standing next to the man she loved, the man who had just told her how much he loved her, in front of people who genuinely cared for both of them. If she had ever needed proof that her optimistic take on life was justified, this was it. She only had to look around to see that their happiness was infectious. Even with all the money in the world to spend on a celebration, nothing could be better than this. It was the happiest night of her life.

The party afterwards was the best fun ever. And as they came together for the last dance of the night the islanders formed a circle around them. They weren't looking for sensation or gossip, they just wanted to join in and wish them well. No one on Isla Del Rey was ever afraid to show their feelings and Rosie would never be frightened to do so again.

They spent the night at the hacienda with the windows open so they could hear the night sounds: owls hooting, cicadas chirruping, as they made love in time to the surf.

'I've got another surprise for you,' Xavier murmured.

'What is it?' she demanded, a smile spreading across her face.

'A proper Christmas, just for you and me—a second honeymoon with no distractions.'

'Christmas?' Rosie's eyes fired with wonder as the child inside her got its dream come true at last.

'Big and brazen,' he insisted, 'with too many gifts, and a turkey that's far too big for us. Mince pies, and Yule logs. Crackers and tinsel. Would you like that?'

'I'd love that,' she said and her eyes filled with tears. 'I love you.'

Much, much later, they talked about the children's centre Xavier had planned, and he told her the hacienda would be the perfect headquarters. He explained what he'd like her to do at the children's centre. 'So, I'm to be an assistant to the superintendent of the facility? That sounds very grand.' Rosie frowned. 'Can I still be barefoot, or do I have to wear a suit?'

'You can wear whatever you like.'

'There's just one thing.'

'Yes?'

She braced herself to tell him. 'I might need maternity leave.'

'Might?' Xavier shot her a wry look. 'I'm counting on it.'

'That's not what I…'

'Are you telling me you're pregnant?' He held her at arm's length to stare into her eyes, as if they would tell him the truth. 'How can you be sure? So soon?' he demanded, taut with hope.

Forget his half of the island—forget everything! His head was reeling at the possibility that Rosie was pregnant. Everything exploded into vivid colour. His fears of parenting evaporated. If he was useless, he could learn. He had Doña Anna's example to draw on and Rosie at his side. No one got a manual with their first child, so he was level pegging with everyone else, learning as he went along.

'It's too soon to be sure,' Rosie warned him, seeing the joy on his face. 'I've just got this feeling…'

'I think we'd better get you checked out.'

'Are you pleased?'

Was he pleased? Whatever he had expected to feel when they had first entered into this so-called arrangement was nothing approaching this. He was speechless and drowning in emotion.

'Xavier? Say something—are you all right?'

'I am beyond all right—beyond happy—beyond anything I've ever felt before. Please, let this be true.' He grasped hold of Rosie's hands when no words seem adequate. 'Do you need to sit down?'

'I'm lying down, in case you hadn't noticed.' They laughed with sheer happiness, and hugged each other. 'And I'm pregnant, not sick,' she said when he eventually let her go. 'If I'm right, you'll get the heir you need.'

'Don't!' he exclaimed, frowning. 'Please don't say that. Don't remind me of what an idiot I've been—it's bad for my ego.' She laughed and kissed him again. 'I've got you, Rosie, and that's all I care about. I've got the woman I want, and the only mother I could ever want for my children. You've made me the happiest man in the world. You'll have the best care available.'

'You don't need to tell me that,' Rosie assured him, catching hold of his hand. 'I've got you.'

EPILOGUE

ROSIE RECEIVED CONFIRMATION from the island's doctor that she was pregnant a short time before Christmas. The doctor also confirmed Rosie's suspicion that sometimes a woman just knew these things. There was no medical reason that could account for that feeling of hers. It was in the bones, he said.

Her baby would be born in the late spring, and, with the whole world at his disposal, Xavier had declared that if they were going to celebrate Christmas properly there must be snow, and so he piloted the jet to the land of cuckoo clocks and chocolate. Even the flight over the snow-clad mountains was spectacular, but Xavier's chalet, with its long winding drive, lined by Christmas trees, each one lit with tiny shimmering lights, was magical. The burnished wood construction, with its steeply sloping roof and quaint painted shutters at every window, was the perfect setting for the perfect Christmas, Rosie thought as they drew up outside. Lanterns glowed on either side of the front door, and a Christmas wreath of pine cones and cinnamon sticks, secured with blousy bows of vivid red ribbon, welcomed them as Xavier helped her out of the rugged four-wheeler.

'What's this?' she asked as he pressed a small box into her hands.

'Your first Christmas present.'

She laughed. 'My first?'

'Get used to it, Señora Del Rio. There are twelve days of Christmas, but you'll have to forgive me in this instance for getting ahead of the game, but I had no alternative if we're to get inside the chalet. Don't worry,' he added, 'some of the gifts might be in kind. I don't want to overburden you with luggage,' he explained with a wicked grin.

'So long as it's not that wretched ring,' she warned, shooting a wary glance at the box.

'Why don't you open it and find out?' Xavier suggested.

She did just that, and pulled out a key.

'Welcome home, Señora Del Rio.'

'I don't understand.'

'This is your house. Any time you want to get away from me you can come here—'

'You're giving me a house?' Rosie exclaimed. She couldn't take it in.

'A Swiss chalet,' he said. 'Just the first of many gifts for my beautiful wife.'

He silenced her protests with a kiss, and made her sigh with pleasure as he caressed her cheek. 'You don't play fair,' she complained softly as he nuzzled the very sensitive skin just below her ear, making her shiver with arousal.

'And I don't take no for an answer, either,' he reminded her.

'But you can't give me a house. It's too much.'

'I can and I have,' he argued firmly. 'This is going to be the best Christmas either of us has ever had.'

'It will be. I promise,' Rosie confirmed, determined to do everything she could to make it so.

'Why don't you open your front door, *señora*?'

'I suppose if this is my house I'd better show you around—'

'Why don't we start with the bedrooms?'

'Do you seriously think we'll get that far...?'

The front door opened on a magical scene. A roaring log fire welcomed them inside the beautiful house, and Xavier carried her over the threshold. Floor-to-ceiling windows overlooked the snow-covered mountains, while the décor in rich, warm shades promised that this would be the cosiest of homes in which to spend the holiday season.

'What's in all these boxes?' Rosie asked as she took stock of them.

'A ready-decorated home would be too easy for you, my beautiful, romantic wife,' Xavier told her as he lowered her down and stripped off her warm coat. 'And so I've provided all the ingredients you could possibly need to dream up whatever scheme you want.'

'Christmas decorations,' she exclaimed. 'Can we decorate the chalet together?'

'I wouldn't have it any other way,' Xavier said as he tossed his heavy outer jacket on a chair. 'Shall we make a start?'

'I meant you should help me with the Christmas decorations,' she chastised him as he brought her into his arms.

'We've got all night for that,' he reminded her, brushing her lips with his.

Rosie couldn't have been happier with their cosy nest. They were in their own little world, far away from the glare of public scrutiny. 'You couldn't have chosen anywhere better. I love it. We can be Mr and Mrs Normal here.'

'Correction—I can be Mr Normal,' he argued. He smiled against her mouth as he whispered, 'There's no hope for you...'

Grabbing hold of his arms, she attempted to give him a little shake, but he was rock. Her need soared. 'That rug looks so neglected...'

They cooked Christmas dinner together with the help of a stack of advice from celebrity chefs who had rushed to offer Xavier their congratulations, no doubt in hope of securing franchises at one of his many hotels. They had to be very strict with themselves to make sure the celebratory meal didn't burn in what had quickly turned into a highly charged second honeymoon. When it came to it, they ended up naked, eating off the same plate on the rug in front of the roaring fire.

Rosie was concerned that her Christmas gift for Xavier wasn't enough. He had assured her on numerous occasions that their baby was more than enough for every Christmas going forward. Their child was a blessing, as well as the most wonderful gift, but in practical terms Rosie wanted him to have something to open on Christmas Day. And how could she ever compete with the chocolate-box-perfect Swiss Chalet he had given her? She could only hope that her modest gifts would please him.

'I've got another small gift for you,' Xavier admitted as Rosie brought out a neatly wrapped package.

'See you, and raise you one,' she said, smiling as she lifted out a bulkier package from under the bed.

'This is the perfect Christmas Day,' Xavier said as he ripped the paper off her first gift. 'Rosie...' He stared down with astonishment at the books she'd given him.

'Do you like them?'

'First editions of my favourite author—are you serious? I love them.'

'Margaret helped me—told me which antiquarian bookshop to use. They're for the library on the island,' she explained. 'You don't have these volumes, do you?'

'Do you know how rare these are?'

She had some idea. It was only when Margaret had insisted that Rosie must enjoy some of the money from her inheritance that she had been able to afford them.

'What's this?' she asked as Xavier handed her a package that looked very much like the one she was about to give to him.

'Open it and see,' he said.

He opened his second gift at the same time, only to discover they'd both had the same idea. Rosie's bright red Christmas sweater had a cross-eyed reindeer on the front, while the one she had given Xavier had a smiling Father Christmas with rosy cheeks and a long grey beard.

'Perfect!' they chorused, laughing as they fell back on the pillows.

'But I don't think we need to put them on just yet, do you?' Xavier murmured, reaching for her.

Five years later...

The sugar-sand beach on sunny Isla Del Rey was packed with islanders, visitors, children, and young people of all ages. The hacienda had been completely renovated, remaining true to its original architectural features, and there was a sturdy handrail on the impeccably maintained cliff path.

Xavier held a barbecue on the beach once a year to

host all the suppliers and buyers, who were big supporters of the island's now famous organic vegetable farm. He cooked and the older children from the thriving Doña Anna Adventure Camp helped him out.

This year's beach-feast was the biggest celebration yet, as it marked the opening of the third building for their international centre. Interested parties had arrived on the island from all over the world to pick up tips on the magic that turned troubled youngsters into confident young people.

Xavier would have said that it was the Rosie touch. Her eternal optimism meant that she had never given up on a child yet. In Rosie's opinion, the success of the centre was all Xavier's doing. He had the drive, the vision, and the practical skills, while she was the dreamer who provided the barefoot fun. Of course, one of their secret weapons was Xavier's trusted financial director, Margaret, who, having semi-retired from full-time work, was helping them to run the centre.

'You're not a bad chef,' Rosie commented with a grin as Elijah, the four-year-old at her feet, clamoured for another treat from Daddy's kitchen. Their two-year-old twins, Lily and Grace, were just happy to take everything in, while the bump in her stomach was too busy having a kick-boxing fest all its own to be in a position to ask for something to munch on.

'Happy?' Xavier asked, wiping his muscular forearm across his brow. He could only grant himself the briefest of breaks, but the break had to be long enough to kiss his wife. That was his rule.

'What do you think?' Rosie teased.

'I think I love you, Señora Del Rio,' Xavier whispered, staring deep into Rosie's amethyst eyes.

'That's a relief,' she teased softly. Holding Xavier's dark, sexy stare, she hitched Elijah up onto one hip. 'Because I adore you, *señor*, and I always will.'

* * * * *

If you enjoyed this story, check out these other great reads from Susan Stephens:
IN THE SHEIKH'S SERVICE
BOUND TO THE TUSCAN BILLIONAIRE
BACK IN THE BRAZILIAN'S BED

And don't miss these other
WEDLOCKED! *themed stories:*
TRAPPED BY VIALLI'S VOWS
by Chantelle Shaw
WEDDED, BEDDED, BETRAYED
by Michelle Smart
Available now!

MILLS & BOON®
MODERN™

POWER, PASSION AND IRRESISTIBLE TEMPTATION

sneak peek at next month's titles...

In stores from 17th November 2016:

A Di Sione for the Greek's Pleasure – Kate Hewitt
and **Married for the Sheikh's Duty** – Tara Pammi
The Greek's Christmas Bride – Lynne Graham *and*
The Desert King's Secret Heir – Annie West

In stores from 1st December 2016:

A Royal Vow of Convenience – Sharon Kendrick
and **The Guardian's Virgin Ward** – Caitlin Crews
The Prince's Pregnant Mistress – Maisey Yates *and*
Surrendering to the Vengeful Italian – Angela Bissell

Just can't wait?
Buy our books online a month before they hit the shops!
www.millsandboon.co.uk

Also available as eBooks.

MILLS & BOON®

EXCLUSIVE EXTRACT

Natalia Di Sione hasn't left the family estate in years,
but she must retrieve her grandfather's lost book of
poems from Angelos Menas! The lives of the brooding
Greek and his daughter were changed irrevocably by a
fire, and Talia finds herself drawn to the formidable
tycoon. She knows the untold pleasure Angelos offers is
limited, but when she leaves with the book, will her
heart remain behind on the island?

Read on for a sneak preview of
A DI SIONE FOR THE GREEK'S PLEASURE
by Kate Hewitt

"Talia…" Angelos's voice broke on her name, and then,
before she could even process what was happening, he pulled
her towards him, his hands hard on her shoulders as his
mouth crashed down on hers and plundered its soft depths.

It had been ten years since she'd been kissed, and then
only a schoolboy's brush. She'd never been kissed like this,
never felt every sense blaze to life, every nerve ending tingle
with awareness, nearly painful in its intensity, as Angelos's
mouth moved on hers and he pulled her tightly to him.

His hard contours collided against her softness, each
point of contact creating an unbearably exquisite ache of
longing as she tangled her hands in his hair and fit her
mouth against his.

She was a clumsy, inexpert kisser, not sure what to do
with her lips or tongue, only knowing that she wanted more
of this. Of him.

She felt his hand slide down to cup her breast, his palm

hot and hard through the thin material of her dress, and a gasp of surprise and delight escaped her.

That small sound of pleasure was enough to jolt Angelos out of his passion-fogged daze, for he dropped his hand and in one awful, abrupt movement tore his mouth from hers and stepped back.

"I'm sorry," he said, his voice coming out in a ragged gasp.

"No…" Talia pressed one shaky hand to her buzzing lips as she tried to blink the world back into focus. "Don't be sorry," she whispered. "It was wonderful."

"I shouldn't have—"

"Why not?" she challenged. She felt frantic with the desperate need to feel and taste him again, and more importantly, not to have him withdraw from her, not just physically, but emotionally. Angelos didn't answer and she forced herself to ask the question again. "Why not, Angelos?"

"Because you are my employee, and I was taking advantage of you," he gritted out. "It was not appropriate…"

"I don't care about appropriate," she cried. She knew she sounded desperate and even pathetic but she didn't care. She wanted him. She *needed* him. "I care about you," she confessed, her voice dropping to a choked whisper, and surprise and something worse flashed across Angelos's face. He shook his head, the movement almost violent and terribly final.

"No, Talia," he told her flatly. "You don't."

Don't miss
A DI SIONE FOR THE GREEK'S PLEASURE
by Kate Hewitt

Available December 2016

MILLS & BOON®

Why shop at millsandboon.co.uk?

Each year, thousands of romance readers find their perfect read at millsandboon.co.uk. That's because we're passionate about bringing you the very best romantic fiction. Here are some of the advantages of shopping at www.millsandboon.co.uk:

Get new books first—you'll be able to buy your favourite books one month before they hit the shops

Get exclusive discounts—you'll also be able to buy our specially created monthly collections, with up to 50% off the RRP

Find your favourite authors—latest news, interviews and new releases for all your favourite authors and series on our website, plus ideas for what to try next

Join in—once you've bought your favourite books, don't forget to register with us to rate, review and join in the discussions

Visit **www.millsandboon.co.uk** for all this and more today!